BETTY CHURCH AND
THE SUFFOLK VAMPIRE

M.R.C. KASASIAN was raised in Lancashire.
He has had careers as varied as a factory hand,
wine waiter, veterinary assistant, fairground
worker and dentist. He is also the author
of the much-loved Gower Street Detective
series, five books featuring personal detective
Sidney Grice and his ward March Middleton.
He lives with his wife, in Suffolk in the
summer and in Malta in the winter.

Also by M.R.C. Kasasian

THE GOWER ST DETECTIVE SERIES

The Mangle Street Murders

The Curse of the House of Foskett

Death Descends on Saturn Villa

The Secrets of Gaslight Lane

Dark Dawn Over Steep House

M. R. C. KASASIAN

Betty Church
AND THE
SUFFOLK VAMPIRE

HEAD of ZEUS

First published in the UK by Head of Zeus in 2018
This paperback edition first published in the UK in 2019
by Head of Zeus Ltd

9 7 5 3 2 4 6 8

A catalogue record for this book is available from the British Library.

ISBN (PB): 9781784978150
ISBN (E): 9781784978129

Printed and bound in Great Britain by
CPI Group (UK) Ltd, Croydon CR0 4YY

Head of Zeus Ltd
First Floor East
5–8 Hardwick Street
London EC1R 4RG

WWW.HEADOFZEUS.COM

For my darling Tiggy

THE FITTING OF THE PEG

All my life I wanted to be a policeman. It wasn't a family tradition. My father was a dentist, as his father was too; my maternal grandfather a publisher of what was then modern poetry; and the women of the family were just that – the women.

It wasn't the uniform either. The Horse Guards looked far more dashing, I thought, and like every quite nice girl, I loved a sailor. But a young policeman gave me a piggyback over a flooded street when I was tiny. He got soaked up to his knees and didn't seem to mind. At that moment I knew that I wanted to be like him, helping people.

It did not occur to me until a teacher ridiculed these hopes that nature had thwarted my ambition. Neither of the Suffolk forces would even consider applications from my sex – the very idea was absurd – but I was not so easily discouraged. I moved to London and became what was, even there, still an oddity – some said an abomination – a policewoman.

I started well enough in the Metropolitan Constabulary, considering I was a curvaceous peg in a square hole. Police officers were supposed to be tall, and I was, but they were not supposed to have long blonde hair, and I did. I passed the training course with distinction and was stationed in Marylebone. This was the posting I had dreamed of, having spent many a childhood hour on my godmother March Middleton's knee in 125 Gower Street thrilled by tales of Aunty M's adventures with her guardian, the irascible personal detective Sidney Grice. It was nearly sixty years since she had gone to live with him and almost as many since she had started publishing her accounts of their investigations.

It was after I caught Hay, the Alkaline Shower Murderer, that my name was put forward for a vacancy and, to my surprise and my colleagues' outrage, at the age of twenty-eight I was made a sergeant – only the ninth woman in the country to reach that rank. And that should have been that but then I foolishly arrested the ringleaders of the Paper Chain Gang – a big mistake because it was hailed in the press as a triumph after it had been Chief Inspector Heartsease's case for the previous five years.

I never wanted to make enemies – I only wanted to be a good copper – but being a successful woman is the best way to make enemies that I know of.

I was thirty-eight when I had my mishap, which meant, of course, that I would have to be invalided out. It was only after leaving hospital that I realised I had a choice: I could feel sorry for myself and do nothing, or feel sorry for myself and go to the one person in the world who might be able to help.

THE LIONS AND THE FLAMESTICK

March Middleton gave her impressions of her first visit to Gower Street in her journal of 1882 and surprisingly little had changed in that time. The hexagonal red-brick hospital still sprouted its turrets to the right. The University College, white and colonnaded like a Greek temple, stood set back on the opposite side of the road, still paved with wooden blocks for quietness though the traffic was more rubber-wheeled than iron-shoed by now. There was, however, still a good sprinkling of horse-drawn carts. The milkman and the coal merchant had no reason to invest in the internal combustion engine.

The people were dressed differently – not a man in spats nor a top hat to be seen and the women showing enough leg to have made Sidney Grice apoplectic.

Gower Street was already all too familiar to me. It had formed part of my Bloomsbury beat when I was a constable and I had made my first arrest on the corner with Cable Street – an unemployed cooper for beating his wife with a cudgel. He had pleaded guilty but, much to my disgust, after hearing what a sharp tongue the woman had, the magistrate had merely bound him over to keep the peace while his wife with a broken jaw and nose was admonished to show more restraint in her language.

Number 125 stood four storeys high near the end of a Georgian terrace and I saw, as I went up four of the six steps to pull on the bell, that the heavy curtains to the right of the black front door were drawn. I once asked March Middleton why she had never mentioned the lions' heads on the doorposts and she had explained that she had not noticed them the first time she visited but, if she had mentioned them in later journals, it would have only drawn attention to her poor skills of observation, something Mr Grice was overly fond of doing already.

The first time I had been there after getting my helmet with its famous Brunswick star, Mr Grice's old maid had met me with, 'I'm supposed to tell visingtors to wipe their feet but I 'spect yours is clean so you can just wipe your boots, Constabell.' At which she clapped her hand over her mouth and came out with a muffled, 'Oh my gawd you're a woman – but I suppositate you know that.'

'It's me, Molly.'

'Everyone is me to themselves,' she had declared wisely, 'expect me. I'm just Molly.'

This time I waited a good two minutes and was just about to tug on the round brass handle again when I heard three bolts being drawn back and was greeted by a woman, about my age I guessed, in a plain black dress with a crisp white apron.

'Oh come in,' she said resignedly, as if I had been pestering her all week for admission. 'I recognise you from your photograph. I'm Jenny.' She ushered me in, shut the door and took my coat.

'Hello, Jenny.' I didn't tell her that Mr G would have blown a gasket at the familiarity of a servant introducing herself.

Jenny was tall. I am well above average at five feet nine and she had a good couple of inches on me; but I was inclined to think she was cheating. Her neck alone gave her an unfair advantage. It rose from her collar like the middle section of a boa constrictor.

'I thought you might be in uniform.' There was something disapproving in the way she told me that. Her nostrils were upturned and her lips thin and I half-expected to see a forked tongue flicking out.

4

Jenny hung my coat next to the great personal detective's old Ulster coat, which was still on its end hook near a stand of his famous walking canes. Sidney Grice had temporarily blinded himself when his gun stick backfired once, and he had stabbed an aristocrat in the foot with his spike stick in Kew one afternoon. I had often wondered which was his swordstick and which one played confusing tunes for they all looked identical to me. But, after nearly starting a blaze with his flame stick, I had been forbidden to touch any of them again and it did not seem right to do so now. I placed my hat on the table alongside seven of March Middleton's laid out, like a milliner's display, in a row.

'I'm off duty.' I was certainly not going to tell her that I might never be on it again.

'Oh.' This didn't seem to be a satisfactory explanation until I raised my sleeve. The maid's head snaked down to inspect this discovery but, finding nothing worth swallowing, reluctantly coiled back.

'How did you do that?'

'I didn't. Is Miss Middlet—'

'Through there,' Jenny broke in with a tip of her head, though that was not going to be my question.

Through there was a site almost sacred in the annals of criminology – Sidney Grice's legendary study and consulting room. Jenny opened the door and I stepped quietly in.

The room was quite dark, for it was still lit by gas, and the mantles were turned low, so it was a while before my eyes adjusted enough to make out the form of my godmother.

'Hello, Betty,' March Middleton greeted me from her armchair to the left of a flickering coal fire.

THE PHANTOM AND THE WOLVES

My godmother had her feet up on a cushion on a low rectangular table and started to slide them off when she saw me enter.

'Please don't get up, Aunty.' I went over to kiss her, shocked at how frail she had become. My godmother was always short and slender but today, in that dim glow, she looked tiny and the hands that took mine were bony and tremulous.

Aunty M put her feet on the spottily charred Persian rug. 'Turn the light up, darling. Let me see you.'

I fiddled with the gas taps, wishing she would get electricity installed. The light those lamps gave out was feeble – hardly enough to read by – and the fumes irritated my throat and eyes almost immediately. Mr G had thought it dangerous to propel electrons into his home but I didn't think his goddaughter agreed.

'You look lovely,' March Middleton said, 'so tall and elegant and that hair – I would give a thousand guineas to have your golden crown and still have a bargain. Show me your arm.'

I rolled up my sleeve for her to inspect the stump of my left forearm with all the appreciation of a connoisseur. 'It is quite slow healing. Does it still hurt?'

'When it's not itching.'

'And you have a phantom limb,' she said sympathetically.

'How did you know that?'

'You put it out to support yourself on the back of the chair when you leaned over before you remembered.'

'I still try to pick things up with my hand sometimes,' I admitted.

'I know it was a much smaller injury but a mesmerist helped me when I lost my toe.' March Middleton laughed softly. 'What a crowd we make, you and I plus Mr G without his eye.'

'Is the mesmerist still working?' I asked.

'Oh no, dear.' Aunty M's eyes twinkled. 'He treated me when I went to visit him in the condemned cell.'

'The last man I visited in jail tried to throttle me,' I told her. 'He very nearly succeeded.' I put my hand to my throat. 'But how are you feeling?' In her guardian's lifetime the chair she was in belonged to him exclusively but when he died she took it over, rather – she had explained – than have strangers sitting in it. I must have been one of the very few children ever to have climbed onto the great man's lap and almost certainly the only one with the temerity to call him Uncle G. I took a wooden chair from the round circular table so that I could sit closer to her.

'I am well.' March waved my concerns away. 'Everybody fusses around me but I wish they would not.'

I hope people fuss around me when I'm coming up to eighty, I thought but said, 'You don't look especially well. Have you seen a doctor?'

'The worthy Dr Picaday comes every day.' March coughed chestily. 'He tries to confiscate my cigarettes. He even tells Jenny to pour away my gin but I know too many horrible ways of murdering people for her to obey that instruction.'

I laughed. 'Shouldn't you be in bed?'

'I was thinking the same myself until Picaday ordered me to it.'

March Middleton had never been a one for obeying commands, and I doubt she would have survived long if she had in what was even more of a man's world than I had ever known.

'Perhaps you could have a little rest later.' I put a hand on her thin arm.

'Perhaps.' My godmother wrinkled her brow. 'I am a little out of touch but only a little. Inspector Franklin still visits most weeks. You have had a difficult time, Betty.'

'More than one,' I admitted wryly.

March Middleton lifted her head, the effort seeming to tire her, but those brown eyes were as quick and sharp as ever.

'But you did not come to me.'

'I did not want to trouble you,' I began hesitatingly and, seeing my godmother so elderly and ailing, I thought it would be unfair to do so now.

March Middleton coughed quietly, almost as if it comforted her to do so. 'I was trapped in that room with Mr G blinded and that *creature* bent on slaughtering us all when—' My godmother chewed her lips and coughed again.

'Please don't,' I whispered, for – though she could not bring herself to publish an account of that terrible day in Grosvenor Square – I had read all the police reports of the events.

'Do you think that whatever you have to tell me can trouble me more than that?'

'Of course not.' I lowered my head. 'But I don't want to add to your worries.'

'Look at me.' For such a little woman March Middleton carried a great air of authority. I did as I was told and she nodded. 'Tell me,' she said just as her maid arrived with tea.

I lifted the cushion aside for Jenny to put her tray on the table before she sidled round to poke the fire, adding a generous shovel of coal.

'Have you not heard that there may be a war coming?' March Middleton grumbled at her extravagance with the fuel.

8

'Indeed I have, Miss,' Jenny hissed. 'I have also heard of catching your death of cold.'

'I am warm enough as it is,' her employer protested. 'If anything, I am too hot.'

'Probably not.' March Middleton still clothed herself in the old Victorian style – though she had long abandoned her bustle – with a dress admittedly a very vibrant pink but long enough to cover the ankles, a glimpse of which would have shocked or aroused the men of her generation. I reminded myself that she would have been sixty in the Roaring Twenties – a bit too old to be a flapper.

'Is she?' The maid fixed me with such a questioning glare that I began to think she was considering swallowing me after all.

'You do feel quite cool,' I told my godmother.

'Young people are never satisfied unless they are steaming,' she retorted without any real crabbiness. She peered over. 'There are no biscuits, not even a digestive. Even you could not have eaten that case the duke sent me yesterday.'

'Doctor's orders.' Jenny slid back round the table.

'Does Dr Picaday pay your wages?' Aunty M enquired tetchily.

'No.' Jenny straightened peristaltically up. 'But are you going to come to your inquest to explain that you made me let you die of a chill or eat all the wrong things?'

'Possibly not.' My godmother coughed and Jenny undulated away, closing the door very quietly, like she was afraid of waking us up. 'Mr G always said I was too soft-hearted. He would have dismissed her on the spot.'

'I'm not sure she would go even if you did,' I said.

Aunty M smiled.

'She frightens me,' I confessed.

'And all the reporters and sensation-seekers who come to my house.' Aunty M toyed with the ring on her finger. 'That is her greatest asset.'

I stirred the tea. 'Doesn't she scare you?'

I waited to be told of how she had faced homicidal maniacs in dark East End alleys but March Middleton laughed. 'A little,' she said.

'Shall I pour?'

'You will but do not dare to try to forbid me the sugar.' My godmother watched me carry out a task she must have performed – though, no doubt, more expertly – at that same table many thousands of times. 'Now.' She took her cup and saucer more steadily than I had expected. 'Tell me.'

I took a breath. 'I know it sounds mad.'

The surface of her tea trembled into concentric rings and my godmother looked at me sharply. 'The best ideas often do.'

'But I want to stay on – in the police, I mean, but...'

'Go on.'

'Not a desk job.'

March Middleton touched her hair. It was grey now but still thick and neatly tied back. 'I was hoping you would say that.'

'They won't listen to me. Is there anything you can do?'

'Perhaps.' My godmother rubbed her thumb and first two fingers together as if she was rolling a cigarette.

The doorbell rang and I heard footsteps coming along the hallway.

'Jenny must have been listening in,' Aunty M observed, then, seeing my puzzlement, explained, 'I heard her dress brush against the bannister, then her footsteps started too loudly as she came back and brushed against it again.'

'We could do with you in the force,' I said but my godmother shrugged.

'It is just a little trick Mr G taught me' – she half-smiled – 'by years of cruelty.'

I heard the front door open, low voices and it closing. Five more footsteps before Jenny reappeared. 'Dr Picaday,' she announced.

March Middleton grimaced. 'I hope he is not going to try to inject me again. His needles are like blunt carpentry nails and I bruise so easily these days.'

'I must go.' I put my chair back in its place. 'I am tiring you.'

'Life tires me now,' Aunty M admitted. 'But you, Betty Church, are a tonic.'

'Thank you, Jenny,' I said. 'I'll be out in a moment.'

Then when we were alone, my godmother said, 'Leave it with me, darling. There are still men of influence who have reason to be grateful to me or fear my knowledge and there is no point in having strings if you do not tug them occasionally.'

I kissed her goodbye.

'Be strong,' she told me with a hug that nearly had me in her lap. 'And be brave. There are wolves out there but even wolves fear fire.'

I kissed her again, this little woman who didn't seem so little any more.

*

A short flabby man with legs that emerged from the folds of his body somewhere around his knees stood in the hall beside the coat hooks, black leather bag in his little pink hand.

'Miss Middleton is very tired,' I told him.

'She is old,' he informed me through flaccid lips that reminded me of an edible bivalve. 'There is no cure for that.'

I stopped myself from adding *except death* as I slipped what there was of my arms into my blue gabardine coat. The doctor had a supercilious manner that I didn't like.

'It's wonderful what they teach you in medical school.' I took my hat off the long side table and tried to let myself out, but Jenny had slithered to the door before me and had it open before I had even tilted my hat a little to the left as was the fashion in that damp anxious summer of 1939.

POISONED CAKE AND THE PUBLIC ENEMY

March Middleton wrote to me. She had made an appointment with Sir Samuel Hoare, the Home Secretary, and, such was the reputation of this woman who had come to London as a penniless orphan from Lancashire, *he* had called upon *her*. Hoare promised nothing – he was too seasoned a politician to do that – but he passed my case down to Commander Jack Bond with instructions to give me a fair hearing.

'Play rough and play dirty,' March Middleton had advised me. So I did. As Bond glowered over a desk the size of a billiard table I mentioned that a certain journalist was very interested in writing a piece about how I had been dismissed for an injury received in the course of my duty.

'Are you trying to blackmail me, Churrch?' He had an odd accent, top crust with a faintly Scottish tinge.

'Oh no, sir.' I tried to exude innocent indignation but I've never been very good at exuding. 'If I were trying to blackmail you I would threaten to tell them about you taking me off the Poisoned Raisin Case when I was about to arrest Sally Spinster. How many people died at that wedding?'

Bond eyed me coolly unaware, I think, that he had snapped the pencil he was toying with.

'You hail frrom East Angliar.'

'I've never denied it.'

'I knew there was something wrong with you.' He looked at his pencil in surprise, then at me accusingly. 'Slackwater, wasn't it?'

'Sackwater.'

Commander Bond threw the pencil clattering into his wastepaper bin, one half bouncing off the rim onto his nice marble hearth. He picked up his pen. 'They've been whingeing about being understaffed in Suffolk for years – always asking for help from Scorrtland Yard.'

He scribbled scratchily on a fresh sheet of headed notepaper.

'A tiny problem there, sir,' I informed him. 'The East Suffolk Constabulary won't accept women.' And I was very glad of that. Sackwater had something in common with Wormwood Scrubs – it was somewhere you tried to escape from and spent the rest of your life hoping never to return to.

'Oh they'll take any old rrubbish these days.' Bond signed his note and blotted it. 'Who knows? You might do some good. They could do with someone to stirr things up a bit, show them which end of a strraw to suck.'

I didn't know the answer to that one myself but I had one more bullet left. I took careful aim and fired. 'Surely that requires somebody senior to a sergeant?'

'I was coming to that,' the commander assured me smoothly, though it was obvious this was one lump of sugar he'd been hoping to keep in his pocket. 'There's prromotion in it forr you, Churrch' – his voice could have cut through steel – 'if you go quietly.' The commander put more feeling into those last four words than James Cagney had into eighty-three minutes of being The Public Enemy.

'Promotion.' I rolled the word around in my mouth and rather liked the taste of it. There were only three women inspectors in the whole Met that I knew of and one of those was rumoured to be quitting to get married. Also it was better to be a good-sized fish in a stagnant pond than a dead one in the ocean that was our capital city.

There was nothing to think about so that's exactly what I did. I cleared my throat. 'When shall I leave, sir?'

Commander Bond blotted his letter. 'Oh no hurrry, no hurrry.' He folded it. 'Finish yourr shift.' He addressed an envelope and glanced up. 'Goodbye.' I got up. 'Just out of interrest,' he asked as I pushed back my chair, 'are you left or right handed?'

I regarded him and then my half-empty sleeve. 'Do I look like I have a choice?'

He slid the letter into an envelope without taking his eyes off me. 'Do I look like I give a damn?' Bond waved the backs of his fingers to demonstrate that he still had ten to shoo me away with.

I went back into the ante-office.

'Loveable, isn't he?' Mary, Bond's secretary, swung the return arm on her typewriter.

'Could you do me a favour?' I asked and, before she could decline, hurried on with, 'His blotting paper needs changing. Do you think you could do that now?'

Mary considered the request and smiled – I hadn't even needed to remind her who got her boyfriend off a petty larceny charge – but then she put a finger to her lips and whispered. 'It's not shut properly – faulty catch.'

I pressed on the handle to open it a little bit more and, very, very carefully, slammed the door.

'Oh.' Mary jammed two keys on her typewriter. 'You startled me.'

'Hope I had the same effect on him.'

But Mary smiled. 'It would take more than that to leave Commander Bond shaken or stirred.'

*

There was no farewell present like Constable Graves had been given and no farewell drink like everybody got, but Sergeant Dover could never let an occasion pass without making a speech.

'I want you to know, Church – and I fink I speak for all of us wivou' esseption – when I say we never 'ated you' – he slowed as he searched for the bon mot – 'personly. In fact,' – he gathered speed like a rickety cart going over the top of a hill – 'you'd have been a good bloke, if you hadn't have been a lady.'

There was a chorus of 'ear-'ears.

'I've tried very hard,' I assured him, 'not to be.'

5

TEA, TENNIS AND CYANIDE,
FORGETTING AND REMEMBERING NAMES

nd so I went back. Nothing much had changed but nothing ever did in the slow death that passed for life in Sackwater.

Old Mr Bell was still in the left luggage office when I deposited my suitcases. He was old Mr Bell when he used to let me *help* in there as a child. 'You've done and gone and missed all the excitement, you have.' He handed me a ticket. 'Mrs Freeman's dog go and attack Mrs Darwin's cat it do and it need three stitches, the dog I mean.'

That was it? That was *all* the excitement? That was what I had missed?

'Blimey,' I breathed. 'Pass me the smelling salts.'

Old Mr Bell rootled in a pigeonhole. 'Hang on,' he said and handed me a bottle.

*

I had time to spare so I ambled about. At least the sun hadn't forgotten how to shine. High Road East still sloped down towards the sea. Green and Green's still offered swimming costumes, fishing rods and postcards that made the North Sea look like the Mediterranean in August. The souvenir shop still stocked painted ashtrays made in Stoke, shells from the South Seas and coral from Australia – all the things you need to remind you of your holiday on the Suffolk coast. Mrs Grundy's rock shop still sold nothing else but that – white spearmint-flavoured sticks painted bright red and run through with letters, the first A so badly printed it looked like Sickwater. The jokes in Joe's Joke Shop were still coated in dust and still not funny and Howland's Café still said *Open* when it was *Closed*, as it almost always was.

But those shop windows looked like mock Tudor now, criss-crossed in black tape to stop, it was hoped, shards shattering inwards. There were sandbags stacked outside the council offices as they had been for the flood of 1912, but these were against a different type of deluge. All this for a war Mr Chamberlain was still telling us was not going to happen.

I nipped into Sammy's Sweets. It had been going since I was a child and I had spent many an hour with nose pressed to the window, assessing the merits of winter mix or humbugs before breaking into my sixpence pocket money.

Sammy Sterne still stood behind the counter in his brown apron, short and bald apart from a few dandelion clock wisps floating on top. Behind him was shelf upon shelf of big screw-topped glass jars filled with every shape, colour and flavour of boiled sugar imaginable – enough to keep my father in business for life.

'Betty,' Sammy greeted me. I had gone in more to say hello to him than buy the produce, but his welcoming grin dropped immediately. 'I am so sorry, I should call you Sergeant, I think.' His accent was as heavy as the day he had stepped off the ferry from Hamburg.

'Actually it's Inspector now,' I told him, 'but I'm still Betty in private.'

The broad smile returned. 'Are you here on leave?'

'I'm being stationed here,' I explained and Sammy shook his fingers, blowing on them as if they were burned.

'That will waken them up a bit,' he chuckled, already weighing out a quarter of aniseed balls and pouring them from the scales bowl into a cone of white paper. I brought out my purse but he refused my coins. 'A welcome home present.' He screwed up the end and handed the little parcel over.

*

Flags still flew hopefully on poles in front of the Grand Hotel – so many nations, so few of which had ever provided visitors – but the German imperial tricolour had already been removed.

For a country still at peace there were a lot of military men about, mainly RAF crew from Hadling Heath Aerodrome, nattily dressed in grey-blue – a big step up from the gaggles of fishermen smelling of mackerel. There was a sprinkling of merchant seamen too for Anglethorpe, north of the estuary, still had a small concrete harbour, though rumours had it the navy was going to block the entrance with mines. Clusters of men in army green trudged with dwindling hopes of finding a pub serving out of hours, especially since the revival of SLAG – originally the Suffolk League Against Gin but now less picky about what they condemned.

I was greatly encouraged to see the first WAAFs making their way up the street. Perhaps the sight of a woman in a military uniform – other than the Salvation Army, which doesn't really count – would not be such a curiosity soon.

The terraced gardens sloped as always down to the promenade, a salty breeze blowing as it must have before the dawn of man. The waves had not stopped stretching and contracting in their pointless labour to scoop and drag the shingle and drop it back in place like the labour of that Greek man who annoyed the gods, whatever his name was. Much of the sand had been washed away and deposited in rival Anglethorpe by a freak storm in 1929 and none of the many storms since then had had the courtesy to return it.

A delivery boy whizzed past, the basket on the front of his bike overfilled with brown paper parcels tied in white string.

The burned-out Pier Pavilion still stood but the actual pier was hardly a half of its former self after being struck by lightning in that same wonderful year. Everyone agreed it was a great shame but nobody agreed to pay for its restoration. Now there was talk of demolishing the whole thing in case Hitler wanted a ride on the narrow-gauge railway.

I had lunch in the Lyons' Tea House at Mafeking Gardens. The little round tables with starched white cloths had not altered. The ancient waitresses still hovered and hobbled, but so tremulously now that I almost felt I should be waiting on them myself. They were affectionately called nippies but it had been a long time since they had done anything resembling nipping. The wireless was on in the kitchen: Reginald Foort playing 'Keep Smiling' on a Wurlitzer.

I had cod and chips – what else at the seaside? – then walked back up the hill, the long way by Tennyson Road.

A young man in a light suit that might have been considered snappy in London five years ago was haranguing a girl as I approached. It was none of my business so I listened in.

'Stupid cow,' he was hissing at her from under his wide-brimmed trilby. 'What the hell d'you want to go and do something like that for?'

'I didn't do it by myself,' she protested. It was obvious she had been crying.

She was a petite strawberry blonde in a pretty, flowery skirt, which made my more demure light-brown dress look positively dowdy.

The man pushed her back against the wall with a hand to her throat. 'Just get rid of it.'

'I can't.' She struggled for breath. 'I don't want to.'

There was something rattish in his face, pointed with long front teeth over a receded chin, but presumably she had seen something in him – possibly his easy charm.

'Do it.' He was almost lifting her off her feet in their new two-tone blue shoes and it quickly became my business. 'Why do my bitches always get in the club?'

The girl started to choke.

'All?' she managed but I didn't like the colour of her at all.

I hurried over. 'Please let go of her, sir.'

'Sod off.' He didn't take his eyes off the girl and I could see her neck blanching under the pressure. He had a black death's head signet ring on his left little finger. I took hold of that finger and prised it back.

'What the fuck?' He let go and the girl gulped for air.

'You can attack me when I let go.' I bent the finger back some more and he doubled up with a gasp. 'But, if you do, the pain you are experiencing now will be nothing compared to what I am capable of inflicting.' I was not sure this was true. He was skinny and I was taller than him. But I knew from experience that little men fight harder and dirtier – they have had to learn to – and I didn't have the authority of my uniform to protect me. 'Are you going to be good?' I applied a little more pressure.

'OK. OK.' He was almost squealing now.

I pushed him before I let go and he stumbled backwards, cradling his hand. His hat fell backwards onto the pavement at his feet and I was half-tempted to toss a penny into it.

'Bitch,' he spat – which was probably his opinion of all women – then added, rather philosophically, I thought, 'There should be some kind of a tablet to stop stupid tarts getting up the duff.'

'There is,' I told him. 'It's called cyanide and you give it to the man. Come on.' I put an arm round the girl's shoulder, steeling myself to turn my back. After six paces I took out my make-up compact to look in the mirror. The man was turning away.

'I only wanted him to do the right thing,' the girl wailed.

'The right thing for him to do would be to take that tablet,' I told her. 'Who is he?'

'Freddy Smart. You're lucky he didn't razor you.'

'From the Smart Gang?'

I knew them of old. Freddy's father ran what amounted to a protection racket, amongst other activities, after the Great War but I thought they had been driven away.

'I always knew he was violent' – the girl massaged her neck – 'but it seemed exciting until he turned on me.'

'What's your name?'

'Millicent.'

I had suffered greatly at the hands of a Sister Millicent but I could hardly blame this girl for that.

'Millicent who?'

'Smith. Why?'

We reached the end of the road.

'Stay away from him, Millicent. If he gives you any trouble, contact the police and ask for Inspector Church.'

She rubbed her throat. 'Will he help?'

'Yes I will,' I promised and continued on my way towards Highroad West.

That Greek man, I remembered as I passed a house where the next Benny Goodman was practising scales on his clarinet, was Sisyphus.

THE BUTTERFLY, THE BAR AND THE BODY

Sackwater Central Police Station was its only police station but they liked to sound like they were in the hub of things. It was a nice old red-brick two-storey building when I first knew it, but now the long once-white sash windows were so far off-white that they might have been smeared with butter, while the central blue-painted door looked like it had withstood a raid by its own officers but only just. The whole building was set back behind a paved area that was turning into a rather fine bowling green.

I took a deep breath, tidied my hair under my brown tilt hat and went in.

The lobby was dark, with all the solid wood shutters closed, except a small frosted rectangular pane of glass at the side, and with no lights on, it took a minute for my eyes to make out anything much. The place was deserted – not an officer to be seen at the desk nor a suspect fidgeting on one of the three benches arranged in rows facing it like backless pews before a pulpit.

The walls – as far as I could judge with the sun streaming in from behind me – were daubed in something like curdled coffee and the floor covered in worn umber lino, coming to a peak in the middle where the edges of two rolls met.

A butterfly escaped over my shoulder.

'Hello,' I called quietly. It seemed disrespectful to disturb the stillness and I still remembered the first time I had gone in there to be given a ticking-off for stealing a helmet, although I was only trying it on for size.

The butterfly flew back in.

I went to the desk. It was one of those tall public bar-type structures fronting a lower work surface. There was a door ajar behind and a passageway either side of the desk leading to the back of the building.

I leaned over to check the register and it was then and there that I saw the corpse.

SCARECROWS AND THE HURDY-GURDY MAN

Before me was the body of a man, well into his sixties I judged, slumped in the spindle-backed chair. By the look of him and the smell of decomposition, he had died some days ago. His skin was grey and had sunk beneath his cheekbones. His head had fallen back, with his jaw hanging down to reveal the stumps of what must have been lower teeth.

He had been dressed – in a hurry it appeared – in an old police sergeant's uniform but it was obviously not his: it hung so loosely on that wasted frame, and no real effort had been made to get the shirt on properly or do up the tie.

March Middleton once told me that one should be more afraid of the living than the dead but I think I would have preferred to be with the living at that particular moment.

There was a green coolie shade hanging on a brown plaited wire from the ceiling above the dead man. I reached over and, brushing the butterfly aside, pulled the short cord. The light clicked on.

'Bwuff.' The dead man opened his eyes. 'What's going on?' He struggled to sit almost upright, screwed and unscrewed his eyes and regarded me blearily. 'Can't you see we're closed?'

'I can't because you aren't,' I replied, trying to pretend that my heart hadn't almost exploded out of my ribcage.

'Eh?' He decoked his throat.

'Inspector Church,' I announced.

The not-as-dead-as-I-thought dead man set about evacuating

his chest, a long but productive process.

'He int come yet,' he rasped at last, still looking like he should have been given a decent burial.

'Inspector Church *is* here,' I assured him, 'only he is a she and that she is me.'

He spat something into a balled-up handkerchief. 'Eh?'

I dealt out my warrant card like a poker player showing the winning ace and the undead man wheezed. He scooped the card up in a poorly preserved hand and held it through the murk to the light over his head.

The sergeant – I was coming to accept that was what he was – scratched the remnants of what was probably a good head of hair when he was alive, but now looked like the undertaker had gummed on some sweepings in a hurry. The flattened tufts pointed in random directions with quite large gaps between them and ranged from old straw to dirty old straw in colour. 'Looks real,' he conceded.

'It is,' I assured him, with feeling, for no man could ever know how hard I had earned it.

The sergeant leaned back and I was not sure if it was him or his chair that creaked so noisily.

'Well, booger me,' he breathed wonderingly.

'Watch your tongue,' I scolded, though I had heard and often spoken worse myself.

'No wha' I mean.' The sergeant stretched his scrawny neck in an oversized collar like a tortoise trying to get out of its shell. 'I int never espied a woman policeman 'fore now.'

'You wouldn't,' I told him. 'Not in Suffolk anyway. I'm the first… of many, I hope.'

'Lor'.' He ran four fingers under his oversized collar. 'Give us a chance to get over you first.'

'Oh you'll never do that,' I assured him, hoping I didn't sound suggestive.

'And you a n'inspector also,' he said wonderingly. 'Whatever will they come up with next?'

'The twentieth century could be arriving any day now,' I warned, adding, before he got too cosy with the idea of me, 'Is that how you greet a superior officer here?'

The sergeant closed his mouth as if the hinges were rusty, scrambled to his feet – it seemed a miracle that he could – and saluted. I had had a sloppier salute once but that was from a hurdy-gurdy man's monkey. 'Sorry, sir.'

'Ma'am,' I corrected him and raised my voice. 'Tuck your shirt in, sergeant, and straighten that tie. You look ragged enough to scare a scarecrow.' My one-time intended father-in-law had told me how his first mate spoke to ratings and it was coming in handy now.

'Yes, madam.' I let that one pass while he made a hurried attempt to plug more shirt into his loose-fitting trousers, but the more he tamped in one side, the more it spilled out of the other.

'What's your name?'

'Frank Briggs, madam.' The sergeant started another salute but changed his mind. 'Ma'am.'

'It's pronounced *mam* not *marm*,' I told him with a growing suspicion that I was wasting my breath. 'And you would be wise to remember that the next time you meet the queen.'

'Mam,' he mouthed sceptically. 'But she be better not comin' tonight. I do have got a darts match on at the Unicorn.'

'What do the others call you?' I asked. 'To your face, I mean.'

'Waaal' – he chewed his cheek – 'the boys do call me Dusty.'

I knew from being raised there that in Suffolk a boy is anything from one day to one hundred years old and not necessarily male.

'Shouldn't it be Dusty Miller?' I asked.

The sergeant looked wounded. 'Can't help my surname,' he mumbled.

'I just thought something like Brigsy would be more normal.'

'I never though' o' tha'.' Briggs chewed the word over. 'But I do believe I like it.' He scratched his ear. 'Brigsy.' He swallowed and digested the name. 'Clever.' He licked his pale-grey lips.

There was a sooty smudge on Briggs's lip and I was about to tell him to wipe it off when I realised it was supposed to be a moustache. There are two kinds of police regulations – the ones that are written down and the ones that everyone obeys. In the second category is the rule that every sergeant shall have a moustache, the bigger and bristlier the better. It is not a rule that I ever adhered to but I have known a couple of women sergeants make more valiant attempts than Sergeant Brigsy Briggs had.

'I am to report to a Superintendent Vesty.' I broke our reveries.

'The superintendent? Oh he don't be coming in much these day.'

'Why not?' I eyed this shambles of a Lazarus in despair.

Sergeant Briggs shrugged. 'Not much call to, I s'pose, since they do move most on us all up to Ainnnglethorpe. They go and goh a new station there.'

'Is anybody else here?' I looked about. Were they all going to jump out shouting *Surprise*? Unlikely since I wasn't expected yet and the average constable wasn't mature enough to behave like a three-year-old.

'Wellll,' Brigsy drawled. 'Inspector Sharkey was but he int now.'

'What's he like?'

The sergeant wrinkled his nose. 'Like his name, I suppose.'

Not to be left out, I wrinkled my nose too. 'Why is there a smell of rotting meat in here?'

Brigsy snuffled like an old bloodhound trying to track itself. 'Tha'll be Constable Walker's beef-paste sandwich. He do drop it down the back of the filin' cabinet one week or two back.'

There was a jemmy hanging on the wall above that cabinet.

'Tell him to undrop it,' I ordered. 'I want to see that sandwich on my desk first thing in the morning.' I wished I hadn't said that last bit but it was too late. Superior officers can say a lot of things but they can't unsay any of them. It looks weak, and you may be weak, but you must never look it. 'Where *is* my office anyway?'

Briggs motioned over his shoulder. 'Tha' room at the back there behind me, tha' do be the back room.' He pointed down a whitewashed corridor to his left. 'The cells and interview rooms do be down there. Tha' corridor' – his right arm swung out, finger crooked like an Old Testament prophet – 'do lead to four pair plus one offices. The end one belong to Supernintendent Vesty for it overlook the garden it do. He do like to tend his roses but only when he do be here.'

'Well, he can't when he isn't,' I reasoned and the sergeant put on some horn-rimmed spectacles, big and square, like the sort of things small boys buy in Joe's Joke Shop to pretend they have X-ray eyes.

'I dunno 'bout tha',' Brigsy decided at last, wiping his glasses on his shirt pocket to look at me again. 'What happened to your arm?' Then, remembering his place, tacked on, 'If I might ask.'

He might and he had and I was used to it by now. 'A crocodile got it,' I told him, 'in Trafalgar Square.'

'Well, I'm blowed,' Brigsy blowed. 'Do they have them in the foun'ains?'

'Not now.' I repinned the sleeve to tidy it up. 'I shot it.'

'Well, booger me.'

'I shall not be doing that.'

'Oh, no, I dint mean…' Sergeant Briggs straightened himself up. He still didn't look good but he didn't look nearly so bad as when he was dead. 'Like a cup of tea, madam?' he asked with a course-you-would crinkling round the eyes and it was then I knew that he and I might possibly jog along.

POOKY AND THE SPITFIRES

'Oh Betty,' my mother greeted me as I deposited my cases. 'When you told us you were coming home, I hoped it meant you were going to get a proper job.'

My mother was nearly as tall as me – or would be, if she wasn't always hunched. Perhaps she was weighed down by her overly ample bosom or by living with her husband. Her hair was wiry in texture and colour and forced back in an Alice band like a prematurely aged head girl.

The door opened and a groggy man staggered across the hall, blood dripping down his chin.

'Bettyboo,' my father greeted me as always, though I wished, as always, that he wouldn't. He glanced at the man. 'Just take a seat back in the waiting room, Mr Freeman. Keep biting on that pack.'

My father was several inches shorter than both of us but made up for it in girth. He claimed to be five feet seven but I would have given him five five plus a bit at most. His features always reminded me of an unfinished clay model: not clearly defined, still dented by the artist's thumb in places.

'Oh he has dribbled on my nice clean floor,' my mother wailed. It *was* a nice floor – a chessboard of Victorian tiles that I could remember roller-skating on – but it was a long time since it had been clean. Cleaning, after all, was our maid Pooky's job, but Pooky had gone off to make Spitfires. We could be needing them soon.

The cocktail of aromas permeating from the surgery was as unmistakeable as it was unpleasant – nitrous oxide, drill-burned dentine and antiseptic – but these were the smells I would always associate with my childhood home.

I glanced at the empty chairs in the waiting room. 'Having a quiet day?' I asked. He had been having a lot of those lately.

'Hamish Peatrie hasn't turned up,' he grumbled. 'That's twice in a row now.'

'That's not like him,' I commented, for I had known him all my life. He owned a junk shop in town.

'Nobody is like anything these days,' my mother mused sagely. 'Oh' – the purpose of my luggage occurred to her. 'Are you expecting to stay?'

'Well, of course I am.'

'You'll have to share,' my father warned. He did like his little joke – even if nobody else did – every time I visited. 'No really, I mean it this time. We've got a dozen evacuees from London arriving on the ferry tomorrow.'

'But evacuations haven't started yet,' I objected, trying not to look at the fluted white pedestal, empty since I had broken the matching urn twenty-eight years ago. It had been left to serve no purpose other than to remind me of my guilt. 'Unless war has been declared while I walked up the road.'

'We've been chosen for a rehearsal,' my mother declared as proudly as if they had been invited to a royal garden party.

'Have you any idea what twelve East End kids will be like?' I asked because I had a very good idea indeed.

'Oh I expect they'll be a bit rough around the edges.' My father waved airily. 'Probably have to teach them how to hold a knife and fork properly.'

'Believe me,' I warned, 'they will know exactly how to hold their knives.'

31

'Also we get seven shillings and sixpence each.' My mother almost skipped. 'That's seven pounds six shillings a week.'

'Eight pounds five shillings,' my father corrected her.

'Four pounds ten shillings,' I corrected them both.

'That can't be right,' my mother assured me. 'Daddy worked it out with a pencil on his headed notepaper.' Silly me. You can't get anything wrong on Daddy's headed notepaper. I picked up my cases. 'Where are you going?'

'Back to meet the superintendent.'

'Used to be a patient of mine,' my father said but he could have said that about a great many people.

'I shall stay with Captain Sultana,' I volunteered since it seemed unlikely they would ask.

'With that horrid man on that horrid boat?' My mother rubbed a bit of saliva in with her shoe.

I had thought Adam's surname was hilarious when I first met him until he explained that Sultana was a common name in Malta and I had better get used to it if we were to be man and wife. We weren't. Policewomen were not allowed to get married and, with him being away so much on some hush-hush official business, I would have had little to compensate me. Captain Carmelo Sultana would have been my father-in-law and he still treated me like a daughter long after I had separated from his son – nearly a year ago now, I realised.

'For now.' I looked at my parents, realising with shock how little they were and how much older they were looking than they should have. 'If you have any trouble you can always ring Dr Gretham.'

He was Tubby to me – but my parents thought it disrespectful to a medical man, even if he had been struck off – and he was the nearest person to the boat with a phone.

'Oh we'll be all right,' my father breezed. 'After all we brought you up, didn't we?'

'If you say so.' I kissed my mother goodbye and was about to kiss my father when he dashed into the waiting room, which was also our sitting room out of hours since it had the only gas fire.

'Put that pack back in, you old fool,' he shouted, 'and stop spitting.' And, when the bills came and the income didn't, he wondered why he was losing patients.

9

THE BUBBLE ON THE BRAIN

Superintendent Vesty was a tall man – well over six feet – with a faded debonair look about him. His uniform, with its gold crown on his epaulettes, was well cut but well worn. His shoes were highly polished, as were his silver buttons. His face was aquiline with a sharply hooked nose, hooded eyes and lean downturned lips and he had an unusually deep tan for Suffolk, contrasting with a bleached wrist visible when he raised his arm to tug his earlobe. Most strikingly, the superintendent had a rectangular indentation occupying most of his forehead where – Brigsy had told me – a steel plate had been put in after an injury received in what we still hoped would be the last ever war. It was difficult to keep myself from staring at it.

He stuck out a hand. 'Welcome to Sackwater, Inspector.' He had a firm grasp but his gaze wandered.

'Thank you, sir.'

'All settled in?' When he bowed his head, the skin sagged forward like a huge blister and I had a horrible thought that, if Brigsy was wrong about the plate, there was little to stop anyone prodding the super in the brain.

I forced myself to look away. 'I'm starting to.'

'Good good. Briggs treating you well?'

'After he got over the shock.'

'Not used to having a woman around the place,' he sympathised, then ruined it by adding, 'especially one so glamorous as yourself.'

'I don't think my looks should enter into it, sir.'

'Quite, quite.' Vesty tugged his right earlobe again. Presumably he did a lot of that because it looked longer than the left. 'Can't blame a chap for admiring a nicely turned calf, though.'

'Actually, I can.'

My superior officer cocked his head like he was listening for something else.

'Pity about the arm, what?' The superintendent touched his head. 'Still hurts you know.' He stroked his fingertips over the depression. 'Well, I'd better have a rest now.'

My superior officer lowered himself into his chair cautiously, like he was expecting it to collapse under his weight, and closed his eyes.

'Will that be all, sir?' I asked uncertainly, but Superintendent Vesty was fast asleep.

I left him to slumber and found Brigsy trying to balance a pencil on its point on his finger.

'Is Joe Paradise still running his taxi?' I asked.

It was only five o'clock but it had been a long day and I had to go two miles with a suitcase.

'Old Joe he do be gooin' strong,' my sergeant assured me.

'Oh good.'

'Only his taxi int,' Brigsy said as mournfully as he might have announced a bereavement. 'It's the sea air gone and got to his suspendsion. Get in everywhere, it do.'

'Is there another service?'

'Of course' – Brigsy brightened – 'there int.' He scratched his chin. 'But if you don't fancy gooin' by foot,' he pondered, 'I've an idea...'

'Oh yes?'

'I've an idea you'll have to,' he finished his sentence.

So I walked. I had only just turned into Gordon Road when I

35

saw what was already a familiar figure in her summery skirt and blue two-tone shoes. She was standing at the bus stop.

'Millicent?' I did not like the way she was bent over.

Millicent Smith turned in response to my call. She had a big bloodstained handkerchief clutched under her nose.

'Go away.' Her left eye was bloodshot and her cheek blackened.

'Did he...?' I began stupidly.

'Yes he did.' She whipped the handkerchief away and I saw that her upper lip was split and swollen and her front left tooth was missing. 'Happy?'

I put my cases down.

'If you make a statement, we can—'

'You can what?' she bawled. 'Arrest the whole family? Will you lock them away for ever? 'Cause you'd have to if I snitched on one of them.' Millicent shook violently. 'Why can't you just leave me alone?'

'I can help you,' I tried again. 'There must be a shelter in the county for women in danger.'

'You think the Smarts don't know where it is?' Millicent covered her mouth. Her words were muffled. 'I know you mean well,' I heard, 'now fuck off.'

10

THE MAD ADMIRAL

Cressida watched my approach through the undergrowth with bright green eyes. It was a Maltese tradition to paint them on the bows of boats. She stood nearly thirty feet to the top of her wheelhouse, supported by railway sleepers sloping in a cradle around her, in the middle of Brindle Bar, which, except at low estuary tides, was really a tiny island off Shingle Cove.

In the winter she was visible from the riverbank but in the height of summer she could hardly be seen. There was a spinney of silver birches at the downstream end of the bar with clumps of rhododendron to give some shelter from the easterly winds. But her main camouflage came from the reeds that grew high in the summer, only dying down slowly as the dark nights closed in.

Nobody knew why he had constructed a houseboat there, for he could never hope to drag such a massive structure into the water. Perhaps he thought the high tide would enable him to float it off – but I suspected he just wanted somewhere he could feel at home and it seemed intrusive to interrogate him.

The captain had set up two speaking tubes: one to the summer house of White Lodge, Tubby Gretham's family seat up the hill, the other on a post nearby on the bank, but I had no need to use either.

'Ahoy,' Captain Sultana bellowed as I waved from the opposite bank, then he was scurrying down the wooden stairs that ran along the starboard side, scattering a dozen hens as he hurried to untie his boat and row steadily across the forty feet or so of slow water between us. '*Qalbi.*' He leaped onto the short jetty to embrace me. 'My heart.' He hadn't needed to translate the word. Adam had taught it to me in happier times.

Carmelo lugged my suitcase to balance on the seat and I scrambled in beside it.

'Madonna – Mother of God.' Although he knew about my mishap, this was the first time the captain had seen me since it happened. 'I shall teach you to scull one-handed. It can be done. You are strong.'

In all the time I knew him Captain Sultana had never cut his hair but kept it tied back to hang in a pigtail behind his old naval cap.

The locals had made the captain welcome enough, for he knew the sea. They respected that but to them he was always – though never to his face – *the Mad Admiral.*

We were soon moored up again and standing on his kingdom. Even as smallholdings go, Brindle Bar was small but, as well as the chickens, he kept rabbits – a favourite food in his native Malta – in pens and stacked cages and grew some vegetables on the gravelly, sandy soil.

'You are staying?'

'If you'll have me.' I dragged my soles over the iron scraper.

'You are staying.' It was a statement this time and I was just about to follow him up the steps when a tousled head of brown hair leaned over the side.

'Hello, Aunty.' It was Adam's nephew not mine, Jimmy. He had started calling me that to annoy me years ago but I was used to it by now.

Oh bloody hell, I thought for I was fond of Jimmy but things had been awkward and I said, even more ungraciously than I intended, 'What are you doing here?'

Jimmy blushed. He was twenty-two but he looked fifteen when he did that. 'Got thrown out of my lodgings,' he mumbled bashfully. 'Sort of set fire to the bed.'

Following Captain Sultana's example, I wiped my shoes repeatedly on the coconut mat at the top, for I knew how lovingly he laboured to keep that main deck polished.

'How?' I looked about me. Everything was spotless, the brass rails gleaming, the glass in the windows of the wheelhouse glittering, the beautifully crafted wheel itself standing uselessly splendid. The old Knights of Malta red flag with a white cross hardly ruffled on the mast high over our heads, a radio aerial poking out at the top.

Captain rolled his eyes and went downstairs – or down below, as he insisted we called it – with my cases.

'Fell asleep with a fag,' Jimmy confessed but immediately rallied with, 'anyway, it's all your fault. You gave me my first cigarette.'

'You told me you were already smoking.'

Jimmy was holding a black-bound book that he had been writing in.

'I thought the police were supposed to be able to tell if people were lying,' he taunted.

'We're not mind readers,' I retorted, 'especially if there isn't much of a mind to read.'

'Just don't do it here.' The captain reappeared. 'Or I'll be using you for bait.'

'Yes, Grandad.' Jimmy found *Great-Uncle* too much of a mouthful.

'He'd make a good worm,' I commented and ducked as the book flew over my head, skimming through the air to land in the undergrowth.

'Oh your poems,' I cried, relieved they had not gone in the water.

39

'Good riddance.' Jimmy flopped into a canvas chair. 'They were rubbish anyway.'

He had shyly shown me some once. I thought they were rather good and if I hadn't glanced out of a porthole in my cabin a few minutes later and spied him beating a path through the nettles on his way to retrieve it, I would have done the job myself.

11

THE CIRCLING OF THE SHARK

The sun was already hot by the time I arrived at Sackwater Central next day. I am proud of my uniform but it was not designed to keep the wearer cool. I was only glad that woollen stockings had recently been abandoned – at least they had as far as I was concerned.

'I int managed to get that san'witch out yet, ma'am,' a constable, introduced by Brigsy as 'Nippy' Walker, greeted me with such a grin you'd have thought not managing was a great achievement.

Nippy had the look of a sparring partner about him – solidly but leanly constructed with a face that looked like he had taken a few knocks, with his right cheekbone flattened and his nose deviated to the left with the bridge dented – but Brigsy had told me over our first cup of tea that Walker had been like that since birth, thanks to a newly trained midwife who was overenthusiastic with her forceps. His hair reminded me of a dune – grittily short at the sides with a clump of trimmed marram grass on the summit.

'How hard did you try?' I took off my peaked cap.

'Not very,' he admitted blithely. 'But Serg dint say you said try hard.'

'In future when I give an order you will carry it out,' I told him as evenly as I could, for I knew from experience that it's fine for a man to shout but a woman who raises her voice is a hysterical banshee.

Nippy chewed that information over. 'Most likely,' he agreed, eyes narrowed to puzzle over the stripes on my epaulettes.

I took a breath. The first door down the left-hand corridor opened and a man stepped out – tall and quite well built, though with a nicely developing paunch. His skin was pale – did none of them ever venture into daylight? – and pocked. His hair was soot-black and slicked back. About a decade older than me, I judged.

'Shark,' Briggs warned through the side of his mouth.

'Sergeant Church,' the newcomer called.

'Well, actually––'

'Shut up,' Inspector Sharkey snapped, so I didn't tell him it was just that I hadn't received my new jacket yet. 'Come into my office.'

So I did, if only to see if he had a bigger desk. He didn't, but he did have a heap of rubbish on it to rival any council tip.

I followed him into a thick, stale fug of cigarette smoke. Like most people I smoke but, like most people in a small room, unless there is a storm or a plague of locusts outside, I generally open the window.

'I think––' I tried again.

'No you don't.' Sharkey circumnavigated me, scrutinising me from every angle. I would be the first to agree that a police officer should always be presentable but I objected to being viewed like a bad sculpture. 'I do the thinking. You obey my orders. Understand?'

'I understand perfectly, Inspector,' I told him. 'But––'

'No buts. Just understand,' he broke in again. He had a touch of cockney in his accent that he was trying to cover up but I didn't think he had quite decided what to cover it with so it kept poking through. 'I deal with the *buts*.' I wished he would deal with the cigarette butts; the ashtray overflowed with them directly onto his green metal desktop. 'You're a bit la-di-da,' he continued. 'What happened to your arm?'

'I come in a kit form,' I told him. 'It's on its way.'

'A wit,' Sharkey remarked as if I was a dog dropping. 'Let's get one thing straight,' he said from behind me. For a second I thought he meant the seam on my stockings, which might well have twisted when I cycled through Treacle Woods to get to work. 'I don't like women in uniform.'

'I hope you are not asking me to turn up without one, Inspector.' I stared straight ahead.

'Don't flatter yourself.' Sharkey spoke over my shoulder. 'It's unnatural.' The inspector spoke moistly into my ear and I refrained from asking if he meant his Brylcreemed hair. Nature at her most bounteous could not have stained it that black but who was I to judge? If truth be told, some of my blondness came out of a bottle.

'What? Like bus conductresses?' I challenged and, while he thought of a response to that, ploughed on with, 'People used to say the same about flying but I like to think it's progress.'

Sharkey withdrew to reappear in front of me, his nose an inch from mine. 'And I like women who think they're clever even less.' His breath was heavy with stale tobacco and booze not quite as stale as it should have been for a working day. I had dealt with whisky coppers before and had hoped not to deal with any more.

'You would prefer me to be stupid?'

Sharkey smirked. His teeth were straight. They would have been nice if he hadn't set about staining them. 'I don't doubt you'll manage to be that without any encouragement from me.'

I gave up trying to hold my breath and said, 'I hope you will treat me with the same respect as you would any other officer, Inspector.'

Sharkey grinned and, mercifully, stepped back.

'Keep hoping, Chapel.' And he had accused me of trying to be funny.

'Church,' I corrected. 'I am at least entitled to be addressed by my correct name.'

The inspector leaned forward and I steeled myself not to wince. He would have taken that as a sign of fear, not nausea.

'While you are under my command, you will be whatever pigging kind of pigging place of worship I decide. You'll be a pigging Greek temple if I say so.' His words sprayed into my face. 'Understood?'

'Quite, Inspector.' I cleared my throat. 'So long as you understand that I shall not be under your command at all.'

'Moving on?' He brightened.

'Moving up,' I told him. 'In fact I already have. When you were first informed that I was being seconded here, I was indeed a sergeant – a bloody good one – but if you had read through some of the mail in your in tray, you would probably find that for the last...' I checked my watch, 'two days and twenty-four minutes, I have been Inspector Church.'

Sharkey's jaw dropped. I didn't think anyone's did outside of a cartoon but Sharkey's fell like the bottom out of a rusty dustbin.

'Which makes us equals, Sharkey. I don't think I'll call you Paul.'

I wondered if he knew the men also called him *Old Scrapie*, a disease of sheep that leads to insanity – though how you can tell if a sheep is mad beats me. It's not going to insist it's Alexander the Great.

'Fuck me.' He could not have been more disbelieving if I had told him that he had a father.

'I shan't be doing that – ever.'

I looked around me – the overfilled wastepaper bin, the stinking ashtray on the rubbish-strewn desk, the bricked-up but unplastered fireplace, the three-quarters-drunk bottle of Johnnie Walker Red Label, the untouched mug of curdled tea. There was a leaning stack of letters on his desk. I shuffled through it to find the only one with a London postmark.

'I think that's probably it.' I thrust the letter into his chest. 'Being an inspector, I believe I'm entitled to think.'

Starkey folded his arms, unfolded them and put his hands on his hips. 'What the hell do we need another inspector for? There's sweet FA to do here already.'

'I can't promise to drum up any business.' I didn't tell him that, when Mary had sent me the blotter I had asked her to change, I had been able to decipher enough to pick out the words *dumping ground*.

'Well, don't expect to be mollycoddled because of your sex,' Sharkey warned.

'I won't if you won't,' I promised and, looking into those jaundiced, capillaried eyes, I wondered which of us hated the other more.

*

'Oh Betty,' my mother wailed when I called in on Felicity House the following week with some fresh eggs courtesy of the captain, who had been shown precious little courtesy by my parents. He had given them eggs and a pair of rabbits in the past without a word of thanks. 'They're horrible. Why didn't you warn us?'

'I tried.'

'They leave messages,' she told me.

'How romantic.'

'No, they poo-poo,' she explained tearfully.

'They act dismissively?' I asked innocently. After all, these were the children I had been evicted for.

'They spend tuppences.'

'I didn't think they had any money.'

'They are not house-trained,' my mother quivered but I

45

had guessed that much by the aromas that had greeted me the moment I arrived. They even overpowered the olfactory treats from the surgery.

My father, hearing voices, came into the hall.

'I blame the police,' he told me. 'In my day, if—'

'You scrumped an apple you got a clip round the ear,' I recited to the accompaniment of sobs from the surgery. I stuck my head in and saw a lady bent over the spittoon. 'Are you all right?'

'Of course she's all right.' My father leaned sideways. 'For goodness' sake, woman,' he called through the open door, 'where would I be if everybody made all that fuss every time I hurt them?'

Exactly where you are now, I thought. I had seen the empty waiting room and the almost empty appointment book many times over the last few years. 'Have you ever thought about trying to be kind to them?' I asked softly.

'Don't be ridiculous,' he snapped. 'I'm a dentist.'

The woman seemed to be choking but my father was telling my mother that she needed to get a cleaner and my mother was telling him to find her one and I was just about to go into the surgery when a crash came from upstairs and a young voice was yelling something that sounded like *cuff* but probably wasn't.

'You little shits,' my father raged. 'I'll have every stinking tooth out of your festering heads if I hear another peek.'

'Peek,' a small voice came back defiantly, followed by the sound of breaking glass.

'Bless,' I said tolerantly and fled before I was forced to make an arrest.

12

THE DIETRICH DAYS

Everybody else had gone, most home, leaving Walker to patrol the town. We had been promised (or threatened with) reinforcements but he was all we needed really. On a normal night Sackwater was as quiet as a grave. Thursday nights were even quieter. Most people had spent their spare cash before payday and, when the pubs were peaceful, so were the streets.

Women officers were not allowed to patrol at night. It would have been beneath my station anyway, but I missed going on the beat in the daytime. It was when I actually got to meet the public I was supposed to be protecting. So, whenever the chance arose, I would do my unofficial rounds, popping into shops and cafés to chat to their owners and customers, getting my face known, building – I hoped – some trust.

There was nothing in the rulebook to say that I couldn't do paperwork at night and, with the threat of war, this had multiplied dramatically. There was talk of registering every person in the kingdom and issuing them with identity cards, and we would be expected to check that people were carrying them. It appeared that, if we had to fight for our freedoms, we must be prepared to surrender them first.

We had seen the power of the Luftwaffe in Spain and apparently our best defence would be to hide from them in the dark. Nobody knew if it was really possible to black out an entire town and so the government decided to have a test run and, if there are dud prizes to be had, Sackwater has always excelled in winning them. We had been at it a week now and were already sick of it.

After Brigsy had gone home, I locked up, turned out the light in the lobby and went back to my office, leaving the door open so I could hear if any of the men returned or the phone rang. It was a good-sized room but before I had even investigated a crime, I was running out of working space with all the files the government had given me. I settled behind my standard metal desk with a mug of tea, plonked my feet on a pulled-out lower drawer and opened the first pamphlet. *What to do in the Event of an Air Raid* looked promising but the bureaucrats of Whitehall could make Armageddon as interesting as a muddy puddle. My eyes were closing and I needed a nicotine boost to help me stay awake. I was just sowing a cigarette paper with a row of Amber Leaf when the front door handle rattled and there was a knock.

Several things bothered me: it was late – the blackout boards were in place with the *Closed* sign up – and also most people knock before they rattle. Not vice versa.

This person was knocking and rattling simultaneously now and then, for good measure, shouting, 'Hello? Is anybody there?' It was a woman.

'Hang on.' I extracted my feet, which had managed to wedge themselves in the drawer, which had managed to half-close itself, and marched into the hall.

'Is this an emergency?' I called through the closed door. It had better be but I hoped it wasn't. We were overstretched enough as it was.

The letter flap hinged up. 'Is that Superintendent Vesty?'

People have often complimented me on my voice. They say it is quite deep and smoky. The depth is my grandfather's fault; he had voice to spare and gave me some of his. The smokiness is my own work with the assistance of Gallagher's rolling tobacco.

A man at a bus stop in Bury St Edmunds once swore he had met Marlene Dietrich and I spoke just like a young her without the accent. Somebody else said I sounded like Greta Garbo. Nobody had ever mistaken me for a man before, though I sometimes wished they would.

I nearly yelled *No, go away* but it would be more satisfying, I decided, to confront the visitor with her own stupidity. Besides, it might be urgent. 'Hold on.'

I should have put the chain on – I'm always telling members of the public that – but, like most of us, I am much better at dispensing wisdom than acting upon it. I pulled the top bolt back, turned the key in the lock and was about to open up when the handle clacked down and the door flew open and a dark shape hurtled into the room.

13

THE INTEGRITY OF MANDIBLES

'BLOODY HELL!' I stumbled backwards.

'Crikey!' The woman sprawled on the floor.

'Crikey?' I cradled my nose. 'Nobody says *crikey* outside a children's story.'

'I do.' The woman flopped about a bit and got onto one elbow like a picnicker and I made a memo to have a word with the cleaner, if she ever turned up. Perhaps she had gone to make Spits too. The caller's mackintosh sleeve was decorated with dark-grey dust and light-grey ash.

'What the hell were you doing?'

'The man said to come in.'

'What man?' I wiggled my nose gingerly and thought I felt it click. 'There is no man. Anyway, I told you to wait.'

'It sounded like come in.' She stuck out a grubby hand. 'Give me a paw. Oh, you have only got one.'

'Really?' I checked myself.

'I would have thought you would have noticed that.' Her fiery red hair had not benefited from her tumble but it looked like it had made up its mind to be naughty a long time ago and I doubted it ever behaved whatever she did to punish it. 'Oh but I expect that was a joke. I'm not very good at those.' She pointed in case I had forgotten the topic of conversation. 'How did you lose it?'

'I lent it to a friend who never gave it back.'

'Just like my copy of *Fenula the Fluffy Kitten*.' My visitor nodded her head, her hair wobbling wildly. 'It took me years to get it back. Neither a borrower nor a lender be, as Daddy always says.'

I touched my face. 'You've broken my nose.' I held out my hand and she scrambled up, using me for handholds like I was a crevasse she had fallen down.

The newcomer stood on tiptoe and put her face close to mine. 'It is not bleeding.' She examined her coat. 'Your floor is filthy as a feather.'

'You're not supposed to lie on it. Anyway' – I wiggled my jaw experimentally – 'even if you did think I said to come in, I didn't say to break the door down.'

'I thought it was stuck.' She smeared the dirt with her hand. 'Why are you doing that with your mandible?'

'To see if it's fractured.'

'It is not. Oh, you're a policewoman as well.' She still had hold of my hand.

'An inspector.' I tapped my sleeve.

'Lummy.'

'As well as what?'

'Me.' The newly alleged WPC performed an elaborate salute. 'Dodo Chivers, woman police constable, reporting for duty, ma'am.'

'You're not due until next week.'

She was a very small girl, short and delicately constructed.

'This is next week,' she reasoned and reached inside her coat to show me a folded letter.

'Temporary accommodation has been found for you with Mr Harold Church at Felicity House, 2 Cormorant Road, Sackwater. You are to report to Sackwater Central Police Station on the first proximo,' I read aloud and handed the letter back. 'This is still August.'

'The twenty-fourth,' Dodo Chivers agreed. 'But proximo

means immediately. Zorro says it in *The Bold Caballero*.' She made a rapier flourish.

'You're probably thinking of pronto.'

'No, his name was Zorro. I have seen the film.'

'Pronto means *now* or *quickly*. Proximo means *next month*,' I explained patiently. 'You're a week early.'

'Oh.' Housewives would be thrilled if their whites came out of the wash with Dodo Chivers' complexion. There was not a blemish to be seen unless you counted one tiny freckle on her right cheek, which I didn't because it only served to emphasise her purity. 'But oh.' Dodo had big violet eyes like prize-winning pansies and they looked like they were going to start spilling.

'Have you come far?'

'One hundred and twenty-eight miles.' Dodo pointed towards the sea.

'Would you like to be more specific?'

'One hundred and twenty-eight and one-quarter miles according to Daddy's Ordnance Survey map. We measured it together in his study with a little wheel on a little stick.'

'Well, you can't go back tonight.'

'I was not thinking of it.' She wrinkled her small Grecian nose.

'Where's your luggage?'

Dodo Chivers clapped a hand over her mouth.

'On the doorstep.'

'Then you had better bring it in,' I said wearily. 'Welcome to Sackwater, Constable Chivers. I'm Inspector Church.'

'That's a coincidence,' she mulled.

'Mr Church is my father,' I said.

'Does that mean we'll be living together and shall we be like sisters?' Dodo jiggled about.

'No and no,' I told her and thought *What the hell? My parents had no room for me but they can accommodate my constable.*

*

'Well, they took our refugees away when they decided this could be an invasion area,' my father explained.

'Good ribbons to them,' my mother said. 'They were dirty and smelly and the language! It was worse than having you home.'

'Thanks a lot.' I pouted.

How do parents do that – turn the most mature of us back into sulky teenagers?

'But they were,' my mother insisted. 'Much much worse.'

'Yes, but I don't want to be a yardstick for bad behaviour.'

'Then don't behave badly,' my mother advised so cheerfully that I would have stamped off to my room, if I had one.

'Anyway, the rent will come in handy since *they* opened,' my father added darkly.

They were the two new dentists at Bradley Court who had poached many of his patients with their cut rates, shiny new anaesthetic equipment and – most damagingly of all – their pleasant chairside manners.

'I would have contributed for my upkeep.' This was worse than when they gave my tricycle to Duncan next door as a reward for his dad repairing it.

'Oh but I'm sure you'll be much more comfortable in that lovely boat.' My mother put a hand to my hair, possibly planning to put it back in plaits, but I pulled away, feeling younger by the minute. 'It looked so much nicer brown.'

'It was never brown.' I felt about twelve now.

'Oh this is super-lovely,' Dodo called down from my bedroom and the next thing I knew I was six, running away from home on my scooter because Mummy wouldn't let me have poached eggs for dinner.

14

THE SHAPE OF THINGS TO COME

cycled as far as I could but none of us had any idea how black a blackout could be until we were obliged to try it on a moonless, starless night. I had a lamp on the front forks of course but almost all the glass was taped over according to the regulations so that it would take a very alert driver to spot its glimmer as he struggled along with his masked headlights, and it did nothing at all to light my way. There had been several crashes already and a number of pedestrians mowed down, one baker's boy fatally. So far we were killing more of each other than the Führer had shown any signs of intending to.

It was after a truck had come straight at me on the wrong side of Pelican Road and I had had to steer into a hawthorn bush that I decided it would be wiser to dismount and walk. I was just disentangling myself when a dark shape flew out. You get quite used to that in the blackout. After all, everything is a dark shape and some of those things have to move. This thing, however, was screaming and running, weaving towards me.

My job entitled me to carry a proper torch, so I did, but there were strict instructions about limiting its use to emergencies. On the first night of the rehearsal a verger was trying to apprehend three boys stealing lead from St John's Church when his waving beam was taken as a signal to our prospective enemy. The next thing he knew, he was hauled off by two ARP wardens to spend a night being interrogated while the boys finished their work at their leisure. Had nobody told the wardens we were still at peace?

I decided to risk it. If war came and the Luftwaffe could see my little torch from ten thousand feet and manage to land a bomb on me we might as well have surrendered before hostilities began. I clicked it on and, shocked by the sudden glare – the beam of a torch in the pitch-dark cuts through it like a searchlight – the shape stopped dead and shielded its eyes. I ran the beam quickly up and down, enough to ascertain that the it was a she, then up the street to check that nobody was in pursuit and clicked the light out. With impeccable timing the clouds parted just enough to let a drizzle of moonlight through.

I leaned my bike against the bush and put out my arm in case the woman decided to run off again.

'I am a police officer,' I said.

'Oh,' she cried. 'Thank God. I have been attacked... inshulted by seep.'

'What do you mean?' I guided her onto the pavement.

'Abooshed.' She waved her hands wildly.

'Ambushed?'

Her fingers plucked the word she wanted from the air but it must have been damaged in the process. 'Abloosed.'

'Do you mean abused?' I leaned towards her and she did not smell of drink. 'Verbally or physically?'

There was blood trickling from under her hairline down her forehead, and she had bruising around both eyes. If she had been wearing a hat, she wasn't now.

'What are you talking about?' she wailed. 'I musht escrape.'

The woman swayed sideways and I just managed to stop her toppling. She had a moustache too, which Brigsy would have been consumed with envy over, if it hadn't been made of blood.

'You need to see a doctor, miss,' I said. 'Come with me.'

'No, no. I'm...' But the woman never decided what she was.

She put a hand to her lip and stared aghast at the result. 'You struck me,' she accused.

'No,' I said firmly. 'You have been attacked by somebody else or had an accident.'

'I was attacked' – her eyes became slits – 'and you, a policemanwoman, stood by and did nothing.' She smeared blood up her cheek with the backs of her fingers. 'You egged them on.'

'You're confused.' I shepherded her back along the way she had come. 'Have you been hit on the head?'

At least she was letting me guide her. 'Please,' she begged, 'I need the po-pol-pleece. I need.' She played statues.

'What is it?' I kept my arm round her shoulder.

'Look.' I tried to follow her stare up the road but she was squirming too much. 'He's coming.' The woman struggled to break free but I twisted her about, grabbing her right wrist in an awkward embrace. 'Save me!'

The pressure on my stump brought involuntary tears but I managed to hold the wriggling woman long enough to look back up the hill and sure enough there was a man, huge – I could hear him panting now and his footsteps smacking on the paving stones and drawing ever closer – hurtling towards us and waving what looked, glinting in the moonlight, unnervingly like a machete.

15

ST JASPAR AND THE SPIES

had been attacked before. You couldn't do my job in London and not be. Officers, good or bad, died heroically or stupidly – the results were the same – at the hands of thieves, murderers or drunks. But I didn't expect it in Sackwater and I did not want to join that roll of honour.

I unwrapped myself from the woman and pushed her towards the bush. I didn't mean her to fall into it but she did. Women police officers didn't carry truncheons and inspectors of either sex never have. I snatched my bike off the pavement, propped it against myself to make some sort of obstacle and grabbed the pump to at least fend off a blow.

'Police, halt!' I bellowed at the top of my voice and, to my relief, the man did. 'Put down your weapon,' I commanded.

'Is that her?' he gasped breathlessly.

'Who is *her* and who are you?' I raised the pump, hoping it looked more threatening than it felt. 'Put the knife down, sir.'

Most men respond better if you show them a respect you don't feel. Maybe it makes them feel they should be the gentlemen they know they aren't.

'Knife?' the man puffed, brandishing the machete.

'Put... it... down,' I instructed. 'Now.' Five seconds more and I would launch myself into him. I probably wouldn't win but at least he wouldn't be expecting it.

'Oh sorry...' The man bent and put his weapon on the

ground. 'I was chopping up old packing cases for firewood when she dropped in.'

'Dropped in?' I repeated doubtfully. 'Doesn't look like you had a cup of tea and a chat.'

'No.' He straightened up. 'She fell through my cellar doors. I'm landlord at the Leg O' Lamb.' He peered over. 'Is she all right?'

'Put the gun down,' the woman directed.

'What gun?' the man and I chorused. He showed her his empty palms. 'She took a nasty tumble,' he told me. 'Knocked out cold she was.'

'So cold.' She hugged herself, sobbing to the man, 'Help me, Officer. This woman shot me.'

'You have not been shot,' I told her. 'Can you remember who you are?'

'Can you?' she challenged. 'Can you remember who I am?'

'What's your name?' I asked the man.

'Saint Jaspar Divers,' he said without a blink then blinked. 'Don't blame me. Blame my parents. Most people call me Jasp.'

'How ingenious.' At least he had got the name right but, just like me, he could have seen it over the pub door. 'Three pints of bitter, half a mild, two rum and waters, a whisky and soda, a double brandy – oh and make one of those bitters a half and have one yourself, landlord,' I rattled off. 'Repeat my order.'

The man did without hesitation. 'Thanks very much. I'll have a half later,' he added. 'Eight shillings and thruppence, please.'

The girl stiffened. 'Did you notice his accent?' she demanded loudly. 'It is German. Did *you* notice hers?' She looked from one to the other. 'It's German. You are German spies. They are spies!' she yelled. 'Help me, they are spies!'

'I am a police officer,' I tried to explain, again.

'Spies!' she repeated with a shriek that might not have wakened the dead but certainly wakened the living. Bedroom sash windows were flying up with yells of 'What's going on?' or 'Call the police!'

'I *am* a police officer,' I called, briefly shining a light on my helmet. 'Everything is under control. Please go back to your beds.'

A dog started barking nearby.

'They are torturing me!' the girl yelled. 'Somebody call the pleesh.'

Another dog joined in.

Another sash rose and a long tube shape poked out. 'Release that woman or I fire,' a man commanded but I didn't even need my torch for that one.

'With a broom?' I sighed as a light went on in the adjacent window.

'Put that light out,' everybody yelled, entering into the spirit of the trial run with commendable enthusiasm, largely, I think, because a rumour had spread that this wasn't really just a practice at all and that Hitler was going to strike before we had a chance to start anything.

'I am coming, *mein Führer*,' the girl shrieked in a remarkably quick change of sides.

'I need to get her to hospital,' I told Saint Jaspar, 'before one of us gets lynched.'

I leaned my bike against the bush again. 'This had better be here when I come back,' I called to the ever-increasing number of heads and looped my arm through the woman's.

'Come along, miss.' Jasp picked up his machete, came over and took her other arm. 'Time to go.'

'Police!' a woman yelled.

'Oh good grief,' I muttered and we went slowly on our way.

16

BONESHAKERS AND THE TENNIS BALL DIET

The Royal Albert Sackwater Infirmary was quiet. The man who had dislocated his jaw demonstrating that he could get a tennis ball in his mouth, but failing to demonstrate that he could get it out again, would have to wait, a nurse who looked like she had eaten everything except that tennis ball told me.

Jasp went back to the Leg O' Lamb. He had shut the doors and not locked them and was worried somebody would get into his cellar.

'You'll be seen in a minute,' she told the girl who greeted the news in a panic.

'We'll be seen,' she cried. 'I told you we should have stayed hidden. Now we'll be shot as spies, *mein Gott in Himmel*.'

'*Bist du Deutscher?*' the nurse said. '*Ich war in Koln.*'

'If you are trying to pass secret messages, you could wait until I've gone,' I suggested. 'Even I can guess at what that means.'

'I knew it,' the girl exclaimed. 'You are both filth columnists. Nurse and policewoman indeed. Well, I can see through that little sub-something.'

'Terfuge,' I finished her word for her, not quite sure why except that I hate unfinished words. They are like songs with the last notes missing or carpets frayed around the edges.

'Terfuge?' the girl repeated, touching her hair thoughtfully. She scrutinised the mess on her fingers. 'Custard,' she decided before she crumpled at the knees.

'Delayed shock?' I suggested after I had helped catch the unconscious figure and dragged her to a trolley.

'Hysteria,' the nurse corrected me. 'The female of the species is a feeble and stupid creature. You have probably noticed as much yourself.'

'Not in any species that I am a part of,' I told her.

'Perhaps,' the nurse conceded, 'but then policewomen are not very observant. Nor are they really female.'

'Fuffinellelpme,' the man with a Slazenger between his jaws interjected, or something to that effect.

My bike was still where I had left it but a note had been tied to the handlebars.

IF YOU LEAVE YOUR VELOCIPEDE HERE AGAIN
I SHALL INFORM THE POLICE.

Velocipede? To the best of my knowledge the word had died before Disraeli. Perhaps I was optimistic to tell Brigsy to expect the twentieth century. It would be a long time coming yet.

17

NETTLES AND THE PRINCESS

My father was still at the kitchen table when I returned to Felicity House the next morning. He was pouring a cup of tea for his guest.

'Good morning, Dad, Dodo,' I said as cheerily as I could for it had not been especially good so far. Jimmy had forgotten to lock the henhouse so I had missed breakfast helping to search for them. Who knew hens were quite so fond of nettle patches? I had found out the hard way.

'Morning.' He glared at me.

Dodo was using my mug, the one nobody else was allowed to use, not even Aunt Philly when she came to stay – and I was very fond of her. I helped myself to my third favourite – Dad had my second.

'Good morning, Betty.' Dodo caught my glance. 'But what is the matter? Do you have a tummsy ache?'

'When you are an inspector you can use my first name,' I said. My rank meant something to me, if not to her.

'Oh but...' Dodo's voice drifted away. Her lower lip drooped.

'I see you've had breakfast,' I added rather obviously.

Dodo brightened. 'Oh yes and we have been having a good old chinwag.' From my father's pained expression, I could guess whose chin had been wagging the most. 'I have told Mr Church all about Daddy's teeth – all the troubles he has had with them having three sets and his gums being weak. Then we discussed

Mummy's teeth – before she departed of course – and I showed him my teeth without even being asked to.'

'She did,' my father confirmed grimly.

'Mr Church said they looked clean though he couldn't see them properly without his tools.' Dodo took the last triangle of toast from the rack. 'I was not sure if I should wear my uniform.'

She had a summer frock on, red paisley with blue trim on the collar and short sleeves – pretty but the neckline was a little low, I thought.

'I don't think so.' I put two slices of bread under the grill. 'Officially you don't start until next week but I can show you around the town,' I suggested and Dodo sprang up, her dress quite short even by more relaxed modern standards.

'I shall go to get ready,' she announced and rushed upstairs.

'Gave me the fright of my life when she came bounding along the corridor this morning,' my father grumbled. 'All that hair, I thought I was being attacked by Coco the Clown.'

*

It was a dull day with a bit of an easterly wind but Dodo declined my suggestion that she bring a coat or wear a cardigan.

'Oh but I never feel the cold,' she assured me as she skipped down the drive in her matching red bonnet, reached the gate then hesitated, 'unless it is actually cold. I think I might change my mind. Do you think I should?'

'I wish you would.'

'I'll be quick as a Quaker.'

I paced the pavement and eventually Dodo returned in exactly the same clothes. 'I changed my mind about changing my mind. I want everyone to see my pretty dress.' Dodo spun so that it flared, rising high up her slender thighs. 'Do you like it, B— Inspector?'

'It's a nice pattern,' I began.

'Daddy said I looked like a princess when I put it on for him.' Dodo giggled. 'But oh what fun we shall have.'

'No we shall not.'

'Where is the sea?' Dodo scanned 360 degrees under the shade of her hand. 'I cannot see the sea.'

'About two hundred yards behind the house.'

She made a telescope with her hands. 'I carrrn't see no sea, cap'ain.'

'Behave.'

We turned left and set off.

'So are we proceeding in a northerly direction?'

'I suppose so.'

'Norrr-therrr-leee.' Dodo brought out a notebook and pencil.

'What are you doing?'

'Practising.' She licked the lead.

'You'll get plenty of that soon enough.'

'How soon? Will it be very?' Dodo stopped, poised to record my reply.

A man in a dark suit and carrying a battered briefcase came towards us.

'Put that notepad away,' I snapped.

'I was just going to write the house names down in block capitals.'

'Now.'

'Little Miss Grumpy.' Dodo rammed the book into her handbag.

'Did you say *yes Inspector*?' Within two minutes Dodo Chivers had transformed me into the terror of the parade ground.

'No I...' Dodo paused. 'Yes, Inspector.'

The man walked by. 'Good morning, sir,' Dodo greeted him merrily.

He looked askance at her then me. 'You're supposed to be getting them off the streets, not pimping them.' He marched on.

Dodo stared at me open-mouthed. 'Are you not going to arrest him?'

'For what?'

'Insulting a police officer.' She shuffled her dress about. 'Insulting two police officers, now I think of it.'

'No.' I kept walking.

'But oh.' The notebook reappeared. 'So it is all right to use offensive language in the North Sea Suffolk resort town of Slackwater.'

'Sackwater.'

'Slackwater sounds nicer. Sackwater does not make sense.' Two sailors were ambling on the opposite pavement. 'I only said *good morning, sir,*' Dodo grumbled. 'It is not as if I said,' her voice rose, taking on a stage cockney barmaid timbre, '*like a nice time, dear?*'

'Not 'arf!' one of them yelled back.

'I'll take the one in the cheeky uniform,' his mate called.

'You'll take a running jump if you know what's good for you,' I threatened, to more hilarity.

'What is this place?' Dodo howled at me. 'A den of sex fiends?'

'Will be when we've spread the word,' the first sailor cackled and both doubled up in mirth.

'Right.' I grabbed hold of Dodo and propelled her away.

'What? Ouchy-wouchy, but you are hurting my arm.'

'Keep walking.' I quick-frogmarched Dodo Chivers to the end of the road, round the corner and to a bench by the bus stop. 'Sit there.' I sat down beside her.

'Are we catching a bus?' Dodo rubbed her arm.

'No we are damned well not.'

'I cannot help but notice' – Dodo edged an inch away from me – 'that you swear rather a lot. Daddy says it is not ladylike.'

'I'm glad you mentioned that.' I edged two inches towards

her. Nobody was going to treat me as if I should be quarantined, least of all a sopping-wet-behind-the-ears constable. 'Because I have news for you, Dolores Davina Porthia Chivers. Two weeks and two days ago you ceased to be a lady. There is no such job as lady police officer. If there was, I would not be eligible because, as you have observed, I am not a lady. The proudest moment of my life was when I became a woman police officer.'

'Mine too.' Dodo sniffed.

'Then start behaving like one.'

Dodo sniffed again. 'I will try.'

'And stop snivelling. WPCs do not snivel.'

'I shall try, truly I shall.' Dodo hiccupped. 'Sorry B— Inspector, I always do that when I am upset.'

She looked so little and forlorn that I almost relented, but no man would have expected or got a cuddle.

'And stop calling me B—Inspector.'

'Sorry, Inspector.'

'That's better.' I got up feeling awful, for I could still remember what an innocent I had been when I started. 'Right, blow your nose, stand up and start again.'

Dodo unclipped her handbag and rummaged about.

'Oh dear I do not appear to have a hankychiefy.'

'Handkerchief,' I corrected, handing her mine.

'Thanker-chief,' Dodo Chivers quipped and I did not know toast could curdle but mine did deep inside me.

18

STARCH AND THE GIRDLE AND
HORRIBLE HOUSE

We waited for the rag and bone man to trot by. He had an upright piano on his cart and a barley-twist chimney pot tied to the wooden rail.

'How tall are you?' I asked as we crossed the road, for Dodo's head hardly seemed to reach my chin.

'Why is that house called Straw House?' She pointed with her left elbow at the tumbledown structure on the corner. 'When it is made of brick.'

'It was built by a man called Thomas Straw,' I told her.

'It would have been more fitting if his name was Thomas Horrible,' she declared with some justification. The roof was sagging badly in the middle and several of the windows were boarded over. 'Because it would be called Horrible House then,' she explained but I was not that easily distracted.

'How tall are you?' I asked, more firmly this time.

'In my shoes?' Dodo enquired innocently.

'No.'

'Oh but I would never ever turn up on duty without them.'

'Bare feet,' I insisted.

'I just made the regulation five feet and four inches.' Dodo jumped with both feet together onto the kerb.

'Walk sensibly. You don't look that tall to me.'

Dodo turned a light pink. 'Can I tell you the truth?'

'Don't ever tell me anything else.'

'I am five foot two and a tweensy bit less,' she admitted. 'But, before you ask and after you ask, I weigh seven stone and twelve pounds.'

'Two pounds under the minimum requirement,' I observed as she broke step to keep up with my longer stride. 'So how did you pass the medical?'

'Promise you will not tell?'

'I'll make you one promise.' I stepped over a furry white dog dropping. 'If you don't explain yourself, I will have you reassessed and out of the force before you get a chance to put on your uniform.'

'I put starch in my hair under the surface so the measuring stick didn't touch my head.'

'And?'

Dodo Chivers blushed. 'I wore big bloomers and the man doctor was too embarrassed to tell me to take them off and I sewed lots of Daddy's fishing weights into a girdle underneath – just over two pounds of them and jolly uncomfortable it was too.' We stopped outside number 6. 'So now you know and you will snitch on me and I will have to go home in disgrace on a choo-choo train.' Dodo hiccupped.

I gazed into the distance, impressed despite myself by her initiative. 'You must be mistaken, Constable Chivers. You are five feet four and weigh eight stone. I think you'll find it says so on your records.'

'Oh,' Dodo cried. 'Thank you, Inspector. I knew you could not really be so horrid as you seem.'

'I wouldn't bet on that,' I warned.

'Oh but I never gamble,' my constable assured me piously, 'except on horse races, greyhound races, card games and, of course, roulette.'

'Of course,' I agreed faintly. We were outside Moulton's Bookstore and I supposed this was as good a place to start as any. 'Come on. I'll introduce you.'

'To a shop?' Dodo wondered and I wished I had not already opened the door.

Moulton's Bookstore had a bow window painted brown but not within living memory. It was a long thin shop, lined either side by sagging shelves crammed with leather-bound food for grubs and mites. Down the central aisle ran four narrow rectangular tables piled with more heavy volumes than anyone could hope to read in a lifetime. Considering they were largely titles such as *The History of Waistcoat Buttons* in two hefty volumes, few – other than Sidney Grice with his love of the esoteric – would have wanted to try.

Teddy, tall and bony, rose from behind his by-the-door counter, where he had been perusing one of his wares.

'Oh good morning, B— Inspector.'

'Tell him off,' Dodo urged before turning to the proprietor with a stern, 'she does not like to be called that.'

'But...' Teddy flapped in confusion.

'But is as but does,' Dodo informed him as if that meant something. 'Daddy says so.'

Something shrivelled. I think it was me.

'Mr Moulton, this is Constable Chivers,' I introduced them.

Teddy propped his tortoiseshell glasses on the knobbly ridge of his brows and his eyes shrank like anemones when the tide goes out.

'You have a lot of books.' Dodo threw out her arms, tipping a propped-up family Bible flat onto the table.

'I am aware of that.' Teddy smiled. He had teeth that looked like they were designed for plucking thistles and a jutting shaven-to-the-point-of-rawness chin.

'Good.' Dodo's eyes flicked from side to side. 'Because there would be something wrong with you if you did not.'

Teddy pushed his brown fringe back but it flopped down again. 'Are you a plainclothes policewoman?'

'Plain?' Dodo straightened indignantly without managing to look any taller. 'You are not exactly Beau Brummell.'

This was true, if uncalled for. Teddy favoured brown corduroy trousers and tweed jackets. The trouble was he favoured them for many years at a stretch.

'Constable Chivers doesn't start until next week,' I explained as she picked up the Bible, knocking an atlas onto the floor in the process.

'Actually I'm waiting for my uniform too,' Teddy said with a proud toss of his head, trying but failing to puff out his sunken chest.

'Are you going to be a clerk?' Dodo stroked her chin. 'You seem well suited to doing something tedious,' she added without malice.

'Air Raid Precautions warden,' he announced, his spectacles rising to share my surprise. 'This will be a war of the people and we will be on the front line in East Anglia.'

'But why?' Dodo picked up the atlas, which had fallen open where Teddy had bookmarked it, and the Bible overbalanced.

'Because we are the closest part of England to Germany.' Teddy pointed to the map.

'No, I mean why are we supposed to rely on someone like you?' Dodo's finger traced the stretch of North Sea separating us from the enemy. It had seemed vast when I crossed it on a ferry but it looked alarmingly slender when I thought of the thousands of bombers poised to hurtle across it. 'We need real men to protect us.'

'Come on.' I grabbed my constable's arm and dragged her out. 'Did you have to be so rude?' I said when we were on the street.

'Oh but...' Dodo stared at me. 'Surely he cannot have taken

offence at that?' She reached back and pushed the door open. 'I'm sorry if I insulted your weedy physique,' she called, pulled the door shut again and rolled her big eyes dreamily. 'I think he rather liked me,' she declared.

'*How to Win Friends and Influence People*,' I muttered.

'That is the name of a book,' Dodo told me. 'Oh I wonder if Mr Moulton stocks it.' She glanced back. 'I could buy it for you, if you like.'

'I don't.'

We passed up Mulberry Road, pausing before we crossed for a bus to go by. It was packed with evacuees, probably from London – children pressing their faces to the window looked out on us, some waving excitedly, some crying, some terrified, some of the younger ones obviously confused. A little girl hugged an even smaller girl. One shaven-headed boy made an obscene gesture.

'They must be boy scouts.' Dodo smiled and gave him the V-sign back.

'Remind me to have a word with you about that later.'

'But where are we going?' Dodo spun a complete revolution on her heel.

'To the hospital.'

She spun again, two turns this time.

'Oh but oh why? Are you poorly-sorely?' Dodo staggered dizzily sideways.

'No but you will be if you don't start acting like an adult.' I stopped outside the main entrance, taken aback by the cruelty of my words until she drove me to the brink of a rage with a stomach-churning, 'Sowwy.'

I let it pass. It was either that or shaking her until bits fell off and I wouldn't wish that on anybody – well, hardly anybody.

*

There was a different nurse on duty. She had the face of an unloved pug.

'The woman who came in last night? She discharged herself this morning.'

'Did she leave a name?' I asked.

'No.' Her projecting lower teeth teetered on nipping my nose.

'Do you know where she went?'

'Of course I do.' The nurse put her hands on her hips. 'She went out of the front door.'

'And then?'

'And then I went off to mind my own business,' the nurse said sourly. 'Just like I'm doing now.' And off she set down the corridor, straight to the vets, I hoped.

'She seemed like a nice lady,' Dodo observed loudly. 'What a pity that she is not.'

19

THE PRICE OF PRIMATES

An army truck had pulled up on High Road West and a dozen youths all still in civvies were scrambling into the back of it.

Two scraggy girls stood at the front of a gaggle of women on the corner, flapping their none-too-clean handkerchiefs.

'Farewell my own true lover,' a scrawny girl sobbed.

'Oi'll write every day, my darlin',' her scrawnier friend vowed tearfully.

A corporal raised and clipped the tailgate and the lorry set off, taking all those boys to their great adventures and leaving me with their mothers waving and weeping and their girlfriends calling endearments that might have been better whispered on the back row of the Trocadero.

'Oh oi'll not be forgettin' him,' the scrawny girl sobbed. 'But thank durg he a'gorn. I'm gaspin' for a cuppa.'

'Oi've got futhers in me crop,' her scrawnier friend agreed.

'What language are they speaking?' Constable Chivers enquired.

'Suffolk,' I told her. 'You won't notice after a while.'

'Gracious, I shall have my work cut out correcting their grammar,' she pondered.

'They will not thank you.' I skirted a smashed bottle of milk.

'Daddy says goodness is its own reward,' Dodo quoted piously as she traipsed obliviously through the puddle and broken glass.

'Let's hope Daddy's right then.' I sighed. I had given up trying to stop Dodo calling her father that and it was probably one of the less annoying of her habits now.

We made our way down Beggar's Lane – more salubrious than the name suggested, a cobbled street with a deep central gutter and bordered by a mix of stables, some still in use, others converted into mews cottages.

Across the road somebody was playing a record – Artie Shaw's 'Begin the Beguine'.

'Oh I love Al Jolson.' Dodo did a twirl. 'The Spaniard that blighted my life,' she warbled loudly.

Number 6 opened straight onto the road and was nicely kept up with a navy-blue door and matching windows either side.

'Oh this is jolly as a jam jar.' Dodo skipped with one foot either side of the channel. 'But why have we stopped here by the sweet little brass sign saying *Bric-a-brac and curios*?'

Apart from my resisting the urge to throttle you?

'A Mr Peatrie, lives above his shop here,' I replied. 'He's almost retired now but he sells odd knick-knacks.'

'As well as bric-a-brac?'

'Yes.'

'And curios?'

'Yes.'

'But oh, Inspector, what is the difference?'

'I don't care.'

'But you do know, do you not?'

Those trusting eyes looked up at me and I realised I had a dilemma. Either I must admit that I didn't, and fall in my constable's esteem, or pretend that I did and think of a reason why I wouldn't tell her.

'I think you should find out for yourself.' I twisted the brass handle.

'To hone my investigative skills?'

Oh for goodness' sake. 'Exactly.'

'And are you going to purchase a knick-knack, bric-a-brac or curio, perhaps as a welcome-to-Slackwater gift for me?' Dodo jiggled about.

'No. It's just that Mr Peatrie hasn't kept his appointments with my father.'

'Crikey.' Dodo gaped. 'You arrest people for missing their appointments?'

'I want to check if he's all right. He dropped his lower denture in for repair and he can't eat much without it.' The bell tinkled genteelly as I opened the door. 'He's a bit deaf.'

'I had an aunt who was deaf,' Dodo told me. 'It made it very difficult for her to hear.'

I waited for a moment, to no avail.

Hamish Peatrie's shop was in a single room that would have once been the front parlour, crammed full of what was mainly junk – a stuffed owl frozen in flight; a stack of mismatched plates, some chipped; another of saucers, ditto; old magazines tied in piles; a box of used postcards with messages from aunts and uncles and schoolchildren and photographs of churches and donkeys. He was a nice old man who used to let me spend hours polishing his brass candlesticks and silver teapots – in retrospect more slave labour than kindliness.

Before the First World War he had owned a much larger shop on High Road West but his son, Danny, was a conscientious objector and Mr P shared his son's convictions. The shop was smashed and looted and he lost almost all his customers. The fact that Danny was killed rescuing a friend who had fallen down the cliffs at Hunstanton did little to assuage the people's righteous anger because the friend was 'conchie' too so they both deserved to die.

'Hello,' I called, 'Mr P.'

'But his name is Mr Peatrie,' Dodo corrected me. 'You told me so yourself.'

'I have always called him Mr P.'

'Except when you call him Mr Peatrie.'

'Yes.'

'Perhaps he is out and has forgotten to lock up or is deafer than you think or having a bath or ill in bed or hiding or sleeping or sulking,' Dodo suggested. 'Or perhaps he is tending to his garden if he has one.'

'Stop jabbering.' I raised my voice. 'Mr P?' Nothing.

'Or dead,' Dodo added dramatically.

'Hello, Mr P.'

'Nobody is replying,' Dodo informed me helpfully.

A furled umbrella projected from a blue-glazed pot. 'Mr Peatrie? Hello.' Again nothing.

'I do not think you should go in, Inspector.' Dodo hovered in the road. 'It might be dangerous.'

'It's a junk shop' – I stepped inside – 'not a snakepit.' There was always a mouldering monkey playing a trumpet in the corner but it had gone now. He had been asking £3 for it but who the hell would have bought that – unless it was for somebody they hated?

'Oh do they have snakey pits in Slackwater?'

'Not yet.'

'But when shall they have them, Inspector Church?'

'Just as soon as they are ready.' I paused. She was making a simple visit into a three-act drama. 'You wait there if you're worried.' After all, she wasn't officially on the force yet.

The shop was deserted.

'Not blooming likely. Excuse my befouled language.' Dodo followed me in.

There was an upright piano with the sheet music for 'Keep

the Home Fires Burning' on the stand. The old war songs were having a revival until we could write some new ones.

'I'll have a look upstairs.'

'I wonder if he is hiding behind this counter on the left-hand side of his emporium, waiting to jump out shouting *boo* to scare us.' She clasped her face in both hands.

'I think that unlikely. He must be nearly eighty.'

'I might take a look.' Dodo crept towards it, then stopped. 'Oh but do I dare to?' she dithered. 'Or do I not?' She put a crooked finger to her temple. 'I do dare,' she decided and poked her head gingerly over. 'Nothing.'

'Good. Now...'

'He could be crouched in the footwell underneath,' she speculated.

'Oh for—' I began as she went behind the counter in a sudden rush.

'Oh!' Dodo jumped and covered her mouth, but not enough to stifle her squawk. 'Dead,' she said through her hand.

'What are you talking about?'

'Dead,' she cried again. 'Dead as a dodo.'

hurried towards my constable. 'Mr Peatrie?'

Dodo shook her head, her hair fluffing out like a red feather duster.

'Then who?' Dodo Chivers had become an obstruction. 'Get out of my way.' She stepped back but only blocked the space between counter and wall even more. 'Move.'

My constable seemed paralysed with shock. I grasped her shoulder, thrust her to one side and pushed past. His stock books were on the floor, the ones where he painstakingly itemised every scrap of rubbish in his shop with details of where he had bought them and who he had sold them to.

'Where?' I demanded and Dodo crooked her finger.

'Spider,' she hissed as if confronted by a grizzly bear rearing up to unzip her abdomen. 'They may be God's creatures but I hate them.' She rummaged through her hair.

'Go away,' I said as evenly as I could.

'Yes, B—Inspector.' She went to stand beside an empty umbrella stand, emitting an odd high whine.

'What are you doing?'

'Humming "I Want to Be Happy" from *No, No, Nanette*!'

'Then stop it.'

'It distracts me.'

'You're distracted enough already. Stop it.'

Dodo took a deep breath. Her cheeks were different shades of pink. 'I am quite recovered now,' she announced, 'despite your unsympathetic attitude.'

'Good.' I came out from behind the counter.

'Perhaps he has gone for a walk or shopping or to the cinema,' Dodo mused. '*Robin Hood* is on – it is awfully good, I hear – with Errol Flynn – he is awfully good too, I hear. Or perhaps he has gone to visit friends or relatives or on holiday.'

I waited for her to finish and, after the proposals of a visit to the doctor's or a religious retreat, she did.

'Shut up,' I said when she already had. Dodo opened her mouth. 'And stay shut up,' I added. 'You are a disgrace, Constable Chivers. Policemen are not frightened of spiders and policewomen are not frightened of anything policemen are not frightened of.'

'Yes but—'

'You will speak when I tell you to and not before. Not only that, policewomen are braver than policemen. When policemen tremble, we stand firm. Got that?'

Dodo nodded dumbly.

'You may say *yes*.'

'Yes, Inspector,' Dodo said meekly.

'We are not silly and we are certainly not soppy,' I instructed. 'We do not use expressions like *crikey* or *heavens-to-Betsy* and you may say *no*, now.'

'No, Inspector.'

'Right,' I said with considerable foreboding. 'Go outside and stay outside.'

'Yes, Inspector.' She meekly obeyed.

'And, if anybody turns up, call me.'

'Yes, Inspector.' Dodo took a deep breath and straightened up. 'It was a whopper though,' she whispered to herself loudly through the open door.

Not surprisingly, I had never been upstairs though Mr P had told me he lived there. Mrs P had run off with a third-rate Armenian author, though her husband let people believe she was dead, even putting little bunches of bluebells occasionally in a milk bottle on the grave of a Maude Peatrie who was buried there in 1748.

The most I had ever seen was the stairs running steeply up on the other side of the solid back door and I remembered thinking how great it would be to toboggan down them on a tea tray but never getting the chance to try.

I turned the handle; the door swung open and Hamish Peatrie shot into the room.

21

THE DIAMOND SLIPPER

stepped aside automatically.

'Oh,' Dodo shouted from the pavement, 'I *knew* you were a prankster.'

But Mr Peatrie's japes did not end there. He did not so much spring out as tumble at my feet.

'Oh,' Dodo repeated, never at a loss for an *Oh*. 'Is he—'

'Dead,' I confirmed and waited for the shrieks.

'Oh, that is all right,' Dodo breathed in relief. 'From the way he is lying with his neck all twisted I thought he must be in awful pain.'

'I think it's broken.' I touched Mr P's cheek. It was stone cold.

'I didn't hear it break.'

'It was already broken,' I told her. 'Come in and shut the door.'

Dodo pranced into the room. 'At last,' she declared merrily, 'a real murder.'

I didn't bother to argue with the *at last* bit.

'I think he just fell downstairs,' I said sadly. I didn't like to think of him lying unfound on the other side of that door. Perhaps other customers had come, given up and gone unknowingly. He was dressed in grey trousers and a brown corduroy jacket.

'Oh but he is only wearing one slipper,' Dodo objected. 'Surely the missing slipper is a vital murder clue. Perhaps the murderer has stolen it because there were diamonds or gold doubloons sewn into the sole or heel.'

I looked up towards the gloomy corridor.

'The other slipper is near the top of the stairs. I imagine it came off, he tripped over it and fell.'

'Should we not be deducing things rather than imagining them?' Dodo brought out her notebook.

'It is what I infer from the evidence as it presents to me.' I crouched wearily to straighten the body up. It was a question of respect. 'He's been dead for a couple of days at least. His body is cold and rigor mortis has worn off.'

And it was only when I rolled Mr P onto his back that I saw two marks just under the left angle of the jaw. Could they have been pressure from somebody's fingers?

'Oh.' Dodo bobbed beside me. 'The wounds of a Vampire.' She clutched my empty sleeve.

'Vampires do not exist.' I prised her fingers away.

'I saw one at the Gaumont.' Dodo grasped my coat belt.

'That was just a film.' I tried but failed to pull free.

'But a true one,' she insisted.

'No.' I loosened her grip. 'Anyway it would have to have really blunt teeth. The skin is hardly broken.'

'Perhaps Mr Peatrie was not delicious,' Dodo suggested. 'He does not look like he was.'

This was an accident, I felt certain, but the coroner would want the cause of death confirmed.

'We'll probably need an autopsy.'

'But we are not dead.' Her grip tightened again.

'For Mr Peatrie.'

'By someone who knows about vampires?'

'Turn the sign to *Closed* and pull down the door blind,' I snapped.

'Oh but—' Dodo Chivers protested but that was all she got to say because I was propelling her out, taking the key off its hook and locking the front door behind us.

82

We called in at Hempson's the undertakers on Cardigan Street. Mr Hempson had only just taken over from his father, who he had buried at a discounted rate but the son had worked in the firm for long enough to know the procedure. He would arrange for the body to be collected and I would inform the coroner.

'Did he have next of kin?' Mr Hempson enquired.

He was a big man, all angular like a painting by Picasso in his cubist period. Even his eyes had an odd rectangularity to them.

'I suppose his wife is, legally.'

'Didn't she elope with an Albanian?' He breathed sorrowfully as if the loss had been mine.

'Armenian.'

'I knew it was something like that.' He nodded gravely. 'Not that I have anything against foreigners. I just can't stand them.'

His hands were flat enough to smooth plaster on a wall.

'I'll put out a request to see if any other forces know where she is,' I promised.

'Nice old boy,' Mr Hempson recalled. 'Had a monkey in his shop which he couldn't bear to part with but he let me have it for a tenner. Threw in the trumpet for another guinea.'

'Lucky you,' I mumbled.

'Indeed.' He nodded gravely again because it was the only way he knew how to nod. 'Bought for our wedding anniversary next week.'

'How romantic,' I murmured and he smiled gravely.

'I thought so too. Mrs Hempson always says I'm a big ape.'

*

'Bit early to be plyin' your trade,' the desk sergeant greeted my companion. 'Where'd'you pick her up?' he asked me.

'Sergeant Briggs meet Constable Chivers,' I introduced her.

Brigsy didn't actually guffaw but he was well on the way to it when he saw that I was not joking. 'Bleedin' hell,' he managed and I waited for Dodo to correct him on his expletive when she marched up to the desk.

'You use as much foul language as you like, Sergeant,' she greeted him gamely. 'That is tickety-boo-boo with me.'

'Tickety-what?' The Shark cruised out from his office. He had not taken kindly to the news that we were to get another woman. 'What's this?' He gestured to our new recruit, who stuck out her hand. 'Hello,' she said. 'My name is Dodo and I am not afraid of spiders.'

Sharkey showed his teeth. 'Just as well,' he said. 'There's one crawling up your leg.'

There was no point in trying to reassure Dodo. Nobody could have heard me above the shrieks. Vesty rushed out to see what the fuss was and I was almost sure he was bearing an invisible pistol.

'Thought it was Jerry.' He slipped his imaginary gun into its imaginary holster.

'Gerry who?' Dodo hitched up her dress. 'Or should that be Gerry whom?'

'Pretty little thing.' Our chief superintendent joined the two men in appraising Dodo's legs.

'It was a joke,' I reassured her.

'No it was not.' Dodo patted herself down. 'Spiders do not have a sense of humour.'

Please don't say Daddy told you that, I prayed.

'Daddy told me that,' our new WPC said.

Why do you never answer my prayers? I never even got that red party dress.

'This is Constable Chivers, sir.' I cringed as I introduced her.

'Ah yes.' He nodded. 'Fido Chivers' girl.'

'Indeed,' I said feebly, for that explained quite a lot. Chief Superintendent Frederick 'Fido' Chivers was a legend in East Anglia and it would have been a remarkably brave officer who rejected his daughter's application. Why on earth had I not made the connection? I chided myself but it was not that uncommon a surname, I decided, and it would have taken quite a leap of the imagination to associate Dodo with the man who broke up the Woodchip Boys of Lowestoft.

Dodo caught sight of our senior officer and clapped as many fingertips as she could over her mouth. 'Oh, your poor head.'

'What?' He touched the concavity as if discovering it for the first time.

'Is it very poorly-sorely, sir?'

'What?' He ran his fingers over the sunken skin. 'Oh I hardly notice it.' And he didn't seem to mind in the least when Dodo Chivers blew his head a kiss.

22

THE RATCATCHER'S DAUGHTER

There were two shapes under sheets in the morgue.

'Angie Harrison.' Tubby Gretham indicated towards the smaller shape.

'The little girl who was found in the village pond at Titchfold?'

'Four years old.' Tubby grimaced. 'No suspicious circumstances, I'm glad to say. The abrasion on her forehead was just what her mother said, something she got two days before in a skipping accident.'

'How sad.' I had been fished out of the sea at a similar age after my father had left me sitting on a breakwater.

'I wanted you to see this.' Tubby lowered the second cover.

Hamish Peatrie's face was waxy and blotchy from the blood draining down but, other than that, he looked peaceful enough, as if ready to be roused for his morning cup of tea. The heavy white sheet was down to just below his nipples. He had been a highly proper man and would not have liked me to be gazing on those and I felt sorry that I had to.

The marks were still visible on Mr P's neck, one no more than a scuff, the other an indentation.

'Here.' Tubby – nursing for me this time – handed me a magnifying glass and I saw the indentation clearly – roughly circular, perhaps a quarter of an inch in diameter and an eighth deep.

'There's no bruising,' I observed.

'So it was received at the time of or after death,' Tubby confirmed. 'Was there anything he could have fallen on?'

'There was nothing on the stairs,' I recalled, 'and the doorknob at the bottom was rounded.'

'Collision with a small blunt object,' Tubby speculated.

'Or pressure.' I speculated too. 'Shine your torch on it.'

'I will if you get your head out of the way.'

'I need to get a closer look.' Tubby slid the torch between me and the body as I lowered my head again, holding my breath. Mr P's corpse was not fresh and had not been embalmed. 'I don't suppose you've got any tracing paper?'

I waited for a sarcastic response.

'Got some greaseproof Boadicea wrapped round my sandwich.' Boadicea was Tubby's pet name for his wife but entirely unmerited. Few women were less likely to go on a murderous rampage than Greta Gretham, despite her married name making her sound like a stutter.

'I only need a couple of square inches.'

Tubby reached into his pocket for a folded sheet. 'Have the lot.'

'You've eaten it already?' I ripped a square off the cleanest corner.

'Don't want to ruin my appetite.'

'Can't imagine that happening.' I laid the paper over the mark and prodded it with a pencil.

Greta was trying to get her husband to lose some weight, little suspecting that he ate her packed lunches for elevenses then still went to the Coach and Horses for his pint with a steak and kidney pie.

'What are you doing?'

'There's a shape, I think it might be a symbol impressed into the concavity and I thought, if I could push the paper in and trace it… Oh, this is much too opaque.'

'I shall complain to Boadicea when I get home.' Tubby thrust the torch at me. 'Hold that.'

'You won't be able to see through it either,' I huffed. 'It looks like some numbers.'

'Not going to try.' Tubby moulded the square over his forefinger, rotating his hand to make a little crinkled cup shape, and snatched my pencil. 'Hold that light still.' And in a few strokes he had copied the lines.

'I didn't know you were an artist.'

'Five years of drawing what you have dissected or can see down a microscope give even a clumsy oaf like me some skills.' Tubby was neither clumsy nor an oaf but he was not a man to fish for compliments. 'Now, let's see.' He flattened the paper out and held it under the torchlight.

I squinted at the marks he had made.

5

G

27

'5G, 27,' I read. 'Doesn't mean much to me.'

Tubby shrugged. 'Nor me.'

The door opened and a nurse popped in. 'Dr Lincoln sends his regards but wishes to know if you want him to do the operation himself,' she announced, then, fearing the reception her words might receive, added, 'it's what he told me to say, Dr Gretham.'

Tubby started guiltily.

'Oh Lord we have a session booked.' He liked to do minor procedures himself, rather than send patients off to Felixstowe or Ipswich. 'Must go.' He washed his hands in the same scratched ceramic sink I had once seen him use to flush out twenty feet of small intestine.

'Thank you for this.' I waved the paper as he pulled off his lab coat and threw it over a hook on the wall.

'Bye, Bet— Inspector.' He bundled off.

'She inspects bets?' I heard the nurse wondering and then there I was with just Hamish Peatrie and poor little Angie Harrison for company.

'Oh Mr P,' I addressed him sadly. 'Don't say you were murdered.'

But Mr Peatrie was saying nothing as I covered him over again, thinking how I could never have imagined, when I polished his brass as a child, that this was how I would wish him goodbye. His mouth was agape like he was about to sing. 'The Ratcatcher's Daughter' was a favourite of his despite its gruesome lyrics – that and 'Danny Boy'.

23

FRANKENSTEIN'S MONSTER AND THE SIGN OF T

On the first of September Constable Rivers joined us. He was a morose man with round shoulders and a strangely receding face. It wasn't so much that his jaw jutted as that the rest of his face had got left behind. Rivers had a toothache in his spine, he told us, clutching his kidneys, arching backwards, gurning and gurgling for several minutes before exhausting his repertoire. Lord knows how he had dragged himself in, he marvelled.

This was Dodo's first day in uniform. Her appearance was more respectable but she still managed to look like a child in fancy dress.

'I had an aunt who had terrible backache,' Dodo sympathised, 'in her gardener.'

Rivers looked at her sideways, unsure if this was a joke, though I suspected it was not.

'Told you he'd be back before payday.' Sergeant Briggs rolled one eye up and the other down and I was about to ask how he did that when the phone rang. Brigsy preened the smudge on his upper lip. I have often wondered why people tend to their appearance for the telephone. Women will almost always check their hair and some even freshen their lipstick before they pick up a receiver. 'Good morning, Sackwater Central Police Station.' He would have made a better receptionist for my father than my mother ever did. 'Oh.'

Brigsy sat straight. 'Oh. I shall s'licit his presence, sir.'

Where on earth had he picked that phrase up from? It was difficult to imagine the sergeant as a guest at a country house party. He laid the receiver on its side and went jerkily, like an emaciated Boris Karloff in full get-up minus the bolt in his neck, to summon my beloved colleague.

Sharkey stomped out of his office, annoyed to have been disturbed. He had probably been doing something important like having a nap.

'Senior Inspector Sharkey,' he rapped into the mouthpiece. This was yet another bone of contention between us. We had enough now to build a skeleton that could take pride of place in the Natural History Museum. True, Old Scrapie had been an inspector four years longer than me, but there is no such rank and I was certainly not going to introduce myself as a junior. 'Right.' There was something in the rise in tone that made me glance over. 'What's the address?' My alleged superior was stretching under his skin like a grub in a cocoon and I hoped he wasn't about to emerge as a new Sharkey, even more horrible than the one we had already seen.

Until recently Briggs could have put the caller through to the office but the connection was faulty and the General Post Office was in no hurry to fix it. They were busy putting new lines in at the town hall so the committees could contact the subcommittees of other committees, thereby winning the war, should it ever be declared.

As I was wondering if there was any point in making a complaint, Shirley Temple crept in, all golden curls, looking about her like a babe lost in the woods. 'I've losted my button,' she piped up timorously. 'My mum will kill me dead or worse.' The little girl held out the lower edge of her cardigan with a trembling hand for me to see the torn thread.

'Where did you lose it?' I asked, briefly forgetting how annoying adults are when they do that.

'Somewhere else,' she told me.

I made a tea signal over Sharkey's head to Brigsy.

'I'll keep an eye out for it,' I promised.

The sergeant fiddled with the scraps on his scalp. 'Do tha' be a Maizonic sign you do just now, madam?'

Sharkey covered the mouthpiece. 'Shut up, the lot of you.'

I delved into my handbag for the bag of aniseed balls and the little girl took at least three, popping them all in her mouth at once. 'Oh thank you.' Her big blue eyes shone with gratitude.

Brigsy peered over at the cardigan. 'If you come in tomorrow first thing,' he whispered, 'my missus do have a tin of buttons. I'll bring it in for you to look through.'

'That's a kind thought,' I commented.

'Oh yes.' The little girl wiped her eyes. 'Thank you very ever so much, General.' She scurried away, her tiny voice piping through the open door. 'She was making the sign for tea, you tosspot.'

Superintendent Vesty drifted out of his office – I hadn't even known he was in the building – tall, slim and very vague, with his usual air of a man wandering from one cocktail party in search of another.

'Everybody happy?' he asked like the perfect host offering to top up our glasses. 'Good. Good.' This was obviously not a question that required an answer but Dodo felt obliged to do so.

'I do not believe there has ever been a time when everyone is happy, sir,' she philosophised.

'Splendid.' Vesty bowed his head, the skin over his plate sagging.

'Oh what a clever trick.' Dodo clapped her hands. 'But quite repulsive,' she decided on second thoughts.

'What?' Vesty looked at her blankly.

'The little girl who just showed us how she can bend her fingers right back,' I improvised hastily.

'Oh I missed that,' Dodo complained.

The super tugged his earlobe. 'Keep up the good work.' Some superior officers come from relatively humble stock and clip their accents like good cigars, a little more with every promotion. One chief inspector in Norfolk was the son of a crab fisherman raised in a shack but his diction made our royal family sound common. Our superintendent was the genuine article though. The Vestys had been landed gentry since before the Norman Conquest.

'And thah door to cell one do be stuck it do, sir,' Brigsy announced. 'Not thah we do have goh anyone to put in it.' He preened his lip-stain thoughtfully. 'Or take out, come to think of it.'

Vesty looked at his sergeant vacantly. 'Got another damned committee meeting,' he muttered as he went on his way.

'Keep your eye on the ball,' I advised softly, for we had all seen the clubs in the back of his Rover.

Sharkey had finished his call. 'Got any big cases on, Church?' he enquired.

Not long ago I thought I had but the coroner had reached a verdict of accidental death for Mr P and he may well have been right. Whatever caused them, those marks on his neck were certainly not deep enough to be fatal.

'I can give you that lost button one,' I offered, pretending not to notice how close he was to bursting. 'Or there's the unidentified boy who pushed a dead lizard through the Baptist minister's letter box.' There was also a stolen rabbit but I was keeping that one for myself.

''Cause I've got a ripe one.' Sharkey smirked. 'A nasty murder by the sound of it.'

'Do you have any nice ones in Suffolk then?' I enquired innocently.

24

THE WASP AND OAK TREE

Bath Road was a pleasant street before the Great War – parallel terraces of four houses, each with a little front garden and a yard at the back – but, for some reason, it had gone downhill. Perhaps it was when Folders, a major employer in Sackwater, moved their bootlace manufacturing business over to Stowmarket so that the working families either became non-working families or moved out.

I knew the road very well because I used to play at my friend Etterly Utter's. Her home had an outside toilet and the tin bath hung on a nail outside, but it was a snug clean house and I was always made welcome there – until the day Etterly climbed into the hollow of an oak tree and was never seen again.

We could easily have walked but Sharkey explained that good policing was all about style and dignity.

'I thought it was all about good policing,' I said sweetly as I mounted the running board.

Sackwater Central had a black Wolseley Wasp with a blue and white police sign on the roof and a bell in front of the chrome radiator grille. My colleague drove, of course. Even if I had wanted to argue about it, I couldn't have changed gear without letting go of the steering wheel and twisting round.

Constable Rivers lounged in the back, his arms over the top of the seat like a gentleman being chauffeured, and Sharkey must have felt that too, for he snarled, 'You're blocking the rear view.' So, with great displays of agony, Rivers shuffled over to sit behind me.

'This is *my* case,' Sharkey reminded me for the third time and pulled over. The engine had hardly had time to warm up.

'And I hope you'll be very happy together.' I hinged the door back and clambered out.

A telegram boy cycled past, hands linked with exaggerated carelessness behind his head, whistling 'Ain't Misbehavin' very loudly and hastily grabbing the handlebar when a wiry mongrel dashed out, snapping at his foot.

Like most of the houses, the front garden of number 15 was just a patch of weeds around a dustbin. It was bordered by what had been a privet hedge but was now a clump of bushes. The brown paint on the woodwork was flaking and the glass in one of the upstairs windows had been replaced with the side of a tea chest giving free advertising space to Tate & Lyle.

Constable Box stood in front of the doorway. He was a giant of a man but his head still looked too large for his body. How he had managed to find a helmet to fit beat me. His face was oddly misshapen, with an earthy texture like some kind of root vegetable grown in the fens to feed cattle. He straightened up as we approached.

'Body's in here, sir,' he announced.

'You'd be a bloody fool standing there if it wasn't,' Sharkey told him pleasantly. 'Door locked?'

'Not now, sir.' Box blinked his sheep-like eyes.

'Then open it, man.'

The constable rotated clockwise – a drawn-out process that reminded me of watching a liner being manoeuvred into dock.

'Was it locked when you arrived?' I tried to peer round at the stained-glass panel. There was a jagged hole in it about the size of a dinner plate.

'Yes, ma'am. I broke the glass with my truncheon. The key was in the keyhole. It's a deadlock.'

'So the glass wasn't already broken?'

'He's just said so,' Sharkey snapped.

'No, ma'am,' Box confirmed.

Box fiddled with the handle, seemingly unused to such complicated devices, and the door swung almost all the way before it hit a shoe.

25

THE NARROW HOUSE

You can't mistake the smell of blood. It hangs thick and sickly and clings to you. After a morning of extractions my father would have to scrub his hands with Lysol to get rid of the stench on his fingers. It seeps into your nose and stays there. The air was heavy with it.

I paused to take in the scene. Most people rush to the body but it's not going anywhere, whereas its surroundings change the minute anyone intrudes on them. The gaslight was still on in the long narrow hall – by no means every house had electricity yet; some still relied on oil lamps – and the floral wallpaper couldn't have been replaced for decades. It would have to be now. It was splattered with clots.

There was a narrow staircase with a worn brown paisley runner going to a half-corridor before turning back on itself. There were two closed cream-painted doors to the left. The right hand would have been a party wall with number 17, the last of that group of houses.

The shoe was on the foot of a young man. He lay on his back on the blue lino in a glistening black pool. If it hadn't been for the same not-quite-sharp suit and the death's head signet ring, it might have taken a while longer to recognise Freddy Smart. As well as his hair having flopped over it, the face was masked in gore. There was a gaping wound just above his Adam's apple and another near the back of his neck below the left ear.

'Somebody's a bit tasty with a knife.' Sharkey whistled as I ran an eye over the door and its frame.

Sharkey had gone through the pool and I followed as closely in his steps as possible.

'Have to be a big one.' I went down on my haunches beside the body, tucking my skirt under my thighs so it didn't trail. 'I'll give you good odds that those two wounds connect. He's been run right through.'

Sharkey caught his breath angrily. 'I didn't say it was a penknife,' he insisted and I saw no point in arguing.

Old Scrapie squatted on the other side. 'Nasty.' He lifted Freddy's left arm by the sleeve of his once-sharp suit and let go. It fell like it would through treacle. 'Rigor's setting in so he's been dead at least four hours.'

'Probably not much longer.' I got a pencil from my handbag. 'If it was in the night, somebody would have been on to him for showing a light. Who discovered him?'

'Neighbour, Mrs Shunter, came round to complain about rats coming under the fence. She saw the body through the glass. You can,' he insisted though I had never denied it. 'Saw it myself through the yellow flower before Box opened up.'

I slid a pencil under Freddy Smart's fringe to lift the caked hair aside.

'Sweet Jesus,' I breathed. His left eye had been gouged into a pulp.

Sharkey shrugged to show he was made of sterner and therefore better stuff. 'Whoever did this will be covered in blood,' my colleague speculated. 'Somebody must have seen him going down the street like that.'

The hair itself was a clotting mass of sticky strands. I walked my fingers through it. The skull felt intact.

I had a thought. 'What if the murderer was never here?'

Sharkey sniffed. 'What then? He was murdered by a ghost? Is that what they teach you in London these days?'

'I don't think anyone else was in this hallway,' I theorised. 'Those footprints in the blood. I'll bet a pound to a penny every one of them is his or ours. There are no bloody prints going towards the back of the hall or on the stairs and there were none on the front step or path when we arrived. If you stabbed this man close up you'd be wading through it.'

'He wasn't stabbed elsewhere and brought here,' Sharkey sneered.

'The door wasn't forced because the lock and woodwork are intact,' I reasoned. Sharkey had got blood on his chin somehow. 'But how could you get out through the front door anyway? The key was in the lock so you couldn't reach it to lock it from outside.'

'What then?'

'This might sound foolish,' I began and he snorted more than loudly enough to let me know that it would be. 'But what if he was stabbed through the letter box?'

Sharkey considered the proposition for just as long as it took him to say, 'Bollocks.' He got to his feet but I stayed down.

'There is blood on the flap,' I argued.

'There's bloody blood every-bloody-where.'

Freddy Smart's hands were clawed and bloodied, with long cuts on the palms and fingers.

I tried a new tack. 'He must have had lots of enemies.'

Sharkey trampled back towards the door, not even glancing to check my observation. 'So how do you deduce that, Miss Marple?'

'Because I know who he is.' I put my pencil into a bag. March Middleton had taught me to carry them and I had thought of her guardian when I saw that gaping socket. 'Freddy Smart.'

'Freddy?' At least I had his attention now. 'He went with his dad, Crake, to America ten years or more ago.'

'Well, he's back now,' I assured my colleague, 'though hardly in the first division, if this is all he can afford. I came across him threatening a young woman the first day I came and I saw her after he beat her up.'

'And I bet you bloody interfered.' Inspector Sharkey wiped his hands on a white-spotted red handkerchief.

'I tried to protect her,' I admitted and Sharkey snorted.

'Nice try, Church.' He pointed to the body. 'I'd love to say that's the result of your meddling but no spurned bitch did that. It'd take a man to kill a Smart. Probably a fight over territory.'

'I—'

'This is my case, Church,' Sharkey interrupted, 'and I decide how to handle it.'

I got to my feet. 'Very well,' I conceded. 'But the assault of Millicent Smith is mine.'

Sharkey stuffed his handkerchief into his jacket pocket and I glimpsed the top of a hip flask poking up.

'Take her.' He flung out an arm mockingly. 'But the culprit of that crime, by your own reckoning, is lying dead at our feet.'

'I need some air,' I said. 'It stinks in here.'

26

THE SACKWATER MARTYR

went to the door.

A round-shouldered woman, hair in rollers under a net, was loitering on the pavement, trussed in a paisley apron, her legs sheathed in the sort of stockings I had been happy to abandon, wrinkled down to her brown carpet slippers.

'That's the neighbour,' Box told me through the corner of his mouth, like it was a secret that had to be kept from the woman herself.

I walked up the path. 'Mrs Shunter?'

'Might be.' Her top denture flopped up and down, semaphoring each word.

'I believe you found the body.'

She folded her arms under her pendant breasts. 'Why d'you believe tha' then?'

'Because I was told you did.'

'And you do believe everything you're told, do you?' She shuffled her arms from side to side as if trying to rock her bosom to sleep. 'Can't be much of a copper, can you?'

'*Did* you find the body?'

'Yes.'

'So I was right to believe it.'

'I could be lyin'.' Her false teeth tried to escape – and who could blame them? – but her lips caught them and returned them to the living hell of Mrs Shunter's mouth. 'I might not even be Mrs Shunter.'

Oh good grief. 'I have been given to believe that you claim to have found the body and you have confirmed that. Assuming, for a moment, that is true—'

'Thah's behher. Now you're thinking logically – like a man would.'

I am thinking of decking you – like a man would. 'How did you find it?'

'Dead.'

I gave up. 'You will go to the police station today and make a full statement.'

'Oh you believe thah, do you?'

'In two words, yes.'

'Thah's one word.'

'The second word is one I can only whisper in my head,' I told her and she blanched.

'I int never been sworn at like thah afore,' she told me, 'except by my kids.' She lowered her bosom. 'Good for you.'

'Who lives here normally?' I didn't know much about Freddy Smart but I knew it wasn't his kind of place.

'Why, the dead woman, of course,' the alleged Mrs Shunter replied. 'Millicent Smith.'

I saw no reason to correct her mistake just yet. 'Alone?'

'Apart from her fancy man who int half as fancy as he make out.'

'Freddy Smart?'

'That's the one.' The woman who tacitly admitted to being Mrs Shunter twisted a roller that was coming undone.

'When did you last see her?'

'Five past eight, through the glass in the door.' She wrapped a rust-coloured lock of hair round the spikes.

'And when did you last see her alive?'

'Just after she lost her tooth. I ask if she gone and been to thah dentist in F'licity House. He's a butcher, if ever I saw one – and I did.'

'What did she say?'

'Nothin'.' She pulled her hairnet down but the roller unrolled with it. 'She do be runnin' for the bus with a suitcase, she do.'

'Do you know where the bus went?'

Mrs Shunter gave up and pulled the roller out. 'Up the road and away.'

'Thank you,' I said. 'You have been almost helpful.'

I went back to the open door, where Rivers was sharing one of Box's roll-ups. Sharkey was cadging a light.

'What purpose do you serve, Constable Rivers?' I demanded and he remembered to rub a kidney.

'It's my back, ma'am. It do be dere.'

Dere, I knew, meant dire. 'That doesn't answer my question.'

'I'm a martyr to it.'

'Nor that. Get it fixed or get another job,' I barked. 'If you want to wear that uniform, do something useful in it for once.'

'Got a bit of a temper, hasn't she?' Sharkey commented from behind as if he was honey personified.

I turned my attention to Box, who quailed a little under my gimlet eye. 'When did you last have a cup of tea?' I asked.

'I do believe it be around about five o' the clock, ma'am,' he replied warily, 'before I start my shift.'

'Then go back to the station. Tell them what's happened and send for Dr Gretham.'

'He's struck off,' Sharkey objected, 'and anyway—' but I was in no mood to be told again whose case it was.

'He knows a corpse when he sees one,' I insisted. We had all heard how Dr Hedges certified Mrs Goodlock as dead on three separate occasions. 'And, anyway, he has been struck on again.' I had a suspicion that wasn't the right term but I was not going to be the one to correct it. 'And you' – I turned back to Constable Box – 'will not stop drinking tea until I get back to the station.'

Box grinned. 'I'll do my level best, ma'am.'

'And you, Rivers' – I re-gimleted my eye – 'will stand and guard this door with your worthless spinal column until you are relieved, if it takes the rest of your miserable so-called career.'

*

We did not exchange a word until Inspector Sharkey had parked on the forecourt.

'Don't you ever humiliate me in front of the men like that again,' he said icily as I put my hand to the handle to get out.

'Do you know what you are?' I asked quietly, deciding to skip the part about him being an arrogant, booze-breathed, poxy bastard. 'A crap copper.'

I braced myself for the onslaught, determined that he was not going to intimidate me. Sharkey's fingers gripped the steering wheel as if it was my throat.

'Know what *you* are, Church?' he spat out venomously. 'Like all jumped-up women who think they can compete with men, a dried-up frustrated old spinster.'

I never understood why spinster is an insult while bachelor sounds rather fun but I decided to debate that with him at a time when we were old and reminiscing fondly by the fireside.

'The difference being that I may not always be a spinster,' I told my colleague. 'But you will always be crap.'

If Sharkey could have squeezed juice out of that steering wheel, he'd have filled a bucket by now. 'Know what you need, Church?' He seethed. 'A fuck.'

I twisted away to open the door.

'But I already work with one,' I told him and swung my feet demurely out onto the running board.

27

THE SIRENS OF SACKWATER

We had had eggs for breakfast for the third time that week. Hetty and Jenny were laying well on the scraps we fed them. If Mrs Perkins didn't buck up soon she would end up in the pot, Captain Sultana threatened.

'Over my dead body,' I said automatically from my torn-out crossword, for she was always the first to charge out of the shed to greet me and I didn't like the idea of eating family.

'Looks like the Poles are massing for a counter-attack,' Jimmy crowed. 'So maybe the Bolshies will think twice about joining in.'

It had been his turn to collect our mail from the Anchor Inn. There was none that morning, being Sunday, but he got yesterday's paper so he bagged the right to read it first, apart from the front page, which was Captain's because this was his boat after all.

'You've changed your tune.' I pencilled *Icarus* into 1 across.

'I only joined because I fancied Emily Butter.' Jimmy's ears reddened as they often did when he told a fib. He had been an enthusiastic, if somewhat naïve, member of the British Communist Party until Joe Stalin signed a pact with his new friend Adolf.

'Where are my glasses?' Captain patted his pockets.

'On your head, Captain,' I told him.

Jimmy flicked through to the sports pages. He was welcome to those. I had yet to find a game that interested me even though I had enjoyed playing them at school.

I looked out of the porthole. It had been a damp summer and the bracken grew thick and tall between the white-barked birch trees. Jimmy had promised to do some scything later. A silver carp, enormous, fat and sluggish, floated on in the late morning sunshine, not fighting on the long steel cable that moored it to a barge downstream.

I leaned back to finish my cigarette.

'I can never do that,' Jimmy admitted enviously. 'Blow smoke rings.' He puckered his lips and puffed like a child blowing out his birthday candles.

'You have the wrong-shaped lips,' I told him, fully aware that many a local girl would disagree with me about that.

Captain checked his huge fob watch. 'It should be on soon.' He struggled out of his rocking chair.

Jimmy was closest but nobody other than Captain was allowed to touch that precious wireless set.

'Get the bottle,' I bossed my courtesy nephew.

'Yes ma'am.' Jimmy sprang up with a mock salute and clutched his head. 'Oh shit-shit-shit. Who put that bloody beam there?' He rubbed his hair furiously. 'It's not funny.'

'It is a bit.' I'd done the same myself many times when I first moved into *Cressida* but, unlike Jimmy, I had learned my lesson. Then I remembered how much it hurt. 'Are you all right?'

'I'll survive.' People who bang their heads always look crossly at everybody else.

'Anyway, you're supposed to be finding somewhere else to live,' I told him firmly.

'Look at that.' Jimmy abruptly changed the subject. 'They always remind me of carp.'

'Do they?' I reached for the bottle. 'It looks like a barrage balloon to me.'

We had been playing pontoon for dried peas while we waited

for the rabbit to cook in the haybox. Jimmy had chosen which was to be eaten on the simple basis that it had bitten his finger when he'd stopped it escaping, but we had left it to Captain to perform the execution.

I poured us all a glass of Captain Sultana's home-made nettle wine. *Fermented weeds*, Jimmy called it derisively, but it had a good taste once you acquired it and a good kick on an empty stomach. In our hearts we knew we would be needing it soon.

The Bush radio was slow in warming up, valves humming and smelling of singed dust.

'Any progress on that murder?' Jimmy swirled his drink around.

'You'll have to ask my esteemed colleague about that,' I replied automatically, transfixed by what we knew but dreading what was to come.

'Oh come on.' The captain twiddled with the tuning dial, the speaker whistling and whining, now a brass band, now some inarticulate gabble, the sounds ebbing and flowing as they battled for our attention. Even with the aerial on the mast we had poor reception down in the estuary.

'Be finished at this rate.' Jimmy paced about but his great-uncle slapped away the hand that was reaching for the tuning knob.

'The British ambassador in Berlin,' surged into the saloon.

'That's him,' Jimmy cried in exasperation. 'You've just gone past it.'

'*Haqq*,' Captain Sultana swore under his breath, tweaking the dial back a fraction for a burst of classical music.

'You can imagine what a bitter blow this is to me,' Mr Chamberlain said, suddenly clear, 'that all my long struggle to win peace has failed.' He sounded like a peeved teacher.

'Oh you poor thing,' Jimmy scoffed.

'What?' Captain Sultana cupped a hand to his ear.

The sound was drifting again but we got the gist. The Germans were wicked, our elected headmaster told us sadly, but he knew we would all play our part with calmness and courage.

I tried to roll a cigarette but the paper split, spilling tobacco all over me.

'Is it…?' the captain asked.

'War,' I confirmed. 'We're at war with Germany.'

Captain Sultana bowed his head and Jimmy stared out of another porthole as Mr Chamberlain ended his lament by calling God's blessing upon us with the certainty that right would prevail.

Class dismissed with permission to die.

It was hardly a surprise but I'd been hoping against hope that Hitler would realise his bluff had been called.

'Yes!' Jimmy clenched his fist. 'And about time too.' He almost danced with excitement.

'We have to do something to stop him, I suppose,' Carmelo conceded sadly.

The last war was still fresh in our memories but his were far more awful than mine, too strong and too numerous to drown in the topped-up glasses of wine he so shakily poured.

'We should have done something sooner,' I said. 'We betrayed the Czechs and let him grow stronger and more confident because we were frightened.'

'What sane man wouldn't be?' Captain pondered. 'Oh those poor boys.' Captain Sultana shuddered. We both knew he meant the ones he had commanded and the ones who would follow suit. He snatched up his glass, draining it in one, but I couldn't face mine. What was I drinking to? I put it down and refilled Carmelo's.

Jimmy shook his head. 'It'll be different this time, Grandad. I've seen a film of the Maginot Line. The French have learned their lesson. It's impregnable. We won't be fighting in the trenches and our ships know how to deal with submarines now. This will be a war of the air – men in machines jousting like knights of old.' Jimmy's eyes shone with zeal for something he could not imagine as he raised his glass in a toast, 'To victory.'

'To Adam,' I countered and we clinked our glasses as the men repeated my words, Jimmy adding 'Uncle'. *Wherever you are*, I mused. Rumour had it that my ex-fiancé was travelling through Italy but Adam's military exploits were always shrouded in mystery.

'I still—' I began to tell his father but his hand passed through my invisible arm.

'Naf,' he said, which meant *I know*.

There would be more announcements later, we were told. In the meantime we had Reginald Foort playing the organ from Langham Place, 'Keep Smiling'. Carmelo turned the set off.

It was then we heard it for the first time, a ghostly wail coming across the water, rising and falling eerily. It was a sound I had prayed so hard not to hear. It came from Anglethorpe and it was joined almost immediately by the sirens of Sackwater.

They were sounding more faintly from Hadling Heath Aerodrome. We could only imagine the frantic activity there but within minutes we saw them, five Hurricanes in a V formation, flying low along the estuary out to sea. Not one of those pilots would have ever fired a shot in anger before and now, on that sunny Sunday afternoon, they were setting out to kill or be killed.

Jimmy was out on the deck waving frantically. 'Go get 'em, boys. Go get 'em.'

'And they call *me* mad,' the Mad Admiral said sadly.

28

THE BEAR AND THE SOCKET

I f you were looking for somebody to play the part of a grizzly bear in your theatrical production, Dr Edward 'Tubby' Gretham was the man for you. He was a huge figure in all three dimensions and all four limbs, his head made all the more massive by a stack of dark-brown hair.

Until recently his face had been almost hidden behind a matching beard but Greta, his wife, persuaded him to shave it off for his second General Medical Council hearing. She had watched him do it, he told me afterwards, stood back and said, 'I don't think I'd have married you if I'd known what you looked like.' So now he was in the process of re-camouflaging himself.

Tubby had the sort of hands you might think were better suited to crushing rocks than being a doctor but, when I had gashed my knee in my teens, he had sutured it for me with delicate stitches that any seamstress would have been proud of and, when he played the piano – which he often did, whether you wanted him to or not – his fingers could flit over the keyboard with astonishing agility, going from a thunderous crash to the lightest of touches in an instant.

The mortuary was in a square red-brick single-storey building round the back of the Royal Albert Sackwater Infirmary, labelled *STORES* to avoid prying eyes, though Tubby loved to entertain friends with tales of delivery men who had blundered into the middle of autopsies – including one who had been thought to be the cadaver on the table.

'Betty,' he greeted me with a grin, because he was just putting down his bone saw and it was not often he got the chance to use it.

Freddy Smart lay naked on his back, even scrawnier than I had imagined. His chest was concave, with the skin sunk between his ribs. His hip bones jutted like miniature ploughs and his bony legs were bowed. He had already been unzipped all down the middle.

'Looks malnourished,' I said in puzzlement, for the Smarts were already re-establishing their empire.

'Had steak and chips for dinner.' Tubby pointed to a wide-topped glass jar labelled *Stomach contents*.

'I met his grandfather once,' I recalled, 'and he was a similar build.'

'The runts of the litter then.' Tubby levered a spatula into his saw-line and the top of the skull came away with a faint ripping sound.

'That's what makes them so dangerous,' I speculated. 'To survive in their world, you have to be tougher than the rest so, if you're weedier, you have to be meaner.'

'Looks like he had a few fights in his time.' Tubby tapped the chest. 'Five ribs broken and mended and an old cranial fracture.' Tubby ran a gloved finger around an oval bulge. 'But I suppose that's an occupational hazard with these chaps. Few healed knife scars as well.' He laid the skull cap aside. 'I've cleaned up the left eye socket. The eyeball had burst from the force of impact with a sharp implement. Most of the vitreous humour burst over his cheek. Messy' – Tubby picked up a pair of surgical scissors to snip through the membranous meninges that wrap all our thoughts – 'and very painful.'

'So he was alive?'

'I should say so.' He was working his spatula around inside

III

the skull like you do when you're trying to get the ham out of a tin in one piece. 'You can see where the blade broke through the bone.' He indicated a letter-box-shaped hole smashed through the back of the socket.

'Would that have gone into his brain?'

'Probably.' He tossed the spatula into a kidney dish. 'We'll see in a minute.'

I stood at his shoulder, trying to keep out of his light, fascinated by the walnut-shaped, wormy grey meat he was handling.

'Strange to think that's all we are,' I commented.

'It may be all you are.' Tubby bent his knees. 'Some of us have immortal souls.' He peered into the top of the skull, pressing the brain down with the flat of his left hand to shine a torch into the space with his right. I saw the beam glow through the shattered back of the socket.

'I thought I saw a glitter. Pass me those forceps... No, the longer ones.' He thrust the torch at me. 'Hold that.' I seemed to have been demoted to mortuary assistant but it was difficult to take offence. When Tubby was involved in fixing an oil leak in his Rudge motorbike once, he had roped the Duke of Kent, who was passing by, into helping and snapped at him for selecting the wrong spanner. 'Keep that torch still.' He was fishing about in the space he had created between the underside of the skull and what I think were the frontal lobes. 'Aha.'

'Have you found something?'

'If I can just...' Tubby's nose was almost buried in Freddy Smart's brain by then as he squinted at whatever he was after. 'Gotcha!' Tubby stood up so suddenly, I had to leap back to avoid being headed in the face and crashed into a trolley of instruments. 'Oh for goodness' sake, woman...' Tubby whipped round, 'Oh...' suddenly realising what was going on and who had been trying to help him, 'oh I'm so sorry.'

I laughed. 'What have you found?'

'This.' In the teeth of his forceps, I saw it glinting, a thin triangle of steel no more than a quarter of an inch at its broken edge and going to a sharp point.

'The tip of the blade?'

Tubby nodded happily. 'Find the rest of this and you have your murder weapon.'

'Can I take it?'

Tubby's face fell. I knew he wanted it for his collection. 'I'll put it in a bottle,' he grumped and rooted about for an empty one.

'I'll try to get it back to you when we're finished,' I promised and Tubby perked up immediately.

'Those incisions on his hands must be from grasping the blade to try to pull it out.'

'Can I have a look?'

'Be my guest.'

I pulled on a pair of thick rubber gloves – much too big for me but they served their purpose – and had a quick look at those hands, still half-closed in their empty grasps. I prised them open just enough to see inside. There were deep cuts running along the palms and inside those hooked fingers.

'What about the neck wound?'

Tubby glanced over. 'Why the singular?'

'I'll let you judge that.' He selected a long narrow spatula and inserted it into the wound above Freddy Smart's Adam's apple. The rounded end slipped in easily and Tubby pressed it gently along. 'The trouble is the track will be filled with hardened clots and the sides of the wound may have collapsed and adhered, so...' he worked the instrument carefully, holding it between thumb and forefinger, 'one must be careful not to create a fresh channel.' He wiggled the spatula daintily, pressing again, and there it was, the rounded end peeking out just below the left ear. 'Well,' he slid it a little further, 'you were right not to say *wounds*.'

I almost punched the air but there is something about the dead that commands more respect than the living.

'Can you tell which direction it entered and exited?'

Tubby picked a broad scalpel similar to the one Julius 'The Surgeon' Carrapticus had threatened me with the day I earned my stripes. 'Possibly.' He started to dissect around the front wound. 'The soft tissues have collapsed inwards at both ends.' He sliced delicately through the skin and muscle beneath. 'Lord, I wish all my patients would be so considerate as not to bleed.' He parted the tissues. 'See that little flap there? That's the epiglottis – the thing that stops your food going down the wrong way.'

I knew that much from reading my grandfather's anatomy book, which was on my father's shelf, but Tubby was never happier than when explaining his craft and I enjoyed him teaching me.

'Most of the time,' I said but he wasn't listening. 'Thought as much.' He scraped the top edge of a white ring of bone. 'See that? It should have a spur sticking out – the greater horn, which attaches to the thyrohyoid ligament.'

'And that does what?'

'Attaches to the thyrohyoid membrane.'

'Of course,' I murmured.

'Now let's see if I can find that horn.'

'So, if it has been broken inwards, the blade must have gone front to back,' I deduced.

'No doubt about it.' Tubby dug deeper into Freddy Smart's throat.

'Would the neck wound have killed him instantly?'

'As near as dammit. Oh, and he had a horizontal contusion here.' Tubby pointed to a faint line about an inch above the eyebrows.

'Perfect,' I breathed.

Tubby paused from his work. 'Why so?'

'It fits in with how I think he died,' I said as he started poking with some tweezers.

'Go on. No, hang on. There it is.' He produced a spicule of bone triumphantly. 'Go on.'

'Tell me if any of this doesn't fit in with what you've found,' I began.

'Don't worry, I shall,' Tubby assured me.

'Freddy...'

'You were on first-name terms?'

'We are now. He is lured to the door. He's too wary to open it to an unexpected visitor so maybe he crouches to peer through the letter box. Perhaps he doesn't realise how clearly he can be seen through the coloured glass. His killer plunges a long-bladed knife or a sword—'

'Sword would fit the bill better.'

'—into Freddy's eye. The tip snaps off and the blade jams. Freddy instinctively grabs it—'

'And cuts his hands.'

'—while the killer wrenches it back, banging Freddy's head on the edge of the letter box—'

'The bruise.'

'—then thrusts straight back and delivers the fatal wound.'

'Bravo.' Tubby clapped, his gloved hands sounding like a performing seal.

'Are you being sarcastic?' I asked warily.

'Not in the least,' he protested. 'That would fit the bill precisely.'

An unworthy thought struck me. 'When you write up your report...'

'To Inspector Sharkey?'

I nodded. 'Do you think you could append that theory to it as your own suggestion?'

Tubby puzzled. 'Surely you deserve the credit for it?'

'Oh, I've already proposed something similar,' I told him and Tubby grinned broadly from deep inside his facial shrubbery.

'I shall lay it on thick,' he assured me.

29

THE MYSTERIOUS MYSTERY OF THE
MYSTERIOUS MISS PRIM

Meanwhile Sharkey still refused to discuss the progress of his murder investigation but, from the men, I gathered that was only because there was none to talk about. I was still determined to interview Millicent Smith but she was nowhere to be seen, so I decided to list her as a missing person. Millicent was young and pretty and we had managed to get a photograph of her from her younger brother, who worked collecting uncharged and delivering recharged wireless batteries in Ipswich. So I had managed to drum up quite a lot of publicity over the case – probably too much, because it fell to me to sift through the mounds of reported sightings of Millicent coming in from all over the country. Two witnesses had definitely seen Millicent Smith in Oxford. Maybe they had but it was two days before I first met her. I pencilled a diagonal cross over the front cover and decided I needed a cup of tea.

Nippy Walker was on the desk and a little old lady sat in the corner when I went to the lobby in search of a brew. She was knitting something startlingly red, far too long to be a scarf but far too stringy to be anything else. It snaked from her rapidly clicking needles onto the floor, curling rather menacingly around her flat little shoes.

'Inspector Church?' she warbled. She had pale mauve hair, coordinating with her paisley mauve dress.

'Yes?' I admitted warily. She looked like the sort of woman who would have the entire force looking for her lost budgerigar.

She put her knitting into her lap. 'I am Miss Prim.'

I stifled a laugh. 'Can I help you?'

'Oh no.' The lady smiled quite sweetly. 'It is I who am here in my humble capacity to help you.'

'In what way?' I pulled the chair next to hers away and around to view her profile. She had not been very carefully constructed, I decided. Her nose dipped at the bridge before rising again to hook round into something you could open tins with. Her lips were caved in, with red cracks radiating at the corners like stained cat's whiskers.

'The murder of Frederick Smart.' She rolled the loose yarn, bringing back horrid memories of hours spent holding out loops of wool for my grandmother to wind into a ball.

'Do you have some information about the case?' I watched her eyes behind her round wire spectacles. They were slow and dull and didn't seem to focus on anything.

'I have better than that.' She slid both needles into the ball. If Miss Prim was trying to tantalise me, she was failing miserably. I was more interested in the sound of a kettle coming to the boil in the back room.

'A confession?' I asked with forlorn hope. It would have to be a detailed one to convince me.

'Oh no.' Her thinner lip quivered. 'I have a theory.' I made no attempt to smother my groan but Miss Prim had wound up the gramophone and she was going to play the record. 'You see, I am a student of human nature,' she began with no visible means of turning her off. 'It comes from years of living alone reading detective novels aloud to my cats.'

'Perhaps you would like to talk to Inspector Sharkey,' I suggested. 'He is in charge of the case.'

The lady made a mewling noise that she had probably learned from one of her tabbies. 'Inspector Sharkey? Oh he is hopeless.' At least she was talking sense now. 'He gave me no credit at all for solving,' her voice sank dramatically, 'the Mystery of the Gardener's Boy's Stolen Bicycle.' She folded her arms with great satisfaction.

'Tha's true enough,' Nippy chipped in. 'He do go and take all the credit for tha' one. Miss Prim told him young Billy Lime gone and stole ih.'

Our visitor unfolded her arms modestly.

'And had he?' I got up.

'No.' Nippy smiled wisely. 'Buh young Billy Thatcher goh-ih-into his head we're searchin' the houses of everyone called Billy and he go and run ow on the street with ih and Inspector Sharkey do catch him bike-handed.'

'All thanks to me.' Miss Prim refolded her arms with even greater satisfaction.

'She do be a marvel, she do,' Nippy endorsed our visitor warmly.

'Then there was the Mystery of the Sabotaged Prize Marrow,' she reminded my constable.

'Oh yes.' He leaned back comfortably, all the better to relate that one. 'Ih—'

'One moment.' I jumped up and marched to the desk. There was only one mystery I was interested in solving – how to get her out of the station. 'Get rid of her,' I whispered.

'Wha'?' He cupped his ear. 'Sorry, I dint catch thah, ma'am.'

I leaned over, snatched up a pencil and wrote in block capitals across a blank charge sheet:

GET RID OF HER.

'Get rid of her,' he read more loudly, I imagined, than Miss Prim narrated to her cats. 'Wha'? You mean murder her?'

'If needs be,' I confirmed and turned back to our incredible old lady. 'I'm sorry, Miss Prim, but we talk in coded messages. You can't be too careful these days.'

'You certainly cannot,' she agreed. 'Did you know that that sweet shop is run by a German spy?'

'We have him under close surveillance,' I assured her.

Our new constable, Anthony Bank-Anthony, wandered through apparently from nowhere and apparently going nowhere. He had joined us from Dudley in the Black Country but insisted he had never acquired the accent. There were various rumours about why he had been offered a transfer, the most popular of which was that he had not so much an eye for the ladies as two hands for them, including his chief constable's daughter.

Bank-Anthony cast his eyes over our visitor.

'Nice ankles,' he purred and I pondered how many more strips I could tear off my men without them disintegrating.

'Oh dear, the phone is ringing in my office.'

Nippy Walker cocked his head in confusion. 'Buh ih int work...'

'I had better answer it,' I said firmly. 'Though it's probably some mad old bat with stupid theories about a murder.'

'There's plenty of those around,' Miss Prim sympathised. 'It's a cross we female detectives have to bear.'

'We?'

'Your men couldn't manage without me,' she prattled on. 'Why, last time I left I distinctly heard Sergeant Briggs talking about somebody losing their Marples.'

'Excuse me. I must take that call.' *Before I have one of us certified.* I hurried down the corridor.

Superintendent Vesty materialised, running his fingers agitatedly over his face.

'Have a care,' he warned. 'The Kaiser is up to his old tricks. We must not let him break us.' He patted the air at shoulder height. 'Hold the line, boys. Steady. Hold your fire.'

30

THE RAT-MAN COMETH

There was a letter – amongst the many on my desk – that caught my attention. It was signed *Millycent Smith* and started off with the statement that she had fled to *Meksigo*, but a staggering number of errors about how she knew me – allegedly we had met in a public house called The Feathers – plus the fact that it was postmarked Woking gave me reasonable grounds for dismissing it as the work of yet another crank. I finished reading the letter and tried to summon up the enthusiasm to peruse a government directive about lost ration books – a feeble joke since, apart from petrol, nothing was actually being rationed or ever would be if Lord Beaverbrook had his way – 'Government Control Gone Mad', his *Daily Express* was raging.

I yawned. There was no reason to stifle it because I was all alone until the door burst open and a small man in a too-long beige trench coat stormed in.

'Here.' Brigsy was close on his heels. 'You can't go marchin' in there.'

'Just have,' the stranger sneered. I had seen that rodential profile – the pointed upper face with long incisors – first when its owner had been throttling Millicent Smith and then when it had been making a mess on the lino in 15 Bath Road. 'Where's Sharkey?'

I leaned forward. 'Get out.'

Old Scrapie was chasing shadows in Stovebury, just the other side of Tringford.

The rat-man walked in. 'Do you know who I am?' He had a you'll-be-sorry-when-you-find-out tone but I had already guessed and remained unrepentant.

'Yes.' I looked into his little pink eyes. 'You are the man who is leaving my office.'

He marched to my desk and I have to say he did a menacing manner very well. If I had been a little girl up an alley at night, I might have been terrified but, when I was a not-very-humble constable, I had been alone in Bridge Street Snooker Hall with Walter Wallis, the Watford Worm Man, when I was not the one wielding a flanged mace. He had refined menacing to such perfection he probably frightened himself. My visitor had a lot of work to do on his act yet.

'Nobody throws me out.' He slammed the heels of his hands onto the papers strewn over my desktop.

'If you do not get out of here I shall arrest you for trespass, threatening behaviour and interfering with the police in the course of their duty,' I warned. 'If you resist arrest, I shall charge you with that too. If you so much as brush against my sergeant on the way out, I shall charge you with assault and, if you do not take your hands off the documents on my desk, I shall charge you with interfering with evidence.'

'I've got something to say to you and you need to listen,' the rat-man blustered but I knew that he knew I wasn't bluffing.

'Go to the desk and make an appointment,' I said steadily.

'You'll regret this.'

'Is that a threat?' I enquired. *Please say yes.*

'It's a prognostication.' He drew back his upper lip.

That's a big word for a little man, I wanted to say and then tell him he had got it wrong – it would have been childish but satisfying. 'Leave.' I leaned back. 'Now.'

'All right,' he sneered, 'keep your arm on.'

I'd heard that one before but he delivered it with great effect and I was just wondering which charge to smash his sneaky, pointy smirk in with first when he spun on his heel.

'Stand firm,' I told Briggs, who was just inside the door, and my sergeant straightened to attention so that our visitor had to squeeze very gingerly past. 'Let me know if he brushes you.'

'Handcuffs at the ready, madam,' Brigsy assured me in his best sergeant manner.

The stranger went into the hall and turned his head towards me.

'Goodbye Mr Smart,' I called.

He narrowed his eyes. 'She knows who I am?'

'She knows all sorts of things about you, sir,' Brigsy told him proudly but without justification as he closed the door.

Two minutes later there was a knock.

'Come in.'

'A Mr Crake Smart to see you, madam.'

'Tell him to wait.' I put my pen down. 'You and I have urgent police business with two cigarettes and a large pot of tea.'

124

31

DESPERADOES OF THE BLACK RANGE

I waited fifteen minutes to make my point before I had Brigsy send Mr Smart back in.

'I want to know what you are doing about my son's murder,' he began.

'I am sorry for your loss, Mr Smart,' I began and I meant it. No matter how horrible Crake was and how vile Freddy, a father had lost his son.

'Sorry?' He snorted. 'Have you any idea what this has done to the family reputation if we can't even protect our own from a little Suffolk slag?'

And, if there was a faint gurgle, it was my sympathy going down the drain.

'Please take a seat.'

Crake Smart pulled his upper lip over his teeth, whipped the light wooden chair back and plonked down to face me. I was pleased to note I had a good head-height advantage without even cheating by using a cushion. 'Well?'

'We are making enquiries,' I told him but, to my astonishment, he did not jump up, say *Thank you very much*, pump my hand and walk off whistling a happy tune.

'What enquiries?' He put his hands out.

'Don't touch the paperwork,' I warned. 'I'm afraid I am unable to discuss the details of our investigation with—'

'I'm his father, for Chrissake.'

'Any potential suspects,' I finished.

Crake Smart lost control over that lip. It sprang up, the teeth sprang forward and he sprang out of his chair. 'Suspect?' he yelled. He had a high voice, rising to referee-whistle shrillness. 'He was my son, for Chrissake!'

'Potential,' I repeated. 'As is everyone until he or she is eliminated.'

'Everyone?' He banged the desk. 'Is your fucking walking-dead sergeant a suspect?'

'If I hadn't been with him at the time of the murder, he could be.' I stood up. No scrawny smalltime smalltown thug was going to think he could dominate me. 'Do you have any information regarding your son's death, Mr Smart?'

'I know that bitch Smith killed him.' Smart leaned towards me. 'And that's all I need to know except where she is.'

'I'd like to know that myself, Mr Smart.' I picked up my wooden ruler. It could make a useful weapon if I needed it. 'What makes you think it was Millicent Smith who killed your son?'

'When a girl tries to trap a man into marrying her,' Crake Smart viewed me with the contempt that all women deserve, 'threatens him when he won't fall for it and runs off the minute he pegs it, it don't take much working out. But let me tell you one thing, copper, she'd better pray you get her first and so had you.'

'I can understand the first part of your threat.' I watched my visitor carefully. There was an iciness in his manner that was more worrying than his temper had been. 'But are you threatening me as well, Mr Smart?'

Smart's mouth twisted. 'Let me tell you something, Inspector Church. There are people in this station who owe me and I may decide to call in that debt.'

I walked round the table to stop within a foot of him to stare down into those dry beady eyes.

'Let *me* tell *you* something, Mr Crake Rutter Smart. I've been a big-game fisher in a big rough ocean. I've caught marlins and great white sharks, creatures that could swallow the likes of you whole and not even spoil their appetites. You think you're in that league? You're not even a big fish in a small pond. You're a tadpole in a puddle and you'd better be careful I don't stamp you out.'

Crake Smart's hands twitched like a cowboy nervously waiting to draw. He seemed to be fighting an urge to attack me and I rather hoped he would. I wouldn't let him off as lightly as I had his son.

'You just wait and see,' he spat.

I strode to the door. 'Get out.'

Smart clenched his fists at his side. He forced his lips together and stormed off. I hoped he had been impressed by my speech and never found its source. It came, as best I could remember, from *Desperadoes of the Black Range*, a book Jimmy had lent me when he was an adolescent. He had joined Adam and me in Birżebbuġa to fish for *lampuki* in the moonlight from a *luzzu* boat with its painted eyes and, later, to grill our catch on the beach when I gave Jimmy his first bottle of Cisk beer and, as I found out later, his first cigarette.

THE SUFFOLK VAMPIRE

The branch line up from Felixstowe was always busy in the summer in peacetime with thousands of trippers, though the majority were going on to Anglethorpe at the end of the line.

I stopped at the red and cream stone-arched entrance.

'Don't you dare call them *puff-puffs*,' I warned my constable.

'As if I would.' Dodo reddened in indignation and I was about to apologise when she added, 'They are choo-choos.'

We were down at the railway station to investigate the theft of a bench. This was about as thrilling as it got on our side of the River Angle estuary apart from the Freddy Smart murder, which my esteemed colleague Sharkey was keeping jealously to himself. Funny how we all longed for big cases. While we claimed to be trying to prevent crime, we were constantly haunted by the fear that we might be successful – just as my father, I supposed, in his battle against tooth decay would not have wanted all his patients to have perfect dentitions, leaving him to twiddle his thumbs even more than he did now.

The 10:28 for Felixstowe was ready to depart, its engine straining and wheels shifting restlessly. Doors were slamming and windows dropping for ratings in second class and officers in first to bid their loved ones farewell. Rumour had it they were off to reinforce the naval blockade but rumours tend to invent themselves. Last week the Germans had definitely parachuted into Norfolk disguised as nuns until they were identified as pilgrims walking to Walsingham. Having gone to a convent school, I could think of a few teachers it would be quite easy to mistake for enemy soldiers. Sister Millicent would probably pass for a Nazi stormtrooper far more easily than she did for a Sister of Chastity.

The heavy chain links clanked and stretched straight and the first puff of smoke threw a mote of soot into the eye of a well-dressed middle-aged lady who had just bade a lukewarm farewell to a corpulent purser. The lady squeaked and did what she was not supposed to but we all do – she rubbed it.

The train shuddered and strained.

'May I be of assistance?' A handsome man of about the same age approached with a clean white handkerchief. 'I'm a doctor.'

The lady was looking up as directed while the handsome man fished behind her lower lid with a starched corner. I saw her lips part and thought he saw it too. He stroked her cheek with his thumb as if that was an essential part of the procedure.

'Oh thank you,' she was quavering.

'How very kind.' Dodo folded her hands over her left breast.

'Except that he's Rufus Verdigris, an accountant,' I told her.

'Oh but oh.' Dodo interlocked her fingers.

'He used to have an office on Hambleton Road,' I told her. 'Until he was committed to St Audry's Hospital for Mental Diseases in Woodbridge but he's harmless enough.'

'How can he be harmless?' Dodo bawled but they were too wrapped up in each other to bother with her. 'If he has a disease it might be contagious, like...' she cast her eyes around for an example, 'toothache or... communism.'

Mr Trime, the stationmaster, marched over to greet us, chest puffed out, his arms pumping like the pistons of one of his locomotives.

'And not before Trime,' Dodo whispered just loud enough for him to glance at her sharply. I blamed Tommy Handley. If he could get away with appalling puns in his *ITMA* Home Service show, everybody else thought they could too.

Mr Trime was a short portly man with a deluxe moustache and wire-framed spectacles who wore his three-piece uniform suit with pride. His manner could be officious and fussy but I liked him. When I was a child he used to let me stand and help Mr Lanter, the porter, collect tickets. Mr Lanter was a sweet man and the railway was his life. Nobody knew how much so until the day he retired, when he lay in his uniform with his head on the track.

'This is a serious business,' Mr Trime assured me seriously and, by Sackwater standards, it was. The previous case I had dealt with for him was a crude – in every sense of the word – drawing somebody had done in the gents just after I had returned. The culprit was still at large and I trembled to think when and where he might strike again. 'It wasn't just any old bench you know. It commemorated something.' The stationmaster's voice rose indignantly. 'But nobody can remember what since the plaque was stolen in 1934.'

'I believe Inspector Sharkey is on that case.' I peered at the empty space where the object of our enquiries had stood and tried to look like I had uncovered an important clue. No doubt Mr G or Aunty March would have the thief behind bars by now just from scrutinising the four clean squares on the paving slab created by the legs.

'Let us hope he does not solve it first,' Dodo pondered. 'A label with nothing to stick it on is like a roar with no lion.' *Thank the gods Daddy didn't say that.* 'Daddy said that,' she concluded.

'It'll probably turn up in somebody's back garden,' I predicted as an engine approached.

Like many edifices in Sackwater the station had been built in expectation of more prosperous times. There was a platform either side of the two tracks, joined by a high cast-iron footbridge. The southbound line from Anglethorpe to Felixstowe had a long brick single-storey slate-roofed building with separate mixed and women-only waiting rooms. It was large enough to house a few families if they didn't mind sharing the public conveniences, though plenty of Suffolk houses would have been glad to have anything better than an unlit, draughty outside privy. The northbound line platform was a much grander affair, with something vaguely Ottoman in the design of the building – two storeys high with a covered walkway supported by pointed arches, echoed in the shapes of the windows and by lighter bricks set into the walls. It had the same facilities plus a ticket office, left luggage, the canteen and the stationmaster's office from which Mr Trime had emerged, pulling on his shiny-peaked, gold-badged cap and dusting himself down.

Mr Trime hauled out his enormous brass fob watch on a heavy chain. 'On the dot,' he said with such satisfaction you might have thought he had driven the 10:42 himself.'

The train pulled in, packed tight – not because of a surge in popularity but because it was down to two carriages, the rest having been requisitioned for troop movements – and the doors at either end of each carriage had hardly opened before passengers started spilling out. The stationmaster and I went into the canteen for much-needed mugs of tea while Dodo dawdled behind to coo at Jeremy, the station's marmalade cat. The door had hardly swung shut behind me when there was a loud crack.

Tilly, the tea lady, released two things – a small yelp and the saucer in her hand. The second of those rolled along the counter and settled, skittering beside a plate of curled sandwiches. The first was smothered too late by her hand.

'Car backfiring,' Mr Trime reassured her but I had heard enough guns in my life to know the difference. It is a sharper, cleaner sound, the one that kills people.

'Stay there.' I spun back onto the platform in time to see about twenty people emerging from the clouds of smoke and steam. They were adults except for a small brown-skinned boy and his sister, slightly apart from the body of people, wide-eyed, holding buckets and spades and hands. The crowd parted and one of the passengers, a middle-aged man in a grey suit, broke from it, crying '*What! What?*' Dodo, helmet askew, appeared to be throttling him. Maybe she was right and insanity *was* contagious.

'What the hell?' I rushed towards them. The man was choking and coughing. He dropped his briefcase to put his hands up to hers but Dodo had a tight grip and showed no inclination to let go.

'Stop struggling,' she scolded but the man was not listening. He clutched at her wrists, staggered two steps sideways and fell onto his left knee, Dodo still gripping him.

'Let go of my hand,' Dodo said firmly and I saw that she had clamped her big white handkerchief over his throat and that it was no longer white but soaked in blood.

The man looked at his hand. *What?* He clawed at the handkerchief. *Oh, oh my God.* His voice was weakening already when he toppled face-up on the platform, his trilby hat flying, blood pumping between their fingers.

I ran towards my constable and the wounded man. Her hand still gripped the side of his neck but his were both clawing the air while his feet were pedalling like somebody running up a ladder. His breath bubbled. I did not like that pumping. It meant arterial blood.

'Get out of my way.' I pushed an old lady, trying to retrieve her spilled shopping, to one side, causing her basket to tip over again.

'Well, really.'

But there was no time to worry about that. I rooted in my handbag for my own handkerchief and pressed it over Dodo's right hand but the cotton was saturated instantly, the blood surging through unchecked.

Somebody appeared at my shoulder. 'Take this.' I didn't need to look up to know that voice.

Jimmy thrust his jacket at me, the sleeve rolled into a pack, and I rammed it over our handkerchiefs. At last the flow slowed but not, I feared, because of our efforts.

'Keep back, please.' Mr Trime, ignoring my instruction to stay put, was herding curious onlookers away. 'Give the man some air.'

The doors closed and the guard, unaware that this was anything more than a passenger tripping up in the rush, blew his whistle. As the train began to pull away, the voice of a woman, a young one by the sound of it, rang out from that direction.

'He's on the bridge. Watch out, he's got a blooming gun!' I looked up to see a stranger, tall, in a floppy-brimmed hat and a long dark coat running over the footbridge, down onto the deserted southbound platform. In a minute he would be through the unmanned exit towards Back Lane. Once there he could easily be lost in the crowds of High Road East. He had a long athletic stride.

'Stop that train,' Mr Trime called with some presence of mind. The porter blew his whistle twice but the back carriage had already cleared the platform and was puffing off to Anglethorpe.

A woman was screaming – I never saw the point of doing that – and the two children were trying to calm her down.

'Oh do be a good lamb,' the little girl begged.

'I'll get him.' Jimmy was off.

'No. Stop!' I shouted – I did not want another death on my hands – but Jimmy sprinted away unheeding. 'Ring for a doctor.' I had never bossed the stationmaster around before. Mr Trime rushed towards his office, his ring of keys clinking as he fished them out. 'And then the police station,' I called after him. 'Tell them there could be a man with a gun on the loose.'

The children had been partially successful until I said that and started their mother off again.

'He shall slay us all,' she shrieked.

'That is quite enough of that nonsense,' the boy reprimanded his mother in a tone he had probably learned from her.

'And then Anglethorpe,' I remembered. 'Tell them to keep all the passengers there for questioning.'

'Did *you* shoot him?' the little boy asked me excitedly but I had no time to deny it.

'Nobody leave the station,' I commanded. 'You can all go into the waiting room.' But I saw that many people were running away or had already fled.

I kept pressing on the wound over Jimmy's pack but there was nothing anyone could have done. The eyes stopped flickering and when the blood stopped flowing it was only because the heart was not pumping it.

'There was no answer at the police station and I couldn't get them at Anglethorpe,' Mr Trime declared. 'They were all out to greet the train and everyone had gone by the time they answered.'

I heard approaching running. Jimmy.

'He got away,' he announced breathlessly. 'I thought I had him on Hamilton Road but I ended up rugby-tackling Mr Amery popping out for his elevenses.'

'The bank manager?' I wished I had seen that on another occasion.

'Probably have to move my account now,' Jimmy pondered ruefully while he leaned over us both for a better view. He smelt of perfumed soap – mine. 'Oh, is he—'

'Yes.' I used the jacket to cover the victim's face. 'I'll see if I can get funds to pay for a new one.'

'Oh don't worry about that.' But I didn't need the look on Jimmy's face to tell me he could ill afford to lose it.

'You'd better go, Jimmy. I know where to find you.'

I got to my feet, ignoring the well-meant offer of a hand. Jimmy could give me a pull-up any time on *Cressida* but the day I see somebody offer one to a police*man* is the day I'll start accepting one on duty. 'But can you call into the police station and tell them what's happened?'

Why the hell had nobody answered the phone? It wasn't time for Brigsy's nap.

'Certainly can.' Shocked though he looked, a part of Jimmy was clearly enjoying the experience.

'Didn't you hear me shout *stop*?'

'Of course.' Jimmy confirmed as he ambled away. 'But I knew you didn't mean it.'

I squeezed Dodo's shoulder. 'He's gone,' I told her and she turned her bloodied face up.

'I tried,' she whispered.

'You did everything you could.' I gave her a hand up. Officers can help each other. 'Go to the ladies. There's a sink and mirror in there – just behind that waiting room.' I lowered my voice. 'You kept a cool head and did a good job just now.'

She pursed her lips and looked at the body. 'It did not do him any good.'

'He was beyond saving.'

'I heard a call for a doctor.' Tubby Gretham came puffing up and Dodo regarded him with loathing.

'Get back,' she snarled with an aggression I hadn't known was in her, 'to unbalancing your ledgers.'

I touched Dodo's arm. 'See if you can clean yourself up a bit.'

'Oh.' She ran her eyes over Tubby. 'I am so sorry. You actually are a doctor.'

Tubby patted his pocket to be sure no stethoscope was sticking out. 'How can you tell?'

'Who else has so many tincture of iodine stains on their hands and suit?' Dodo asked simply and walked off towards the waiting room.

'We'll make a policewoman of her yet,' I told my friend as she disappeared inside.

He walked round the dead man. 'I hear he was shot.'

'A gun was fired.' I lifted the jacket off. 'But I'm not sure it hit him.'

The dead man's face had a diffident expression, almost like he was embarrassed by the fuss.

'Well, he didn't die of a heart attack,' Tubby observed.

'A bullet at close range would have passed straight through.' I turned the head a little to show the neck on the other side undamaged and took the makeshift pack away. The clots pulled off with Dodo's handkerchief and the injury was quite cleanly exposed now.

Tubby squatted beside me, his knees crackling like dry twigs. He smelt strongly of pipe tobacco and I rather liked it.

'Puncture wounds from a sharp instrument,' he diagnosed. 'Two of them but we'll need a proper PM to confirm that, of course.' Tubby glowed at the thought of another outing for his bone saw. 'People seem to be getting into the habit of being stabbed in the neck lately.'

'Or somebody is getting into the habit of doing it,' I pondered grimly.

Tubby stood creakily. 'So how's your new constable getting on?'

'Oh help,' we heard. I started towards the voice with Tubby Gretham on my heels. 'Spider.' It was hissing in terror.

'I think she's just answered that question herself,' Tubby said drily.

THE VERMIN OF FLEET STREET

D odo did her best. She had washed her face and hands but her clothes were beyond wiping down. I sent her home.

'But I only have one uniform,' she moaned. 'And it will take at least a day to get laundered.'

'Come in your civvies tomorrow and I'll find you something to do at the station,' I said. 'Only wear a longer dress this time.'

'Oh but Constable Bank-Anthony said using less material helps the war effort,' she told me, 'and he thinks I should do even more of that.'

'I bet he did.'

I went to clean myself up. My uniform was a mess but it would have to do for now. I kept my spare at work ever since a family of field mice had made a nest in the pocket of my best overcoat on *Cressida*.

Bank-Anthony or Bantony as he had been rechristened – not entirely to his satisfaction – turned up, his usual dapper self. He always managed to look as if his uniform had been made by his personal tailor, even when he had accidentally put on Walker's coat when they were going out once – and Nippy was a few sizes smaller.

'Bluddy 'ell,' Bantony breathed.

'Mind your tongue,' I warned him. It was not that such profanities would never get past my tonsils but there were plenty of people around who would be shocked by such language, especially from an officer of the law.

'What 'appened to 'im?'

'He died.'

'Oi can see that.' Bantony was looking at me oddly but I would worry about that another time.

I felt inside the dead man's jacket pocket and found a pigskin wallet – three pounds and one ten-shilling note. In the other pocket was a silver cardholder. I pressed a button and the lid sprang open to reveal:

Mr Ardom Dapper, Seed Merchant, 16 Brace Street, Tringford.
Telephone Tringford 24

printed on white cards in that whorled style that passes as posh. I flicked through them. The rest of the cards were the same and, therefore, probably his.

'See if you can find the bullet,' I told Bantony and he rotated his head as if the projectile might be buzzing about it like a persistent gnat.

'It could be anywhere.'

'It could not be in Japan,' I pointed out, pedantically, I knew, but that was the bad influence of Mr G, who lived for the literal. 'Look for any sign of it hitting anything.'

Bantony trailed off like a schoolboy on an errand when he wanted to be playing football. It was a lot to ask of one man but with Dodo Chivers gone and our other constables off assisting the redoubtable Sharkey on his energetic but so-far-fruitless quest, there was no one left to help him.

Mr Trime came over. 'The next train from Anglethorpe is due in five minutes,' he warned.

'I'm sorry but it can't stop here.'

'I thought as much,' he said. 'I've already rung to warn them to hold back but is it all right if it passes through? It'll be on platform 2.' We were on number 1.

'I don't see why not, if we can screen the body,' I agreed and he went off in search of something to use.

A breeze ruffled the surface of a blood puddle and I shooed Jeremy, the station cat, away from lapping a rivulet flowing off into a cracked slab. Jeremy shrugged. I didn't know cats could do that but he put Maurice Chevalier to shame with his display of nonchalance.

The stationmaster returned with a porter. They were both laden with blankets.

'I thought we could cover the body and drape some over the bench,' Mr Trime explained.

I laid a blue blanket over Ardom Dapper who was now labelled *Property of East Anglian Coastal Railways*. The train hurtled through, windows filled with the surprised faces of passengers who had been expecting to disembark.

Bantony rejoined me to say he couldn't find anything.

'I thought you probably wouldn't,' I told him and he bridled, unsure if I was getting at him, but I wasn't.

'Your witnesses are getting restless,' Mr Trime reminded me.

'Oh yes.' I had almost forgotten about them. I went over to the waiting room. Of the dozen or so I had instructed to stay only three women were left.

'They all said they had better things to do,' Mrs Harvey, the postmistress, explained. 'But I made them write down their details.' She passed me a slip of paper.

'Potatoes, onions,' I deciphered.

'On the other side,' she huffed and I turned her shopping list over.

'Well, the last one is fake.' I prodded *Hurmun Gurring, Burlin* with my finger.

'The cheeky madam,' Mrs Harvey seethed. She was a big woman and swelled in indignation like a bullfrog.

'Tell them what we saw, Mrs H,' an almost-as-large woman in a faded floral dress urged.

Mrs H folded her arms as people do when about to launch into an anecdote, but she was mercifully brief. 'The man running away,' she declared. 'We all got a good look. He was a tall foreign-looking gent in a long black cloak.'

'It was a coat,' I corrected her.

'I know what I did see,' Mrs H insisted and the others heartily agreed.

I should have known better than to leave them all together to gossip.

'And a bat flew away,' the last woman, large but not up to her companions' standards, volunteered. She had a turban on. They were all the rage since factory girls started using them to protect their hair from machinery but she looked like a pantomime sultan in hers.

'Probably a pigeon,' I reasoned but was instantly voted down. They knew what they had seen and a bloodsucking winged mammal was by far the most likely creature to be flapping around the East Anglian skies.

'I know a vampire when I do see one,' the almost-as-large woman insisted because, of course, she had seen oh so many of them recently.

*

A tall middle-aged man in a crumpled light-grey suit stepped forward as I got to the station exit. He was laden with an enormous camera, all the paraphernalia on leather straps round his neck – flash and meters and cylinders for spare lenses and film – all sorts of things that Jimmy would have happily spent all day discussing but didn't interest me in the least.

'Inspector Church?'

'Yes?' I agreed warily.

'Gregson of the *Sackwater and District Gazette.*' He put out a hand and I took it. He had a strong grip and direct gaze with dark-blue eyes in the shade of his fedora.

'I'm afraid you can't go into the station, Mr Gregson.' I took my hand away.

'Might I ask you a few questions?'

'You can but you will have to walk with me and I'm not promising to answer them.'

'Thank you.' He had quite a deep melodious voice that reminded me of a trombone – Tommy Dorsey in a mellow mood maybe.

'You are very polite for a reporter,' I commented, as I set off.

'Would I get a better response if I wasn't?' He had a quick easy smile that lifted ten years from his lightly creased face and, without waiting for an answer, went ahead with, 'Is it true there's been a murder?'

I was not walking especially quickly but he seemed to have some trouble keeping up.

'There has been a violent death in suspicious circumstances,' I conceded.

'Can you tell me who the victim was?'

'Not until the family have been informed.'

'Or how he died?'

'The same applies.' I stopped and he did too, gasping for breath. 'Are you all right?'

'Yes.' Gregson supported himself with an outstretched arm on a lamp post. 'Sorry, just out of hospital. Had half a lungectomy – or whatever they call it.'

'TB?'

'"Fraid so.'

'Should you be out?'

'If I'm not, the paper isn't.'

'Are you that important?'

'I like them to think so.' He straightened up, staggering sideways into my shoulder – the right one, fortunately. 'Sorry.'

'That's two more apologies than I ever had from the press before.' I watched him with some concern and he flashed that smile again, though a little apologetically this time.

'We are not all – what did your godfather used to call us?'

Sidney Grice was actually the godfather of my godmother but it wasn't worth quibbling about.

'The Vermin of Fleet Street,' I reminded him.

Gregson grinned. 'I like to think of myself as the Scribe of Straight Street.'

I had been into their Straight Street office once to place an advertisement for a lost tortoise and I had been most annoyed, after having spent sixpence, to get back to find her trundling home again.

'Well, Mr Gregson,' I said. 'Let's see how accurately and honestly you report this event. I'm sorry there is nothing much else I can tell you at present.'

'I'll do my best,' he vowed and I felt fairly sure he meant it, but I had trusted reporters in the past to my regret. 'I can give you one scoop,' I realised. 'Police wish to interview a tall man in a long black coat and a floppy-brimmed hat seen running from the scene.'

I didn't mention the gun. Perhaps I should have but I didn't want to start a panic and I couldn't help but believe that whoever fired that gun would have hit somebody or something if they had been aiming towards the dead man.

Gregson lit up. 'The murderer?'

'Did I say there was a murder?'

The newspaperman smiled. 'You can't blame me for trying.'

He was right about that, I couldn't. I was only surprised he hadn't tried harder.

After a coughing fit, Gregson made his way back to his office, declining my offer of assistance, and he was as good as his word. The headlines in the *Gazette* were a muted:

UNFORTUNATE INCIDENT AT
SACKWATER RAILWAY STATION

but the other papers felt no need for such restraint. Bella Lugosi's *Dracula* film was still showing in various venues around the country and clearly Dodo was not the only one to have seen it, for the *Anglethorpe Advertiser* trumpeted:

VAMPIRE MURDERS SACKWATER
MAN IN BROAD DAYLIGHT

and, as if that was not bad enough, the *Suffolk Courier* proclaimed libellously:

POLICE STAND BY WHILE VAMPIRE
STRIKES AGAIN

Again? I skimmed through the article. Apparently Freddy Smart had also been killed by one of Dracula's acolytes. No wonder Sharkey was having trouble with his enquiries, I pondered. He was looking for a human being. It was the *East Anglian Chronicle* that really went out of their way to reassure its readers though, with the understated announcement:

SUFFOLK GRIPPED IN VAMPIRE TERROR

And I had thought we only had the Nazis to worry about.

34

SHAPES ACROSS THE MOON

Inspector Sharkey had been looking distinctly peaky recently. The long hours he was putting in trying to solve the Freddy Smart murder were not being rewarded. The Shark had rounded up every criminal on his books – including a member of the newly formed Oil Drum Gang, only to find out it was a musical comedy act – and he was getting nowhere. If anybody had any information about the murder of Freddy Smart, they were in no hurry to share it with Old Scrapie and the value of his kudos in the town was rapidly dwindling into overdraft.

Torn between envy of my getting a case to rival his and delight at my messing it up, my colleague took the second course.

'Nobody saw anything that I didn't,' I told him in response to a gloating enquiry.

'So you didn't give chase to the killer?' Sharkey ripped open a fresh pack of ten Senior Service.

'I thought it more important to try to save a man's life than to catch his attacker,' I explained.

My colleague tilted back in his chair to strike a Winners match on the wall. The plaster was streaked in red lines beside him and the green lino splattered with black-rimmed craters from snapped-off heads when he had struck too hard.

'And, in the end, you lost both of them,' he reminded me with great satisfaction.

'I do have one lead,' I told him and, in response to a scowl, continued, 'I hear the Oil Drum Gang might be behind it.' I only wished I knew one of their songs to whistle as I left his office.

*

Vesty was going into his office. 'Ah, Church, a word if you please.'

And suddenly I was the child going into the headmaster's office.

'Is something the matter, sir?'

'Close the door.' He installed himself behind his desk, which was at least twice the size of mine, every letter or file neatly stacked in piles all the same height and each, as far as I could judge, exactly half an inch apart like mosaic tiles waiting to be grouted. 'Take a seat.' Vesty wired a pair of half-rim glasses onto his rather splendidly hewn nose and picked up a sheet of paper. 'Had a memo this morning about you.' He peered over the top of the lenses. 'You women, I mean.'

'Oh yes?' I said politely.

'Yes.' He turned it over. 'Ah here we are.' His voice changed, as people's voices do when they read something out. 'A female police officer is in all matters subordinate to the male.' He folded the document in three. 'To précis – a woman cannot give orders to a man and must accept instruction from him, even if he be lower in rank.'

I knew about this because, unlike most of my colleagues, I actually read the regulations, but I had hoped nobody else would find out. It meant that I was certainly inferior to Sharkey and, even more gratingly, in theory – and probably in practice – Walker or Rivers could give me orders and I knew that I could not work in such circumstances.

'You will receive my resignation before the end of the day, sir,' I told him.

Vesty banged his ear so hard it made me wince to watch.

145

'Damn this tinnitus.' He removed his glasses and continued, 'This leaves me with a bit of a quandary.'

'But I have just solved it for you.' I almost wept in frustration at the stupidity and injustice of it all.

'I hoped you would,' he said and I felt my trimmed fingernails dig into my palms below his line of vision. 'Because the problem is, I have nowhere to file this memo.' He waved a hand like he was summoning a taxi. 'As you can see, my office is completely chock-a-block.' He lowered his arm slowly. 'Bit of an imposition, I know,' he hinged the wires of his spectacles flat with great care, 'but I wonder if you might file it for me.'

I stared at my superior. 'I think I can manage that, sir.'

'Thank you.' Vesty passed it over. 'Keep up the good work.'

I opened my mouth and got as far as, 'Then...' before Vesty looked up sharply.

'That will be all, thank you, Inspector.'

*

Brigsy had gone home and I was about to when I picked up the phone as I passed his desk. Before I could speak, an overly well-modulated voice said, 'Briggs, you old son of a sodomite, Fergusson from Anglethorpe – you know, the proper police station over the water. Hear you've got another juicy case on with that new girl trying to run the shop. Need a hand? I can pop over and cast the old beads over it if you like. Give it the benefit et cetera.'

'Booger off,' I said and hung up before he could work out that my very best Brigsy imitation was not very good at all.

Our blackout boards were slightly warped and I wedged the front few pages of a memorandum into the gap between them in case anyone came in during the night. I could think of a few people who would revel in the chance to report the police to the authorities.

I called in at Felicity House on the way back to *Cressida*. The hall floor was so greasy as to be slippery now and, with my excellent convent education, I could have written my name in the dust on the table.

'What on earth did you do to your little friend?' my mother demanded. 'She came home looking like your father had done a full clearance.'

'She did,' my father concurred.

'She is not my *little friend*,' I objected. 'She is a serving police officer.'

'Even policewomen have feelings,' my mother scolded.

'Well, it's taken you many a year to recognise that,' I snapped.

'Don't be such a silly, Bettyboo,' my father put in helpfully. 'We've only known her a few weeks.'

'Happy weeks.' My mother clasped her hands in a silent prayer of thanksgiving.

'But you haven't even been to see if the poor little thing is all right,' my father accused.

'But that's why I'm here now.'

'Oh.' My mother propped up her bosom. 'Not to see us then?'

'Well, of course that too.' *Police inspector slaughters parents*, I thought but patted the air between us down. 'Is she in my room?'

'Well, it's her room now,' my father pointed out.

'Nobody would blame me,' I said, unintentionally, aloud.

'If you're talking about that expensive white fluted pedestal,' my father called as I set foot on the first step, 'we most certainly would.'

'And don't make a mess,' my mother's voice followed me.

'Speaking of messes' – I paused on the third step – 'have you thought about getting a cleaner?'

'We had Pooky,' my mother reminded me.

'Yes but—'

'She left to make Spitfires,' my father explained ploddingly as if we had only just met.

'There are other cleaners.' Even the bannister rail left a grubby mark on my hand.

'Where?' He looked around.

'I can't be having strangers in my house.' My mother was wild-eyed, as if a horde of them was battering the door down to rape, pillage and smash the sacred pedestal.

It was useless, I knew, to argue that their income depended on having strangers in the house.

'Perhaps you could do a little bit yourself,' I suggested gently.

'Cleaning?' She could not have been more indignant if I had suggested she tried her hand at prostitution. 'What am I – a skivvy?'

'Is that all she is to you?' My father looked almost as shocked. 'You are talking about your mother, for heaven's sake.'

I carried on up.

'Where did we go wrong?' my mother's voice followed me.

'We mustn't blame ourselves,' he reassured her.

For the first time in my life I knocked on my own bedroom door.

'Come in if you're good-looking.' Dodo was sitting on the floor in my blue dressing gown with my dolls and teddy bears in a circle all around her. 'Oh hello, B—Inspector,' she beamed. 'I've made lots of new friends today. Say hello, Archibald.' She made the balding teddy wave a paw.

'It's Mr Fluffly,' I bawled and wished, instantly, that I hadn't, but if there was one thing Mr F hated doing, it was performing tricks.

35

THE SACKWATER SLAYINGS, AL JOLSON
AND THE KAISER

always arrived early for work. It gave me a chance to check the first post and get some paperwork done – plus it kept the men on their toes, knowing I was there and able to check they weren't finishing the night shift early or starting the morning shift late. Brigsy usually beat me to it but he had the advantage of living round the corner. *I do be round the bend, I do*, he would tell people, bemused by their sniggers.

'Let me know when Constable Chivers turns up,' I told him as he stirred the pot.

'You'll know as soon as I do,' he forecast with raised eyes.

Ever since Dodo had heard the 'Three Little Fishies' song she had taken to announcing her arrival with a *boopety boop ditty boopa* – her own approximation of the tune and lyrics.

I took my enamelled mug to my office and shuffled through the files. A vampire attack on a child in nearby Tringford had turned out to be a stray cat but the village constable – clearly feeling he was missing out – had seen fit to put in a report. A bat in a retired wrestler's bedroom for which he called out the fire brigade (there being no anti-vampire service in Suffolk) was exactly that, a tiny harmless pipistrelle bat.

There was something I had been meaning to ask since the day I came. 'Why' – I nodded towards it – 'do we have a jemmy on the wall behind the filing cabinet?'

'Somebody drop ih here seven year gone by' – Brigsy stood up slowly like the mummy encumbered by its bandages – 'and we do be awaiting him coming back to look for ih we do.'

'Is that likely?'

'Well.' The sergeant leaned on his desk like a landlord ready to regale his customers with a well-honed anecdote. 'You may well ask me thah. A month or so back you may well ask me if it's likely we have a lady inspector and my answer would be the same.'

The front door opened a crack and a little face poked through.

'Tuppin' 'ell,' Brigsy groaned.

'May I gain admittance?' a voice to match the face enquired.

'Just this once let me say *no*,' Brigsy begged between gritted teeth.

'Come in, Miss Grim,' I called.

'Prim.' She crept into the lobby. 'I shan't disturb you.'

'Oh good.' I slipped crabwise towards my office but Miss Prim scuttled cockroach-wise to cut off my escape.

'But I know you have been avoiding me.'

'Well—' I hadn't actually given her much thought since we met.

'Because you are too shy or stubborn or silly to ask my advice.'

Or too sane.

'I am a trained police officer—' I began indignantly.

'Yes but that is the trouble.' Miss Prim pulled a crooked finger through the air. 'You are looking for clues when you should be listening to your feelings.'

'I shall bear that in mind,' I assured her, confident that while a defendant's lawyer might criticise evidence, he would, of course, never dream of questioning feminine intuition.

'But fear not,' she piped up.

'Thank you very much, I won't.' I made another unsuccessful break for freedom but nobody could have told Miss Prim that little old ladies do not have lightning reactions, for her furled umbrella shot out like a rapier, blocking off the last line of my retreat.

'Because I am here to help.' A light smile slinked over her atrophied lips. 'I have given a great deal of thought to the Sackwater Slayings, as I shall refer to them in my memoirs, and it appears to me that you have forgotten, as the murderer intended you to, about the real crime.'

I didn't want to but something made me ask, 'Which is?'

Miss Prim's spectacle lenses glinted in the light over the desk.

'Have you forgotten already?' She sniffed reproachfully. 'Why, the crime at the station, of course.'

'But that was a murder too,' I objected and Miss Prim tinkled in amusement.

'Oh no, my dear. I am referring to the memorial bench.'

Miss Prim tapped the bench at her side, in case I had forgotten what the word meant.

'So you think the murders were committed to distract attention from its theft?'

The tinkle became a neigh. 'Isn't it obvious? I dare say you have hardly given that crime a thought since you allowed yourself to be distracted by the vampire.'

'There is no vampire, Miss Prim,' I insisted. 'And, even if there was, why would a vampire steal a railway bench?'

'Haven't you understood a word I said?' Miss Prim closed her eyes patiently. 'To distract you from your murder investigations, of course.'

Brigsy cleared his throat. 'I did hear talk of a foreign man in the Copper Kettle in Tringford boastin' 'bout havin' a new bench, I did,' he recited in oddly flat tones. Brigsy sighed heavily. 'If Inspector Church allows me, I'll be on the twenty-past bus and in that café snoopin' about this very day.'

'I can't possibly spare you, Sergeant,' I said and he did a passable imitation of a man imitating somebody looking disappointed. 'And

I shan't allow anyone else to go there and take all the glory either.'

'Well, I've detained you long enough,' Miss Prim said more truthfully than she probably realised and skipped off as agilely as her aged skeleton allowed.

'Inspired,' I told Brigsy.

'Who is?' he asked suspiciously.

'You.'

'Had a bath night afore last.' He bristled as much as any man with no bristles can.

The door opened again.

'Like Piccalilli Circus,' Brigsy complained, betraying the fact that he had never even been to London by transforming one of its most famous squares into a jar of tangy relish.

It was Sammy Sterne, the sweet-shop owner, and he looked utterly miserable.

'I have been told to report here.' He handed me two envelopes with the royal crest stamped on them and my heart sank, for I had seen a few of those already. 'Yesterday I'm a good citizen – good enough to pay taxes at least.' He flapped his hands. 'Today I'm an enemy alien.'

'You don't have a British passport?' I asked.

'I never got round to it,' he admitted.

'What about Mrs Sterne?' I tried without hope.

'She has taken to her bed,' he told me unhappily.

Brigsy read the letters. 'She do be ordered to attend,' he pointed out, ruefully, for we all knew Abbie Sterne. She made cakes for the children's Christmas party, even though it was hardly her festival.

'I tried to tell her.' Sammy waved his hands around his head. 'But she is overcome with terror we will have to go through it again.'

They had been interned in the last war but I had hoped they would have been naturalised by now.

'Don't worry,' I said. 'I'll call in later, if that's all right, to sort out the paperwork.'

'Thank you.' Sammy clasped my hand in both of his and I felt something being pressed into it before he trudged off, a jolly man who had made the mistake of coming from the wrong race in both the country of his birth and the country that had all but adopted him. I glanced down. It was a little bag of gobstoppers.

Sharkey was hovering as usual. He didn't do many things well but he was very good at that. I was only glad he hadn't seen me accepting a bribe. 'Stinking Krauts,' he sneered. 'Should have gone back to their own country.'

'They would not be welcome in the Reich,' I pointed out and Sharkey sniffed.

'Hitler is right about one thing,' he said. 'They caused the last war and now they've caused another.'

'What?' I burst out. 'You think the Kaiser was a Jew?'

'No but he was controlled by Jewish bankers and they own or control all the armaments factories.'

'You don't mind buying cigarettes from Mr Abrahams,' I pointed out.

'Has he been in yet?' Sharkey reached over for the book.

'No and he won't be,' I told him. 'He was born here.'

'Still a Jew.'

'We are not fighting the Jews.' I swallowed a gutful of obscenities.

'Not yet but we will be.'

'I can't argue with you.' I viewed the man with renewed disgust.

'Because you know I'm right.'

'Because I'm not going to tell you exactly what I think of ignorant bigots in front of a fellow officer.'

Briggs perked up. 'Don't you mind me, madam.'

Constable Walker burst in, his sandy hair – never sleek – wildly flopping over his face. His complexion – usually Sackwater grey – was ripe russet. His sheep eyes rolled and his arms windmilled like Al Jolson blaring that he was on his way to Swanee to see his mammy and tell her how he loved her.

'Muh.' Walker leaned on the doorpost, bent over fighting for breath. 'Muh.' He looked worse than Gregson with half a lung missing. 'Murder,' he managed at last.

36

BREAKFAST WITH POOKY

Sharkey was there before me because I had to go round the desk.

'Murder?' He grasped the constable's shoulders. 'Who? Where? Speak up, man.'

Walker got his breathing almost under control.

'Mr Sk-Skotter Jackson, the accountant on Dogeye Lane.'

'How and when?' I hurried over.

'Stabbed,' Walker panted. 'Ju-just found him.'

'Another?' Sharkey's eyes flicked from side to side. Even he must have realised he was biting off more than he could chew. He hesitated.

'Your case. I'll help,' I conceded to close the deal quickly. Better to be second fiddle than left out of the orchestra.

Sharkey nodded and we dashed to the back room.

'Who's there now?' I called over my shoulder, praying he had not left the scene unattended.

'Constable Bank-Anthony...' Walker swallowed, 'sent me for help, ma'am.'

I was just slipping my gas-mask strap over my shoulder when another little face poked anxiously in.

'Is she here yet?'

'What the hell do you call this?' The Shark pointed at the wall.

Dodo quailed. 'The station clock, sir.'

Sharkey inhaled.

'You go ahead,' I told him hastily before he really let rip. 'I'll deal with her and catch up with you.'

My fellow inspector needed no more encouragement. With a little luck, he could persuade the press that he had been first on the scene and it was a good while since his photo had been in the *Gazette*. 'She'd better have a bloody good excuse.' He ripped the door from Dodo's grasp. 'Well come on, man.'

Walker had been in the process of unfastening his chinstrap but he hastily clipped it up again and followed.

'Oh.' Dodo winced as if I had raised a hand to her.

'So why *are* you late?' I asked as patiently as I could. 'It's by no means the first time either.'

'It is the ninth,' Dodo agreed miserably, 'and usually it is because Mrs Church does not like me to set off without a delicious and nourishing cooked breakfast in my tumbly and Mr Church wants to chitter-chatter and it seems rude to cut his wizard stories and side-splitting jokes short.'

My mother had never cooked me a breakfast. I didn't even know she could. It was a job that had begun and ended with Pooky. Also my father could have won prizes for monosyllabic grumpiness in the morning.

'So what happened today?' I asked, trying not to sound as jealous as I felt.

'Oh.' Dodo turned a sheepish pink. 'The bus was late.'

She shuffled towards the desk.

'You may have forgotten,' I reminded her, 'that I know exactly where you live, having lived there myself for many years, and you do *not* need a bus to get from Felicity House to Sackwater Central.'

'But I was not there last night.' Dodo turned a good Suffolk pink – the sort of thing you see on the walls of thatched cottages.

'Aye-aye,' Brigsy chortled in the knowing way of men who know nothing.

'So where were you?' I asked.

'I went to see Daddy. He was in Ipswich on business but the train was cancelled because of that explosion at Felixstowe and I had to get a bus and it was late,' Dodo recited to an invisible audience over my head.

That much rang true. We had all heard how a munitions train at Felixstowe docks had blown up three days ago and I knew there had been a senior police officers' conference in Ipswich over the weekend. There was another coming up soon that Superintendent Vesty had roped me into, Lord knew why. I had never been to a meeting yet where the main purpose wasn't to arrange the next meeting.

'I haven't got time for this,' I said. 'But you will not be late again.'

The pink was streaked with white now.

'Oh but what will happen to me if I am?'

I fixed her eyes – no easy feat because they were flitting everywhere. 'Listen to me, Constable Chivers. You will *not* be late again. Now come with me. We have a murder to investigate.'

'On Dogeye Lane?' Dodo stepped back, catching the rim of her helmet on the wall. 'Ouchy.'

'I told you not to say that.'

'I am sorry to disagree, ma'am' – Dodo folded her arms – 'especially on such a lovely morning, but you told me not to say *ouchy-wouchy.*'

'*Ouch* will suffice in future.' I put on my helmet. 'How did you know it was on Dogeye Lane?'

'Oh.' Dodo Chivers twiddled her thumbs. 'I heard somebody say it.'

She was right about one thing. It was a lovely autumn day.

'Who?'

'Um, Nippy Walker.'

'Well, let's see if you can be one yourself.' I strode briskly off, Dodo trotting at my heel like a faithful terrier full of mischief and tricks. I had a reason for staying back to admonish my constable other than saving her from being skinned alive. I wanted to prove something and, after they had got the car out and running and gone round the block and down busy High Road East, I still had a chance to do so. We cut through Jericho Alley, breaking into a gentle trot.

'Cannot we slow down, Inspector?'

'Of course we can,' I agreed, 'but we shan't.'

'Oh but your gorgeous legs are longer than my gorgeous legs.'

Life was too short to correct her on everything she said, besides which I liked to think she was right. We stopped.

'Don't look like you've been running,' I ordered.

'Oh but I am breathless as a badger,' she panted.

'Don't look it.' I was breathing a little faster than usual myself but determined to appear fresh and relaxed as I strolled out onto Dogeye Lane, just as Old Scrapie was parking the Wolseley outside the chandler's shop, cleverly called – wait for it – The Chandler's Shop.

37

DEATH ON DOGEYE LANE

I f Sharkey was miffed at our prompt arrival, he was not going to show it.

'Took your time.' He glanced at a crowd of curious onlookers. 'Go about your business,' he commanded and they pressed forward.

Near the back stood Jimmy, with his flop of brown hair and dark-red lips. The two scrawny girls were eyeing him with intent, I thought, as he gave me an odd little wave.

What are you doing here? I turned away.

Constable Box stood on the threshold of a small terraced flint building,

SKOTTER HEATH JACKSON,
CHARTERED ACCOUNTANT

engraved into a brass plate on the wall. He had made a speciality of doing that.

Dogeye Lane was a narrow street and sloped upwards quite sharply. As a child I loved freewheeling on my bike down it, the cobbles nearly shaking the teeth out of my mouth – until the time I crashed into the back of a cart pulled by Pickles, the donkey delivering pickles.

'Morning, sir, ma'am.'

'Clear these people away.'

'Under what authority?' a tall, corpulent man in a purple-brown

Harris tweed suit piped up. I recognised him as Sir Malcolm Butterworth. He was slumming it, mingling with the hoi polloi.

'Under the authority of a clip round the ear.' Sharkey raised his hand but dropped it when he realised who he was talking to. 'Beasty' Butterworth owned Mawleigh Mansion and a few thousand acres around it and sat on the bench as a justice of the peace.

'Can I quote you on that, Inspector?' Gregson of the *Gazette* emerged in a blue blazer, notebook in one hand, pencil in the other, photographic equipment dangling round his neck.

'No, you may pigging not.'

'Pigging.' Gregson made a squiggle with his pencil.

'Put that bloody pad away.' Sharkey stepped towards him.

'Mind your language,' a woman in a hairnet complained. 'I brought my boy to witness a good wholesome murder, not that kind of filth.' She looked about. 'Where's the little skitter gone now?'

Gregson – clearly a man of many talents – fiddled with a light meter while out-elbowing a young man in a leather jacket who was trying to elbow him out of the way.

'Who you pushing?' the youth demanded.

'I rather thought it was you,' the reporter replied.

'Clear off, all of you.' Sharkey tried to wave them away, but the crowd was swelling now with locals anxious not to miss the entertainment.

'This is exactly the sort of police state we are fighting against,' Beasty Butterworth remarked, rather oddly for a man of his legal standing, I thought.

We hadn't done much fighting so far – at least not on land – but his remark was rewarded with an enthusiastic round of applause and a muttering of *Nazi* pronounced *naahsee*, as our First Lord of the Admiralty, Winston, was in the habit of saying it.

'Why you—' the Shark raised a hand. I do not suppose he would have struck the boy, at least not in public, but he was interrupted again anyway.

'Hold it.' The man from the *Gazette* raised one of his three cameras and pressed the shutter. 'Gotcha.'

'What?' Sharkey's purple indignation would have made a much better picture, I felt, but the cameraman had turned his attention elsewhere.

'And you too, please. The public will love to see a police*woman* on the front page.'

I am not especially vain – just ordinarily so – but Adam had told me that my left profile was my best, so I turned and had almost managed to put on my best staring-into-the-distance expression before the shutter clicked again. And it was only when the cameraman said, 'Could we have the skirt raised a fraction?' that I realised his attention had been on Dodo, leaning seductively against a bollard.

'No you could not,' I snapped before she even thought of complying.

'So how long have you been a lady policeman?' Gregson of the *Gazette* asked.

'I am a woman police officer,' Dodo told him with great dignity and I left her to explain the difference.

Constable Box saluted smartly but with his left hand. He often confused them. 'If you look at your thumbs, the right one should be whiter from sucking it,' Dodo had explained once and, sure enough, hers was, with two little dents where her lower teeth had dug into the back of it. Unfortunately his wasn't. 'I suck both thumbs,' he had explained, 'in turn.'

'Morning, ma'am.' Instead of rotating, Box stepped aside. We had rehearsed that back at the station, and he was perfect on his opening performance. 'Not a pretty sight.'

This was something we warned the public about, not each other.

'Oh you can't help your looks,' I told him kindly and Box slid further along, back against the bamboo-pattern paper as if the wall would collapse without his support.

Behind me Old Scrapie posed manfully on the step but the attention of the crowd and press was taken by the little skitter walking around Dodo on his hands.

There was a tiny hall with a quarrystone floor going straight to the planked back door. These were fishermen's houses once and some still were, but many had been converted into little shops or small businesses for they were cheap to buy, very cheap to rent and convenient for the town centre. There was one door to the left pulled to and the rest was wooden stairs, painted in scuffed cream.

'First floor, ma'am,' Box told me.

'Officer, come quickly,' a well-clipped gentleman's voice rang out behind me but I ignored it. If anyone was going to be summoned in such a peremptory manner, I would prefer it to be my beloved fellow inspector.

I went up to a landing, the same size as the hall, which was no great size at all, lit only by light from the sole door, hanging off its hinges to my left with Bantony leaning against its doorpost like he was waiting for a date.

38

SNORKELLING IN GOZO

The door was open, the lock breaking through the woodwork and the frame splintered. I put my head inside. The curtains were still closed, billowing inwards in a draught just enough to let flickers of faint daylight in but not enough to see anything except an ominous lump behind the desk to my left.

'Who found him?' I stepped into the room.

'Oy did, ma'am. Mrs Milligan, 'is secretary, called for 'elp when she found 'is office door locked and saw that.' My constable pointed to a thick rusty-red trickle stagnating over the threshold.

'And you charged the door down?'

Bantony rubbed his shoulder ruefully. 'What else could Oy do?'

'You had two choices,' I told him. 'God did not give policemen outsized feet and the East Suffolk Constabulary did not give him outsized boots to be a ballet dancer. A well-aimed kick at the lock would have torn it off its screws.'

'And the second thing?' Bantony rotated his arm stiffly.

'There's an iron merchant's just down the road. You could have borrowed a jemmy and jacked it open without breaking into a sweat.'

'Oy acted on moy initiative.' Bantony sniffed as if that raised his actions above criticism.

'Were the curtains closed like this when you arrived?'

'Yes, ma'am,' Bantony said. 'I opened them for a bit then pulled them again.'

'So is the window open or closed?'

'Closed and locked, ma'am.'

'Did you touch anything?' I looked at the tiny droplets of sweat on his upper lip.

'Hardly been in there, ma'am,' Bantony assured me so defensively you'd have thought it was a very naughty thing indeed for a policeman to enter a crime scene. 'Well, Oy went in – of course – but Oy didn't touch anythink.' Bantony adopted his Oy'm-a-good-boy-Oy-am demeanour.

'So when we dust the place down we won't find a single dab to match any of Constable Anthony Bank-Anthony's fingerprints?' I clarified.

'Well, of course I *touched* a few things. Yow can't help touchin' things.' He was starting to sound like William Brown explaining to his irate mother how a treasured ornament sort of broke itself. 'But Oy didn't interfere with anythink.'

I did a breathing exercise Adam had taught me when we went snorkelling in Gozo. 'What exactly did you touch?'

'Well, the door handle on the inside, of course,' Bantony began.

'Why?'

'Well, yow do, don't yow?' he told me.

'No I don't.'

'It's for luck,' he explained. 'Yow tap a door handle on both sides for luck.'

'Be damned lucky for the murderer if you've obliterated his only print,' I snapped. 'What else? What else did you touch, tap or maybe rub to summon a genie?'

Bantony chewed his lips one at a time, clearly confused. This was not in the least what women were for.

'Oy prolly touched the desk and chair and Oy went to the window and put moy hands on the ledge when Oy looked out.'

'And did you see anything out there worth mauling the sill for?'

Bantony did a breathing exercise he must have taught himself.

It was quick and sharp, the sort of noise you make when you burn yourself ironing – before you make all the other noises.

'No, ma'am.'

'Right.' I stepped over the threshold. 'Stay where you are.' I waited a minute for my eyes to adjust to the gloom. 'One day I shall buy you a pair of gloves.'

'Oh can Oy have black leather ones?' Bantony brightened. 'The girls loike them.'

'No you can't.' I had become very good at snarling lately.

'She is never very cheerful first thing in the morning,' Dodo Chivers had whispered to him once. 'Her dear little mummy told me that.'

I got out my handkerchief and, aware that Bantony was willing me to be careless, used it to flick up the dolly switch and turn the light on.

'Oh,' I commented uninformatively. *Shit*, I breathed in my head.

You see a lot of death in my job but that doesn't mean you get used to it and it doesn't mean you have to like it.

39

THE MAN IN A PINSTRIPE SUIT

The ominous lump was, as I knew it would be, a man. He was slumped backwards, wearing a pinstripe suit, in a high-backed chair behind a leather-topped desk. He might have been staring at the ceiling for inspiration if it wasn't for the two gaping wounds in his throat, just to the right of centre.

The trickle on the threshold had flowed from a puddle around the dead man's feet. With exemplary care my constable had not trampled all over it – though, knowing Bantony, he probably had a fastidious rather than a procedural motive.

'Open the curtains.'

Constable Bank-Anthony crossed to the window at the front of the building, holding his right arm across himself as if it was in a sling. A blackout board had been propped against the wall.

I took a look at the room – a small office with two upright pine chairs for customers facing the dead man across his desk, a green metal filing cabinet, the bare floor painted cream and grey Anaglypta wallpaper. There was a picture over the unlit gas fire set into the chimney breast of Edward VIII looking rather silly in bales of braid and sporting more medals than the average battalion. Had nobody told the dead man we had gained a new and better king three years ago?

The man himself was probably in his mid-thirties. He had a good head of wavy gingery hair, neatly barbered, and the suit was well tailored, though heavily stained now.

'Why is there no blood on the desk?' I wondered aloud. 'It doesn't look like he was dragged here.' I crouched, pulling my skirt over my knees to avoid my sergeant's leering gaze.

'What is it?' Bantony watched me reach under the pedestal.

There were footsteps in the hall.

'It looks like' – I pulled it out – 'a sack.'

It was a jute one, the sort of thing you might get grain in, and it was encrusted in gore. I held it up towards the window. There were five vertical rips in it, each about an inch long.

'The murderer put this over his head before stabbing him,' I said.

The holes were only on one side of the sack and corresponded roughly to the dead man's wounds.

'To stop 'im strugglink?' Bantony hazarded.

'Partly,' I agreed. 'Also it stops the murderer getting splattered with blood. I suppose this is definitely Skotter Heath Jackson?'

'Mrs Milligan identifoid 'im.' Bantony brushed some dust off his sleeves.

'Where is Mrs Milligan now?'

Bantony jerked his head like he was trying to shake water out of his ear. 'Down there.' He pointed so vaguely that for a minute I thought he meant under the floorboards.

'Is she all right?'

My constable considered the matter. 'Not bad,' he decided, 'bit old for moy but quoite trim.'

I breathed hard and tried again. 'Is she all right being left sitting by herself?'

Bantony shrugged. 'What else could oy do?'

'You could have comforted her. Her boss doesn't need consoling.'

'Oy was lookin' fer clues.'

'And did you find any?' I held up the sack as an example.

'One,' Bantony declared, proud as a cat presenting its owner with a disembowelled mouse, and I went to look – five footprints in the blood on the other side of the body, four of them smudged but one quite clear – a flat round-toed shoe with parallel cleats in the sole.

'Do *not* let anybody near that. Guard it with your career,' I instructed. 'We need a police photographer.'

'Do we 'ave one?' Bantony rolled his head back.

'Of course.' I glanced at the blotter. It was fresh and blank. 'He starts in about ten years' time.' I went back onto the landing. 'And don't touch anything.' Another thought struck me. 'Where on earth has Chivers got to?' I raised my voice to a bellow. 'Constable Chivers!'

And from downstairs I heard, 'Here I am, Inspector.'

I peered over the bannister but could see no sign of her. 'What are you doing?'

'Talking to Mr Jackson's secretary.'

'Get Mr Gregson of the *Gazette*.'

A little face appeared at the bottom of the stairs, peering up. 'Do you mean arrest him?' She glowed with excitement.

'No, I mean ask him to come in.'

'Shall I tell him bossily, like...' her voice rose half an octave, 'You there, come here this instant.'

'Constable Box,' I called over her head. 'Can you do it?'

'Might the inspector have a word, please, sir?'

'Ohhh.' Dodo swung her left leg sulkily. 'I could have done that.'

'Go back to Mrs Milligan.'

'Yes ma'am.' She was a thousandth of a decibel off stamping.

Gregson squeezed past Box. One day I would see if East Suffolk did a stepping-out-of-the-way course and send our sturdy constable on it. He had already forgotten the lesson I had given him.

As I went down a thought struck me. 'Where's Inspector Sharkey?' I asked Box.

I had expected Old Scrapie to be hot on my heels, barging me out of the way.

'I think I can answer that.' Gregson grinned. 'There was a sighting of a German spy signalling from the allotments.'

I could not imagine Old Scrapie passing up that opportunity. He would be national news if he arrested a Nazi.

'So why didn't you go?' I asked suspiciously.

'Well...' Gregson looked a little, but only a little, abashed. 'This is only a theory but maybe it was a quiet news day even by Sackwater standards so somebody started that rumour before he heard about this story.'

'You do know it's an offence to waste police time?' I asked as sternly as I could manage.

'Certainly do.' He adopted that guilelessly innocent look that only the guilty can carry off successfully. 'And the moment you capture the villain, the *Gazette* will be strident in its condemnation of him.'

I smothered a smile. 'Want another scoop?'

'If it's the one about the duck warning the farmer about the fox, that's already in tomorrow's edition under Dauntless Duck Foxes Fox at French's Farm.' His eyes were Oxford blue, almost black in the dull, Box-filtered light.

'I think you can hold the front page,' I prophesied and those dark eyes flashed.

'So it's true.' His face was alive with excitement and his finger underlined the air between us as he underlined his headline. 'The Suffolk Vampire Strikes Again.'

169

40

THE FATE OF THE EEL

was only surprised Gregson had taken so long to ask. A London reporter would have copy on his editor's desk by now.

'No,' I said. 'As you well know, he doesn't exist.'

'Do you believe in the Loch Ness Monster?'

'No.'

'Neither do I but he sells papers.' This was a healthier and more assertive man than the one I had met at the station.

I hesitated. Perhaps this wasn't such a good idea. 'As, I'm sure you know, there has been a murder.'

'Skotter Heath Jackson?'

'Yes.'

'And Mrs Milligan?'

'No.'

Gregson clicked his tongue. 'Pity.'

'You don't like Mrs Milligan?'

'I don't know her but a double slaying would have tripled circulation.'

'If I let you up there will you promise to take one photo of the clue that I point out to you and nothing else and not write anything about what you see up there without putting it past me?' I waited for his outburst about freedom of the press and democracy. It was a speech they must all be taught in the Journalists' School of Hypocrisy.

'Yes,' he said simply.

'Why?' I asked warily.

'Because if I say no, I'll be back on the street with no more story than any casual bystander got. Also, if I break my word, you'll never give me any information again. So' – he swung the lever to wind on his film – 'what is it? An axe?' His ambitions soared. 'The bloodied corpse?'

'A footprint.'

Gregson's face fell until he found a glimmer of hope. 'In the blood?'

'Yes.'

'Excellent! That has to be a front page.' His finger drew again. 'Footprint of a Murderer.'

'Only if you prefix it with "Is This The" and end with a question mark,' I advised for both our sakes. 'Can you manage the stairs?'

'Race you.' He looked up them wryly.

'You'll have to give me a good start,' I replied and we set off, me first, the reporter taking the steps one at a time and pausing on each to replenish his oxygen.

I stopped near the top. 'It's not a pretty sight.'

'It is from where I'm standing.'

'Is that an attempt at charm?' I reached the landing.

'The British press never lie.'

'The British press just has.' I went into the room.

'Who's that?' Bantony tried to look busy but, having been told not to touch anything, he had nothing to look busy about.

'A reporter from the *Gazette*.'

'Why's he wobbling?'

I spun round and leaped out just in time to catch Gregson's lapel as he swayed and staggered backwards towards the abyss.

*

'Maybe a bit too ambitious,' Gregson said after I had sat him on the top step and got him to put his head between his knees.

'I'm sorry.' I put a steadying hand on his shoulder. 'I shouldn't have asked you to do that.'

'Not just the bellows.' Gregson raised his head. 'I've never seen a murder before,' he admitted bashfully.

'Can I have a go with your camera then?'

'Certainly not.' Gregson clutched it protectively to him. 'I'll be all right.'

I helped him up. 'Tell me if you feel dizzy.'

'I'll be all right,' he repeated tetchily. Obviously the very idea that he might not be was an unwarranted slur on his manliness and, if there's one thing you must never do with a man's masculinity, it's slur on it.

Gregson tugged the bottom of his blue blazer down. I don't really like blazers but at least it was single-breasted and didn't have anchors on the brass buttons. Gregson dusted his beige trousers and tipped the brim of his panama down, like George Raft on a killing spree only not quite as menacing. He tightened the knot of his earthy-green and lemon-yellow striped tie, inflated his chest and marched in.

Gregson of the *Gazette* did himself credit. He was pale and tense but he kept on his feet this time, had a closer look at the body, whistled once and said, 'Nasty.' He took three photos of the footprint, two of them with popping flashbulbs.

He scanned the area, mesmerised by Skotter Heath Jackson's corpse now.

'We'd better discuss what I can and can't reveal. I wouldn't want to mess up your investigation. Dinner tonight?'

Was he trying to pick me up? Even if he wasn't it would be far more professional to tell him to go to the station. Gregson smiled. He was not a handsome man and he had a crumpled air, possibly due to his illness. Adam was the kind of man fortune tellers tell every girl she will meet: tall (by Maltese standards), dark and very handsome, but Adam was not there and Gregson was. Gregson had a winning smile and, for today at least, it won.

'I'll meet you for a drink,' I decided.

'Do you know the Compasses?'

'I certainly do.' I'd been thrown out of there by Walsaw Welch for trying to buy a drink underage but there was a different landlord now. Walsaw had choked to death trying to swallow a live eel for a bet. The eel survived long enough to be the main attraction of a stew.

'Shall we say eight?'

'Perfect,' I said.

'Yes you are.'

'Very nearly,' I agreed.

I saw him out. His eyes were cobalt in the sunshine, I noticed, with golden flecks in them.

41

THE BONE-HANDLED KNIFE

I went to the downstairs office, where Dodo was holding the hand of a woman seated behind a typewriter at a small wooden desk. Her hair was greying round the roots and coming unclipped.

'Mrs Milligan came in just before nine. Mr Jackson, her employer, usually came in around eight because he got the early bus from Tringford where he lived. The door was locked so she thought he might be late until she saw the blood. He left before her last night. I was just asking Mrs Milligan if she knows anyone called Lavender Wicks.'

'Who—' I began.

'Mrs Milligan,' Dodo replied with great patience.

'No, who is—' I tried again.

'I have already told you that I don't.' The woman looked up. 'I hope you catch the bastard and I hope you string him up.' Her face was blotchy and streaked with tears and, from the dent in the bridge of her nose, she normally wore glasses.

'Do you have any idea who it could be?' I asked but she shook her head.

Her wire-framed spectacles lay hinged open between old splots of ink on the desk's pine top.

'No.'

'Did he have any enemies? Anyone who complained too much about his bill or blamed him for their taxes?'

'Why on earth would anybody do that?' she demanded as if I had done so myself. 'He was a good accountant and considerate

174

employer. Everybody liked him – except the cleaner, who left in a paddy because he asked her to wipe the skirting boards. I believe she is making parts for Spitfires now.'

'Did she make any threats?'

Mrs Milligan grasped a lethal-looking bone-handled knife. 'Called him a dunt chop-logger-head.' She slit open the letter.

'How very rude.' Dodo tossed her head indignantly. 'Unless, of course, he was one.'

'Was he married?'

'Of course.'

'Happily?'

'With three sons. Somebody will have to tell them.'

'I can do that,' I said. 'Do you know his home address?'

'The Chestnuts, Moss Lane, Tringford.' She exhaled shudderingly. 'If he hadn't come back to work yesterday he would still be alive now.'

'He'd been away?'

'With a terrible cold.' She picked up an unopened letter. 'He took a whole week off. He hated doing that.'

'I'm sorry,' I said, 'but can I see your shoe?'

'What? Oh for goodness' sake.' Mrs Milligan twisted round in her chair, sticking her right foot out as if she would have liked to kick me with her pointed stiletto. Even before I asked, I knew I was wasting my time.

'And if you could lift it, please.' There were no cleats and no dried blood. 'Do you have any other shoes here?'

'What a stupid question.'

Don't ever let me catch you scrumping apples, I thought, but said, 'Some women wear shoes for walking to work and change when they get there.'

'I don't.'

I paused, puzzled by her lack of cooperation.

'Do you resent my trying to catch your employer's killer, Mrs Milligan?'

'I resent you treating me like a suspect.'

'I am trying to eliminate you as one.'

'Then kindly do so.'

'Daphne is very upset,' Dodo explained helpfully. 'She's never had an employer murdered before.'

'Oh this is such a waste of time,' Mrs apparently-Daphne Milligan burst out. 'We all know you won't catch him and you'll end up blaming it on the Suffolk Vampire.'

42

THE STAKING OF CAREERS

t was with some difficulty that I persuaded Mrs Milligan that she had to leave the premises. She was paid to stay until five, she told me, and looked more shocked than by anything else when I told her, 'Not any more.'

Dodo brought out her notebook. She had already almost filled it with her tiny neat handwriting. She licked the pencil and began to print. 'The suspect wore a brown coat,' she murmured.

'What?' Mrs Milligan tied then untied her belt in confusion.

'Goodbye, Daphne.' Dodo wiggled her fingers. 'I hope you have better luck with your next employer.'

'Thank you,' Mrs Milligan said to my surprise and trudged out of the front door when I held it open for her.

'Hold it... Lovely,' I heard Gregson say. 'Is there anything you would like to say to our readers, madam?'

Mrs Milligan growled something and I caught sight of him flinching.

'I don't think I could print that.' Gregson put his notebook away. 'I'm not even sure I could spell it.'

I shut the door. 'I hear Inspector Sharkey has gone in pursuit of a German spy.'

'Oh yes. A new waitress rang Slackwater Central from Henrietta's Café,' Dodo told me airily as if that was an everyday event. 'Only...' She hesitated.

'Only what?'

'I think she heard that nice little man from the sweet shop

talking and jumped to the wrong conclusion. I saw him come out of the café on my way from the bus stop.'

Exactly how many spies can there be in this town? They must outnumber the trippers.

'But you didn't tell Inspector Sharkey?'

Dodo twiddled the lower brass button of her jacket. 'I thought we might manage better without him.'

'How unprofessional,' I scolded and gave her a wink.

'Oh dear,' Dodo said, 'have you got pixie dust in your eye?'

* * *

Sharkey didn't exactly froth at the mouth – I've never seen anyone do that unless they've overdone the tooth powder – but he did the closest thing I've ever seen to it without the bubbles.

'Bloody wild goose chase,' he fumed. 'It was that damned Kraut off to clean out his fucking doves. It's a bloody joke.'

'Geese bleeding? Doves making babies? I don't understand' – Dodo wrinkled her brow – 'why that's a joke.'

'Mr Sterne keeps racing pigeons,' I told her. 'He has quite a few prizes for them but they are his babies really, the children he and Mrs Sterne never had.'

Sharkey rounded on me. 'You set it up, didn't you?'

'When and how?' I didn't need to ask *why* because it was obvious he thought I was stealing his case.

'When this brainless mopsy turned up late again.'

'I shall look that word up later,' Dodo warned. 'You are not supposed to abuse fellow officers.'

'And while you're about it, look up the word *late*,' he retorted, with some justification, I thought.

'We only have one phone so I would have had to make the call in front of all the men,' I pointed out but it was obvious that even Scrapie did not really believe his own accusation.

'Dammit.' He clenched himself together.

'The body is still there,' I reminded him. 'We haven't disturbed anything and we can tell you what Mrs Milligan, the victim's secretary, said. We even have a photo of what might be the murderer's footprint.'

'The murderer left a photograph of his footprint?' Dodo asked incredulously.

'No, I got Mr Gregson to take a picture.'

Sharkey leaped at my words. 'You let that man from the *Gazette* into the crime scene?'

'I know I did,' I said. 'But he will not publish anything without my permission.'

Sharkey folded his arms. 'And you believe that?'

'I will stake my career on it,' I asserted, aware that I already had.

43

THE DRAGON'S TEETH

Dodo almost but not quite skipped as we turned onto High Road East. 'I see the sea and the sea sees me,' she chanted merrily, oblivious to the curious stares of the public. 'Where to now, boss?' She had taken to calling me that lately and I didn't mind. At least it was better than binspector.

'Dolly's Café,' I told her.

'Are you expecting to find a clue there?'

'I am expecting to find a good pot of coffee and two iced buns.'

'Is one of the buns for me?' Dodo wondered. 'I'm as hungry as a haberdashery.'

'It might be, if you tell me who Lavender Wicks is.'

'I do not know.' Dodo put a hand to her helmet. She was having trouble with her new one. We had been issued with the military type, *POLICE* printed in black letters on the front, and you can't pack as much hair into one of those as you can into the peacetime peaked helmet. People think it's a myth that constables keep snacks in their helmets. I certainly used to, though I soon learned the hard way that it's not a good idea to store chocolate in one on a hot summer's day.

I thought I had given up hard hats for soft when I swapped my stripes for pips but the east coast could soon, as Teddy Moulton had predicted, be our first line of defence and we were all dressing like soldiers now.

'Then why did you ask Mrs Milligan if she did?'

'I thought she might.'

I stopped and pointed. Across the gap at the bottom of the road a destroyer glided, grey in the grey North Sea.

'Goodness.' Dodo crossed her fingers. 'Good luck, boys.' She waved both arms high above her head.

'I don't think they can see you.'

'But they have telescopes,' Dodo objected, 'and look, those children on the prom-prom-prom are waving too.'

I could not help but wonder how many of those on that ship would survive the battles that must surely come and, feeling a bit self-conscious but even more proud, I gave them a salute.

Dodo blew her nose. 'Sorry, boss.' She hiccupped.

'You're allowed a tear for those men,' I told her as we walked slowly on until we were at the seafront and the ship was disappearing around Angle Promontory.

The bell tinkled merrily as I pushed open the door.

'My boy's on that ship,' Dolly, daughter of the original owner, told us, cups and saucers rattling with pride as she set them on the gingham tablecloth.

'God keep him safe,' I said and she chuckled sideways. The left side of her face had been paralysed since she had been attacked by a dromedary when there was a failed attempt to outdo Anglethorpe's donkey rides. The creature had escaped soon afterwards, never to be seen again. Presumably it was washed out to sea. It's hard to imagine nobody would notice a camel roaming the Suffolk countryside, though rumours had been rife that Bressinghall's, the butchers, were putting it into their sausages.

'It's Adolf's lads you want to worry about when my Alfie gets a crack at them.' She placed the pot with the handle towards my constable.

'Lavender Wicks,' I reminded Dodo.

'Oh yes.' She dabbed the icing on her bun with her little fingertip. 'Of Treetops House, Pinfold Lane. I found this.' She

slid a red booklet across the table like a croupier and I did not
need to turn it over to know what it was.

I opened the cover.

```
DL2 No A 70827 Suffolk County Council
Traffic Acts 1930 and 1934

Driver's Licence

Lavender Wicks

Of: Treetops House, Pinfold Lane,

is hereby licensed to drive a motor vehicle
of any description from 5th February 1939
until 4th February 1940 inclusive.

Fee of 5/- received.

The Controller, Taxation Department, County
Hall, Ipswich.

Usual Signature of licensee: L F Wicks
```

On the opposite page under the stamped,

BURY ST EDMUNDS COUNTY COURT

was handwritten in Indian ink:

Date: 9th August 1939

Offence: Exceeding the speed limit in a built-up area

Date of Offence: 2nd August 1939

Order: Fine of £1.10/- and endorsement of licence.

A signature that looked like *A Sniff* but probably said *A. Smith*,
then 'Clerk to the Justices'.

And the stamped warning:

```
Must not be removed or defaced.
```

'Where did you find this?'

'On the floor in the hall, near Mrs Milligan's office door.'

'And why didn't you tell Inspector Sharkey?'

Dodo rubbed her front teeth with the knuckle of her thumb. 'I forgot.'

'No you didn't.' I was not going to tell her the thumb habit was one of the things she did when she fibbed.

Dodo clipped and unclipped her handbag. 'I wanted to tell you first.'

'Have you any idea how angry Inspector Sharkey will be when he finds you've been holding back evidence?'

She repeated the handbag process. 'Will he be as big a crosspatch as when I spilled ink on his trousers?'

'Bigger.'

'Oh dearie-dearie me.' Dodo changed colour a few times before settling on white with a hint of fuchsia. She dabbed the pot with the tip of her little finger. 'Shall I pour?'

'Can you without spilling it on the cloth?'

'Possibly.' She nibbled her right thumb.

'I'll pour.'

'I can manage the milk.' Dodo confidently slopped it into my saucer. 'He will be busy this afternoon, will he not?'

'And this evening, writing his report,' I confirmed.

'When would he least like to be disturbed?' She took a lump of sugar in the silver tongs, swooped it through the air and dropped it into her tea like she was bombing it, splashing her beverage onto the cloth.

'In the evening,' I said with some confidence. 'He'll be tired and even more grouchy than usual. One of the very few things we have in common is we both hate paperwork.'

'That is when I shall tell him,' Dodo decided and stirred a whirlpool into her tea. 'Shall we go and see if Mrs or Miss Lavender Wicks is home?'

'Why not?' I agreed, unwilling to admit I could think of nothing more useful to do. The best lead I had for the killing of Ardom Dapper at the railway station was a definite sighting of the Suffolk Vampire in the vicarage gardens, which had turned out to be a cassock on the washing line. I had no reliable information either on the whereabouts of Millicent Smith. Some of the reports coming in now were so bizarre as to be insane or mischievous. An account of her on a balcony in Rome with Mussolini could have fitted into either category.

'Why not indeed?' Dodo pondered over her coffee. 'Well...' She grasped her chin. 'She might not be at home and we will have had a wasted journey. She might be at home but hiding in her cellar, if she has one, and we will have had a wasted journey. She might—'

'It was a rhetorical question,' I interrupted before she could tell me Lavender Wicks might be a mermaid and forcing me to explain why mermaids can't drive cars.

'Oh.' She raised the cup to peer at me over the rim. 'I am not very good at spotting those. I am good at spotting dropped licences and gentian violet stains though. Also I once spotted a dolphin going down Oxford Street. It was in a glass case though and not very difficult to spot. Why are you pointing to the tip of your nose?'

'I am doing a shush sign.'

Dodo's lower lip slipped out. 'Is that because you want me to shush?'

'I want you to enjoy your coffee in peace.' I lied over the *you* bit.

'Oh thank you, boss.' She smiled so prettily that the man on the next table slopped his tea down his shirt.

'What a nice man.' Dodo's voice rang around the café. 'He did not even swear when he behaved in such a stupid clumsy way.'

I rolled a cigarette.

'I do not want to preach…' Dodo folded her hands primly.

Oh yes you do, I thought. 'Then don't.' I inhaled the smoke deeply but the pleasure was gone, Dodo watching every puff in much the same way as a child might view her father getting roaring drunk. I pinched off the end. 'Is it all right if I drink my coffee?'

'Oh but you simply must,' Dodo urged and even the desire to do that withered.

I gulped it down, trying to pretend I wasn't scalding my throat, and stood up. 'Come on. We have work to do.'

'Oh but I have hardly commenced mine.' Dodo's pansy eyes brimmed as if I had stolen her Christmas present. For a second I nearly relented but it was bad enough being disapproved of by my parents without my usurper following suit.

'Maybe you shouldn't have spent so long not wanting to preach,' I suggested, shocked at how nastily my words came out.

Dodo's lower lip trembled.

Oh for Pete's sake, how are you going to cope with the abuse the average criminal will give you? I wondered in dismay but only said, 'Drink up while I go to the ladies.'

My constable looked about. 'But there are not any ladies here.'

I put a half-crown on the tablecloth, went through the door at the back and relit my cigarette, feeling rather like I had at school when Sister Millicent was on the prowl.

Dodo was dabbing her lips when I came back.

'I told the waitress you do not want any change,' she told me brightly as we stepped onto the street.

I can think of one change I would like right now.

There were soldiers near the water's edge, packing huge bales of razor wire under the pier and stretching it between conical concrete blocks designed to stop tanks rolling up the beach.

'What are those cementy things?' Dodo pointed with both hands.

'They call them dragon's teeth.' I watched the timber groyne I used to dive off being bulldozed into splintered planks.

'Well, they shouldn't,' Dodo said crossly. 'It's very misleading.'

44

THE MANGLED SHEEP MURDER

Pinfold Lane was an unmade private road on the outskirts of town. It was built into the edge of the sandhills and they were making determined attempts to reclaim their territory. The surface of the lane was sprinkled with sand and it was piling up at the sides. The houses were almost all expensive-looking dormer bungalows.

We had taken a number 16 bus to the end of the road. It would have been an easy cycle ride but there was no such thing as an easy cycle ride for Dodo. 'Bicycles are a teensy-weensy bit too wibberly-wobberly for little old me,' she had said when I had suggested she got one.

'Why did they not put some of this sand on the beach?' Dodo asked reasonably enough.

'It's too light,' I said. 'If the wind didn't blow it straight back, the tide would wash it all out to sea.'

To prove my first point, a low gust swirled eddies around our ankles.

'You know a great many things,' Dodo remarked, adding, before I got too swollen-headed, 'I presume that is because you have been alive so long.'

I wanted to tell her she would not reach my venerable age if she kept saying things like that but I only said, 'Probably.'

Treetops House stood at the end on the left, just before Pinfold Lane disappeared into the dunes with only a faint dip to indicate where it was intended to go. Two storeys high with a flat roof,

Treetops House was built in white concrete with steel-framed windows and a straight-fronted curved-sided upper balcony on pillars on its left-hand side.

There was a curving flower bed at the front, walled also in white concrete and planted with heathers and alpines. A double garage was attached on the right-hand side and I wondered if it was being used. Petrol rationing had already led many people to put their cars on blocks for the duration.

Dodo wrote *DODO* in the sand with her toe. 'Would it not be simply toooo thrilling if Lavender Wicks were to be married to Thurston Wicks, the film star?'

'I hardly think he would be living in Sackwater.' I watched her name blow away. 'Even if he did, it would be somewhere like Mallard Road.'

I rang the bell and waited.

'Perhaps—' Dodo began, but I was spared any bizarre theories about what the inhabitants might be up to by the door swinging open.

'Yes?'

'Pooky,' I said in surprise.

'Miss Betty.' She drew back, taller and bonier than ever, her long frizzly grey hair dragged fiercely back under a starched white hat.

'You are supposed to be making Submarine Spitfire aeroplanes,' Dodo said accusingly, as if this was her maid caught in the act of betrayal.

'Supermarine,' I corrected but neither of them was listening to me.

'I'm just visiting.' Pooky glared at us both defiantly.

'In a maid's uniform?' I objected and she tugged at her apron.

'It's all I have left.' Pooky put her hands into her pockets – something my mother was always scolding her for. 'The rest of my clothes got burned in a fire.'

'But you left your old uniform in lovely old Felicity House. It was black and white and threadbare – the uniform, not the house,' Dodo pointed out. 'I know because I have played dressing-up games in it.'

'Are you playing one now?' Pooky sneered in a tone she usually reserved for men.

'I do not believe I am,' Dodo replied with less confidence than she should have.

Pooky's dress was a nice claret with an apron whiter and crisper than a communion wafer.

'You want the truth?' Pooky crossed her osseous arms and, without waiting to find out if I did or not, gave it to me anyway. 'You were a lovely sweet girl, Miss Betty, a pleasure to work for. I would have gone to the end of the garden for you, I would. Remember the fun we had with that old mangle?' I didn't remember the mangle, let alone its entertainment value, but – unlike Dodo Chivers – I usually recognise a dollop of rhetoric. 'When we put your toy sheep through to dry and its innards exploded out. And the pastry cutter? Remember what we did with that? Oh' – she clasped her hands ecstatically – 'but your parents, they were produced in a very different factory from very different raw materials indeed. How can I put this kindly? Your parents were a couple of shitters.'

Pooky crossed her arms with a beatific glow as if she had just delivered an affectionate eulogy. I remembered Lucinda Lamb now, how I had cried and how my mother had sewed her up in the way she did everything – really badly.

'I believe Miss or Mrs Lavender Wicks resides here,' I said nicely.

'Mrs Lavender Wicks do,' Pooky admitted, taken aback by my failure to endorse her remarks.

'Is she at home?' I enquired. 'By which I mean is she here and not that servant rubbish about not being at home to me.'

'She—' Pooky began.

'Do *not* attempt to shelter her,' Dodo warned fiercely. 'In time of war it is a capital offence to impede the police in the execution of their duty.'

It wasn't but Pooky probably didn't know that. She probably didn't know what a capital offence was either.

'She—' Pooky began again but Dodo had not quite finished.

'No matter how nice her name is, which it is, isn't it?'

'—is at home,' Pooky finished.

'Then kindly inform your mistress that we wish to speak to her,' I instructed and Pooky looked at me sideways, the way she used to look at the grocer's boy when he dipped into the biscuit barrel.

'You've gone and changed since the day we met,' she rumbled.

I hoped so. The first time Pooky clapped eyes on me I was in swaddling clothes and squalling because my father had accidentally sat on me. This time she seemed about to shut me out.

'Oh please, Pooky dear,' Dodo beseeched and my parents' old maid softened.

'Just takes a bit of *manners*,' she lectured me and stood back to admit us. 'And don't forget to wipe your feet,' she scolded, 'properly.'

45

THE DANCE OF THE DEAD

We entered a big rectangular hall with Tiffany electric light fittings. It was decorated from the walls to the woodwork and ceiling to the deep-piled fitted carpet in tiny variations on white.

'Wait here whilst I solicit her presence,' Pooky told us with a well-oiled but never-before-seen curtsy and I wondered, from her choice of words, if she knew Brigsy or if they had seen the same film or attended the same finishing school.

Pooky passed through a door at the end.

'Oh but this is lovely.' Dodo swirled like Cinderella at the ball, caught sight of herself in one of the six white-framed long mirrors and swirled again in the opposite direction. 'White as a walrus.'

Pooky reappeared. 'Mrs Wicks will see you now.'

'Oh I feel fizzy.' Dodo staggered sideways.

'Feel dizzy,' I corrected her.

'Oh poor you.'

Lavender Wicks was getting up from one of four long white boxy sofas arranged around a low aluminium-legged rectangular glass table. She was quite a tall young woman, about my height and athletically built with long well-toned well-tanned legs that she showed off below a short white cotton skirt. Her matching shirt was unbuttoned far enough to give a good glimpse of her generous proportions. If Captain Scott had had so much white in his house he might never have felt the need to leave home. Even the baby grand piano by the French windows was the colour of fresh snow.

'Oh, you knit.' Dodo pounced on a ball of white wool impaled on two lethal-looking needles. 'I love knitting and needlework and making all things pretty.'

Lavender Wicks smiled uncertainly. 'Is something wrong?' She had hair more platinum than Jean Harlow, flowing from a centre parting in those natural waves that only hours with a very expensive hairdresser can produce.

Dodo picked up the knitting. 'No, it looks quite good to me.'

'Nothing to be alarmed about,' I said. 'I'm Inspector Church of Sackwater Central Police Station and this is—'

'Dodo,' Dodo burst out, running her fingers over the embryonic scarf or pullover or sock dangling limply from a needle.

'Constable Chivers,' I insisted.

'That purl could be a little tighter,' Dodo commented.

'It's about your driving—' I began.

'Oh crikey.' Lavender Wicks covered her mouth, giving the lie to my claim that nobody else ever used that word, and in the corner of my eye, Dodo smirked. 'I wasn't really speeding very much, no more than about fiftyish along Looms Lane and I was in a fearful rush for a party.'

The room stretched about thirty feet to a wall of windows looking out towards the pinewoods but had a slightly claustrophobic feel, I felt, because the ceiling had not been raised in proportion to its scale.

'Looms Lane is a thirty-miles-per-hour area,' I told her, 'but that's not why I've come. I am talking about your driving licence, Mrs Wicks.'

'Blimey.' Lavender Wicks uncovered her mouth, her beautiful bow lips pouting in a way that might have worked better on Bantony than me. He would have been like a rutting stag by now. 'This sounds,' her voice dropped to a melodramatic hiss, 'serious.'

'It is,' I assured her.

'Oh.' Lavender Wicks proved that she could be sensible after all. 'Please take a seat.' She indicated a chaise longue facing hers over that table, the glass etched with elegantly dressed, impossibly slim boyish women. There were long wall mirrors bearing similar designs. 'I think I might need to.' I waited for her to sit before I did but Dodo plonked herself immediately beside her, extracting the needles from the ball. 'Have you found it?'

'Yes, at—' Dodo began and shot a hand to her own mouth, nearly piercing her ear in the process.

'Just the licence?'

'What else should we have found?' I asked carefully.

'Well, everything, I hoped – my purse, the money, my chequebook, my scent bottle, gold cigarette case.'

'Are you saying you lost your handbag?'

'But I have already told you.' She wrinkled her nose until it resembled a question mark.

'Ooh,' Dodo objected. 'What a whopper.'

Inside I cringed. Outside I said, 'You told us no such thing, Mrs Wicks.'

'Well, not you personally.' Lavender Wicks flicked her finger like she was tapping the ash off a cigarette. 'I left my handbag in Corker's Coffee House and reported it to Anglethorpe Police Station last Tuesday.'

I made a mental note to check that.

'Can I show her?' Dodo asked and, when I nodded, whipped it out of her own bag, trumpeting *to-to-to-toot* triumphantly before handing it to her bemused hostess.

'Dolores Chivers,' she read in further bemusement.

'Give that here.' Dodo snatched it off her and delved in for another.

Lavender Wicks flicked open the red cover. 'That's mine,' she confirmed. 'Where did you find it?'

'Were you by yourself?' I ploughed on.

'With my husband, Thurston,' Lavender Wicks confirmed. 'Until he went to work.'

'Oh!' Dodo shrieked. 'So it *is* Thurston Wicks. Oh I love him.'

'So do I.' Lavender smiled coyly.

'Ajax Clarke, Private Eye.' Dodo almost swooned. 'He solves crimes.'

'So do we,' I reminded her.

'He has fights without spilling his cocktail.'

'I've never done that,' I conceded.

'Which is why nobody pays to watch you at work.' Lavender half-winked and I was working on a clever retort that many criminals had paid as a result of my work when Dodo burst out with, 'Oh is he making another *Ajax Clarke, Private Eye* film even as we speak?'

I remembered Ajax Clarke, the suave English gentleman who sported a monocle and went around the world teaching foreigners a lesson they wouldn't forget in a hurry. I thought I had seen two of that series but found them a little dull.

Lavender shook her lovely locks. 'Thurston got bored with that role. He wanted something that stretched him so he gave it to Crispin Staples.'

'Crispin Staples.' Dodo clasped her hands under her chin. 'Oh but he is so deliciously handsome.'

Lavender Wicks tisked. 'Thurston is doing what he can for the war effort,' she informed us. 'He is appearing in government information films – what to do in the event of an air raid or a gas attack – that sort of thing. He wanted to re-enlist in his old regiment but, since Thurston hurt his back filming *The Dead Don't Dance*, he has been classed as unfit.'

'Where were you on Wednesday morning before nine o'clock?' I asked.

Lavender Wicks yawned. 'That's an easy one. In bed.'

'Here?'

'Yes, of course.'

'It's not an *of course* answer,' Dodo told her severely. 'Most people don't sleep here though this is a lovely house.' My constable clicked the needles contentedly. 'Or could be with a bit of decorating.'

'By yourself?' I ploughed on.

'With my husband,' Lavender Wicks said, 'until he went to work.'

'You don't wear a wedding ring,' I observed.

'Neither do you.'

'I'm not married.'

'Really?' Lavender Wicks eyed me for longer than I felt she needed to. 'I'd have thought you would have been snapped up years ago.'

I very nearly was on two occasions but I only said, 'I didn't want to be snapped.'

'Anyway,' Dodo chipped in helpfully, 'Inspector Church does not have a hand to put a wedding ring on.'

'Why don't you wear a false arm?'

'Why don't you?'

Lavender Wicks caressed her own left arm, shivering at the sensation. 'I don't need to.'

'Neither do I.' I did sometimes but that was none of her business.

Dodo looked up from her knitting. 'Are you keeping to the same number of rows for now?'

'What?' Lavender Wicks glanced at her distractedly. 'Yes, I suppose so.'

'What time did your husband go to work that morning?' I returned to the matter in hand.

'What is this about? Six thirty as always. Wilson was here.'

'Whom?' Dodo asked abstractedly and this didn't seem the time to point out that she should have said *who*.

'My maid,' Lavender Wicks explained icily. I had never thought of Pooky as having a surname and, now that I thought of it, Pooky was unlikely to be her real Christian name.

'Do you know Skotter Heath Jackson?' I enquired.

'Did,' Dodo corrected me at the risk of being run through with one or both of those needles.

'It's all right,' Lavender Wicks assured me. 'I'd have to be dead myself not to know that he is.'

'Who' – Dodo performed some complicated manoeuvre, twiddling one needle around the other – 'told you, Mrs Lavender Wicks of Treetops House, Pinfold Lane?'

'Do you send her to entertain children's parties?' Lavender Wicks asked me.

'Who told you?' I asked quietly. Quiet gets more attention than loud. Loud gives people the excuse to take umbrage, shout back and demand to see their briefs or solicitors depending on their social stratum.

'Everyone knows.' She reclined with her arm along the back of the sofa as if about to make a move on Dodo, who was leaning forward, intent on her task. 'Beasty Butterworth rang me, if you must know.'

'Yes we simply must,' Dodo assured her.

'And did you know Skotter Heath Jackson?' I pressed.

'No.'

'Did you ever go to his office?'

Lavender Wicks's periwinkle eyes met mine coolly. 'No.'

'Oh but why?' Dodo protested. 'Did I find your licence there?'

'Did you?' Lavender Wicks didn't wait for an answer. 'I have not the faintest idea.' She pulled her arm away. 'Are you telling me I'm a suspect?'

I regarded her carefully. 'I have not told you anything, Mrs Wicks, but now I shall. Constable Chivers found your driving licence at the scene of a murder.'

Lavender Wicks flapped her hands. 'Then somebody stole it without my knowing and then dropped it there.'

'A clever but stupid thief,' I murmured and Lavender Wicks sprang up.

'Oh you made me slip a stitch.' Dodo jumped.

'I think you should go,' Lavender Wicks said firmly. 'If you wish to communicate with me again, please do so through Mr Ventnor, my husband's solicitor.'

She was too posh to have a brief.

Pooky saw us out. 'Bugger off.' She flapped her arms. 'Filthy pests.' I turned in surprise and saw she was shooing a tabby cat away. 'Belongs to that old widow opposite but it do come and do its business on our front drive, it do.'

There was a bungalow across the way at the end of a long lawned rear garden backing onto Pinfold Lane. It must have faced Featherstone Lane, I calculated. The door of the potting shed was open and I glimpsed an elderly lady putting a broom away.

The cat yawned and licked a paw.

'Oh and give all my love to your parents,' Pooky called as we set off.

'She doesn't know my parents,' Dodo pointed out but she seemed preoccupied so I didn't bother to explain.

We were twenty yards back up the lane, kicking sand, before Dodo, unable to contain herself any more, burst out with, 'That is her. That is the Suffolk Vampire.'

46

THE TRAIN TO ISTANBUL

t was useless, I knew by now, to insist there was no vampire. I kept walking, Dodo Chivers darting around me like an excitable terrier.

'Mrs Wicks or her maid?'

'Lavender Wicks, of course.' Dodo skipped backwards in front of me.

'And what leads you to that conclusion, Constable Chivers?'

The sand was getting a bit annoying now, sweeping low over my shoes and sneaking inside them.

'Five reasons,' Dodo expounded.

'Tell me one of them.' I was not sure I could stomach two.

'All that white is intended to make us think she is pure,' Constable Chivers declared. 'The lady doth protest too much, methinks.'

'*Hamlet*,' I recognised the quote.

'Daddy,' she corrected me. 'He used to say it when I did not want to eat my liver – I mean the liver he had put on my plate, not my own liver. That would be self-cannibalisation.'

'What is your point…' I struggled to remember what we were supposed to be discussing, 'about her protesting too much?'

'Oh yes.' Dodo stopped to pick up a pine cone. 'Only the impure try to appear to be pure. The pure recognise their own impurities.'

'Your father?'

'Dolores Davina Porthia Chivers,' she told me with great satisfaction.

'Pretending to be or imagining you are purer than you are

doesn't make you a murderess,' I reasoned. 'It makes you a hypocrite or delusional.'

'Ah but' – Dodo wagged a finger like a maths teacher with an innumerate child – 'here comes my second reason.'

There was a small ditch on the left-hand side of the road and I wondered if I could accidentally tip my constable into it.

'Go on.' Talking to Dodo felt increasingly like using my father's professional services – a painful experience best got over and done with.

'Did you not see the way she looked straight at you with her lovely periwinkle eyes?'

'What of it?'

'That's what guilty people do. I read it in Miss Middleton's invigorating factual account of *Murder on the Train to Istanbul*. Innocent people do not try to stare you out.'

The wind whipped a sudden miniature sandstorm into my face just as I was opening my mouth. I coughed and turned away to spit into a roadside clump of marram grass.

'Yucky-wucky.' Dodo peered over at my expectoration.

'It's not an infallible law.'

'Well, it should be.' Dodo whirled to walk on ahead of me, rising high on her toes like the ostrich I had seen at Anglethorpe Zoo once. 'And...' She tucked her thumbs into her armpits in imitation wings.

'Stop it,' I commanded and Dodo froze.

'Which bit?'

'All of it – the walking, the flapping, the spinning round – all of it,' I snapped. 'You are embarrassing me.'

Dodo rotated very slowly. 'But there are no witnesses to my eccentric display, boss,' she pointed out meekly.

'If you know it's eccentric why do you do it?' I brushed past her and marched on up the lane.

'Oh but I do so love to,' Dodo cried. 'It is just a little weakness of mine.'

'Indulge it at home.'

'I shall,' Dodo vowed, catching up with me. 'Mother and Father do not mind in the least.'

'Mother and...' I was almost speechless.

'Well, I cannot keep calling them Mr and Mrs Church.' She was walking so normally now it looked abnormal. 'And it would be impertinent to use their first names, which, as you probably know, are Harold and Muriel.'

'Most people, wanting to use a courtesy title, use *Uncle* and *Aunt*,' I objected.

'I did suggest calling them *Aunty* and *Uncle*,' Dodo assured me, arms swinging in a paradeground fashion, 'but they said they preferred *Father* and *Mother* because I was like the daughter they never had.'

This was going too far, even by my parents' standards.

'They *have* got a daughter,' I insisted icily, '*me*.'

'Oh yes,' Dodo agreed heartily. 'They have got a daughter but I am like the one they have not got.' And I was still trying to work out if that was better or worse when she came out with, 'And – the third of my quintet of reasons – Lavender Wicks said she forgot her handbag. What woman ever ever *ever* forgets her handbag?'

She gazed at me triumphantly for this was the ace serve that gave her game, set and match.

'I have,' I admitted. 'A few times.'

'Oh.' Dodo scratched under her steel helmet.

'Have you not ever?'

'Well, yes but that is only because I am silly.' Dodo started to hum Hoagy Carmichael's 'Stardust' but had only got as far as 'dreaming' when she thought of a different subject. 'Knitting is so relaxing. You should take it up, boss.'

'And how do you suggest I hold the needles?'

'You will work it out,' she replied with touching faith. Dodo clasped her hands behind her back. 'Anyway, I still think she did it.'

'You need a bit more evidence than that.'

'Oh good.' Dodo spun again, realised and blushed. 'I thought you were going to tell me I need a lot more evidence. A bit of evidence should be very easy to find— oh.' She worked her mouth. 'I understand why you did it now.' And, twisting her face away, Constable Chivers spat a mouthful of sand into the side of a dune.

'Fourthly,' she pressed on, 'Lavender Wicks is magically beautiful – her hair, her face, her figure, her... everything. And I have seen enough films to know that beautiful women are innocent and marry the hero in the end.'

A gust whipped the sand into my face and into my nostrils. 'And that makes her guilty how?' I blew my nose.

'Because,' Dodo wagged her finger, 'you might not know this but films are not true. So,' she was in school debating-society mode, 'if something is not true it must be untrue.'

'Well—'

'Ergo' – there was no stopping her by now – 'if films say beautiful women are always innocent, they must be always guilty. Are you pretending to be Fu Manchu?'

'No, I'm trying to stop sand getting into my eyes.'

'You are wise to do that,' Dodo said approvingly, 'because it can really stingle.'

'What' – it would be easier to get this over with, I decided – 'is your last reason?'

'Ah!' Dodo exclaimed triumphantly. 'Lavender Wicks has a nose that bends into a sort of upside down question mark when she turns it up,' she recalled excitedly, 'and I have never known an innocent person to do that in all my weeks as a woman police officer. That is what we are trained to do, is it not, Inspector Church – to use our experience?'

'Yes, but to use it sensibly.' I sighed.

'Oh but they did not tell me that.' She sighed as well. 'Do you think Mrs Wicks was in the movies too? I am almost slightly sure I saw her in something.'

'I didn't recognise her.' I watched a lizard scuttle behind a clump of marram grass.

'Yes but you did not even really know who Thurston was.' Dodo bent over to get rid of some more sand. She stood up with a meditative air. 'I rather like spitting,' my constable decided.

47

THE KING'S OAK

Dodo fell quiet as we made our way back to Sackwater Central, intent on counting her footsteps, until we reached the Soundings. This was a nice square in the middle of Old Sackwater, as the locals called the genteel Georgian part of the resort, which had later become swamped by Victorian attempts to cash in on the railway boom. Four neat, flat-roofed terraces boxed the area in, with roads leading out at each corner.

There were iron-framed wood-slatted benches around the edges of the green but the drizzle and gathering gloom were enough to deter people from using them. I had my first proper kiss on one that encircled the trunk of an elm, with Richard McLoughlin. All the girls went weak at the sight of Richard striding past in his cricket whites and were corroded with envy when he paid attention to me but I felt sick afterwards. It was a disconcertingly slurpy experience. Three years later, Richard lost both legs at Passchendaele and became a pathetic figure, pulling himself along the streets with weights on a low trolley, until he wheeled himself – whether by accident or design nobody knew – under a speeding truck.

In the middle of this stood the King's Oak, an ancient tree hollowed by an inverted V that, as a child, I loved to slip through and climb up the inside of the trunk, emerging at the top to sit on one of the few remaining branches. I was ten the last time I had hidden inside it, having been too terrified to go in any more after the mysterious fate met by my friend Etterly, from Bath

Road. Some said she had been eaten by the tree but that was silly. Others said that she still haunted the King's Oak and they had heard her calling out at night, which I didn't believe either but, when you hear stories from usually reliable people, you can never quite dismiss them.

'Why does that tree have a door?' Dodo broke my reverie. 'Does somebody live in it?'

At least she hadn't asked if they were goblins.

'No. It's to stop any children getting in,' I explained. 'A friend of mine, a little girl called Etterly Utter, hid in there when we were playing once and nobody saw her coming out. She disappeared.'

'Goblins,' Dodo declared firmly but, after a pause, conceded, 'probably.'

There were moves to chop the tree down after Etterly's disappearance but residents of the Soundings objected. It was an ancient tree of great historical significance – though no one was quite sure what that significance was – and so it was reprieved. As a compromise a pine-plank door was fitted to seal the entrance, but vandals had smashed the locks off and nobody had bothered to replace them.

'Don't suggest that to the men,' I advised as we left the square.

'I shall not,' Dodo assured me. 'Oh, I forgot my footstep count. Shall we go back and start again?'

'No.'

We walked down Slaughterhouse Lane.

'The men are very silly about that sort of thing. Do you not agree?' Dodo piped up but I had no idea what sort of thing she meant until she declared, 'They do not believe in goblins, elves, imps or fairies. I know they do not because I have asked them all.'

'Oh good grief.'

We went past the police box on Derby Street and into Tiny Rupert Square.

'But you believe in fairies, do you not, boss?' Dodo looked at me anxiously with her pale face and puppy eyes.

'That lane' – I pointed – 'is called Divine Alley. It's a good shortcut to the seafront but there's no official right of way so Bressinghall's the butcher's often block the far end with their van. You can't see it until you get round the bend so it's usually quicker to go the longer way round.'

'Are you avoiding the question?' Dodo asked.

'They have a dog called Gripper,' I battled on.

'Oh.' Dodo jumped with a crooked arm raised as if the hound was leaping up at her. 'Is it very fierce?'

'It tries to be but it has no teeth,' I told her.

'I suppose they could change its name,' Dodo pondered, 'to Gumbo like Gumbo Marx in the Marx Brothers.'

'Gummo Marx,' I corrected her.

'I know it does.' Dodo brayed at the hilarity of her pun that very nearly made sense. I cringed, but at least we had got off the subject of fairies.

'You do believe in elves, do you not, boss?' Dodo entreated.

*

A workman was painting the top of a pillar box yellow on the corner of High Road West and Hamilton Road.

'How very pretty,' Dodo cried, 'it would be if it were a different colour.'

'Gas detector paint,' he informed us, though it obviously didn't detect the fumes from his foul clay pipe, for the mix was still jaundiced.

'What colour does it go if we have an attack?' I asked.

'Red.'

I thought about that. 'But pillar boxes are red already so how will we know if the top has gone red with gas or never been painted yellow in the first place?'

The workman sucked on his pipe musingly. 'Dunno,' he decided at last and, clearly satisfied with his answer, set back to work, humming 'The Lambeth Walk'. I think Constable Chivers would have danced a few steps to it if she hadn't caught my warning look and, unusually, realised what it meant.

*

Sergeant Briggs was gainfully employed when we got back to the station. He was showing Constable Walker how to make a paper boat from an unused charge sheet and screwed it up far too late for me to miss.

'Is Inspector Sharkey back yet?' I asked and his expression changed to that of a suffering saint.

'He do be in his office, madam.'

'And he can stay in there,' Nippy Walker contributed with feeling.

'It is not for you to decide if Inspector Sharkey can or cannot stay in his office,' I scolded and he straightened up. This was a little worrying. I was getting to enjoy the feeling of power. Was this what happened to Hitler when he soared to the rank of corporal?

'Flew at me like a mad dog, though, he did, jest 'cause I ask if he do catch his spy,' Walker protested.

'Near bit his head off and chewed it into cud,' Brigsy confirmed.

'Do you want to leave it until the morning?' I asked Dodo, who was hopping from foot to foot like a child needing to be excused.

'Oh but this is perfect,' she cried. 'Oh please let me tell him about the licence now, Inspector, and *please* let me tell him alone.'

I had intended to offer to go in as referee but, if my constable was determined to throw herself to the shark, she might be better learning the hard way.

Dodo hesitated. 'But will you stand nearby in case he attacks me, Inspector?'

'He won't but yes, I will.' We went down the corridor, Dodo creeping noisily on tiptoes to the door. She knocked, three good raps.

'Come in,' we heard.

She rapped four times.

'Come in.'

She rapped another five. 'It is I, Inspector Sharkey, Constable Chivers.'

'I said *come in*.'

'Can I come in?' She rattled the handle as she had when we first met.

'Come *in*, dammit.' They probably heard that at the desk.

Was Constable Chivers anxious to die? She counted softly to six.

'I think he's suitably cross,' she whispered and went inside, leaving the door wide open. I stood just out of direct sight and risked intermittent peeks round the frame.

'Are you busy, Inspector Paul Sharkey?'

'Yes I am and don't use my Christian name.'

'Are you very-wery busy-wizzy?'

'Yes I bloody am.'

'Is your energy sapped to the point of exhaustion after spending half the day chasing after imaginary spies, sir?'

I was a bit less confident that he wouldn't attack her now. Sharkey drew a breath. 'What do you want, Chivers?'

'I thought you might like a chat, Inspector Sharkey.'

'No I bloody wouldn't.'

'You do curse rather a lot,' Dodo observed.

'I haven't begun yet,' he warned.

'So what would you like to chat about?' she prattled merrily.

'Are you stupid or what?'

I sneaked another look.

'You have often said I am,' Dodo reminded him. 'Stupid, I mean, not the *or what* bit.' She threw out her arms like a circus performer working up applause. 'You will never guess what I found today.'

'No I won't because I'm not going to try. What—'

'Do you not want to know what I foundy-woundy, Inspector Sharkey?'

'No I bloody don't.' He brought the side of his fist down on the desk. 'Clear off.'

'Or with whom I had a chat with about it after you had finished running around after imaginary spies?'

'Get… out.'

'Yes, Inspector Sharkey, sir.' Dodo scurried away, closing the door firmly behind her.

'He cannot say I did not try,' she whispered to me and seemed to have fairy dust in both her eyes. She never did learn to wink with one.

48

THE PRISONERS

Sammy Sterne opened the door of his home, a nice little bungalow though the sea view had been obstructed by a block of Art Deco apartments on Promontory Road.

Abbie Sterne sat in a rocking chair with a blanket over her knees, long white hair pinned into plaits rolled onto the top of her head, granny glasses perched low on her nose.

'I am sorry about this,' I told them both. 'But I shall petition the authorities on your behalf.'

'A police inspector, Abbie,' Sammy beamed, 'they will listen to her.'

'In the meantime,' I continued, hardly able to look at either of them, 'there are various emergency restrictions, I'm afraid. You must hand over any binoculars, telescopes, cameras or radio transmitters that you have. Do you own a car?'

'A Morris Minor,' Sammy told me. 'A good British car.'

'Then you will have to give me the keys. Somebody will come to collect it.'

'You are stealing our car?' Abbie asked in disbelief.

'It will be put into a pound for the duration,' I told her.

Sammy shrugged. 'We can't get petrol anyway.'

'There is a curfew,' I continued. 'You must not leave your home between seven at night and eight in the morning.'

'We are prisoners in our own home.' Abbie clutched the blanket in both fists.

I took a breath. 'And you must give up your pigeons,' I told

Sammy. The government was worried they could be used to communicate with the enemy.

Sammy blinked. 'Shall they be put in a pound for the duration?'

I swallowed. 'I think the army will use them for messages.'

Sammy closed his eyes and nodded three times and there was a new hurt when he opened them again. 'I see.'

'There are some forms we have to fill out,' I struggled on. 'It shouldn't take long.'

And afterwards, when Sammy Sterne showed me to the door, he asked, 'If you are told to arrest us – Abbie and me – will you do it?'

'I hope it would be me,' I said and he nodded again but very slowly.

I had thought about resigning. After all, I hadn't joined the police force to behave like the Gestapo. But I knew it would not save them and I also knew how Sharkey might treat them if he was given the job.

Sammy held out his hands, palms open upwards, as if he was going to embrace me.

'Shalom,' he said as I stepped outside but I was afraid it would be a long time before any of us saw the peace he was wishing for.

49

THE CLEVER DOG PRIZE

The Compasses was a long thin pub with a door at either end, a bar along one wall and a row of stools against it. There was little room for anything else. For this reason it was popular with drinkers, who would sit in solemn lines up at the bar, but less popular with those who wanted to play darts or cribbage or even socialise, since it was difficult to chat to anyone other than your immediate neighbours. So I was slightly surprised when Gregson suggested it.

'Is this your local?' I asked.

He was standing in the doorway, smoking the stump of a cigarette.

'Not for much longer.' He was wearing the same blazer and slacks as before, but I had changed into a dress, not to impress him but because I didn't think it proper to be seen boozing in uniform. 'They've just told me no women allowed inside and I don't think you'd pass as a bloke somehow.' He surveyed me. 'First time I've seen you out of uniform.'

'Only the third time you've seen me.'

'Do you want to go to the Ship?'

'In a word, no.' The Ship used to be an old-fashioned spit and sawdust place but they didn't have the sawdust any more. 'Have they still got the summer house here?' I hadn't been back since my disgrace. 'We could sit in there.'

Gregson's face uncrumpled briefly. 'What'll you have?'

'A pint of bitter, if you let me buy the next one.'

I went round into the back garden. The summer house was really just a three-sided shelter designed for people watching the bowls, but the green had been so neglected you would have had trouble finding the jack if you tried to play now. I sat on the bench behind a long board table watching a pigeon stealing thatch from the roof for its nest until Gregson came out with two tankards, stumbling over a molehill, slopping beer down his sleeves and cursing under his breath. I didn't have to be a lip-reader to work out what he was saying.

He put his load on the table and we clinked glasses in a toast. 'Cigarette?' I offered.

'I have to ask you.' Gregson watched, fascinated, while I rolled it one-handed. 'What happened to the arm?'

'Am I being interviewed?'

Gregson made that innocent face that men always make when they aren't.

He changed tack. 'What's your first name?'

'Betty.'

'Short for?'

'Betty. What's yours?'

'Toby, short for Tobias.'

'Wasn't Tobias Gregson a detective in Sherlock Holmes?'

Toby rubbed the back of his neck. 'My father was a fan of Arthur Conan Doyle.'

'My godmother's godfather had a feud with him. He claimed Doyle plagiarised his life.'

'Sidney Grice.' Toby clicked his fingers. 'I meant to ask if you actually knew him.'

'Quite well.' I took a sip of my bitter. There wasn't much head on it but it tasted all right.

'Was he as horrible as everybody says?'

'More so.' I wiped my mouth with the back of my hand. 'But

he was brave, honest and extraordinarily intelligent and he was always very kind to me, even when I broke his Grice Patent Self-Buttoning Waistcoat... No, really.'

Toby laughed. 'So March Middleton is your godmother? I'd love to interview her before she dies.'

'You may have trouble afterwards,' I pointed out, wondering – not for the first time – if a little bit of Uncle G had rubbed off on me. 'But she doesn't trust the press, I'm afraid.'

'Is it true that she secretly had a child?'

'Anything Miss Middleton wants you to know about her is in her books.' I took another drink. 'How long have you been a reporter?'

Toby Gregson dabbed his lips with a white handkerchief. He obviously had better manners than me. 'Since I was four.' He ran his finger round an old ring stain. 'My father, who was proprietor and editor, sent me to crawl under the trestle tables at Tringford Summer Fête and find out who the judges were going to award prizes to so we could all go home and he could get it in the next edition before people lost interest. I couldn't hear everything they said, so there was a bit of a fuss when the *Gazette* announced that the best sponge cake had been baked by Mrs Pooey.'

I coughed on my beer. 'And your father didn't doubt you?'

'He was more sceptical about the clever dog prize going to a collie owned by Jillian Thick and that one was true.' He paused for another drink. 'Then my father had a stroke so I reluctantly promised to look after the *Gazette* until he got better. I'd have thought twice if I'd known he'd take so long about it – five years so far.'

That, I thought, would explain his lack of killer instinct.

'So you are acting editor, reporter and photographer,' I observed. 'You seem to be a one-man band.'

'Not in the least.' Toby tossed his head in mock indignation.

'There's a lady who covers births and marriages, if they're in the right order, and we have a vicar who writes nature notes, book reviews, recipes and horoscopes under four different names.'

'What about Ethel Proudfoot?' I asked. Ethel had been the agony aunt when I was in my teens and I had written to her about a boy who never noticed me. She had advised taking up ballroom dancing but I didn't and, anyway, another, less spotty boy had noticed me by then.

'That used to be Dad,' Gregson admitted. 'Now it's me, though Mum chips in with practical household tips.' He drained his pint.

'So what did you do before all this?'

'I'm a violinist.'

I drew back involuntarily. I used to go out with a musician – a pianist – until it became obvious I wasn't the only piece in his repertoire.

'In an orchestra?'

'In the Cool Club. Perhaps you've heard of us.'

'I'm afraid not.'

'We were on at the Pier Pavilion.'

'Before or after it burned down?' I stopped, taken aback at my own rudeness, but Toby chuckled. 'You can't pin that on me.'

I noticed now that he had linear calluses on his right fingertips – something my auspicious god-relatives would have spotted instantly – so he was left-handed.

'So you play band music?'

'We based ourselves on the Quintette du Hot Club de France.'

'The French play jazz?'

'You haven't heard of Stéphane Grappelli and Django Reinhardt?' Toby was shocked. 'Sister, you've got a lot to learn.'

'I like jazz,' I protested. 'It's just I've never heard any French bands.' I drained my pint. 'Did you manage to make a living out of your music?'

'No.' Toby finished his. 'But I made a life out of it.'

I put my glass over a knot hole and then, remembering what we were there for, said 'Did the photo come out all right?'

'I'll show you when I've got another drink in.'

'You'll have to get it,' I slapped two shillings on the top, 'but it's my round.'

'Never been bought a drink by a woman before,' Toby Gregson commented.

'I think you'll find there's a lot of things women will be doing differently before this war is over.'

'Do you think it'll begin?' Toby's face crumpled even more. 'I hear Chamberlain's going to sue for peace by giving some of our colonies to the Germans.'

'There was a girl at my school who used to make other girls give her their pocket money,' I recalled, 'and I'm ashamed to say that I gave her mine. But when the smallest girl in our class, Davina Divine, refused, everybody else realised they could too. You have to stand up to bullies or they just demand more and more.'

'We need a strong man.' Toby stood up.

'Churchill's the man for me,' I said. 'I'm just worried he might be too old.'

'Didn't do us much good in the last war,' Toby argued. 'Gallipoli for a start.'

'If Chamberlain met Hitler again he'd polish his shoes,' I said. 'Winston would break his jaw.'

'I'll get the drinks.' Toby scooped up my florin and, when we were settled again, he unclipped his satchel and brought out a large buff envelope.

'We had a choice between cutting down to two pages or going weekly with eight,' he told me, 'in anticipation of paper shortages. There was sweet damn all to fill a daily anyway. Even the fox story had to be embellished. All the duck did was quack and wake the dog.' He slid out a developed photo. 'Came out quite well, I think.'

I held it out into the evening light. 'Very well,' I agreed. 'You can see the cleats clearly.' I handed it back.

'And this is my draft.'

It was typed on a sheet of white foolscap.

```
        MURDER OF SACKWATER ACCOUNTANT

The idyllic seaside resort of Sackwater was
shocked on Wednesday by news of the murder
of local businessman Skotter Heath Jackson,
Chartered Accountant in his office at 14
Dogeye Lane.
```

I skimmed through. He had given few details but lots of quotes from locals about what a wonderful man Skotter Jackson had been, and then on page 2:

```
    IS THIS THE FOOTPRINT OF A MURDERER?
```

was printed over a space for the picture and mention of a reward.

'Fifty pounds,' I read out. 'Who's giving that?'

'A group of local businessmen. They're worried holidaymakers will get frightened away.'

'Holidaymakers?' I repeated incredulously. 'What on earth would they come here for? The burned-out pier? The signs saying *Danger Mines* on the barbed-wire sand-free beach?'

Toby Gregson shrugged. 'It's their money.'

'You haven't mentioned vampires,' I said with gratitude and Gregson wheezed painfully.

'Would you ever trust me again if I did?'

'No but you don't need me to tell you it would sell more papers.'

'In the short run.' He rubbed his chest. 'But I won't be the one looking silly when you catch the killer and you might be more inclined to let me know first. Plus I need another photo.'

'Of?' I asked suspiciously.

'You,' he said, 'in uniform.'

'All right.' I was never averse to a bit of publicity. 'Did you get one of Inspector Sharkey?'

'Old Scrapie?' Toby tossed his head. 'He's not very photogenic.'

'How did you know he was called that?'

Toby grasped the handle of his tankard. 'You are sitting next to the man who christened him.'

I laughed. *I thought it was more imaginative than their usual nicknames.* 'Do you have any family?'

'Only my parents. My wife left me for a rat-catcher – no, really. They live in Harwich now with his mother. How about you?'

'A spinster of this and every other parish,' I told him.

'Good,' I thought I heard him say softly to himself.

I leaned back and he leaned back and we watched the sun sink behind the sand dunes and the lengthening shadows of the thinly scattered pines in the distance, comfortable together, like the old married couple neither of us were.

50

THE OTHER SIDE OF FURY HILL

The nights were drawing in and it was only just about light enough to risk riding my bike – crow-time, as the locals called it, when the birds return to their nests. I pedalled out of town, up the side of Fury Hill – quite a climb by Suffolk standards – all the way to the gate that used to guard the entrance to Treacle Woods but now hung off its hinges.

There I dismounted. The track was too steep and dark to risk hurtling down it, especially one-handed with a heavy satchel of paperwork over my shoulder. I parked my bike in the old hide that Tubby Gretham's father had built to watch badgers. The sett was deserted now and curtained with cobwebs, much as my mother was allowing Felicity House to become.

Carmelo had been as good as his word, giving me sculling lessons on my very first day. The secret was, he had instructed, to put the oar in the rope notch at the stern and move it to and fro in a figure of eight. It was hard work and required a lot of wrist action. At first the boat swayed crazily from side to side but I was soon confident enough to make the short distance from Shingle Bay to Brindle Bar without capsizing.

The important thing to remember was to loop a rope over a post as you set off, to trail after you so that whoever was on the other bank could haul the boat back if they needed it. Jimmy had forgotten once and been subjected to a torrent of Maltese references to his mother's son by a Carmelo who had stood bellowing in the rain for twenty minutes before I heard him over *Cressida*'s noisy conversation with a stiff wind.

The poultry had been locked away and Mrs Perkins clucked reproachfully at me from her prison as I climbed the steps wearily. It was unlikely, we thought, that a fox would bother to swim the channel, but foxes were notorious for doing unlikely things. Captain swore he had seen one crouched under the seat one night, trying to hitch a ride until he chased it away with an oar. But seafaring men are not renowned for understating their stories.

Captain Sultana sat at the pointy bit – as Jimmy and I insisted on calling the bow, to annoy him – smoking his favourite briar stuffed with what always smelt like old rags to me. He must have watched me struggle across but knew better than to offer help.

'*Qalbi*, you are weary,' he told me as I bent to kiss his cheek. Apart from that tobacco, he smelt of the sea, as if the salt had soaked into his leathery skin over the years.

'I thought there would be no work in Sackwater.' I rested my backside against the railing.

'No rest for the wicked,' he quoted.

'The wicked are probably snug in their beds while we scurry about looking for them.' I leaned back, feasting my eye on the illuminated vault of the earth. 'What a beautiful night.'

Without the glare from nearby towns and villages, we were getting some wondrous skies. The captain took out his pipe and pointed with the stem and I knew that he was going to name all the stars in the galaxy.

'Like a drink?' I asked hurriedly.

'I shall wait for dinner. You have one.'

I went below.

Jimmy was in the galley with a pot bubbling on the range. 'Oh hello, Aunty. I was just making a sort-of stew.'

'Sounds nice,' I said uncertainly for it didn't smell good. 'What sort is *sort of*?'

'Bully beef.'

'Yummy.'

He churned his creation with a large wooden spoon. 'Any luck with that stabbing?'

'Not much.' I slumped onto a stool. 'What were you doing at the station anyway?'

'Oh just seeing a friend off.' Jimmy's ears went red and he wiped his hands on a tea towel, a little too casually, it seemed to me. 'You look dead beat.'

'So the captain told me.'

Jimmy looked at me a bit warily, I thought. 'He hasn't told you anything else?'

'What have you been up to?'

'Nothing... well nothing bad... Honestly.'

If I knew one thing about Jimmy it was, when he said *Honestly*, he never lied.

'Is it just me or is it hot in here?'

'Hot? You could make ice cream in here.' He looked at me in concern. 'Sit there.' He pulled out a chair from the pine table, opened an overhead cupboard and took out a bottle. He poured two large measures of Scotch with a splash of water in each. 'Welcome home.'

I took a large draught and slumped. 'Oh Jimmy, what would I do without you?'

Jimmy swirled his whisky around the tumbler. 'Well, you're about to find out.'

I knew what he was going to tell me but I only said, 'Oh yes?' After all, I was not interrogating him.

'I popped into the Anchor at lunchtime,' he told me. 'They had some mail for me.' He took a drink.

'Go on,' I encouraged him.

'My papers have come through.'

'For the RAF?'

'No, the Women's Institute,' he joked weakly. 'They're taking me off the list of reserves.'

'But that's marvellous.'

Jimmy smiled wryly. 'It would have been.'

'If you're thinking about the captain…'

'I've done a lot of jobs in the last few weeks he can't do by himself.' Jimmy brushed back the fringe flopping over his eye. 'That rope for the rowing boat, mending the fence, re-roofing the hutches. How will he cope?'

'He coped alone before and he's got me now.'

'Yes but he's getting older and you… well, you've only got one hand.'

'Which is more than enough to spank you with,' I teased but Jimmy was serious. 'I'll try again with the false arm and anyway I can help pay towards any hired help we need. Tubby's always willing to assist when he's available.'

Jimmy put the lid back on the cast-iron pot. 'And how often is that, now he's back at work?'

'About as often as you, when you're not chasing local girls, I should say.' I put my glass down.

'They chase me,' he said with some justification and I got up, ducking under the great oak beam that had so often been his tormentor.

'We'll be fine.' I gave Jimmy a hug, keeping my stump well clear. It was sore enough already without getting knocked. 'It's what you've always wanted and I'm very happy for you.'

And I was but I was not happy for me. I had got used to having Jimmy around and – if truth be told – I was frightened for him. There were boys even younger than him in the forces but Jimmy was a dreamer. He had been raised on stories of knights of the air, the Red Baron and chivalry in the Great War, and I had a feeling this war would not be run by gentlemen, but I pulled back so he could see my best smile before I hugged him again. Courtesy Aunts are a bit like hens. They fuss and brood over the chicks – but I never saw Mrs Perkins with a tear in her eye.

*

'It was his news to give,' the captain told me when we were having a nightcap in the wheelhouse.

'Of course it was.' I sipped on my limoncello, an Italian drink very popular in Malta. Captain Sultana made his own with thick-skinned warty lemons from his home town of Birżebbuġa, known to the English as *Pretty Bay*. I didn't ask where the alcohol came from but it was powerful stuff. Perhaps it would help ease the pain and the headache I had had all day.

'I can't imagine Jimmy killing anyone,' I meditated.

'Nor I,' the captain agreed. 'When Jimmy was twelve he came to stay and my sister asked him to go out and get our last rabbit for the pot. He was gone a long time and when he came back he said he was sorry but the rabbit had escaped. Karmena was furious and nearly took a stick to him. I told her, remember he is not used to handling rabbits. I didn't tell her I had seen him put it over the wall and shoo it away.'

'That sounds like Jimmy.' I smiled.

'I fear for him,' his great-uncle said.

'Jimmy?' I tried to chuckle. 'He's a natural flier, from what his wing commander told me. Jimmy can look after himself.'

'He is but he can't.' The captain tossed his liqueur back.

'No he can't,' I agreed, 'but we can't keep him here.'

'A caged bird dies slowly,' he ruminated.

'Is that a Maltese proverb?'

'No, it's a clue in your crossword,' Captain Sultana told me, 'but I can't remember how many letters.'

51

THE CROWN OF THORNS

The mornings were getting colder but we liked to eat our breakfast in the wheelhouse when we could, watching the geese skein over the estuary as the low mists – or *dags*, as the locals called them – melted in the soft autumn sun.

Jimmy was busy packing, unpacking and repacking his few possessions. The lower ranks could use rucksacks big enough to smuggle a petite brunette into their dormitories but an officer was a gentleman and carried a small leather suitcase – or so Jimmy told me, with his vast experience of such matters.

I had tried to sneak a present in – *A Further Range*, the poems of Robert Frost in a nice burgundy cover with gold letters – but of course he had seen it now, and my inscription.

'Will you really miss me?' he had asked.

'Be glad to see the back of you,' I had told him and hurried back on deck.

The whistle blew and Carmelo strode over to answer it. He still had a rolling gait, though his seafaring days had been long over when I first met him. 'Bridge,' he bellowed and put the tube to his ear, then back to his mouth. 'Stand by.' He held the tube towards me. 'It's for you.'

'Ahoy,' I shouted sheepishly into the horn. Captain had forbidden me to say *hello*.

The message was faint, being relayed from the summer house up the hill. At nearly 300 feet it took strong lungs to even blow the whistle, let alone hold a conversation. 'OK. Thanks. I'll be up,' I yelled and put the cap back over the mouthpiece. 'I have a phone call.'

I grabbed my old tan coat.

'Must be important.' I had given very few people Tubby Gretham's number and then only with strict instructions not to abuse his generosity. Tubby was one of the few people in the area to have a phone, thanks to his profession. A disagreement with the General Medical Council may have deprived him of his livelihood for a time but he never lost the line.

'If I'm not back in twenty minutes, can you tell Jimmy I'll see him at the station?' I asked Carmelo. 'I know he's got some people he wants to see in town first. Are you sure you won't go?'

'He won't want a silly old fool blubbing on his shoulder,' the captain said. 'I'll say goodbye here.'

I clambered down the wooden steps to the earth still wet with dew.

Tubby was coming lumbering awkwardly down the hill, shambling even more like a bear than usual, his open duffle coat flapping about him.

'I'm sorry you've been disturbed.'

'I'm not.' Tubby was almost luminous with excitement. 'Do you know who it is? – Of course you don't – it's your godmother, March Middleton, *the* March Middleton.' I knew he was an admirer but a fifteen-year-old girl meeting Bing Crosby could not have been more thrilled. 'And you will never guess – of course you won't – she promised to send me an inscribed – inscribed, mark you, not just signed – copy of *The Breathing Horse*!' If it were humanly possible, Dr Gretham would have evaporated with the joy bubbling out of him. 'We must hurry,' he urged, giving me a little shove in the back. 'She said she would ring back in ten minutes and you can't keep *March Middleton* waiting.'

Tubby turned back up the hill, still jabbering. A rabbit popped out of the old warren burrowed into the side of the woods. 'I told her how much I admired her forensic skills and she said you had told her about that emergency operation I did on Dandy Tremaine and she' – he took a breath – '*complimented* me on it. Oh Betty...' He swept his arms out, a love-struck boy after his first date.

I followed him up the wide strip that his grandfather had cut through Treacle Woods to give a clear view from White Lodge at the top. Barbed wire was wrapped like thorns round a broken fence rail.

We drew level with the summer house and I almost came a cropper on a collapsed molehill camouflaged under a pile of leaves, only saving myself by performing a split leap Margot Fonteyn would have been proud of, though landing a little less gracefully.

'How's the arm?' Tubby chuckled at my antics.

'Still hurting.' I trod cautiously.

He flicked at a pine cone with his stick but missed like the bad golfer that he was.

'I'll take a look at it later.'

'Thank you.'

'Any progress on the railway station stabbing?'

'Not much.'

'I have a theory.' Tubby hesitated. 'Why are you groaning?'

'I was clearing my throat.'

The good doctor cast a sceptical eye. 'What if the murderer had fired darts from a blowpipe?'

'I think we might have noticed them sticking out,' I objected.

'Ah yes' – he wagged a finger – 'but here's the clever bit...' He shot me a glance.

'Got a bit of a tickle.' I rubbed my neck. In every theory the public ever gave me there was always a *clever bit*. I hoped he was not going to suggest the darts were on fishing lines for the killer to reel them in again. Miss Prim had written to me with that one.

'What if the darts were made of ice? No, hear me out. The temperature of the blood combined with the pressure of your peculiar constable's tourniquet would have melted them away.'

'You got that from *Death on the Amazon*,' I pointed out.

If there was one thing that had made the life of a police officer more difficult over the last decade, it was the explosion of whodunnits with their bizarre murders and unconvincing explanations. The only redeeming factor was that most of the best ones were written by women.

'That's what Boadicea said,' Tubby mused. 'But the murderer could have read the book too. It's great stuff. Lady Olga Slayer wrote it, you know.'

'I do.'

'Ask your godmother what she thinks of my theory,' Tubby urged.

'I shall,' I promised and whispered, 'not.'

'I heard that.'

'So did I. Did she say what she was calling for?' I asked.

Tubby looked more shocked than when he had come away from the first GMC hearing. 'I couldn't ask Miss Middleton something like that.'

'But she sounded all right?'

'She sounded wonderful.' Tubby smiled beatifically. 'And she was very nice when I told her she had got her left and right cardiac ventricles the wrong way round when she wrote about one of her solo investigations in *The Woman Vanishes*.'

'Was this before or after she promised you the book?' I wondered.

'Oh ages before,' Tubby puffed. We were near the top by then. 'Miss Middleton explained that she had got it right but somebody had altered it and that all editors and proofreaders are lazy, ignorant and incompetent parasites sucking at the author's lifeblood.'

'Really?' I had thought she had a high opinion of her publishers,

Antonia and Nicola Cheetah in particular, and it was not like Aunty M to be unkind.

'Well, she said that is what Mr Grice told her.'

It did sound more like him than her. Tubby kicked another pine cone, scuffing it sideways.

'Watch out, Billy Walker,' I murmured.

'Didn't know you liked football.'

'I don't. Carmelo and Jimmy do.' They had not been at all happy that the England team had been ordered to give the Nazi salute in Berlin but were partially mollified by our side winning 6–3.

'Jimmy found a job yet? A proper one, I mean.'

I knew what Tubby thought of Jimmy's aspirations to be a writer.

'He joins the RAF today.'

I was Tubby's chance to say *Really?* so he did. 'Is that why you're all dolled up?'

'I'm seeing him off.'

'Not Annie' – Tubby grinned – 'or Milly or Jayne?'

'All busy, I'm afraid.'

Once there had been sheep cropping the path. Now there was only Boris, an ancient billy goat glaring accusingly from a patch of brown bracken, and the grass was knee-high in places until we reached the lawn that I had seen Greta scything last autumn.

We went through the side door straight into the kitchen, where Greta greeted me with a steaming mug.

'How are you now?' I took the coffee gratefully from her knobbly-knuckled hands.

Greta had had a nasty bout of bronchitis to add to her miseries.

'Cold.' She pulled her quilted coat around her shoulders.

'No natural insulation,' Tubby grunted as if being delicately built was something his wife did out of naughtiness.

'But not as cold as you must be in that boat,' Greta went on.

'It's actually quite warm,' I assured her but didn't like to add that it was a lot warmer and more sheltered than the draughty hilltop pile they lived in.

'You wait for winter,' she warned. 'But it's the captain I worry about.'

'Carmelo?' Tubby snorted. 'An old seadog like him can withstand a great deal worse than the British winter.'

'Is that your considered medical opinion?' I stood closer to the range.

'It's what he told me to say,' Tubby admitted and the telephone rang. 'That'll be her.' He beamed, like a child hearing sleigh bells on Christmas Eve, and I quit my cosy perch for the unheated, high-ceilinged, oak-panelled wind tunnel they called the hall.

52

MANICURE MURDERS AND THE IDLE BUNCH

t was a good clear line from London, much better than we got from one side of Sackwater to the other.

'Hello, Betty.'

The greeting was cheery enough.

'Is everything all right?' I asked anxiously.

'Oh yes, dear. I did tell Edward to reassure you.'

It took me a second to realise that *Edward* was Tubby. My godmother had been engaged to an Edward, a long time ago in India.

'I believe you promised him a book.'

'I hope he did not think I was being patronising.'

'Oh, he's like two lambs with four tails,' I assured her. 'If you write *To Dear Tubby* he'll be like a flock of them.'

'Of course, darling. He was telling me about his wife,' Aunty M said. Tubby never talked about Greta to strangers. It was not until his hearing that I'd realised how bad she was. 'I did not want to be presumptuous but, if they would like to consult with Professor Bronowski, I'm sure I can arrange it.'

'Thank you, Aunty, I'll let him know.'

'And he can always ring me here. I did enjoy our chat.'

'You might have to have your phone disconnected if I tell him that,' I warned and my godmother chuckled.

'The reason I rang,' she told me, 'is because I read about that awful business on Sackwater Station and I believe you were there.'

I briefly explained what had happened.

'It is just that it reminded me dreadfully of a similar case we had in Euston Square underground station in 1927,' March Middleton continued. 'I am only surprised that the press did not pick up on it – though I should not be, really. They are an idle bunch on the whole – the Camden Vampire, they called it here.'

'I remember the case,' I told her. 'But I was involved in the Manicure Murders at the time.' They were called that because the killer neatly trimmed all his victims' fingernails, leading one scurrilous newspaper to dub him *Jack the Snipper.* 'Do you think your vampire and mine could be the same man?'

'No, darling, I do not,' Aunty M assured me. 'We caught and hanged him and I am absolutely certain we got the right man. It is just the similarities were so striking that I wondered if this might be a *crime de copié*. It may be nothing but I can let you have the files, if you like. His name was Vernon Willowdale.'

'Oh yes, I've heard of him. That would be very helpful,' I said.

'Or very unhelpful, if it is just a coincidence. I shall have them sent to you as soon as possible,' she promised. 'Now, how is the arm and then I want all your gossip, the more scandalous the better. The people I meet these days are so well behaved in my presence, I might be the queen in church.'

'My arm is fine,' I lied. 'Do you remember me telling you about Caroline Foster who I went to school with?'

'The one with two lovers?' I could almost see Aunty M perk up.

'Well, now it turns out she has three husbands.' I perched on the edge of the telephone table. This could be a long call.

*

It was only later I realised that Aunty M and Dodo had one thing in common. They never *didn'ted* their *did nots* or turned their *are nots* into *aren'ts*. My godmother was Victorian but what was Dodo's excuse?

'I wish I'd asked her to write *To Tubby* on it,' Tubby moaned. 'But I didn't have the nerve to ask.'

'Even if you had, I can't imagine she would,' Greta told him.

'Have you ever heard of Professor Bronowski?' I asked them both.

'Tubby wrote to ask him for an opinion,' Greta sighed, 'but then that stupid brainless pompous committee interfered and said he couldn't take referrals from a struck-off doctor, so he wouldn't see me.'

'I think he might now,' I said but Greta was looking at me oddly.

'Are you all right, Betty?' Her husband was flicking something.

'Yes of course,' I told her.

'Just going to pop this under your tongue.' Tubby slipped a thermometer into my mouth. 'Roll up your sleeve, please.' All at once we were back in his surgery and I was an embarrassed teenager.

'Oh dear,' Greta said.

'Oh dear indeed,' Tubby seconded. 'That wound is very angry. I don't want to prod it and hurt you but I think you have sequestra – bone fragments breaking free – also' – he whipped the thermometer out – 'you have a fever – 101 degrees. You need to get it X-rayed and cleaned up properly under an anaesthetic.'

'I'll get it looked at when I have time,' I told him.

'Do you have time to lose the rest of your arm?' he cross-examined me. 'Or even – and I am not being melodramatic here – your life?' And I knew he was right. It was just that I had a nearly-nephew to wave off and a murderer to catch and neither would wait for me to feel better.

53

THE MIRACLE OF MESOPOTAMIA

Jimmy waited on the platform, looking even taller in his uniform, though he was tall enough for most purposes already. He stood a good head above the hordes of servicemen, mostly new recruits with their mothers, and, were it not for my heels, he would have had an inch or two's advantage over me.

I glanced at the platform. It had been well hosed down and scrubbed since that murder and I forced myself not to look again. I was not there in my official capacity.

Jimmy looked terrific in his grey-blue uniform, the black band on his sleeve with a thin blue band inside it denoting his rank as pilot officer. His peaked hat with the brass badge was tipped very slightly to one side. He spent ages fiddling with that so as to look rakish but not scruffy.

'Very smart.' I adjusted his tie though he had knotted it perfectly and saw him shift a little in embarrassment, this boy, hardly old enough to vote, setting out to be a warrior.

'Is the jacket OK?' He tugged it down. 'It hung a bit baggily so I got Mr Tubwall to take it in.'

I stepped back, hoping Jimmy would not get into trouble or be mocked. The jacket was noticeably waisted now and I was almost sure it wasn't meant to be.

'You look splendid.'

'So do you.' Jimmy grinned. I had put a blue floral dress on with long sleeves and a white glove to hide my false arm, with the other glove wedged between the wooden fingers to look like

I had just pulled it off. I had been feeling under the weather lately and looking a bit grey. Women police officers in uniform do not wear make-up, but I was off duty so I had taken the opportunity to brighten myself up. 'It's a long time since I've seen you in a frock.' He was looking at me more like his uncle used to and I couldn't pretend I minded.

I had padded my stump as best I could but any careless movement still brought a tear to my eyes.

A little boy prodded Jimmy's leg. 'Are you a German?'

'Don't be dizzy.' His older sister rolled her eyes like Emily, the china doll I used to have before Dodo appropriated her and renamed her Cynthia. 'He's one of those brave boys in blue that Mummy likes so much.'

'Are you going to kill Nazis?' The boy was awestruck.

'Every blessed one of them,' Jimmy vowed as their mother dragged them away.

Jimmy puffed out his cheeks. 'Pity the captain didn't come. He's still got an old uniform.'

I glanced away. 'You know he hates goodbyes.' And, though I did not say it, so did I.

Jimmy unbuttoned his left breast pocket. 'He gave me this last night, from Dad.' And slipped out the old cigarette case. We all knew his father's story of how the dent was caused by an Ottoman bayonet in the Mesopotamian campaign.

'That should keep you safe.'

Jimmy slipped it back. 'You don't believe that stuff, do you?'

'It worked for him.' I smiled with a reassurance I didn't feel as I watched Jimmy put the case back over his heart. 'Maybe he'll get in touch when he knows you've joined up.'

'I shan't tell him,' Jimmy vowed, 'and you mustn't.'

A squadron leader paused. 'Hello, pal. I say, what a stunner.' He eyed me up and down and up again, pausing at the third button of my dress. I had left the top two undone. 'Just to brief you, we've commandeered the front two compartments for the RAF.' He said *RAF* as if it were a one-syllable word, then zipped past and swung his soft leather bag into the train.

'You will be careful, won't you?' I touched Jimmy's hand.

Jimmy laughed and rubbed the back of his neck.

'It's not about being careful, Aunty. It's about killing Jerries.'

I didn't like to say that they would be doing their best to kill him too, nor that the Luftwaffe was the biggest air force in the world with pilots who had had combat experience, whereas Jimmy had only trained in peacetime and never been fired upon.

The brake joints hissed like a pantomime audience when the villain makes an appearance.

'Come on, chum,' another officer called from on board. 'Say goodbye to your girl. We're ready for take-off.'

There was a self-consciousness in these uniformed youths' choices of words that was rather endearing, like boys trying to adopt their new school's slang.

'Wouldn't want to leave her behind,' another shouted while a soldier, leaning out of the train, yelled, 'Wouldn't want to leave her front either!' to general catcalls.

Jimmy glanced over his shoulder. 'Well, I'll be off then.' He pecked me on the cheek and peered over my head. 'Don't take this amiss but I was rather hoping one of my girls would come. Gives a chap a bit more kudos with a girl to see him off.'

'I'd give her more to remember me by than that if she were mine,' the squadron leader scoffed.

'No, she's not—' Jimmy began but I put a finger to his lips and a hand behind his head and winked and the light dawned, but still Jimmy hesitated.

'You don't mean…' but he never said what I didn't mean for he knew full well that I did.

'Kudos,' I mouthed and stroked his face.

Jimmy took a breath. 'Bye, darling.' And took me in his arms to kiss me near the mouth, but I was too quick for him.

'I say.' Jimmy blushed and just managed to stop the sound that his lips were making of *Aunty*.

'Once more,' I whispered and he held me tighter and kissed me properly and longer the second time.

'Gawd, get some solvent. They're glued together,' a sailor cackled, throwing his knapsack into a second-class carriage.

'And a crowbar,' one of his friends whooped.

'Be lucky.' I kissed Jimmy a third time before I let go of his head and he released me. If he was feigning reluctance, he did it very convincingly.

'Gosh,' he breathed and I was only relieved that nobody else heard him and that he wasn't blushing any more.

Jimmy grinned. 'I'm glad you're not really—'

'Don't miss your train,' I broke in and he stepped back.

The guard blew his whistle and flapped a green flag on a stick and Jimmy snatched up his suitcase and turned.

'Welllll, she's a bit super-delicious.' The squadron leader leered. 'Has she got any sisters?'

Jimmy said something I didn't catch but I was happy to see that it got a good laugh. He heaved his case in and followed it.

I couldn't see Jimmy because his comrades were leaning out of the window.

One roared, 'Stick around, sweetheart. I'll finish the job for him when I come back.'

Doors were slamming. The engine strained and the wheels shifted restlessly.

'Oh he's more than capable of doing that himself,' I assured Jimmy's new pal, settling into my newly expanded not-really-an-aunty duties rather well, I thought.

The two scraggy girls I had seen waving the truck off were there, flapping their even-less-clean handkerchiefs at two different sweethearts.

'Farewell my own true lover,' the scrawny girl sobbed. She was getting very good at that.

'Oi'll write every day, my darlin',' her scrawnier friend vowed tearfully, though a little less convincingly, I felt.

The train drudged off. So many people must be waving bravely to their loved ones throughout the country, with no way of knowing what might lie ahead. It was just the pain shooting up to my shoulder, I told myself, that brought tears to my eyes.

Mr Trime came across. 'Was that your sweetheart?' he asked solicitously as the two girls went off in search of a cuppa.

'I was just doing my bit for morale,' I told him.

'That's the spirit,' he said uncertainly.

'I expect that munitions train blowing up has caused you a few headaches,' I said but the stationmaster shook his head.

'Luckily it was just on the dock line so we weren't affected at all.' He clicked the lid shut on his East Anglia Line hunter watch and slipped it back into his waistcoat.

But Dodo told me they cancelled her train, I remembered. Why would she lie to me about being late? Had she had a romantic assignation? She had seemed even more dreamy than usual lately.

I went out and onto High Road West.

A newspaper vendor bellowed hoarsely, 'Brave Poles defy Hitler in Warsaw!'

Not for much longer, I thought in dismay. Then Hitler could turn his attention to us. Evening was falling on our empire, or so he proclaimed, while a new dawn rose over the Thousand-Year Reich.

Rufus Verdigris, the accountant and would-be doctor, came rushing up. 'Damn and blast, I've missed it.' His clean white handkerchief poked neatly at the ready from the breast pocket of his well-pressed pinstripe suit. 'Last time,' he confided, 'a man got grit in his eye and asked if I could help. What a sauce!'

54

WAVES THROUGH THE ETHER

Every police force I have ever visited runs off tea and Sackwater Central was no exception. That morning it was Dodo's turn to make it but, having sampled her previous concoctions, Bantony had volunteered to brew a pot himself. I was just explaining to Constable Box, disconsolate at having no nickname, that, using cockney rhyming slang, he could call himself Sticks, when Inspector Sharkey made an appearance, so white with excitement he could have stood naked – horrible thought – in the corner of Lavender Wicks's sitting room without being spotted.

'What's happened?' I was not going to wait for him to play some silly game, but then the end door opened and Superintendent Vesty drifted in, secateurs in hand.

'One Easter Sunday when I was six and ill in bed,' he told the assembly, 'my older brother Bernard came to my room with a black thread and told me to pull it as hard as I could. Being a tractable child, I did as I was bid, whereupon I was alarmed to hear a loud crash accompanied by the sounds of smashing.

'"Now you're in for it," my brother Bernard cachinnated and thereupon absconded.

'My father came out of his oak-lined study where he was writing a paper on the perils of transmitting radio waves through the ether, to discover that his fine collection of Yorkshire glass and the fine Yorkshire cabinet in which it was stored had been shattered beyond repair. My brother had tied the other end of the thread to the top of that fine Yorkshire cabinet in which his fine collection of Yorkshire glass was stored.

'"Who capsized that fine Yorkshire cabinet in which my fine collection of Yorkshire glass was stored?"

'I was unable to perpetrate a deceit and responded, "I did, Father."

'"Why did you capsize that fine Yorkshire cabinet in which my fine collection of Yorkshire glass was stored?"

'"My brother Bernard told me to," I explained, certain that the righteousness of my statement would remove the cloak of guilt from my shoulders and place it upon my brother Bernard's, but my father sent me to fetch his hazel switch and thrashed me until I bled.' Vesty's voice trembled and his secateurs-free hand rose to point shakily at the ghost of Easter Past. 'The incident has played upon my mind every minute of every waking day since. Filthy business. It broke my heart.' He swept that hand back over his head as if he still had more than a dandelion clock-head floating upon it. 'But it did not break me.'

There was a long silence.

'How awful,' I broke it and the superintendent seemed to notice me for the first time.

'Jolly nice to see a couple of pretty faces around the place. Keep up the good work,' he told us and returned to his office.

'What the hell was that about?' Sharkey huffed and for once he spoke for almost all of us.

'Oh, did you not understand, Inspector Sharkey?' Dodo enquired. 'It was about Easter Sunday when Superintendent Vesty was six years old.'

'What happened?' I asked Old Scrapie again.

'Superintendent Vesty's brother—' Dodo began again.

'Shut up!' Sharkey shouted and Dodo opened her mouth but thought better of it.

'I was talking to Inspector Sharkey,' I explained.

'But how was I to know that?' she quivered.

'Because I was facing him with my back to you,' I told her. 'Now be quiet.'

'There was an arrest yesterday in Paris.'

'*Vraiment*?' I asked, to his bafflement. 'Just the one?'

'Of a man answering to the description of the Sackwater Station killer.'

'What?' Brigsy's cadaverous face gaped. 'With a cloak and bloodshot eyes and long bat teeth?'

'I'm talking about proper witnesses,' Sharkey snarled.

'Well, I was one of those and the description I gave wasn't exactly detailed,' I objected.

The Shark waved a fin. 'Other people saw a man hobbling down Hamilton Road with blood around his mouth.'

'I think that was probably Mr Amery from Martins Bank,' I suggested. 'He hit his nose on the kerb when he was detained by a member of the public in error.' I omitted to mention who had rugby-tackled his probably-ex-by-now manager and that I knew him – but the Shark had the scent of a suspect and was not to be deterred.

'He says he can reveal details of how it was done but he will only do so to the officer in charge of the case.'

It was actually my case but I knew Sharkey was about to flex his seniority muscles and that I had two choices. I could put in a protest with our superintendent and, having a better figure than Old Scrapie, could probably win my plea – or I could let him go on another wild goose chase and make an even bigger idiot of himself.

'That would be you, Inspector Sharkey,' I said generously and the creature beneath his skin moved.

'Never been to Paris,' he admitted. 'Never been abroad.'

'Not even in the last war?' Rivers asked. 'That's what did do my back in fer me and I've been—'

'—a martyr to it ever since.' Brigsy completed the phrase we all knew so well. If Rivers had been playing a record the needle would have cut through it by now.

Sharkey stiffened. 'I was doing important war work here but I can't talk about it – Official Secrets Act.'

The rest of us exchanged unofficial secret glances.

'Take a mosquito net,' I advised, 'and you'll need a pith helmet.'

'Very funny.' Starkey eyed me contemptuously. 'Think I don't know that nets will be provided?'

'They speak French in Paris,' Dodo informed him helpfully. '*Gooten morgan* – that means *hello* and—'

'I don't think—' I began but Sharkey shushed me.

'I'd better write some of these down.'

'*Sprekensee English, swinehunt?*' Dodo continued. 'Do you speak English, please.' Her face was deadly serious and Sharkey was scribbling furiously.

'A lot of words are just stolen from English with *en* added on to them like *come* is *comen* and *go* is *goen*,' Dodo recalled. 'Oh yes and *Give me a coffee, waitress* is *Gibbon me eye-nun fickin, smutzig hundin.*'

'Where did you learn French, Dodo?' I asked.

'From a man I met on a train when I was sixteen and a bit,' she told me. 'He was very kind and said I could sit on his knee but I explained that in England we sit on the empty seats – though they are not empty once you have sat upon them.'

'Oy 'ad an uncle who goo for Paris,' Bantony declared, 'but 'e never arrived.'

'What happened?' Starkey asked with a tinge of unease.

''E changed 'is moind,' Bantony explained, 'and went ter Blackpool instead.'

Vesty wandered back out, carrying a trug this time with rose cuttings on it, and I hoped he wasn't going to serenade us all.

'That story I told you all a moment ago.' He shuffled his feet. 'Just between ourselves, what?'

'Of course, sir,' I assured him. 'In fact, with that Hurricane flying over, we didn't really hear much of it.'

'Hurricane?' He wrinkled his brow.

'It is a type of aeroplane, Superintendent Vesty, sir,' Dodo explained, 'but I don't remember hearing—'

'Then try to,' I butted in and turned back to our chief. 'Inspector Sharkey is leaving us for…'

Vesty clapped like a child at panto, no mean feat with the flower basket over his left arm. 'Excellent, excellent.' He stuck out his hand, striking the Shark in his midline bulge. 'Well, good luck, Scrapie, as I believe you are affectionately known. I can't pretend I've ever liked you but I wish you all the best.'

'A few days,' I ended weakly.

55

GREEN STRAWBERRIES AND THE
WAY TO ROTTERDAM

Dodo sat in the back room with an enormous mug of tea in one hand and a book in the other.

'What's that?' I asked, checking the kettle to find she had drained it.

'A mug of tea, boss.'

'The book.' I put the kettle under the tap.

'Oh it's my very favourite.' Dodo Chivers radiated happiness. '*Fenula the Fluffy Kitten*. Have you read it?'

'No.'

'Do not worry,' Dodo reassured me. 'I shall lend it to you when I have finished though I must warn you, it is very sad in the middle.'

'I don't think you should read it here,' I advised, putting the kettle on the stove and lighting the gas ring.

'Oh but I have got past the bit that makes my nose tickle,' she assured me.

'If the men see you reading it they will make fun,' I warned, looking in vain for a clean mug. Somebody had used mine and left a stained ring halfway down.

'But they would not make fun of how Fenula got lost in the Fairy Forest but was rescued by a golden butterfly,' she protested.

'I'm afraid they would.' I washed out my mug – not as easy

as it sounds when one of your hands is in a jar of formalin in your cabin.

'But surely-to-Sudbury not when Fenula ate too many green strawberries and got tumbly-ache?'

'Even then.'

Walker ambled in.

'You heartless beast,' Dodo scolded him.

'What?' He showed his open hands in a gesture of guiltlessness. 'You can't have found that spider I put in your locker yet. Oh...' Walker looked for a verbal escape route. 'Not that I have.' He scrambled through it unconvincingly.

'Good,' Dodo said. 'Then I will not have to tell Inspector Church what you used her mug for.'

Walker cleared his throat. 'I'll just go and make sure nobody else put one in.'

I sniffed my tea. 'What *did* he use it for?'

'Catching the spider,' she told me, but I had seen people panic less than Walker when they were being arrested for murder.

I poured my tea away and resolved to bring a fresh mug in the next day.

Dodo slid her book into her handbag and I glimpsed two spikes sticking out from under her handkerchief. They were much too thick to be knitting needles.

'What's that?'

'Nothing.' Dodo Chivers snapped her bag shut without even glancing to see what I had meant.

*

The important thing I forgot that night was to loop the rope but it was late and I was tired, wet, grumpy and still feeling feverish. We had had heavy rain for the best part of a week now and, while *Cressida* was waterproof, my clothing when I was walking and

244

cycling to and from work was not and the water had a clever knack of finding a way inside it.

In the half-moon's light I could see the water was up a good few inches, and hear it racing, but I was not alarmed. I pointed my boat upstream to the west as Carmelo had shown me and set off. The boat wobbled as it always did for the first couple of strokes – but it didn't stop wobbling. It started to spin and I found I had very little control over it. I was drifting downstream and all my efforts could do nothing to correct my course. The current was too strong.

I passed the easterly tip of the bar but if I could just steer landwards a bit, I would hit the last horn of the bay. If not, there was nothing much between me and the estuary flowing into the open sea, with the first stop being Rotterdam a couple of hundred miles of the North Sea away. I dipped the oar deeper to use it as a rudder, turning the nose of the boat inwards, but I couldn't turn it far enough fast enough. I was almost parallel and about to be swept outwards into the middle of the estuary. I heaved on the oar but it was useless. Twice I slipped, clattering onto my back over the bench. The second time I caught my stump and screamed in pain and rage at my stupidity and clumsiness and in frustration at my powerlessness. Short of suicide, few of us can choose the time and manner of our deaths, but all I knew was I did not want to end up capsized in the freezing waves of the Atlantic Ocean, another dogfish-chewed bloated corpse to be washed up wherever the tides might take me.

For some reason, I thought of Sharkey and how he would gloat. *Takes a man to handle a boat*, he would say, and the fury that this thought aroused in me gave greater strength to my arm than any amount of terror could have done. I dipped the oar back into the water and leaned, my foot on the side of the boat, straining with all my might until the tip of the boat turned. It was too late to hit land. Even with an outboard motor I doubt I could have done that. But there was a fallen tree jutting from that horn. In the summer, Jimmy, Carmelo and I had sat fishing on it with our feet in the water. They had been most annoyed when, after their patient – but unnecessary – tutorials I caught the first fish, a fat whiting that they never managed to equal.

I could just make out the shadow of the trunk, I thought, remembering Carmelo telling me to watch how the ripples in the water broke over low obstructions in order to avoid them, but I would do everything in my power not to avoid this one. I sculled literally for my life and felt the underside of the boat scrape over some submerged branches. It was only then that I knew I could save myself. If the current started to push me out again I would leap into those branches and cling onto them all night if I had to. But I managed to turn the boat a fraction more and bump the port side of it into the body of the tree. Hooking the rope loosely round my ankle, I scrambled out onto the trunk, determined not to lose the captain's boat with numb fingers. I tied the rope to a broken limb in nothing a nautical man would recognise as a knot but what I felt confident would do the same job, then crawled up the trunk until I hit the roots. The ground was just about visible as I slithered down, face towards the tree, skirt rising, stockings shredded, but at least I was on solid, if muddy, ground and able to use the roots to haul myself up the bank and feel my way through the low shrubs back to Shingle Bay.

Carmelo heard my shouts.

'Madonna.' I couldn't see but I knew he would be crossing himself when he heard my account of what had happened.

'Go to the house. Stay the night with Tubby,' he shouted from the prow. 'He will help rescue *Genevieve* in the morning.'

I had forgotten the rowing boat had a name and hoped I had secured her properly. Nothing with a name like that deserved to bump into one of the mines both sides were sowing like grain over the oceans to reap their grim harvests.

The rain started up again but more heavily as I trudged up the open vista that led past the summer house and across the lawn to White Lodge, the welcome of true friends, dry towels, a thick, itchy dressing gown, a welcome mug of hot sweet coffee and a very welcome very large tot of brandy.

'Now tell her off,' Greta urged, not for the first time, and Tubby proceeded to do so. He was a forceful man but, worse than that, he made sense.

'I *will* get it seen to,' I promised and I meant it – just as soon as I could – but it felt a bit better after they had bathed it and dressed it and he had given me a draught of something that I shouldn't really have had after alcohol. The tree trunk was only mildly less comfortable than the bed they gave me and I knew I would toss and turn all night, but the next thing I saw was sunlight coming into the room with Greta bringing me a mug of tea and telling me I was to stay in bed, and it was only after I had marched across the lawn in Tubby's dressing gown with no shoes on that she could be persuaded to give me back my uniform.

March Middleton once told me she would retire the day all the criminals did. I would have my operation as soon as I caught the so-called Suffolk Vampire.

t was a lovely clear morning. The water was still and steaming lightly. Two white swans sailed snootily by, five cygnets in their wake, grey-brown and fluffy, already as big as their parents. A water rat splashed in from the bank. Carmelo used to trap them, convinced that they ate eggs and chicks, until I found a book to confirm they were voles and vegetarian.

The captain had taken a walk into town – a rare excursion for him but he had to collect his identity card – and I was setting up my easel, something I hadn't done for a long time, to do my Suffolk's-answer-to-Monet routine when the launch came. It was not often the coastguard came this far up the estuary unless they were checking a report of suspicious activity. The boat edged carefully along – there were a few submerged sandbanks in the area of Brindle Bar – a watcher pushing the prow away from an obstruction with a quant pole.

'Morning, ma'am,' the coastguardsman called from behind the wheel. He was well protected against the elements in his yellow oilskin coat with matching sou'wester. 'Lookin' for an Inspector Church.'

'You have found her,' I told him and he nodded his shaggy head.

'Thought so.' He flapped his left sleeve, which was fuller than mine. 'Bu' I've be told to put you a question to make doubly sure.' He rooted and tapped around inside his outer clothing like he was searching for a flea before bringing out a twice-folded sheet of paper. 'Here it is. I've been told to read it exact.' He unfolded the paper. 'Dunno wha' ih do mean though.' He cleared his throat. 'What did Molly say when she told you about the' – he brought the message closer to his eyes – 'in-vis-ual elephant?… whatever tha' mean. You have to say ih exact.'

'Oh, Miss Betsy, if I hadntn't not seen it with my own eyes I wouldntn't not have disbelieved it,' I yelled, much to the surprise of an otter taking an early dip.

The coastguardsman was mouthing the written words as I said them. 'Is thah some secret code?'

'No, it's just Miss Middleton's old maid.'

'Is that safe to tie up on?' He pointed to the small wooden jetty Stanislaw Stanislavski, the previous occupant of our island, had constructed forty years ago, driving oak beams into the river bed.

'I only know it's strong enough to stand on,' I replied, which was as helpful as I could be. Nothing bigger than a rowing boat had moored on Brindle Bar in my time there. 'But you're welcome to try.'

I walked to the end, the water waking up in lazy eddies around the piles, and the bowhook (I think he was called) threw me a rope (or was it a cable or a line?). The captain would be disappointed in me, I thought, as I looped whatever it was over the mooring post, hurrying back before they put the structure to the test. The boat edged in, the reeds bending and snapping under it, and I felt a non-proprietorial pride in seeing our pier stand firm.

'Dint think this place was lived in, I dint.' The coastguardsman heaved himself up. There were three others on deck now.

'The owner tends to keep himself to himself.' I stepped aside to allow him onto land. 'How can I help?'

'We've goh some records for you, we do.' He looked over my shoulder at *Cressida*, who made his boat look very insignificant even if she couldn't float. 'Ih was the only way Miss Middleton could think of getting them to you. Lord knows we owe her a favour or two from over the years.'

'We usually get deliveries sent to the local pub,' I told him, feeling a bit guilty at his wasted journey.

He guffawed like I was a very good music hall turn. 'Not like this you don't.' He called back over his shoulder. 'OK men, this do be ih.'

One of the men lifted a hatch and climbed down and a minute later a tea chest rose through the opening. His companions heaved it out.

'I didn't realise there were so many files,' I said.

The coastguardsman snorted. 'Got three more on them, we do,' he told me as the two men staggered ashore.

*

'Oh darling, I am sorry, how stupid but you cannot blame them too much. They are only men,' March Middleton mocked gently when I rang from Sackwater Central to thank her. Brigsy wasn't overly happy about my using *his* phone but this was police business. 'I told them to send you just the summary. It should be in a Grice's Lilac folder with my stamp on it. I didn't want to trust it to the post after they lost Harry Hobdell's face. Lord knows where that ended up.' She chuckled grimly. 'Not in some unfortunate's morning mail, I hope.'

'So it's all right if I use the phone to ring *my* aunty?' Bantony rested his elbow on the desk like he was waiting for his pint.

'When your aunty is Miss Middleton, yes,' I told him.

'When will that be?' Brigsy mused.

Bantony's normally immaculate jacket was bulging.

'What's that in your pockets?' I questioned him.

Bantony patted himself in surprise. 'Onions,' he admitted at last.

'Why?' I had a feeling I knew the answer to that one already.

Bantony looked abashed. 'Oy couldn't get any garlic.'

'There are no vampires in Sackwater,' I insisted. 'Take them out at once.'

'Nippy 'as a crucifix under 'is 'elmet.' Bantony emptied his pockets resentfully. 'And 'im and Box and Bantony 'ave ordered leather collars.'

'Well, you can tell them from me, if I catch anyone wearing one he will be strung up by it,' I warned.

'And Rivers carries a bokkle of 'oly water,' Bantony declared in a great show of solidarity with his fellow officers. 'And Serg—'

'What's taking so long with tha' tea, Walker?' Brigsy bellowed. 'Making the water yourself?' He stopped and lowered his voice. 'Oh, tha' dint come out quite right.'

I let his interruption pass. Quite honestly I didn't care what anti-vampire measure Sergeant Briggs had adopted, so long as he wasn't carrying a revolver loaded with silver bullets.

57

THE DESTRUCTION OF LININGS

The day after Sharkey set off on his adventure we were joined by identical twins, Constables Algernon and Lysander Grinder-Snipe – ungracefully tall and skinny with gangling legs and dangling arms, unpolished sapphire eyes and floppy long yellow hair, like badly painted poster boys for the Hitler Youth.

'How will I tell you apart?' I asked.

'We 'ave different names,' one explained.

'I'm Lysander and I don't like being called Sandy,' the one I was going to call Sandy, whether he liked it or not, introduced himself.

'I'm Algernon and I don't like being called Algy,' the one I was going to call Algy, whether he liked it or not, introduced himself.

Their accents did not quite match the gentility of their names.

'Where are you from?' I found their letters of transference on my desk.

'Lancashire, ma'am,' they chorused and, being from the north, they correctly pronounced it *mam* rather than *marm* but made it sound like I was their mother.

'Whereabouts in Lancashire?' I pressed.

'Parbold, mam,' they chorused.

'A small village,' Sandy explained.

'Near Wigan,' Algy clarified.

'Born—' Sandy began.

'And bred,' Algy completed.

'Oh I have been to Parbold,' I remembered happily. Aunty M had been raised in the Grange, on the top of Parbold Hill, and

I had enjoyed some lovely holidays there. 'You must know of March Middleton.'

The twins looked at each other in alarm.

'Must weh?' Sandy asked.

'Nobody told us we 'ad to,' Algy protested.

'Ohhh dear,' they choroused.

'No, I meant that you probably have.'

'Phew.' They wiped their brows in exaggerated relief.

'We 'aven't 'eard of 'er,' Sandy confessed.

'At all,' Algy confirmed.

I was surprised because it was a small village and my godmother was the only famous person to come from it, except for Joshua Beetle who invented a device for putting the stones back into olives but lost his fortune manufacturing it.

I tried again. 'Is the Stocks Tavern still open?'

They looked at their watches.

'Not at this time,' Sandy told me.

'Of day,' his twin contributed.

They stood to attention, shoulders thrown so far back in an effort to puff out their puffed in chests that they were leaning slightly backwards.

'At ease,' I said and they flopped, arms hanging loosely, backs bent, heads lolling.

'So what brings you to Suffolk?' I tried and they exchanged we've-got-a-right-one-here looks.

'Nothing brings uz 'ere, mam,' said the one I was almost sure was Sandy – for they had taken my *at ease* as an invitation to shuffle about while I was looking through their paperwork.

'We're already 'ere,' the one who was probably Algy explained, because Sandy seemed to be the one who always spoke first.

I gave up and announced, 'We'll put you on patrol together to start with.'

'Huzzah,' they cried with peculiarly emphasised 'h's.

I battled on. 'Constable Walker can show you the route, then you can take over the seafront beat.' I felt a bit guilty giving them that. Nobody liked it but somebody had to do it. Even in the summer the promenade could be windswept. In the winter it was lashed by gales straight from Siberia, bringing whatever little treats their climate had to offer.

'Hoorah,' Algy piped, breaking the Sandy-speaks-first rule the moment I had made it.

'Hooray,' Sandy chirped and they both clapped hands three times.

I suppose I should have been glad of anything we were given but, with Sharkey being away and Vesty seemingly on the brink of nervous collapse, we had gone from being top-heavy to top-light. As the only inspector at Sackwater Central, I had one sergeant – Briggs – and six constables – Dodo Chivers, the Grinder-Snipe twins, Nippy Walker, Bantony and – when he turned up – Rivers. Clearly Brigsy couldn't man the desk twenty-four hours a day and I didn't like leaving a constable in charge to deal with any more imaginary spies and certainly not in the unlikely instance that we had a real one.

We really needed one or two more sergeants but – while there was no shortage of people who were lucky to have their jobs – there was nobody I felt able to recommend for promotion.

Unfortunately *Cressida* was too far out for me to be readily available so there was only one thing for it – I would have to stay with my parents again at Felicity House.

*

'But where would you sleep?' My mother ran a finger over the hall table, cutting a shining canal in the grey landscape of its surface. 'You can't have Dear Dodo's room now that she's settled in.'

'That still leaves four empty bedrooms,' I pointed out.

My mother drew her toe over the floor as if setting up the oche for a game of darts. 'It's not very convenient – all that extra bedding to wash.'

'It's a lot of extra work for your mother.' My father blew through his empty meerschaum. 'She might even have to start cleaning the house soon.'

My mother welcomed this news as a personal affront, shuffling her folded arms under her bosom.

'I still have my sleeping bag in the attic,' I reminded them. 'I can use that.'

'But we have it all so nice and cosy here,' my mother moaned. 'And you know your father needs a good night's sleep, now that he's decided to try being nice to patients. He won't get that with your coming and going at all hours.'

'I wouldn't disturb you.' I sniffed. 'I have my own key.'

There was an odd, not very pleasant aroma on top of all the horrible dental smells I had grown up with.

'Ah yes.' My father inserted a fluffy cleaner into the mouthpiece. 'I was coming to that. It would be much easier if Dear Dodo had her own key.'

'I can get another one cut for her,' I offered.

'I do think you're being rather unfair' – my father pulled the cleaner out – it was thick with tar and dried spittle 'expecting poor Dodo to live with a superior officer.'

'Only superior in rank,' my mother chipped in.

I sniffed again. 'What's that smell?'

'What smell?' my mother asked edgily.

'I can't smell anything.' My father blew a cloud of ash out of the bowl. Years of Whisky Flake had destroyed the lining of his nose.

'Like rotten eggs.'

'The drains,' my mother said, a little too abruptly, I thought.

'You should get them looked at.'

'Always bossing us about.' My mother tried to rub the oche line out with her foot but made it into an uncoiled spring.

The front door opened. 'Hello, Motherkins and Fatherkins, your fairy princess is returned to the nest.' Dodo skipped in. 'Oh hello, Inspector.'

'Inspector,' my mother repeated pointedly to me. 'That's exactly what your father means.' Before oozing, 'Hello, Dodipops.'

'Hello, Doadie-Woadie.' My father grinned soppily.

'Have 'oo had a howwid day?' Motherkins took Dodipops's jacket and put it on a hanger on my hook. 'Shall Mumpsywoomp make 'oo your favourite mug of cocoa?'

I went to the stairs.

'And where do you think you are going?' my father demanded in his not-too-old-for-a-slap-young-lady voice.

'To get my camping things.' I was going to add a sarcastic *Poppsywoppsy* but my tongue had shrivelled and was unable to form the word.

58

THE HURTING OF THE HAT

t was time for tea – as if it wasn't always – and I was enjoying mine with a smoke, made all the more welcome by it being one of Brigsy's cigarettes, when he told me.

'You do have had a couple of calls from Gregson of the *Gazette* asking if you'll meet him.'

I greeted the news warily. A tame newspaper editor was a rare and valuable asset but the trouble was I had enjoyed being with Toby more than I should for a professional relationship.

The phone rang.

'If that's Mr Gregson tell him I'm busy but I'll get back to him,' I decided quickly.

Sergeant Briggs picked up the receiver like a bomb disposal expert might remove a fuse. 'Sackwater Central Police Station.'

'Why are we called Central when we are the only police station in town?' Dodo asked loudly.

'Shush.' Brigsy put a hand over the earpiece.

I moved a few feet back.

'Ohhh,' Dodo sighed. 'Have I made you cross as a Christmas tree?'

'I see,' Brigsy was saying.

'No.' Where the hell did she get these similes? I decided not to ask. 'It's just so that Sergeant Briggs can hear better.'

'I see.' Brigsy was making pencilled notes.

'Oh, is moving away from people a cure for deafness?' Dodo wondered.

'No.' I waited for her to shuffle towards me. 'Apparently there used to be two police stations in town – Sackwater Coastal and Sackwater Central.'

Dodo waved a paw. 'I think I can guess which one closed down.'

'I see,' Brigsy said twice more, then, 'I do be about to replace the receiver now. Goodbye.'

'That was a phone call—' he began.

'I think even Inspector Church could have worked that out,' Dodo broke in.

'From Ainnnglethorpe,' he continued.

'*Even?*' I seethed.

'About a handbag handed in on the nineteenth.'

'Well, you aren't odd so you must be even,' Dodo reasoned.

'Only they forgot to pass them on,' Brigsy announced.

'Though you do have a slightly odd number of hands,' she pondered.

'The message and the bag,' Brigsy carried on, apparently unaware of any interruptions. 'Though now they've passed the message on they're sendin' the bag today.'

'Being minus half an arm doesn't mean I don't know when there's been a phone call,' I protested.

'Eh?' Brigsy said.

'Handbag?' I queried.

'Yes.' Brigsy took the phone off the front ledge of his desk, putting it down behind just in case anyone was thinking of using it or even looking at it.

'Did they say whose it was?'

'They?' The sergeant scratched his cranial floor-sweepings. 'There was only one person, madam.'

'I think what Inspector Church means is *did they say whose it was?*' Dodo clarified.

'I do not need you to explain what I am saying,' I snapped. 'Especially when you haven't.' It came out a lot nastier than it was meant to but Dodo was unperturbed.

'You do when you're talking to Mummikins and Poppsicles,' she argued and I wondered briefly if it was possible for my head to explode.

'Did your caller tell you who the bag belonged to?' I asked patiently. *And please don't just say yes*.

'Yes.' Brigsy looked at me expectantly as if we were playing tennis and I was about to serve.

'The inspector means *Did your caller tell you who the bag belonged to?*' Dodo told him, having forgotten what I didn't need almost as soon as I had told her I didn't need it.

Brigsy consulted his jottings. 'A Mrs Lavender Wicks,' he announced. 'They found a chequebook with her name on it.'

'Mrs Lavender Wicks,' Dodo translated for me. 'Lavender Wicks!' She twirled around the room. 'I told you she was the murderess.'

'She told us she had lost her handbag on the very same day that it was handed in to Anglethorpe Police Station,' I reminded her. 'In what way does that make her guilty of anything other than carelessness?'

'Don't you see, ma'am?' She skipped backwards, tripping over the ridge in the lino and sitting down heavily on the middle bench. 'Owsy-wowsy.'

'Are you all right?' I hurried over.

'She int never all right, she int,' Brigsy informed me.

'Ouchy-wouchy.' She rubbed her right ankle. 'I seem to have strained it.'

'Sprained.'

'Oh.' She looked alarmed. 'Do you really think so?'

'Can you put your weight on it?'

Dodo put her foot up on the front bench. 'I left my weight at home.' She flexed her macaroni arms. 'See how it has built up my biceps?'

'Can you stand on that foot?'

'I used to be able to,' she cogitated. 'Let me see.' She put her right foot on the floor. 'Crikey,' she screwed up her little face, 'that hurts like a hat.'

'We need to get a doctor to look at it,' I decided despairingly. I didn't have time to take her and I couldn't spare Brigsy. We would be a constable down now and, hopeless as she was, at least Dodo Chivers made up our numbers.

Dodo put her foot up again. 'Talking about Lavender Wicks,' she said chattily, 'I still think this points to her guilt.'

'Why?' I paced the room.

'Because,' she explained simply, 'she was telling the truth, which murderers do to throw you off the scent. I think we should visit her, boss, to see how she tangles herself up in the web of her own truthfulness.'

'Well, you are in no state to walk that far,' I told her.

Constable Bank-Anthony was coming up the right-hand corridor from the back door, probably in the hope I wouldn't see him arriving twenty minutes late.

'Then will you go?' Dodo begged.

'Anyone can return her handbag.'

Bantony spotted me, stiffened, then carried on with exaggerated nonchalance.

'Yes but she needs to be asked penetrating questions like *Where did you get the sack from?* Then we can see if she remembers to ask which sack you mean,' Dodo insisted. 'She's guilty, boss, even if she is rich and kind to her maid and breathtakingly beautiful.'

'Oy can take 'er bag back, if you give me 'er details,' Bantony offered gallantly.

'You can take Constable Chivers to hospital,' I told him. 'She has sprained an ankle.'

'Oh dear.' Bantony crouched to have a closer look. 'Oh that does look sore.'

It looked the same as the other ankle through her stockings.

'It is ever so poorly-sorely,' she told him.

'Put your arms round my neck,' Bantony told her. 'Let's get yow up.'

Bantony put his arms round Dodo and she struggled up. 'Don't let go of me.'

'Oy won't.' He held her very close. 'Can yow put your weight on it?'

'I left that at home.'

'Oh yow poor little thing.' Bantony swept Dodo up.

'Oh it's just like being carried over the threshold,' she chirped.

Her dress had risen over her knees and fallen up her thighs but Bantony can't have noticed, even though he was looking down intently, otherwise he would have told her to pull it down again.

59

MAYHEM ON SPECTRE LANE AND
JIMMY IN WONDERLAND

never understood why camp beds, which seem like the pinnacle of luxury living when you're in your teenage years in the middle of a field, feel like they actually are that field when you're in your thirties and indoors. The frame – when I managed to assemble it – had gone wonky and the canvas was sagging in the middle.

The sleeping bag was too small for me now but I couldn't get into it in my skirt anyway and I was not going to strip off with the threat of a beat officer coming back for a not-very-quick cuppa, especially as I had to keep the office door open to listen for callers. I used the bag as a mattress, hung my jacket on the coat stand and lay on my back wondering if the cracked ceiling was likely to collapse on top of me and whether I would survive if it did. Toby Gregson might sell a few extra copies if I didn't.

The thought of Toby made me smile, something I suddenly realised I hardly ever did any more. At school Miss Dubois had called me *Sunshine* because of my cheery demeanour and the name had caught on. I would probably be *Stormcloud* now. Perhaps I should try to be nicer to the men and maybe I would if they would stop behaving like naughty children in kindergarten. I closed my eyes.

Jimmy was beginning to get very tired of sitting with his aunt on the bank and not having anything to do. Once or twice he peeped into the book I was reading.

'What's the point of a book,' Jimmy with Adam's face yawned, 'with no action or dialogue?'

'It's the revised regulations.' I turned the page.

'Sounds thrilling.' He unbuttoned his shirt. His chest was bronzed from the intense Maltese sun.

Watching the sea stretch and slide sleepily back over the shingle, it was difficult to keep my eyes open. I knew I must at all costs but I couldn't remember why. I only knew the blade was coming towards me and I was trying to shout *No!* but Miss Dubois was clanging the handbell that signalled the end of break and I was just wondering why she was there when I realised it was the phone ringing.

I tumbled off my bed – helped by the whole thing tipping sideways as I rolled over – scrambled to my feet and hurried to the phone. If this was Mr Leatherbarrow insisting that the tree stump in the field behind him was a Nazi paratrooper, I abandoned any thought of being anything other than nasty.

'Sackwater Central Police Station.'

'Mam come quickleh.' I recognised those northern tones immediately as one of two possibilities.

'Snipe?'

'Grinder-Snipe, mam,' the voice corrected. The twins were adamant that they did not want to lose half of their double-barrels. The average life being no more than three score years and ten, we were all determined that they would.

'Which one?'

'Constable Lysander Grinder-Snipe, mam.'

'What's happened?'

'It 'as not 'appened.' His voice was high with excitement. 'It *is* 'appening.'

I glanced at the station clock. It was ten to three. 'What is?'

'May'em, mam, murder and may'em in the 'Ouse of 'Orrors.'

60

THE HOUSE OF HORRORS

The House of Horrors stood on Jacob's Point, the highest part of Sackwater, eighty yards from the cliffs. It had been over a hundred yards until the storm of 1929 finished the work of years of erosion, tearing an undermined chunk of Suffolk off into the North Sea. A winding footpath had been carved up from Cliff Road and given the suitably spooky name of Spectre Lane.

According to the regulations I should have told Sandy I couldn't go out after dark, but there wasn't a rulebook written that would have kept me inside that night.

The path was too steep and gravelled for me to pedal up and it was illegal to leave a bike unattended in case Heinrich Himmler parachuted in without enough money for his bus fare, so I dismounted and pushed my bike with some difficulty by the stem of the handlebars.

An eight-year-old Betty Church had chickened out of going in. She had sat on the grass trying to eat a toffee apple with her little fingers in her ears to block out the shrieks of the girls while Pooky went inside with her young man – a hay-boy from Great Medding – with Pooky's dishevelled, breathless state on exiting twenty minutes later confirming my fears that it was a place where terrible things happened to anyone foolhardy enough to enter. By the time I wasn't so scared, I was too old not to have felt silly, so I had never been inside.

The House of Horrors had been built by Erasmus Calendar, an Edwardian entrepreneur who had intended to build a whole village of gruesome *attractions* from the Red Barn to Bluebeard's Castle; but, after finding his wife having an all-too-corporeal relationship with one of his hired ghosts, he slew them both with a handy executioner's axe, then hanged himself on the gallows conveniently constructed in the same room. This turned out to be an exceedingly shrewd move, for business – sluggish up to that point – boomed. There is nothing like a real murder to pull in the crowds, so his grieving son did not try too hard to discourage rumours that the house was genuinely haunted now, even putting about a story that a young man who had sneaked in to spend the night there for a bet was found, white-haired and raving mad, the next morning, only to rush off and plunge over the cliff, joining the other ghosts, who were doubtless delighted to have someone who could make up a four at bridge.

In time, though, interest palled. The Chamber of Horrors in good old Anglethorpe had the mummified hands of Justin 'Jack' Waldorf the Nursery Rhyme Killer and the pail of water in which he drowned Jill Vinegar.

Arriving at the top, breathing harder than Pooky had, with the house silhouetted in a full moon, I could see why the House of Horrors had kept its reputation. It stuck, towering, up into the night, all dark turrets, blocked-out arched windows, tall chimneys tilting at odd angles and – incongruously, I thought – crenellations with gargoyles made of ghouls' faces. If there ever had been such a thing as the Suffolk Vampire this might have been where he had his lair.

The House of Horrors was built of wood painted to look like brick, though the corrosive salt air had rather spoiled the effect because nailed planks were clearly visible in places and the sign over the door now read:

USE OF HORROR

At the top the path widened to encircle the house. A gibbet stood to the left, the disintegrating corpse in its cage disintegrating even more than it was supposed to. A pirate swung from a beam to the right, rather forlorn since children had stolen his hook. I could probably have done with that myself. A woman in a long dress was about to be beheaded by a masked and muscular man in a sleeveless jerkin and looking commendably calm about it. A man with a ruff had just been given the treatment, his concrete head looking distinctly indignant at being held aloft by his nemesis. He was minus a nose and chin, as if the executioner had taken a few wild practice swings before finding the neck.

Since I was last there two more figures had been added, swaying wildly in the gusting east wind, but these ones were waving their arms and rushing towards me.

'Ohhh, mam, thank goodness,' Sandy gasped like he had been struggling up a steep incline with a Raleigh Ladies' Popular No. 27.

'Ohhh, mam, thank 'eavens.' Algy could not have spluttered more if he had just been rescued from the foaming ocean crashing a hundred feet below, smashing the rocks into more shingle to drag up and down the beaches.

'Right,' I puffed, because I had been doing all that Raleigh Ladies' Popular stuff. 'What's all this about?'

'Ohhh mam, it were,' they said in unison before daringly going their separate ways with Sandy's 'orrible and Algy's terrible.

'What was?' The wind was being naughtier than Pooky's hay-boy, trying to lift my skirt and peek underneath. I slapped it away and held the front down.

'Screamin'.' Sandy mimed it with his mouth stretched wider than the man with a Slazenger in his tonsils had managed.

'And devilish lafter.' Algy threw his arms down and out like a pole-carrying tightrope walker almost slipping into the Niagara Falls. 'Like this.' He took a deep breath. 'Hahahahahahahaha.'

He sounded more like an asthmatic pug than the Lord of the Flies.

'No, Algernon.' Sandy put a delicate hand on his brother's sleeve. 'It were more like…' Big breath. 'Hahahahahahahaha,' exactly like his twin.

'Lysander, you are right, as always.' Algy bowed his head stiffly.

'How long did these screams and laughs go on for?' I propped my bike against Anne Boleyn's or Mary Queen of Scots' or Lady Jane Grey's block.

'Oh for ever,' the twins chorused.

'Don't be silly.' I tucked my skirt in and held it between my knees. 'Even Dr Goebbels's speeches have a beginning and an end.' I stretched my pinned sleeve down off my stump and tried to pretend my arm didn't feel as sore as it kept telling me it did.

'We 'eard it when we was on the cliff path.' Sandy waved elegantly towards the track.

'We did.' Algy put his hands on his hips.

'What were you doing up here anyway?' My stump felt damp but I didn't want to look in front of the men.

'Oh, we often come this way,' Sandy told me.

'The sea air is so invigorating.' Algy inhaled appreciatively.

'And the stars,' Sandy enthused.

'Oh the stars, the stars, the luvleh stars,' Algy rhapsodised.

'But it's not part of your beat.' I strode to the iron-studded massive front door with a normal-sized door inset into the left-hand leaf. Both were locked.

'Rules and Regulations state that an officer may modify 'is route at 'is discretion should circumstances require 'im to do so,' Sandy quoted, some of his words lost in a sudden gust of wind, and I was about to follow that up when we were interrupted by a scream.

I jumped. 'What the…'

It was a woman, I was almost sure of that, and she sounded absolutely terrified.

Police officers do not, unless one is rescuing the other from drowning, clutch each other. They just don't. Sandy and Algy did. They embraced like long-separated lovers. 'That's it,' they screeched but even they could not compete with the long, piercing shriek. It came from inside the house and filled the air, flying out over the cliffs and over the waves and bouncing around the bay.

'Pull yourselves together,' I scolded.

'Ohhh but we can't,' Sandy trembled and, before his twin could corroborate that, there came the laugh. It was even louder than the scream, wild and demonic, pausing only to let the scream begin again.

'Let go of each other this instant,' I commanded and the noises stopped.

Algy shook. 'Ohhh but—'

'Now!' I shouted and they were just disentangling themselves when there was another gust of wind and the screaming started again.

'Ohhhh there's a maniac in there,' Sandy quivered.

'Cue the laugh.' I clicked my fingers and it started again.

'Oh 'eck.' Algy looked about for an escape route, which didn't take much planning – a run in any direction would have done it, though over the cliff might have been a bit risky.

'Pause laugh for scream,' I shouted over the racket and to their astonishment it was done. 'Listen,' I instructed. 'It only happens when there's a gust of wind from the north. It must be setting something off.'

'A recording,' Sandy deduced.

'It does sound the same every time,' Algy realised.

'And if you listen next time, you'll hear a click in the second scream where it's scratched.'

Sandy giggled. 'Oh silly uz.' He punched his brother playfully on the arm.

'Ow,' said Algy, rubbing it. 'You know that's my sore arm since I 'ad that injection.'

'But that were fourteen year ago.' Sandy joined in the rubbing. 'Oh mam, what a couple of twits you must think we are.'

'If I had any doubts about your fitness to wear those uniforms, you have both confirmed them tonight,' I said severely.

'Oh thank you so much, mam,' Sandy burst out.

'No. I—'

'For a moment I thought you was going to give us the sack.' Algy sagged in relief.

'I need to see you both in my office in the morning,' I told them with a heavy heart. They were nice young men, I was sure, but there was a bit more to the work of a copper than being a sweetheart.

'Oh that's luvleh.' Sandy almost did a Dodo skip.

'Yes, thank you, mam.' Algy actually did one. 'We've never been invited into an inspector's office except—'

'—to be told off,' Sandy completed the sentence. 'Oh well, I suppose we should get back on our proper beat.'

'Except,' I told them, 'that, every time the noises start, a light shows from upstairs.'

'Surely not?' Sandy said in surprise. 'We would 'ave noticed.'

Algy nodded vigorously. 'We are trained to notice things – like 'ow you, mam, hold yer fork in yer right 'and.'

The wind was blowing across from Anglethorpe again. Scream, laugh, scream complete with click – and all the time a flicker of light from the seaward side.

'We'll have the coastguard and the ARP accusing us of signalling to enemy submarines.'

'Oh but that would be so unfair,' Sandy protested.

'A travesty of justice,' Algy joined in.

'We are completely innocent,' Sandy said, with his brother repeating every word as he spoke, in a weird echo effect.

'Is there any other way into the house?' I asked and they looked at me blankly. 'Is the back door locked?'

'Oh we 'aven't been all round,' Sandy told me.

'You two go round clockwise. I'll go the opposite way—'

'Anticlockwise, mam,' Algy told me helpfully.

'And we will meet round the back,' I continued. 'Look for any other doors or windows it might be possible to open.' I set off, glancing back when I reached the corner. 'Go on then.'

The Grinder-Snipes looked at each other dubiously.

'It's ever so spookeh,' they synchronised.

'Constable Chivers has got more guts than the two of you put together,' I goaded and they gaped like beached codfish.

'Oh that's wounding,' Sandy pouted.

'You've 'urt uz feelings,' Algy sulked.

'If you do not buckle down and start doing your duty right now—' but I didn't need to finish my threat – which was just as well since I hadn't decided what it was – because they scampered off in a very unpolicemanlike way but at least in the right direction.

I felt the wind change – not through some great meteorological skill but by the fact that while it had been cheekily tugging at the side of my skirt, now it made a sudden grab for it as I rounded the corner. I thought about shouting a warning but they were big boys and it was about time somebody treated them that way. The scream, expected though it was, still startled me. It was louder now and shriller and I didn't remember anything like that from when I was waiting for Pooky all that time ago.

A flickering beam of light was coming through the side of the building.

The house was square and huge, maybe forty feet along each side. I clicked on my torch briefly and spotted Maria Marten lying on her back ten feet away, trying to fend off the knife of her lover William Corder. This must have been intended to go in the replica of the Red Barn where the real murder took place. Twenty thousand people watched Corder being hanged in Bury St Edmunds and thousands queued to view his partially dissected body. I wondered who the real brutes were in this sordid case. At least it took my mind off wondering why I was stumbling round a failed fairground attraction listening to silly sound effects in the middle of the night.

The light was just above me now and I saw that it came from a gap between the boards. One of them had swung sideways on a rusty nail. If I could push that loose plank back in, maybe I could block the light out and get the owner – whoever that was – to sort it out in the morning. I grasped the board and twisted it. The nail snapped and a section of wall about two feet wide and three high came away in my hand. I dropped it to the ground. The screams started up again and, of course, the light came flooding out now. I stood with my back to it to plug the gap.

'Constables,' I yelled above a Vincent Price cackle.

'Was that Old Stumpy calling, Lysander?'

'I do believe it was, Algernon.'

The laugh stopped and I heard the click louder this time.

'Yes mam?' the Grinder-Snipe chorus chorused.

'Come here at once.'

'Yes mam.'

I heard crunching on the gravel and two figures appeared, stopped and grabbed each other's arms.

'Oh Lysander, 'e's murdering her.'

'No, it's—' I tried to explain about Maria Marten but Sandy was yelling, 'Not if I have anything tuh do with it, Algernon,' and hurtling at William Corder, going low into a rugby tackle that would have sent Mr Corder flying if he hadn't been made of concrete.

There was a sickening thud. 'Ohhhh,' Sandy wailed. 'I've gone and fractured me pelvis.' He rubbed his shoulder.

'Do you need a cuddle, Lysander?'

'I need an ambulance, Algernon.'

'Oh for Pete's sake just come here,' I snapped. 'You pair of buffoons.'

It was a stupid thing to have done but I could not help but feel some pride and gratitude that Sandy hadn't hesitated to tackle what he believed to be an armed man in order to save my life. Sandy's moment of heroism was over though and he was massaging himself and mewling like a kitten as they came up to me.

'Salute me with your left arm,' I commanded and they both obeyed.

'Is that a permanent instruction, mam?' Sandy asked.

'No, it was to check that your collarbone wasn't broken and it isn't.'

'But why are you backed against the wall, mam?' Algy eyed me uncertainly.

'It's because she's frightened,' Sandy explained.

'No I—'

''Oo wouldn't be?'

'Our old dad wouldn't.'

''E might be a bit,' Algy theorised, 'if—'

'It's because this board has snapped off and I'm blocking the light.' I butted it. 'While it's still quiet in there, I'm going inside to see if I can turn the electricity off. You, Sandy, will take my place in case it comes on again.'

'But won't that be dangerous, mam?' Algy looked anxiously at his brother. ''E could get attacked from be'ind.'

'No he couldn't,' I insisted. 'Because you are coming in with me, Constable Algernon Grinder-Snipe.' I couldn't see if Algy blanched but I think it was a fairly safe bet that he did. 'I will need to hold my torch in there. How many hands do you think that leaves me to fiddle with any switches or fuses?'

'Ooh I know the answer to that one.' Sandy raised his arm to attract the teacher's attention.

'She was asking me,' Algy insisted in a rare instance of sibling rivalry and his arm shot up too. 'None, Miss— mam.'

'And,' I continued, 'if you come with me, how many hands will be available then? You can both take a stab at that one.'

'Two,' they cried in delight at their joint cleverness.

'Go jointly to the top of the class,' I murmured. 'Right. Let's get inside.'

61

THE HUMILITY OF HEROES

stepped away from the hole. It was smaller than I thought and I had to squeeze through, right hand first with my torch on, but I managed without too much loss of dignity except for laddering both stockings. I had a small allowance for those, granted by men who thought that nylons could last as long as a pair of trousers did for them.

'Damn it.' I found myself in a mock-up of a bedroom and it took a moment to realise that the couple lying on top of the eiderdown represented Ressel and Fosalanda Phidgeton, who had been found with their skull caps sawn off and then replaced, their brains having been removed and swapped over. They were killed by their son Fossellum, who, exhausted by their constant bickering, thought it would help them see things from each other's point of view. To the best of my knowledge he was still in Broadmoor Hospital, where he was writing an authoritative atlas of cerebral anatomy. His manikin had a moth-eaten wig and wielded a saw he could have used to fell a medium-sized oak tree.

Algy, for his own private reasons, had decided to scramble through feet first and was waving them in the air like a capsized beetle, unable to find the ground. I took a leg to guide it down and he squeaked.

'It's me,' I said and left him to it. 'Excuse me.' I stepped over the corpse of a Red Indian sprawled on the floor in a tattered ostrich-feather headdress. He must have been dumped from another display. I didn't recall Sitting Bull having a role in Fossellum's deranged deeds.

'Push please, Lysander.'

'I am pushing, my dear Algernon.'

The next room flowed straight off the one I was in, the lathes having been ripped from the partition wall leaving the studwork frame. This was probably from when a small group of local businessmen had made a half-hearted attempt at renovation. They had done nothing to get rid of the foul smell and I wondered if rats had crawled under the floorboards to die, as I was beginning to think they must have in Felicity House.

Here was an execution chamber – more blocks with King Charles I and Sir Walter Raleigh awaiting decapitation with dignity and axes. To the left was a guillotine, Marie Antoinette waiting saint-like for her turn. To the right was a scaffold, the feet of a woman swaying in the shadows. The wind gusted through the enlarged gap and there was a click, a light went on and the screaming started again. That was getting annoying now. It was then I saw that one foot of the hanging woman was nudging a lever that must have operated everything. I glanced up at her and stepped backwards, tripping over a basket of heads and sprawling on my back, cracking my head on the lower edge of the guillotine. The frame shuddered and the headlock of the stocks fell, pinning me by the neck face upwards. The blade above me juddered and *I only knew the blade was coming towards me and I was trying to shout, No!*

'No!' I yelled and somebody else was yelling too, flinging himself on top of me and saying, 'Ohhh bluddy 'ell that 'urt.' And Algy was climbing off me and rubbing his back as the demonic laughter died away. 'Are you oreet, mam?'

I suspected he had bruised my ribs but it seemed churlish to mention it.

'Yes, thank you, Algernon.' I got up with as much dignity as I could muster, which was almost none at all.

The blade, when I looked at it, was blunt but it was heavy and would almost certainly have killed me. Algy couldn't have known it wasn't razor sharp and yet he had unhesitatingly followed his brother's example.

Algy was rebuttoning his collar, which had come open. 'That were ever so brave of meh, weren't it, mam?' If he had glowed any more, Algy would have been in breach of blackout regulations.

'Yes it was,' I agreed.

'But I don't think we'll tell Sandy or anyone else,' he decided. 'It would make you luke foolish and you are the least foolish person I know.'

My skirt had revolved forty-five degrees. 'Thank you, Algy.' I unrevolved it.

'Besides.' He polished his shoes on the backs of his trousers. 'It's the first time I've ever been brave and 'eroes don't boast.' He tried to strike a manly pose but looked more like he had put his spine out. 'But if you could maybe drop an 'int to Sandy that—' Algy looked up at the hanging manikin. He was blocking my view and I was just about to assure Algy that I would tell Sandy his twin had been courageous when my constable let out a squeak, staggered sideways and fell in a faint over the basket of heads.

I thought I had been mistaken at first glance but, along with the pretty, flowery skirt, the two-tone blue shoes were enough to give me my suspicions... and it was the missing tooth that seemed to confirm them. The face was too alive with maggots, however, for me to be absolutely sure that this was the body of Millicent Smith.

62

MAGGOTS AND THE FINAL SLEEP

Dawn was rising as Tubby Gretham arrived and it would have been a lovely fresh morning if it wasn't for the job he had to do.

I had unbolted the back door from the inside so at least the doctor didn't have to try to enter through the hole in the wall. A camel would have had better luck with a needle.

'Assuming she was alive when the noose went round her neck and he or they didn't just hang her corpse, it has to be murder,' I said. 'Her hands are tied behind her back and her ankles strapped, so she couldn't have removed the safety bolt and pulled the lever herself.'

'Well, the quality of murder has certainly gone up since you came back,' he said drily. 'If I were a detective you would be high on my list of suspects.'

'I might well bring myself in for questioning,' I agreed as we stood viewing Millicent's body still hanging on the scaffold. 'Can you tell how she died yet?'

'No.' Tubby climbed the steps and peered closer. He didn't seem to mind the smell but a devotion to pipe-smoking had probably taken the edge off it.

I would have appreciated a breath of fresh air but I started to follow him. The light seeping through the back door and the hole in the wall was stronger now and I could use my torch to improve it without fear of breaking the blackout.

Liquids of putrefaction had trickled down what I felt certain were Millicent Smith's legs and pooled in a greasy stain on the floorboards beneath. The backs of her shoes were scuffed and, on closer examination, ripped.

'Been dead a good few weeks,' Tubby commented. 'Read an interesting paper by Dr Simpson – heard of him?'

'The pathologist? Yes, he helped me with a case.'

Tubby hmphed in a mix of esteem and envy. 'You seem to have mixed with all the greats.'

It was Keith Simpson who had confirmed my suspicion that Molly Chatterton had been sliced into the sandwiches being sold to football fans at White Hart Lane.

'What was the article about?'

'Rates of decay in different conditions.' Tubby strolled around the trapdoor. 'He's made a study of the life cycle of the blowfly. I shall reread it and maybe drop him a line.'

He got some forceps out of his battered old leather medical bag and picked a fat writhing worm-like creature out of Millicent's gaping mouth.

'You could give him a ring,' I suggested. 'I've still got his number at Guy's.'

'Oh I couldn't do that.' Tubby was shocked. 'He's *famous*.'

I poked my head between two cross-beams supporting the platform, praying that no maggots were going to drop and nothing was going to drip on me. The structure was so roughly made I found it difficult to believe that it really was, as the placard proclaimed:

THE ACTUAL GALLOWS WHERE
DR CRIPPEN MET HIS END

Also Pentonville Prison was not in the habit of selling the furniture of execution to showmen.

'Seen something interesting?' He peered over the railing.

'Pass me those forceps,' I growled. 'No, the longer ones.'

'Ever heard of *please*?' Tubby grumped. 'Oh I see – that was supposed to be me.'

He handed them down to my waiting hand and I stretched to the back of the scaffold. There was something hanging on a nail.

'Gotcha.' I pulled out from under there, trying but failing not to retch. March Middleton recommended drops of camphor held over the nose in a handkerchief for these occasions but I had not expected, when I got that silly phone call, to be dealing with a rotting cadaver.

'What is it?' Tubby had put his horn-rimmed glasses on and they definitely did not suit him.

'A scrap of blue leather.' I held it up. 'And I will bet a pound to a farthing it will fit the rip in the back of her shoe.'

'So she was kicking her legs,' Tubby deduced, 'and very much alive and conscious when they strung her up.'

'She must have been strangled.' I pictured poor Millicent, dragged terrified up those steps, trussed on that trapdoor without even the mercy of a hood, watching them stepping back and pulling the lever, the jolt of pain that failed to break her neck, choking and writhing until she eventually passed into her final sleep.

63

THE LOST 'T'S OF SUFFOLK

went outside.

'Are you all right?' Tubby came up behind me.

'How can you be so unfeeling? I don't mean callous. I mean… matter-of-fact?' I exclaimed in bafflement. The Dr Gretham I knew was a kind and sensitive man.

'I've seen what people do to people and I've seen worse.' He took a deep breath and I saw that he was very far from tranquil. 'I'm sure you have too.' A muscle was ticing in his right cheek. 'When men are coming to you, mutilated, screaming in pain and terror, looking for you to save them when you know they have seconds to live, you learn to mask it.' He took off his glasses and pinched the bridge of his nose.

Greta had told me once that he came back from the Great War a changed man, that he cried out in his sleep but would never talk about it.

'I'm sorry.' I touched his arm.

'You have to do the same.' He stared out to the heaving, tossing sea. 'With your men. You can't cry like you did when…' His voice trailed away and at first I thought he was being tactful, but then I realised his attention was elsewhere.

'What is it?' I looked at him.

'Just a thought.' Tubby scratched his ear. 'If she was kicking like that, why didn't she knock the gramophone over?'

'I've met Albert Pierrepoint, the hangman, a couple of times,' I told Tubby Gretham and he sighed enviously. 'And he told me how they soak the rope and hang weights on it the night before an execution otherwise it's too elastic. I don't suppose the killers bothered doing that.'

'So it would have stretched with her weight until her feet were close to the machine and a strong sea wind set her swinging against it,' he realised.

Rivers was labouring up the path as if he were the first man to scale Everest.

'Gorr,' he gasped as he approached. 'My back and me dint wan' ta do that again in a hurry.'

'That's a shame,' I commiserated. 'Because you're both going to have to.'

'Wha'?'

One day I shall start a search for all the lost 't's of Suffolk. There must be countless millions of them lying rusting in the countryside when they could be collected for the war effort.

'Go to Hempson's the undertakers on Cardigan Street and tell them we want a standard pine coffin and a hearse to take a body to the morgue,' I instructed.

'Wha'?'

'Go to the *Gazette* office on Straight Street,' I continued, 'and ask Mr Gregson if he is willing to take some photos that he can never publish and, if so, can he come here immediately.'

'Bu'—'

'Now.' I pointed down the hill like that painting by Millais of a man telling two unhappy boys to Go West.

'Gorr.' Rivers, seeming to have exhausted his vocabulary for the time being, groaned, turned round. 'Oh,' he remembered, 'tha' Dozy Dodo rang in. She say to tell you she do be off sick with her poorly-sorely ankle.' And, with those glad tidings, Rivers set off back down Spectre Lane, which didn't look remotely spectral in the daylight. Even the House of Horrors looked like what it was – a shabby timber shed in need of demolition. It was only the knowledge of what was inside that appalled me now.

'I don't know how you do it,' Tubby snorted. 'And those twins of yours, with all due respect, they're a couple of...' He hesitated to insult my men to my face.

'Charlies,' I filled the pause and he half-smiled. I had sent the Grinder-Snipes home. If they were to do the night shift again they would need some sleep. 'I don't know what to do about them,' I confessed.

'Can you afford to lose them?' Tubby brought out his pipe – an old briar, already primed with shag.

'I'm not sure I can afford to keep them.'

'As bad as that?' He brought out a box of Swan Vestas.

'Worse than Constable Chivers.'

Tubby laughed. 'At least she had her wits about her when that seed merchant got stabbed at the station.'

'I suppose so.' I fell silent as the image replayed in my head – Ardom Dapper struggling as Dodo clutched him by the throat.

Tubby struck a match, cradling the flames in his hands, as only an experienced pipe smoker can, against the gusts whipping over the cliffs.

64

FRENCH MANICURES AND THE FAMOUS GRASSHOPPER

Pooky – or Wilson as she was now – came to the door of Treetops House.

'I'll tell her you're here.' She made to close it but I stuck a foot in.

'It is an offence to impede the police in the execution of their duty,' I warned, suddenly aware that I was paraphrasing Dodo without mentioning the war or capital punishment.

Pooky's eyes narrowed like they did when she was deciding whether to shop me for breaking that urn in Felicity House and decided that she would, ignoring my pleas for her to back up my story of a goat rushing in and how my parents should thank me for saving the fluted white pedestal. 'Wait there,' she said, stomping away without bothering to tell me she would solicit any presences.

I pushed the door open to watch Pooky/Wilson clump through the whiteness in her nice claret dress and the apron and wondered how she managed to keep it all so immaculate. Even in her heyday my parents' hall never looked anything better than not-too-bad. Pooky went past the sitting-room door this time and through the next one on the right.

There were low voices and she returned. 'You are to come straight through.' So – like every good girl should – I wiped my feet thoroughly before following.

Lavender Wicks reclined on a pink-cushioned high-backed

sofa in a pink-walled room with pink carpet and curtains. She wore a black dress, so skimpy that no one could possibly have accused her of wasting material.

Lavender was leafing through a magazine. *No knitting for victory today then.*

'Inspector Church.' She held out her long elegant hands with pink-bodied, white-tipped French-manicured fingernails that had not seen a day's housework in many a year. 'When your sergeant rang, I didn't expect you to bring my bag in person.'

Apart from an aluminium and glass table in front of her and another against the wall, there was no other furniture in the room.

'I wanted to see you—' I began.

'Oh how sweet,' Lavender Wicks cooed. 'Do take a seat. I thought we might be cosier in my snug.' She curled her legs up to make room for me. But I don't get cosy with members of the public. I perched on the open end of the sofa, skirt demurely over my knees. If Lavender was trying to embarrass me, she would have to try harder than that. There was a faint bruise on her well-toned left calf.

'I wanted to see you,' I began again, 'to check that everything is there.' I held the black bag up. 'I take it this is yours.'

There was a large picture of Lavender above the fireplace. She was in a long fur coat and laughing in the way that women only do for photographers. Nobody except a dentist needs to see that many teeth.

'Goodness, it looks bulging, doesn't it?' She giggled.

'Not as bad as mine.' I had my bag in my lap.

Lavender Wicks smiled. She had a very nice smile, clean and straight. It might almost be called radiant but I didn't like it. It was like a lightbulb. She could turn it on and off at will, which is a useful trick but no less of a trick for all that.

'Yes but I expect you have handcuffs in yours.' She brushed

the battered black leather with her forefinger and I put it on the floor.

'Women officers don't carry them,' I told her, glancing at the framed photos on the tables, all of Lavender alone or with male stars I didn't recognise except for David Niven in a dinner jacket.

'Pity,' she purred. 'It would be quite an experience' – she swallowed – 'being manacled by a lady officer.'

'I'm sure somebody will be happy to handcuff you.' I pointed to her bag. 'Would you like to check the contents?'

Was that Charles Laughton on the set of *Mutiny on the Bounty*? I resisted the urge to look closer.

Lavender sat up, unclipped the gold clasp and rooted. She lifted out the chequebook Brigsy had told me about and leafed through it, the famous grasshopper on the top of a shield instantly recognisable as the Martins Bank symbol. 'No cheques missing. I've only used one.' She put it down on the table in front of us, followed by a slim leather-bound diary – after quickly flicking through it – a gold lighter, a silver scent bottle with a cut-glass stopper, a gold cigarette case engraved *LW* and a white lace handkerchief embroidered with her initials. Soon she had the table littered with treasures including a petite silver hip flask. She ran her fingers round the lining. 'It seems to be all there,' she announced and tossed the empty bag onto her pile. 'How curious.'

It was exceedingly curious but I wanted to know why Lavender Wicks thought it was. 'In what way?' I asked.

Lavender leaned towards me. 'If I stole a handbag—'

'What makes you think it was stolen?'

I thought the man she was arm in arm with might be Laurence Olivier. Whoever it was looked bored.

'Your sergeant told me it was found in a ladies' cloakroom,' she replied. 'If you found a handbag in a café you would hand

285

it to the cashier on the assumption that the owner would return for it.'

'Go on,' I encouraged her.

'But, if you had stolen the bag, you would take the cheques or...' she stretched forward for her diary to reveal two pound notes and one ten shilling folded inside it, 'the money. A driving licence is not much good to anyone, especially now we have identity cards.'

She tossed the diary back on the table and leaned back, closer to me this time.

'It is odd,' I agreed.

'Especially as the licence was found near the scene of a murder.' She said that last word as if it was delicious.

'Do you have any idea how it got there?'

Most members of the public think of murder as exciting and I daresay the murderer and the victim find the experience stimulating too. It varies in its degree of cruelty from a sudden unthinking blow in the heat of the moment – what the French sensibly class as a *crime passionnel* – to calculated sadism but, to a police officer, murder is grim. It is sordid and represents thousands of man-hours of work and – if I am honest about it – unless there are witnesses, a fingerprint or a confession, the chances of catching the killer are slim.

'Do you have any idea how it got there?' I asked.

'I've thought a lot about that.' Lavender patted her upper arms like you might a favourite dog. 'And the only explanation I can think of is that somebody took my bag just to get my licence – after all, they discarded everything else – then deliberately left the licence on the scene.' She rubbed her arms tenderly.

'Where did you have your bag in Corker's Coffee House?'

'It was careless of me, I know.' Lavender grasped her shoulders. 'But I've been going there for years. I just put it on the floor by my chair with a pile of shopping and I was sitting by the door, so I suppose anyone going past could have just picked it up and walked off with it.'

'Were you with anybody?'

'No.' Lavender lowered her hands into her lap. 'I can usually bump into someone I know but the café was heaving with RAF men and women. I think they had an outing from Hadling Heath.'

'So the waitresses are unlikely to remember their customers from that morning,' I surmised.

'Do you know what I think?' Lavender put her legs up again, her knees half an inch from my thighs. 'I think somebody with a grudge tried to frame me.'

'Do you have any idea why someone might do that?'

'I have no enemies that I know of' – Lavender Wicks shrugged – 'though many a girl would like to sink her claws into my husband. Thurston must have acquired a few. People think show business is glamorous but it's hard work and it's ruthless. Speak to anyone who does amateur dramatics and they will tell you of the petty jealousies that people have over who has got the most lines or the best costume. The film industry is the same a thousand times over. That's why I was so glad to get out of it.'

'You were in films?' Looking at my hostess afresh, I supposed I should not have been surprised. She was certainly pretty enough.

'Only for a while,' she told me. 'I worked under my studio name, Lavender Lalique.'

'Constable Chivers thought she might have seen you in something,' I recalled.

'Oh I doubt it.' Lavender chuckled. 'I was never a star like Thurston. In fact I only had my name on the bottom of the credits three times.' She laughed again softly. 'If truth be told, I hated it – hours of hanging about to speak two lines, one of which would be cut. Directors never noticed me but Thurston did. It was a whirlwind romance and we were married within six weeks. Perhaps you read about it in the *New Movie Magazine*.'

'I'm afraid not.' It was not a publication I subscribed to. 'Did anyone in particular bear a grudge against your husband?'

Lavender stretched lazily. 'George Raft was said to be furious that Thurston landed the lead in *I Fought the Mob* but then George got *Scarface*, which more than made up for that.'

'What brought you to Sackwater?' I wondered. 'We are not exactly convenient for anywhere.'

'Which is exactly why we chose it.' Lavender brushed a hair from her bosom. 'Nobody pesters us here. Most people don't even know who we are. No ghastly rounds of cocktail mornings or pointless parties, the only aim of which is to impress people whose only aim is to impress you.' She left her hand where it was. 'We still have a house in Chelsea but London is such a bore, especially with this phoney war dragging everyone down.'

How awful for you.

'How long have you been married?' I put a hand to my shirt. The way she had looked at me made me feel a button might be undone. It wasn't.

'Ten years next January.'

'But no children?'

'If you had a figure like mine would you destroy it with babies?' Lavender Wicks fluttered her eyelashes. 'But what am I saying? You do have a figure like mine.'

This was not the sort of conversation policewomen have with members of the public.

'Will your husband be home later today?'

'No. Why?' She yawned ostentatiously. 'Are you worried we might be disturbed? Wilson never comes in while I have… guests.'

'Perhaps you could get Mr Wicks to give me a call when he does come home.'

Lavender stretched languidly. 'I know what people think.'

I had a kitten called Cinders when I was little and she was very clever but she couldn't purr as nicely as Mrs Wicks.

'They think I married Thurston for his money – he is nearly twenty years older than me, after all – but I love my husband, Inspector Church. He is a generous man – he gave me all this. OK, I go to a lot of parties without him, but he is always working away and there is no point trying to keep me in a cage for I simply won't be kept. Thurston knows he can trust me. I never even look at other men and he has no problems with my having' – the smile switch clicked on and off so quickly I was worried she would fuse – 'girlfriends.' She tugged playfully at my sleeve.

'Please don't touch me, madam. I'm a police officer.'

'Madam? Oh I like that.' Lavender Wicks sidled up close. 'Does it hurt?'

More things hurt than she could imagine but she was not a woman I would choose to confide in.

'Yes.'

'Can I see it?'

'No.'

'Perhaps I could make you feel...' Lavender Wicks licked her lips, 'better.'

'I doubt it.'

'When all this is over why don't you visit me? You can come in uniform and perhaps you could borrow a truncheon.'

'I'm afraid I won't be doing that.'

'Afraid?'

'Just a turn of phrase, madam.'

'If you say so.' Lavender Wicks stroked her thigh, which was just as well. I wasn't going to stroke it for her.

*

'You were quick,' Pooky commented. 'Usually, when she uses the snug, her guests stay for hours. Stupid, I call it. All that furniture in the white sitting room and they have to squash next to her on that little sofa.'

'Does she have many guests?'

Pooky shrugged. 'Lots of Wrens recently. She likes women in uniform a lot. Very patriotic, she is.'

65

THE SACKWATER PIRATE

put out an order to bring in Freddy Smart's father, Crake, for questioning and, unusually, it was Rivers who tracked him down – or, rather, bumped into him. Rivers had nipped round the back of the Coach and Horses for a smoke – one of the many things officers are not supposed to do in uniform but do anyway – when Crake came out from an illegal out-of-hours drinking session and almost fell into his arms.

'Ain't an offence to buy a drink. It's an offence to sell it,' he told me and I could not be bothered to argue about that. We were in the interview room with Dodo Chivers in attendance, notebook at the ready and pencil poised.

'We have found Millicent Smith,' I declared and the flitting smirk he greeted that news with confirmed any faint doubts I may have had.

'Oh yeah?' Smart tipped his chair back. 'Where was she?'

'Why the past tense?' I leaned towards him.

Smart could have said he meant *Where was she when you found her?*' But he stumbled with 'I meant *is*' proving that, if ever a man did not deserve his surname, it was this one.

'Do you want to talk to her?' I asked.

'What?' He rallied his scattered thoughts. 'No.'

'Why not?'

Crake Smart tipped his chair forward again. 'Yeah all right then. Bring her in,' he agreed. 'But I read about the House of Horrors and I'll give good odds it's her.'

'You must have needed help,' I said.

Smart blinked. 'Prove it,' he challenged.

'You made one mistake,' I told him and his face ticced.

'Oh yeah?' He sat up straight.

'Killing her on my patch,' I told him and he relaxed.

'Is that it?'

Dodo stopped scribbling and said, 'It is enough to have you dancing on the end of a rope,' a little too piratically for my tastes but I couldn't argue with the sentiment behind it.

I stood up.

'I have never yet not got my man, Mr Smart,' I lied shamelessly. 'Especially when I already know who he is.'

Crake Smart's smirk was a great deal less convincing this time, I thought, as I bade him a fond farewell.

66

THE TENANT AND THE CRONE

was sitting at my desk, my eyes heavy and head drooping. We were always told that the Germans were obsessed by rules but this time we were going to out-regulation them on every front. There had been an explosion of orders, information and advice that I was expected to read through. When the men or members of the public asked what to do in an emergency, I could hardly say that I thought I had seen a memo and could they hang on while I looked it up.

One communication did grab my attention though. It was from the Aliens Department of the Home Office and concerned the Sternes. They were to be taken in without warning at our earliest opportunity in coordination with the army. It might take a while to organise that, I decided.

The office phones had been reconnected and mine was right beside my ear as I slumped over a memo about a conference in Ipswich I had to attend, complete with minutes of the last meeting. The bell burst into life and, if I hadn't been 100 per cent awake, I was now.

'Ohhh mam...'

'Algy?'

'Lysander, mam. Oh please come quick. There's screamin' and all sorts of a tuh-do. Ohhh it's reet 'orrid it is.'

I exhaled, then took a deep breath. 'Are you back at the House of Horrors?'

'Ohhh I wish we was,' Sandy replied with feeling. 'It's the Royal George 'Otel.'

I knew the Royal George by sight – a mock-Gothic pile on the promenade – and by reputation as somewhere that didn't care too much what its guests got up to, providing they paid their bills.

'Are you there now?'

'No, mam. They don't 'ave a telephone so I'm using the police box on Clayton Road.'

It would have been quicker to have come back to the station but the twins had a hopeless sense of direction. Their beat went along mainly parallel roads but they had still managed to get lost many times.

'What *exactly* is happening?' I asked firmly.

'A man is being murdered,' Sandy Grinder-Snipe shrieked so manically you might have thought that he was the man in question.

'Well, run back and put a stop to it.' The last time I read *Duties and Obligations of a Police Officer* this was one of the things we were supposed to do.

'But we can't gain access tuh the room.' Sandy was sounding more northern and even more girly with every word. 'Algernon is there and trying so very 'ard but 'e's wearying apace and growing exceedingly bothered and distressed.'

Oh dear God, what have I done to deserve this? I prayed silently. If it was that broken greengrocer's window, that was an accident but I would own up and pay for it.

'Calm down, Snipe,' I said, continuing to talk over his indignant *Grinder-Snipe, mam.* He was not quite hysterical enough to forget to take umbrage over that. 'How do you know somebody is being murdered?'

I could hear my constable taking a breath before reeling off at great speed, 'The man in the Blue Room were shouting and Mrs Andrews, the proprietress, knocked on the door but she couldn't

294

gerr in 'cause the door were locked on the inside and the noises continued, grunts and groans and panting and—'

'Get to the point, Snipe,' I butted in, sowing a row of tobacco strands.

'Grinder-Snipe. I'm just setting the scene, mam.'

'You're not writing a three-bogging-part novel. What is *happening*?' I licked the paper.

'Mrs Andrews called the police – that's me and Algy – and we went in and knocked and the noises were just disgusting.' He took a gasp. 'Oh it's all tooo tooo 'orrible. We didn't know what tuh do, mam, but we couldn't tell Mrs Andrews that so we whispered in each other's ears. Then Algernon suggested that I rang you. So I did.'

'Oh good grief.' My cigarette paper split. 'OK, I'll come and take a look. In the meantime, go back and help Algy,' I instructed his twin. 'And on the way, knock up Rivers. He's at...' I leafed through our address book. 'Sixteen Ash Street off Victoria Road – that's the side road opposite the Trocadero cinema – and tell him I don't care how much his back hurts, he is to take over your beat.'

Rivers was as close to useless as it's possible to get without being certifiably useless, I knew, but we had to have somebody on the street. Besides which, why should he lie snug in bed when I couldn't?

''E won't be very pleased tuh see me,' Sandy predicted anxiously.

'Neither shall I,' I warned him. 'Go.'

'Yes, mam.'

'Have you gone?'

'Not quite yet, mam.'

'Go now.'

'Yes—'

I put the receiver down.

Within a minute, I had my jacket, coat and helmet on, had

grabbed the jemmy – which nobody had turned up to claim yet – slung my gas mask over my shoulder and was out on the forecourt.

It was a drizzly night, the much-needed moon only a mean sliver between heavy splashes of grey.

My bicycle was just round the side, behind a low wall out of sight of anyone who might be tempted to borrow it. I heaved it over, stuck the jemmy under my belt and set off, pedalling as fast as I dared down Tenniel Road to Bishops Street, where I stopped outside number 4, a terraced property indistinguishable – apart from the number and the pillar-box red paintwork – from any other on that long straight road. I could only identify it for certain by a very quick flash of the torch.

Feeling a little guilty, I tapped on the door. There was no reply. I tapped harder and waited – nothing. I rapped and kept rapping until I saw some movement in the right of the two upstairs windows – the blackout curtain being removed and the sash window going up. An ancient crone stuck her head out, toothless as far as I could see without the benefit of my father's equipment, and wearing a cotton cap tied under her chin in a style Charlotte Brontë might have regarded as old-fashioned.

'Yes?' Her voice was so quavering it was a wonder she had managed to make the effort. I didn't know Sergeant Briggs lived with his mother – or was it his grandmother? I decided to play it safe.

'Mrs Briggs?'

She cupped her ear. 'You'll have to speak up, dear.'

'I need to speak to your son on police business.'

'What's the little beggar been up to now?' She pecked at the air with her hook nose.

'Nothing…' I paused in confusion. Had I got the wrong house? 'Frank Briggs, I mean.'

'I know what the bleedin' bleeder's name is,' she snapped.

'Wait there.' Her head disappeared but other heads appeared in other windows across the street. I waited. There was a bit of a scuffle, then two heads appeared – the crone again, holding a lad of about fourteen by the ear. 'What do you been up to now?'

'Nowt, Mum, honest,' the lad wailed. ''Part from smokin' and drinkin' and puttin' dog poo in Mrs Glitter's shoppin' basket oh and thah dead newt through that vicar's letter box.'

At least that last one was one case I could close.

'There's been a mistake,' I called up. 'I'm looking for Sergeant Frank Briggs.'

'What?' The crone was incredulous. 'Why didn't you say so?' Her head disappeared before I could explain why I hadn't said so and I heard two slaps. 'That's for the smoking and that's for the drinking and this…' There was a barrage of slaps Buddy Rich would have broken into a sweat to produce on his drums, 'is for the shit, you little shit.'

No slaps for the newt then?

Brigsy stuck a head out.

'I have to go to the Royal George,' I told him. 'So I need you to coordinate things.'

'Righto,' he agreed with a disconcerting lack of curiosity. He glanced behind himself, then back at me. 'Sorry about the confusion with my missus,' he told me confidentially, 'only we have separate bedrooms.' My mind raced with polite ways of saying I didn't blame him but came up with none before he explained, 'To stop me pestering her.'

I didn't even try to think of an answer to that one. 'I'll give you a ring as soon as I know anything.'

'But we don't have a phone, madam.'

'At the station.'

'I'll have to get dressed,' Brigsy protested because that was an insurmountable obstacle.

'Yes you will,' I agreed and, remounting my bike, pedalled away to High Road East, turning right along the promenade at the bottom.

It was still raining, lightly, but heavily enough for the sea breeze to blow it into my eyes, making me squint. It was then I discovered yet another reason God gave us two hands. I couldn't hold my collar to stop the water trickling down my neck.

The Royal George Hotel was not as grand as the Grand but more Gothic, a high-Victorian structure with proper towers and real turrets looking distinctly menacing in the moonlight. If there was such a thing as the Sackwater Vampire, I thought as I dismounted, *this* would be where he had his lair. The House of Horrors would have to look for another tenant.

67

THE INNOCENCE OF FELONS

Bantony stood under the portico with Nippy Walker, neither of whom had been included in my instructions.

'Why are you here?'

'Oy got woken too so Oy thought Oy'd come,' Bantony told me. 'Been lodging with Rivers since me landlady threw me out fer giving 'er daughter a bit of a seeing-to.'

'A bit of what?' Nippy Walker queried.

''Ow's-yow-father,' Bantony rephrased it.

'He's dead,' Nippy told him cheerily.

'Why are you here, Walker?' I demanded. 'Don't tell me you've been misbehaving as well?'

'Chance'd be a foyne thing.' Bantony smirked. 'Oy was passink 'is dump and I thought 'e might as well come too.' Bantony smirked again at Nippy's scowl. Nippy liked his sleep, as I had discovered many times on going into the back room.

'You told me she said I was to come,' Walker said indignantly.

'Yow must 'ave mis'eard me,' Bantony said with all the innocence of a felon caught climbing out of a window with a sack of swag.

'And in fourteen hours' time, when everyone is exhausted, who will man the station or walk the beat? You think Box and Chivers can run the town between them?' I demanded to blank looks. 'Chivers can't even walk without a stick.'

'Well...' Bantony began and I knew that whatever he was going to say would be useless.

'This is ridiculous,' I fumed. 'Almost an entire station called out to ask two hotel guests to have relations a bit more quietly.'

'They've got family with them?' Nippy scratched behind his helmet. 'Is that why they're so noisy?'

'Oh good grief.' I gritted my teeth and was just about to go into the hotel when the door burst open and Sandy Grinder-Snipe burst out.

This was two too many bursts. If there was one thing you didn't do in the war it was rip back curtains with the lights on. If there was another – and there was – it was fling a door wide open. In blackout conditions it was like turning on Blackpool Illuminations.

'Oh mam—' Sandy Snipe began.

'Turn that bloody light out,' I yelled, all at once the pride of the ARP, and somebody inside did and, in another all-at-once, we were back in an even blacker blackness.

'Oh mam—' Sandy Grinder-Snipe began again.

'Shut up,' I snapped, groping my way to where I judged the doorway was.

'Oooh, that tickles.' Sandy Grinder-Snipe giggled.

'Oh for…' Repeatable words failed me. I was only glad it wasn't Bantony I had fumbled. I recoiled to think what he would have made of that.

The door pulled outwards and there was a heavy curtain across it. I slid through it sideways so as not to let Hermann Göring see where I was, doubtless at the top of his list of intended targets.

Come friendly bombs and fall on Sackwater. Even if it didn't scan, it had a nice ring to it, I thought.

'Right,' I barked. 'I want everybody inside and I want them inside *now*.' A sar'major could not have driven his men over the top more effectively than that, for there was a stumbling, pushing stampede to obey me. 'Is everybody in?'

'Yes ma'am,' Bantony replied because, of course, he was everybody.

'Yes ma'am,' the others chorused.

I felt behind me, relieved to find I had grabbed the curtain this time and not part of a constable, and pulled it across. 'Turn the light on.' Somebody did. There was a dusty chandelier overhead with four bulbs fused, one missing and one remembering and doing what it was born to do. And, there with her hand on the switch on the wall, was a striking woman aged about fifty, I guessed, hair curled in a light blue rinse, a well-chiselled jaw and nose, her cheekbones just prominent enough to cast shadows that would have been the envy of the Marlene Dietrich I allegedly sounded like.

A man stood stiffly by as well, in his sixties and stubby in a faded red livery.

It was a square lobby, dark-oak panelled with a lighter-panelled reception desk straight ahead, a pigeon-holed structure and a board of keys on hooks behind it.

'Hello,' I said but that was all I said.

I expected to introduce myself. I didn't expect to be stopped by such a terrible scream.

68

SPIKES AND THE EXTINGUISHING OF HOPE

Everybody froze – you can't help it – but I like to think I thawed first.

'Was that—?' I was going to ask if that was the same noise they had heard before.

'The vampire!' Constable Lysander Grinder-Snipe ejaculated because it is the sworn duty of every serving police officer to terrify members of the public.

'What?' The woman gaped in horror.

'Upstairs?' I asked.

She nodded dumbly.

'Lead the way, Snipe,' I rapped.

'Grinder-Snipe,' he muttered.

'Lead the way.' *Damn you*, I added under my breath.

'Up there?' Sandy looked about in the panic he had done his best to nurture.

I pushed him aside, racing up the cantilevered staircase on the left-hand side of the lobby, aware of heavy feet pounding the threadbare fleur-de-lis carpet behind me. At the top was a galleried landing.

'To the left,' the woman called – more useful and cool-headed than the 50 per cent of my double-barrelled twins had been so far. 'There's a light switch just inside the arch on your left.' I turned through the open archway, felt a dolly switch and flicked it down to find myself at the end of the corridor going off to my right.

From down the corridor came a whimper. Halfway along, in the middle of the floor, down on his haunches, was Algy.

I rushed up. 'Are you injured?' But he was busy trying to curl into a ball, his head between his knees clamping his hands over his ears to block out another louder, longer, higher scream.

'Ohhh poooor Algernon.' Sandy hurried up. ''E's always bin 'ighly strung.'

'Stand up.' I prodded Algy with my foot but my attention was on room 14. I tried the handle. It turned but the door was locked. I knelt, peered through the keyhole and slipped out a hairgrip. The key was still in but it was turned too far for me to wiggle it out.

At least the screaming had stopped.

'Get the porter,' I yelled at Bantony. Sandy was down by his brother, giving him a cuddle. 'Stand up, the pair of you,' I commanded. 'You are officers of the law.'

I hammered on the top right of the four bevelled panels and called out, 'Police. Open up.'

'I tried that.' Sandy struggled up and held out his hand to help his twin to his feet.

'Be quiet. I'm trying to listen.' I put my ear to the door and thought I heard rustling.

'Open the door or we shall break it down!' I bellowed. I have quite a strong voice. Nobody had trouble hearing me in school plays, except Mrs Whetbarrow when Johnny Harrison had poured melted candle wax into her ear trumpet for a joke.

'I tried that' – Algy rubbed his shoulder – 'but it's ever so strong. Solid mahogany, George said.'

'Who's George?' I asked automatically, giving the door an experimental kick. It didn't even rattle.

'I am, Inspector,' the porter declared as he came through the arch.

'What does this room overlook?' I asked.

'The back garden,' he told me, 'but you can't get in there. The side gate is padlocked with spikes over the top and all the ground-floor windows are barred. Mrs Gillian Andrews on reception is the owner, with Mr Francis Andrews, but he has gone on holiday with the keys to the back door and gate since he found chambermaids were inviting gentlemen callers in.' His voice dropped so low I could only just make out, 'I think he suspected Mrs A was doing the same thing.'

'Wouldn't mind a bit of that myself,' Bantony murmured because this was exactly the time for barrack room talk.

'Out of your league, son,' George told him because, apparently, it was exactly that time.

The Grinder-Snipes were making baby noises to each other.

'Shut up,' I snapped, 'the pair of you.'

Algy shushed Sandy and Sandy shushed Algy and they cut the noise to a few low hisses.

I put my ear to the door again and heard some shuffling. 'How many people in there?' I asked the porter.

'A couple checked in,' he told me, 'Mr and Mrs Herring.'

'Is there a fire escape?'

'No, ma'am.'

'Or a ledge someone could get along from the next room?'

'I'm afeared not.'

A faint hope. 'It isn't an interconnecting room, is it?'

'No, ma'am.' Faint hope extinguished.

'How many other guests in the hotel?'

'None, ma'am, and no staff live in but for me and Mrs A.'

I unsheathed the jemmy from my belt. 'Anyone know how to use this?'

'Oy certainly do.' Bantony eyed the whimpering twins in disgust.

I slapped the jemmy into his hand – perhaps a bit too hard,

for he winced. 'Then use it.' Inspectors don't break doors down. They order it done.

Bantony took the jemmy in both hands and twisted his body round, ramming the flat blade in between door and post just above the lock. It stuck in deep. He leaned into the bar, put one foot on the opposite post and pushed, the muscles of his neck fanning out with the strain.

'Come on, yow bastard,' he grunted and was rewarded with a sharp cracking as the wood splintered away and the door hinged open a fraction.

There was a plaintive sob.

'Stand away from the door. We are coming in,' I warned and nodded to Bantony, who looked at me quizzically. 'Well, kick it, man.'

To give Bantony credit, he made a good run at it and managed a flying kick with both feet before landing on his side. 'Shit.' He rolled onto his back as the door crashed open. It hit against something hard, partially rebounding.

Somebody was choking and there was the sound of drumming feet and a sharp whispered, 'Die, bitch, die!', then the sound of a spade being plunged into earth – though I had a sickening sureness that it was not a spade nor was it earth – and a gurgled gasp.

There was a light on in the room. I put my head through the gap and saw a wall of wood. A wardrobe had been dragged behind the door.

'You twins,' I rapped. 'Put your shoulders to the door.' They looked at me and each other as if I had suggested they leaped into a vat of boiling pitch. 'Do it now, God damn you.'

As one they went to the door. 'Use your other shoulder, Algy,' Sandy advised, 'as that one is so sore.'

I could hear more scuffling.

The twins swapped sides and gave a little shove.

'Get that fucking door open, you mincing ninnies,' I screeched. This was no time to worry about hurting their feelings.

And, rather than pouting as I expected, the twins put their backs into the job now. They were not very hefty but they were tall and quite athletically built and, as they heaved with all their might, the wardrobe ground back, twisting away a foot or two until the door opened about halfway. 'It's jammed, mam,' Sandy said. They were so unusually purple now that Sidney Grice might have patented their colour.

'Stand back.' I brushed past them into the opening, ripping my jacket off, throwing it to the floor and pulling my chest in as much as I could, wedging myself, back to the wall, in the tight space they had managed to create.

A window slid and slammed but, though my head was facing forward, I could see nothing except the side of an unmade bed and an old iron fireplace to my right. I wriggled wildly. The lock was hanging loose and a bent screw caught on my shirt, digging into my waist.

'Let me.' I was aware of Bantony behind my left shoulder straining at the wardrobe.

'Hang on,' I said, trying to twist the lock away, but I couldn't. I took a fistful of shirt and yanked. There was a ripping noise and I heard a button bounce over the floorboards. 'OK but don't touch my arm.' Even in all the mayhem I was aware of it throbbing.

Bantony had his knee up against my hip and was pushing so hard that I let out an involuntary yelp but I had to get through and, with one final squeeze and pull from me and violent shove from him, I did, tumbling into the room to see the closed window and the disarrayed bed and the horror that was upon it.

'Bloody hell,' I breathed, for that is exactly what it was.

69

THE SLICING OF THE NIGHT

found myself in a small room – maybe fifteen feet square, some sort of big orange leaves on the wallpaper, putty-coloured fitted, frayed carpet, the wardrobe halfway across the doorway at an angle and, straight ahead, a double bed, bedding strewn about, soaked in blood, and on top of it all, the bloody bodies of a woman and a man.

I ran to the window and wrenched up the lower sash. It was slightly warped and a struggle to do one-handed but I got it fully open. It was just that every snag was wasting precious seconds. I stuck my head out. There was no natural light at all out there now. I rushed back to the door.

'Is she dead? Has the killer gone?' Bantony asked.

'They are both dead. Give me a torch.'

Another delay, then, 'Here, mam,' Sandy Grinder-Snipe said and a long-fingered elegant hand passed one through the gap. The lens had been largely painted out.

'A proper one,' I shouted. 'Look in my handbag.'

More shufflings until my torch appeared. I snatched it and dashed back to the window, clicking the switch as I went. My beam sliced through the night as I worked it to and fro. It was a small garden laid mainly to an unkempt lawn with flower beds along every border. The sides were walled in solid red brick with no visible breaks. In the back right-hand corner was a wooden octagon.

'Is the summer house kept locked?' I shouted.

'I don't know, mam,' Algy called back. 'One moment, I'll ask... No, Sandy doesn't know either.'

'Ask George, you halfwit,' I yelled.

'It is, Inspector,' George called back. 'And it's full of garden furniture so nobody could get inside it.'

I would swap this man for any one of my constables, I thought fleetingly.

'Is it possible to get behind it?'

'No, ma'am. It's right against the wall and the side gate is flush with the back of the hotel so there is no passage anyone could hide down either.'

Any two of them, I thought, training my beam from side to side, ploughing furrows in the dark. There was nobody there.

'Could anyone break back into the hotel on the ground floor?'

'All barred,' George assured me. 'So is the cellar.'

'What's behind the back wall?'

'Donkey Lane,' George shouted. 'It's an alley between Paget Street and Fallow Road.'

'Twins.' I ran the beam carefully around the back bed and thought I saw a broken rosebush. 'Go out to the front door. One of you turn left, the other right. Go down those two streets until you meet in the middle of Donkey Lane. If you see anyone – and I mean anyone at all – detain them. Check every back garden you can get into. See if there's anyone hiding. Look for any abandoned ladders. Have a good look at the back wall for signs someone climbed over it – scuffs, bits of ripped clothing, footprints if it's muddy out there – and don't trample over any. Once you've done that, come back here.'

'You'll know when you're at the back of this hotel because there's a metal plaque on the gate,' George told them, earning his sergeant's stripes already.

'What if the maniac is still out there?' Algy queried nervously.

'You will exercise your authority and arrest him,' I bellowed. 'Now go.'

'Oy can't get in.' Bantony was grunting and struggling with the door.

'Stay where you are,' I ordered. The last thing I needed was somebody coming in messing things up and distracting me. 'Are you still there, George?'

'Yes, Inspector.'

'My constable will give you his key for the police box. The phone will automatically put you through to Sackwater Central. Sergeant Briggs will answer. Tell him two people have been murdered and their killer is on the loose. Briggs is to gather every officer he can get hold of at the station and to inform the police at Anglethorpe and Felixstowe Police Stations. Got that?'

'Yes ma'am.'

I didn't get him to repeat it because I knew that he had.

It was time to give my attention to the bodies.

70

THE SLAUGHTER AND THE SORROW

The couple lay on their backs, the woman – young, petite, pretty if you could see past the long slashes in her face, peroxide-blonde if you ignored the blood soaking into her hair – was on the left near the window. Her nightdress had pulled down from the top and up from the bottom into a crude cummerbund. There must have been fifty knife wounds visible at a glance, including one just below her small left breast, gaping between her ribs. I touched her arm. It was still hot. Her head was turned towards her companion.

The man was naked with numerous bruises, weals and cuts all over him, particularly his face and upper arms, but most striking of all was the sight of his throat. It had two puncture wounds about an inch apart on the left-hand side. I turned the woman's head and found two similar injuries in her neck too. I drew a breath. It was becoming increasingly difficult not to believe in the Suffolk Vampire when I kept coming across his victims.

Both were spread-eagled, waxy-grey skins glistening with straw-coloured serum seeping around great gouts and clotted streams of blood. They had been tied with braided cord by the wrists and ankles to the brass bedstead. Both had soiled themselves.

The couple's mouths had been stuffed with what looked like their stockings. His was held in place by a blue tie with yellow diagonal stripes, knotted round the back of the head. From the depth the cords had cut into both the victims' flesh and the way the headboard was tipped forward it was apparent that they had struggled desperately during their ordeals. His arm was still hot too.

'Are yow all right, mam?' Bantony called anxiously.

'Yes. I'm looking for her handbag.'

Bantony got an arm through and gave me a wave like he had just spotted me at a party. 'Oy don't fink she'll be needink it.'

'No,' I agreed, 'but I do. There are more secrets in the average woman's handbag than in a filing cabinet in the vaults of the War Office.' I was gabbling, I knew, but I had to say something to break the silence of death. A brown leather strap curled from under the dressing table. 'Ah there it is.' I rooted through. She would have hated me doing that.

A heavy chest of drawers had been pushed behind the wardrobe. I grabbed one side and managed to rotate it away. 'Try the wardrobe now.'

Part of the problem, I discovered, was a rucked-up rug and I did my best to hold it straight with my foot as I pulled on the wardrobe while Bantony strained again, heaving it round far enough to force his way into the room.

He stopped. 'Probably best if Oy stay on guard, ma'am.'

'What?' Was the whole force going mad? If I had had any doubts they were about to be dispelled.

There were sounds of raised voices and feet trampling upstairs. I went to the doorway. Sandy and Algy were frogmarching a man along the corridor.

'You said to stop anyone we found,' they chorused, as proud as two cats bringing in pigeons.

'Ruddy maniacs.' Constable Rivers hobbled between them. 'Take months for my back to recover from this.'

*

I went downstairs. Bantony, being the one I distrusted least, had taken all the staff's and victims' details.

'Did you check their identity cards?' I asked the receptionist.

Gillian Andrews cleared her throat. 'Well, of course. Mr Grant Herring and Mrs Elizabeth Herring.' She turned the guestbook for me to read. 'See. I made a note of his number. She forgot hers but they were together so it didn't matter.'

'Yes it did and no she didn't.' I showed her the card I had found in the handbag. 'She was a Mrs Timothea Cutter.'

'Was?' The receptionist's jaw muscles tensed. 'What has happened?'

'They have both been murdered.'

Gillian Andrews sat down heavily. 'I thought it must be something like that.' She looked distinctly queasy. 'Have you caught the murderer?' She jumped nervously. 'Is he still in the hotel?'

'He got away through the window.'

'But it's on the second floor.'

'I am aware of that,' I snapped. 'But are you aware that, in barring every exit, you have broken enough fire regulations to get this place closed immediately and land you and your husband in court?'

'It's all his doing,' she protested, disloyally but probably – in view of what George had muttered – truthfully.

'If we could have got round the back it is possible we could have stopped the murders and caught the criminal but, because of your actions, two people died who might have been saved and their killer has escaped,' I reminded her, though she could hardly have forgotten.

'Oh dear God.' Gillian Andrews clamped a hand over her mouth and strained her head forward as if she was going to be sick. 'I didn't know. I didn't think.'

'The law is there for a reason,' I told her firmly. 'I shall not make trouble for you over this but I can't guarantee the courts will not.'

'I wasn't to know that would happen,' she cried.

'And do you know when there will be a fire and how guests can escape?' I demanded.

'Guests?' Gillian Andrews spread out her hands to indicate the vast hordes not milling around us. I took her point. This was the Royal George Hotel, Sackwater, after all, not the Ritz, Paris.

'From what George told me, I take it you have nobody else staying here.'

Gillian Andrews gestured to the book. 'Another man did come in but he went straight out again,' she told me. 'He said he had the wrong hotel.' She gritted her teeth. 'More likely he took one look and decided to go to the Grand. Wouldn't be the first time it's happened to us either.'

I looked at the sign over the passageway to the right of the desk:

NON-RESIDENTS WELCOME

'What about the bar?' I asked. 'Did that have any customers?'

Gillian Andrews made a piffing sound. 'Three,' she said. 'Mr Simms, the headmaster of St Joseph's School, and his wife, plus a woman.'

I hardly needed to ask from the way she expelled the last word. 'What kind of a woman?'

'The kind that hangs around hotel bars,' she replied. 'Stayed about an hour with a port and lemon, then left.'

'By herself?'

Gillian Andrews sniggered. 'I think Mrs Simms would have had something to say if she wasn't.'

'I'm glad you find humour in the situation,' I said sourly. 'I will need to speak to you and George another time,' I pressed on, ignoring her indignant gasp. 'In the meantime, you must write down everything that happened this evening. I don't care how trivial, irrelevant or embarrassing it may be.'

'Embarrassing?' She looked blank.

'If you had sex or went to the WC,' I said. 'And get George to do the same – in separate rooms with no conferring.' I watched her hand tremble as she picked up her pen. 'If I find even a hint that you have colluded with each other, I will see you prosecuted for perverting the course of justice.'

'I've learned my lesson,' she vowed and, looking straight into those troubled eyes, I believed that she probably had.

71

THE CREEPING OF NECROSIS

The constables stood behind the desk in a row, like naughty children.

'Right,' I began. 'We are going to get invaded by half the East Suffolk Constabulary and most of the British press today. A double murder and another vampire scare...' I paused. It was just the long night that had made me feel dizzy. Where was I? Oh yes. 'But before we go into details of how we are going to deal with the situation, there are serious problems within the station itself and last night proved that I cannot keep ignoring them.'

'Can't we do this separate?' Bantony pleaded.

'I am not going through this four times.' I marched up and down, inspecting them. 'What's wrong with you all?'

'Well, I've got a sore shoulder,' Algy told me.

'And I've got a chill in my stomach,' Sandy added, 'and a stubbed toe.'

'And I—' Bantony began, not to be left out.

'I mean as people,' I broke in before I was subjected to an encyclopaedia of symptoms. They looked blank. 'Are you all snivelling cowards?' I demanded.

'*We* are,' the twins chorused.

'That's why we became policemen,' Sandy confessed. 'We knew there was a good chance of a war coming.'

'And we was terrified of being called up,' Algy explained.

'It can still be arranged,' I threatened. 'And you, Constable Bank-Anthony – wanting to guard the door indeed.'

'Well, it works for Box.' Bantony jerked a thumb at his colleague.

'You rat.' Box clenched his massive fists.

'Unclench them,' I said. 'Explain yourself, Bank-Anthony.'

Bantony hung his head. 'Oy know Oy put it about that Oy was transferred because Oy'm a bit of a ladies' man.' He swallowed. 'And Oy am,' he added defiantly. 'But the real reason Oy left Dudley was...' He swallowed again. 'Oy don't like blood. Oy mean Oy really don't like it.' His Black Country was getting so thick I had trouble translating it.

'But you were all right at the railway station.'

'Oy didn't really look at 'im,' Bantony admitted. 'Oy just shot quick glances and then concentrated moy attention on yow well-turned ankles, begging yow pardon, ma'am.'

'Oh good grief.' I took a quick stroll around him clockwise.

'So why weren't you just made to resign?'

Bantony smirked. 'Isabella, the chief constable's daughter, took a bit of a shoyne to me. She said, if they sacked me she would strip off starkers on the town 'all steps.' He went a bit dreamy. 'Almost be worth getting sacked fer that.'

I perambulated around Box. 'And you?'

Box stared straight ahead over me. 'Well, I int bothered by any old drop of blood,' he said gamely. 'You could bring a bucket of it in here, you could, ma'am, and I wouldn't go swooning like a soppy Dudley girl – no offence, Bantony. It's bodies I can't tolerate – dead ones, I do mean – I'm not bothered by living ones.'

'So that's why you always stand outside.' I stopped to look in his big blank eyes. 'So why weren't you dismissed?'

'Don't like to boast, ma'am.'

'Try,' I urged.

Box blushed. 'Got the KPM,' he confessed.

'The what?' the twins queried.

'The King's Police Medal,' I explained, much impressed. At most 120 were issued every year throughout the whole country, empire and Commonwealth. 'What did you get it for, Constable Box?'

Box turned a brighter red. 'Got some children from a fire in Bury St Edmunds, I did, but it int much.' He coughed.

'I think it must have been,' I argued but it was obvious that Box didn't want to give any more details. 'So why did you get transferred?'

'New superintendent,' Box said. 'Orders me into a morgue, he do. I refuse. He puts me on a warning – official hearing – the full works.'

'But they can't sack a hero for cowardice so they dump you here, out of the way,' I concluded in disgust.

'What about you, ma'am?' Bantony probed, now that we were getting all confessional.

'Hush now, boy.' Box flapped a hand, then whispered – they kept doing that. Had somebody put it about that I was deaf? – 'You know about her trouble.'

I would have thought it was a bit obvious what my trouble had been until Bantony tapped his nostril and said, 'Oh yes. Oy'd forgotten that for a mo.'

There was something about the way he said 'that' with never a glance at my pinned-up sleeve that made me uncomfortable.

'Forgotten what?'

Box shifted uncomfortably. 'Tint none of our business what trouble you got up to with takin' bribes and things.'

'Bribes and *what* things?' I demanded. 'What *things*?'

'Well just bribes mainly, I think,' Box mumbled. 'But we int here to judge you, ma'am.'

'Where did that story start?' I looked Box straight in his troubled face.

'Well, everyone sort of know it,' he mumbled, 'but I do think it was Inspector—'

'Sharkey,' I pounced. 'Well, let me tell you, and I hope you will spread this truth as readily as you spread the lie. I have never taken or even been accused of taking a bribe. If Sharkey told you I had, he is a shit-faced liar.'

The bit about his face probably wasn't very professional but I was not feeling very professional at that moment.

I ripped off my jacket, wincing as I jarred my stump. 'Want to see why I'm here?' I unpinned my shirtsleeve and pulled it up, the dressing flapping loose as I did so. '*That* is why I am here. That and no other reason.'

Bantony staggered back and shielded his eyes like a sinner on Judgement Day but Box slipped on his old wire-framed glasses and bent over to take a closer look.

'Does that bit o' bone normally stick through your skin, ma'am?'

I was feeling hot and sick already and the arm was hurting like hell and I got quite a shock when I saw the state of it but, if Box hadn't accidentally poked the wound, I probably wouldn't have fainted.

*

Mr Cactopopus washed his hands and I couldn't help but notice how he did that much more thoroughly after he had examined me than before. He had not had Tubby's scruples about hurting me when he prodded the stump about.

'A great pity they didn't take it off at the elbow.' He tutted. 'A tragedy.'

'It wasn't a surgical procedure,' I reminded him. Besides, I was rather glad to have retained my forearm. It might come in useful if ever I got used to that damned prosthesis.

He had a cairn of scabs on the side of his nose, with tiny yellow and orange fungi sprouting on its slopes.

'You have what we surgeons call *creeping necrosis*. It is working its way slowly but inexorably up your limb. We could remove the sequestra and trim the bone but we would have to do it again in a few months' time. The kindest thing would be to amputate the rest before septicaemia sets in.'

This didn't seem like a very kind thing to me.

I couldn't take my eyes off that growth.

'So right up to the elbow?' I clarified with a horrible certainty that he would say *yes*.

'Oh no,' Mr Cactopopus said with a chuckle, to my relief, before he added, 'up to the shoulder.'

For a split second, I thought it was his peculiar sense of humour – this, after all, was a man who wore checked trousers and was starting a botanical garden on his face – but then I realised he was laughing at my stupidity.

'I shall seek a second opinion.' I put my shirt back on and the jollity dropped stone dead at his feet.

'I am the foremost in my field.' His manner was menacing now, but I have dealt with a drunken mob of philatelists in my time so I am not that easily scared.

'Nevertheless.' I had not liked the way he had watched me unbutton my shirt and I didn't like the way he watched me button it either.

'If you do not take my advice you will die,' he snarled so unpleasantly I half-thought he meant to do the job himself.

'We shall all die, Mr Cactopopolopolus,' I told him, getting all tangled up with my fingers, my buttons and my words. 'But I would prefer not to at the hand' – I was not going to acknowledge that he gloried in having two – 'of an egocentric surgeon who cultivates slime mould on his nostrils.'

Mr Cactopopus touched his flourishing nasal rock garden in wonder. 'Is that what it is?' He tweaked it between his finger and thumb. 'I've been worried sick about that.' He opened the middle drawer of his desk and brought out some headed notepaper. 'Thank you so much.' His eyes welled with gratitude as he unscrewed the cap of his fountain pen. 'Now, where would you like to be referred?'

72

THE DIFFERENCE

should have been on sick leave but there was one job to do before I left and before Sharkey got the chance. I had been in touch with a Major Harris from the Great Molefield Barracks and had arranged for his men to be there at 9 a.m. but, when I turned up at half past eight, their truck was already parked outside the Sternes' bungalow.

A dapper but stout officer strode towards me, swagger stick tucked under his arm.

'Church? Harris.' He touched his cap with his stick and I returned with the best salute I could muster.

'You're early.' I had wanted time to prepare them.

'Surprise, the first rule of attack,' he rapped.

'They are an elderly and much loved local couple,' I informed him. 'Not a division of panzers.'

'The enemy is the enemy,' he informed me. 'And fraternisation is an offence.'

People like you are the offence, I thought but said, 'I believe it is my job to detain them.'

'Send a couple of men in with you,' he decided, 'and a couple round the back in case they make a run for it.'

'Mrs Sterne can hardly walk,' I told him. 'I don't need your men.'

I walked up the drive but before I could knock on it the front door opened.

'Inspector Church.' Sammy stood in a long black woollen coat and homburg hat. 'Did you think we would put up a fight?'

I drew close and said quietly, 'I'm sorry, Sammy, but I have to take you into custody and hand you over to the army.'

'Mr Sterne,' he corrected me and I nodded.

'You are allowed one suitcase each, though they will examine the contents to make sure there are no weapons or radios. I believe you were sent a list.'

'Tell me something.' Sammy unbent. There was pain in his eyes. 'What is different between what you are doing and what Hitler does?'

'You are not being arrested for being Jewish. You are being detained because you are a German national,' I pointed out unhappily.

'To be imprisoned with all the Nazis?' Sammy raised his voice and I was aware of some movement behind me. Two privates had come up the drive, rifles over their shoulders.

'Get back,' I snapped but they stood their ground and I knew I had no authority over them.

'What?' Sammy shouted. 'Will you drag me out in chains?'

'If you resist they might,' I warned as Abbie Sterne hobbled into their hall on two walking sticks.

'Shush now.' She nudged her husband. 'You asked her to come,' she reminded him in a whisper.

'Good morning, Mrs Sterne,' I greeted her as steadily as I could.

'Good morning, Inspector.' She looked me in the eye. 'Thank you for coming. We have turned off the gas, water and electricity.'

'If you give me the keys, I will lock up,' I promised.

'And will you guard it while we are away?' Sammy demanded. 'Or will we come back to find it wrecked and looted like last time?'

Why in God's name didn't you apply for citizenship? I thought. *Half the town would have vouched for you.*

'I have a nephew who will come this afternoon with some

friends and board it up,' I said. 'And I will instruct the beat officers to keep an eye on the place.'

But I knew there was little we could do to protect their home. Sammy's shopfront had been smashed that morning, the shelves ransacked and the walls daubed with swastikas, but I saw no point in telling him. Only God knew if they would live long enough to return.

My arm was throbbing dreadfully. I felt hot and sick but not, I thought, just because of the infection.

A private stepped forward and I was about to try to restrain him when he put out his hand.

'Can I help you with your bag, ma'am?' he offered and Abbie smiled.

'That's the difference,' she told Sammy and I hoped she was right and didn't see the two small boys across the road goose-stepping, right arms out straight and left first two fingers on their lips in imitation moustaches.

73

THE VISITORS

f it hadn't been for the fact that I was in hospital, I might have quite enjoyed my stay at UCH in London. The pain had eased considerably after the operation and Mr O'Sullivan, the surgeon, assured me he had had to remove very little of my stump to get back to clean bone. He would try a new kind of arm on me, he promised, which was much lighter than the ironmongery I had been sent home with before.

I must get complete rest, Mr O insisted. I had been banned from reading any newspapers and all visitors were put on their honour not to talk about work.

Aunty M came twice every day. Sometimes we chattered non-stop. Sometimes she just sat beside me, holding my hand. We were comfortable in either situation and I could not help wishing that I had known her in her youth and shared some of her – less distressing – adventures. March Middleton never stopped working, though, and it was she who discovered why all the patients' false teeth had gone missing.

Carmelo came every week, despite the expense coupled with the difficulties he had with the public and officials thinking he was a Nazi. The Maltese accent sounds nothing like the German – it is more melodious with Italian influences – but all foreigners were Germans in many people's eyes and the fact that the captain had British citizenship only served to reinforce their suspicions.

Jimmy came. He had matured – sort of – though there was still something of the schoolboy about him. He had had a couple of skirmishes, he told me, but not killed any Huns yet. His moustache had come on well. He had trimmed it into a very natty Clark Gable style and, going by how the nurses greeted him, I was not the only one who approved. Jimmy still called me *Aunty* but his manner towards me was more sympathetic than it used to be and, when he left, he gave me a long kiss goodbye. I can't pretend I discouraged it – if truth be told, I was disappointed there was only one. I was lonely and bored, in need of affection. I would have a serious talk with him when I got out.

Dodo came in a long fur coat – a present from Daddy, she told me – and a short tight-fitting dress that a passing junior doctor seemed to thoroughly approve of. Dodo inspected the lady in the next bed, who had been in a coma for four days, peeling back both upper eyelids with her thumbs. 'She does not look well.'

'That's why she's in hospital.'

Everything was tickety-wickety-boo-boo, Dodo assured me, dumping a huge handbag on my feet and her coat over my knees. No, they hadn't found the Suffolk Vampire yet.

'Don't call him that.'

'Everybody else does – even the *London Times*.' She stood peering down like I was the corpse at a wake.

'He is not a vampire,' I insisted. 'When we catch him, I guarantee he will have a reflection.'

'I suppose he will have plenty of time to reflect in prison,' Dodo agreed. 'Anyway, boss, I have been given strict instructions by Dr O'Sullivan not to talk about it.'

'Mr.'

'Missed who?'

'He's a *Mr* not a *Dr*.'

'Oh heavens to Halesworth.' Dodo threw up her arms in horror. 'You let a man who is not a doctor operate on your arm?' She shuddered more violently than if I had thrown a bucket of iced water over her and I almost wished I could. 'No wonder you only have one hand.'

'He's a surgeon. They call surgeons *Mr.*'

'Oh.' She calmed herself down. 'I see.' Dodo pulled up the strap on her dress, though it hadn't fallen down. 'I think I would still want a doctor to look after me.'

Though time lay heavy on my hands I did not have enough of it to pursue those thoughts.

'Anyway, Mr O'Sullivan is not your senior officer,' I pointed out.

'I promised.' She crossed her heart on the right-hand side.

I decided to change tack. 'How did Inspector Sharkey get on in Paris?'

'He has not actually returned to our cosy nest yet,' she told me.

'Really?' My feelings oscillated between hoping the murderer had been caught and hoping Old Scrapie wouldn't be the one to have done it. 'What happened?'

'Superintendent Vesty told us that Inspector Sharkey was arrested as a spy,' Dodo recited so matter-of-factly anyone listening in would have thought it was something my colleague made a habit of.

'Why?' *Had he tried to photograph the Maginot Line?* I wondered, though I couldn't quite imagine Sharkey as a tourist with a Brownie camera.

'Apparently – and this is only hearsay so it must be true – he kept speaking to people in German.'

'*Gooten morgan*,' I remembered.

'Exactly.' Dodo pounced on my words triumphantly. 'If he had stuck to what I taught him, Old Scabies would have been safe as a sausage. He wanted Superintendent Vesty to come and vouch for him,' she continued. 'But the super has been so busy recently he has not had time.'

It did not sound like Vesty to be deliberately callous. 'Busy doing what?'

'Fortifying his desk with piles of books mainly.' Dodo patted her hair all round for no reason I could think of. 'I think all this talk of war has upset him. His head has been hurting a lot.'

'Has he seen a doctor?'

'Dr Jackson comes every day.' Dodo pulled a hair out from the side of her head. 'He is a proper doctor and he says Mr Vesty just needs a rest.' She scrutinised the hair. 'Oh, I thought it felt black.'

'How are the other men getting on?' I was not sure I wanted to know.

'Oh very well,' she assured me. 'The twins made their first arrests last week.'

'Really?'

'Yes.' Dodo sat on the edge of the bed. 'They had an argument about who looked more like the other and arrested each other for insulting a police officer.'

'Please tell me that's a joke.'

'I will if you want' – Dodo picked at a loose thread on my blanket – 'but it is not. Brigsy told them to drop the charges or he would arrest them both for wasting police time and so they did but they are still as snappy as sardines with one another.' She peeked at my bandaged stump. 'Would you like me to rub that for you, boss?'

'I would not,' I told her firmly.

'Oh' – she knotted her fingers in disappointment – 'but I have recently discovered I have healing hands.'

'How?' I looked at the clock. There were still twenty minutes before visiting time was over.

'Bantony told me.' Dodo simpered. 'He gets terrible cramps and I am the only one that can massage them away.'

'And whereabouts does he get these cramps?'

'Oh, usually in the back room when the station is quiet.' She crept her fingers over the top blanket towards me.

'Do not even think about it,' I warned.

'I cannot stop myself thinking,' Dodo protested and I refrained from telling her that she usually managed.

'What part of him gets cramped?' I persisted.

'Oh, it varies.' Dodo put her fingers into reverse. 'It started with his shoulder and then it was his arm and yesterday it was his thigh – but just his inner thigh, which was just as well. Outside thighs are rather embarrassing, do you not think, Inspector Church?'

'I think you should stop massaging Constable Bank-Anthony,' I said. 'In fact, that's an order.'

'Except his tummy?' Dodo returned to tugging on the thread.

'Any part of him.'

Dodo wrinkled her nose. 'Are you allowed to give orders from your bed?'

'Yes.'

Dodo thought about that, thought of a response then thought better of it.

'I suppose,' she said brightly and that seemed to be all she was going to say until she chirped, 'I did not promise Mr O'Sullivan not to tell you about another interesting case.'

I shuffled up a bit on my pillows. 'Go on then.'

'What?' Dodo had pulled a good couple of feet of thread out by then. 'Promise Mr O'Sullivan not to tell you about another interesting case?'

'No.' I reached for the carafe on my side table. 'Tell me about it.'

'Well.' Dodo wrapped the thread round her left hand to get a better grip. 'Navigable – that is my clever nickname for Rivers – read about it first and showed it to Briggs – that is my clever nickname for Brigsy – who showed it to Superintendent Vesty – I do not have a nickname for him as I believe that to be disrespectful, though Shirty and Vesty would be clever and amusing – who rang them up but they said it was their case and none of our business.'

The end-of-visiting bell tinkled and all the visitors stood immediately because they knew Matron would ban them if they didn't.

'Is that the bell for tea?' Dodo perked up hopefully.

'Time to go,' I said and Dodo Chivers – just when she might have started saying something interesting – jumped off the bed.

'I have brought you something to read, boss.'

Oh please not Fenula the Fluffy Kitten.

'Oh yes?'

'Yes.' She plonked the bag heavily on my stomach.

'Ow.'

'Oh sorry. I thought it was your stumpy-wumpy that hurt.'

'I don't have a stumpy-wumpy,' I snapped, 'and it doesn't mean the rest of me is immune to pain.'

'Immune is an interesting word,' Dodo mused as she unclipped her almost-suitcase-sized bag. 'Daddy says it comes from the Latin word *immunis* so it must be true.'

She lifted out a stack of papers tied in brown string and dumped it on my chest.

'Ouch,' I said, unheard.

'A lot of our words come from Latin – like bungalow.'

'Bengali,' I corrected and Dodo brayed so loudly that the ward fell quiet.

'Oh I do not think that is a Latin word.' She clipped her bag up again. 'I had better go.' Dodo swung her bag off me. 'Goodness, this feels light as a lifeguard now.' She bent low over me as if to give me a kiss and I was just wondering if I should stand on my dignity and forbid it when her nose touched my forehead. 'Oh, is that a grey hair?'

'Where?' I asked stupidly.

'On your head.' Dodo straightened up. 'There is a big hole in your blanket now,' she told me with a cheerful wave.

*

At three we had what was described as afternoon tea – liquid tannin with a slice of dry bread cut into four triangles.

I nibbled the bread and took a look at the file. It was headed *The Dunworthy Hotel* but it didn't look like a holiday brochure. I flicked through to the end.

'What?' I felt the papers being whisked out of my hands.

'No work until you are better.' Matron stuffed them under her arm.

'Give those back!' I yelled, waking the old lady in the bed next to mine from her coma.

'Doctor's orders,' Matron told me with grim satisfaction.

'Oh I've missed my tea,' the old lady realised. 'Thank goodness.'

THE PREVALENCE OF UNICORNS

protested vigorously about the confiscation of police files but anyone worried about the police state would be better focusing their attention on the medical state. In a hospital Doctor's word is law except when Matron is fiercer and, when these two teamed up, a battalion of grenadiers could not have made them give me back those papers until they were handed over in a large brown envelope as I stepped out of the front door into Gower Street.

I stuffed them in my suitcase and turned my attention to March Middleton, who had brought Jenny along to carry my bag and who took it upon herself to scold all the ragged children crowding round my godmother for the sixpences and sweets she was always dispensing.

There followed five days of rest, gin and gossip. While I had been lying uselessly in bed, Aunty M, with the assistance of her new microscope and two burly Glaswegian perfumiers, had caught the Bloomsbury Butcher and she had a great deal to tell me about that.

'I still feel guilty smoking in the house.' She handed me a Turkish from her father's gold case and laughed lightly. 'But that doesn't stop me doing it.'

At the end of the five days, much invigorated by her company and largesse, I was helped into a taxi for Liverpool Street with strict instructions to contact her immediately if I felt unwell.

The station was packed with servicemen and women saying

goodbye to their loved ones, waving through the smoke and steam and shouting over barriers and from platforms above the whistle of engines and clatter of carriages about taking care of themselves and how they would write every day. Such scenes had become part of our everyday lives by then.

Sergeant Jim Foxley was there, keeping an eye on things. I knew him from my Met days – a pinch-faced man in his forties with flickering eyes, jaundiced skin and tight lips – the sort of face you might expect to see on a *Wanted for Murder* poster, but he was a decent, unassuming man, a good copper who had done a great deal to make the station safer since setting up a not-quite-official office at the station.

'Even if you get on, you'll never get a seat,' he predicted. 'But most of 'em 'ave to be back at camp before dark, so you might find the next train less busy.'

Jim invited me to join him in his room for a cup of tea, all the more welcome for the generous measure of brandy he added to it and the flickering coal fire we settled beside.

We chatted a bit about how I liked Suffolk – more than it liked me, I suspected – and whether they would let me stay – I was not sure I wanted to.

'You should.' This was as close as I would get to being told I was a good copper. The men don't say it to each other so they certainly won't say it to a female.

I offered Jim a cigarette and he took it gratefully before telling me he had been ordered by his doctor to give them up.

'Don't suppose they see many women police in that neck of the woods.'

'Rarer than unicorns,' I agreed.

'Took a while to get used to 'em 'ere.' He struck a match on the sandpaper of his Webb's matches to offer me a light.

'And you are one of the few who have managed,' I told Jim

332

and he was just sucking greedily on his smoke when he was called out to deal with a drunk and disorderly on platform 5.

   With nothing better to do, I settled back to look through the case notes that Dodo had given me what felt like a long time ago.

75

DEATH AT THE DUNWORTHY

Police reports tend to be heavy going, badly written and generously padded with irrelevancies.

This report, however, was a model in brevity. Either somebody had painstakingly condensed it or, more likely, the Essex Constabulary were being frugal with what information they were willing to share. Either way it was relatively easy to extract the gist of the events.

On the night of Tuesday 3 October a young man and woman checked into the Dunworthy Hotel, Bocking, in Essex. They gave their names as Mr and Mrs Ian Henshaw of Bath Avenue, Sackwater.

The lady was described by Maggie Morgan-White, the receptionist, as petite in a green dress and overcoat. She had a mustard headscarf, little finches flitting over it, pulled further forward than usual and dark glasses, worn, she explained, because she was suffering from a migraine.

Mr Henshaw was tall, well built and smartly attired in a well-cut grey suit with wide lapels. He had a fedora hat on, which he had pulled over his eyes in the style of an American gangster.

Harry Bright, the night porter, took them with their one case up to room 14 on the first floor. The man gave Harry a very generous five-shilling tip, saying that he would like his shoes polished later. The woman, Harry reported, seemed to be annoyed about this. It was Mr Henshaw's insistence that they were not to be disturbed *under any circumstances* that made Harry Bright wary – so much so that, when he went downstairs, he discussed his concerns with Maggie.

At ten thirty Harry Bright locked the front door for the night. He then did the rounds of the hotel. There were five other rooms occupied and all of them had put at least one pair of shoes in the corridor. When he went to room 14, a black pair had been left outside the door and, as Harry went to collect them, he heard noises that he later described as creaking bedsprings, grunts and moans.

Harry went to his office to make himself a mug of tea before setting to work with his brushes. About an hour later he returned all the polished shoes to their owners. As the porter approached room 14 again, he heard more noises. The grunts were louder now and increasingly like cries, but Harry had heard and seen many unsavoury things in his career and was just deciding that he would mind his own business when Maggie Morgan-White came down from her attic room, greatly perturbed about the sounds reaching her room. She was almost certain she had heard a cry for help.

Harry knocked. He put his ear to the panel and heard some bustling about and footsteps, then a gruff voice replied, quite close to the other side of the door, 'I told you we were not to be disturbed.'

Needless to say, this did not allay their fears and, when Maggie called out to enquire if Mrs Henshaw was all right, they heard a few more groans cut off almost immediately and a distinct cry of pain.

Harry called out a warning before using his spare key to unlock the door.

The woman was shrieking now, 'What have you done to him?'

The door opened two inches before it hit the wardrobe that had been dragged across it.

'What are you doing?' the same voice shrieked. 'No. Don't hang me… please.'

Those last words were choked as Harry began to force his way through. There was the sound of a slap, a yelp and then a low hoarse, 'Come on or I'll snap your pretty neck,' more scuffling and then a strangled cough.

Harry got a hand in to turn the light on but that was all he could do. There was no response to his enquiries now. He squeezed his way through and found the lower sash window had been fully raised, the curtains drawn back. The walls were splattered with blood, the recently replaced carpet sticky with it.

Ian Henshaw lay naked on the bed, spread-eagled on his back by thin cords at the wrists and ankles to the brass bedstead, covered in bruises, weals and cuts. A gag had been forced into his mouth. It was later found to have been made from two rolled-up men's stockings held in place by the blue tie Ian Henshaw had been wearing when he checked in. The tie was knotted round the back of the head. His hands were blackened by the tightness of the ligatures.

Of the woman there was no sign until Harry looked out of the window and saw two figures receding into the shadows of the small back garden. The taller figure appeared to be dragging that of the woman away.

It was then that a third figure appeared, Noble Jones, an ARP warden in a fury at the showing of a light and, by the time Harry Bright had managed to explain the situation and persuade the warden to turn his own torch on to search for them, the two figures had disappeared.

While Harry Bright shut the window, turned the light out and locked the door, Maggie Morgan-White rang the police.

Inspector Jack Clements at Braintree Police Station was the first officer at the scene but it was too big a case for the local force

336

and it was not long before the chief constable of Essex, realising his men had no experience of such crimes, requested help from Scotland Yard.

Suffolk was the neighbouring county but, in police terms, it was a different world and forces were alarmingly reluctant to share information with each other. The kidnapping received national coverage in the press, though, and even the flotsam that washed up into sleepy Sackwater in the guise of policemen could not help but see the striking similarities with events at the Royal George Hotel.

Of especial interest was that the body of Ian Henshaw was identified by his wife. Mrs Henshaw had been at home all the time. It seemed her husband had borrowed her ID card for the night. The identity of the missing woman, therefore, remained a mystery.

The post-mortem report recorded many injuries, detailing lacerations, bruises and cigarette burns received while Ian Henshaw was still alive, but the pathologist was confident that the cause of death was the two deep puncture wounds he had noted about an inch and a half apart on the left side of the victim's neck. In a footnote he remarked that these were similar to those in reports he had read of the Suffolk Vampire.

*

Jim returned. His tea had gone cold but he was not going to let a tot of alcohol go to waste.

'Couple of squaddies found they were both saying goodbye to the same sweetheart,' he grinned, 'and, by the look of 'er, one of 'em will be a daddy before too long.'

'Had a word with the guard on the twenty-five-past. 'E'll take you in 'is van if you don't mind sitting on the luggage.'

'Thanks, Jim.' I shuffled the papers awkwardly back into the envelope. 'But I've had a change of plan.'

76

THE SOCKS AND THE PSALMS

Rail travel at night was no fun in wartime. Apart from the cold, the whole train was blacked out, the windows being painted over except for rectangular peepholes. That night the clouds only parted enough to give brief glimpses of a crescent moon glinting weakly on the iced landscape. All the station names had been removed and at every one voices could be heard demanding to know where we were. There was an air raid alert at Chelmsford, so we were shunted into a siding for an hour until the all-clear sounded – another false alarm, thank goodness.

I changed at Witham – another long wait in a draughty ladies' waiting room; the canteen was closed and there was no fire in the grate – with two overly grand, sanctimonious women who berated me about how I should be knitting socks for sailors until I politely asked them to show me how I could. After that they went back to clicking their lethal-looking needles while tossing quotes from the psalms to each other as if it was a competitive sport. When the train finally steamed in, I went into a smoking compartment and choked quietly rather than listen to any more of that. I counted the three stops but still appreciated hearing a voice announce, 'Braintree. This is Braintree,' in direct contravention of government directions to confuse enemy spies who had probably studied their route more thoroughly than the average hapless traveller.

The few other passengers who disembarked with me soon disappeared into the night. I waylaid a porter hurrying back into his cosy office.

'Where can I get a taxi?'

'Witham.' He wiped his nose on the back of his hand.

Witham was the best part of ten miles away and I had been through it to get where I was.

'I need to get to the Dunworthy Hotel.'

He smirked. 'Can you walk?'

'Well, I didn't fly from the train.'

'Up the road, turn right, into town, head towards Bocking and through. 'Bout a mile or two.'

There's a bit of a difference between a mile or two on a wintry night but, having no choice, I trudged off, head down against a cold wind that was driving iced air into my eyes. I soon began to wish I was in uniform. Though not especially stylish, the thick woollen skirt, blouse and coat were better protection against the elements than anything more fashionable.

The roads were quiet – petrol rationing had seen to that – but an army truck pulled up, green canvas flapping over an iron frame. The driver slid across to open his window.

'Like a lift, darlin'?' He was a cheery-looking man with more than the regulation number of chins and unlikely, I thought, to cause me any trouble.

'Are you going past the Dunworthy Hotel?'

'I am now.' He winked.

I clambered into his cab, my coat and skirt rising halfway up my thighs and I could not really begrudge the man, a corporal, his appreciative glance before we set off, the light from his partly painted-over headlamps giving worryingly little view of the road ahead. He seemed to know his way, though – at least I hoped he did from the speed he got up through the narrow streets.

'The Dunworthy? You must be desperate,' he chatted as we quit the little market town of Braintree.

'I have business there.'

Bocking was much as I imagined it, not so much sleepy as comatose.

He pulled up near a factory, a massive structure that seemed out of keeping with its semi-rural setting – Courtaulds, I realised, famous for its silk. It was probably making parachutes now. ''Ow about doin' a little business with me first?'

'I would love to.' I reached into my handbag. 'If it's police business you're after.'

'Eh?'

I flipped open my lighter – the Brass Zippo Windproof that Adam had given me – and spun the wheel to light the wick, just long enough for him to see my warrant card.

'It was an innocent question,' he protested.

'Tell that to your wife,' I suggested.

'What? I ain't—' But he stopped when I tapped the photograph he had wedged on the dashboard.

'If that's you with your mother,' I said, 'why are you being showered with confetti?'

He sniffed. 'Most girls like a man in uniform.'

'I work with men in uniform. The novelty soon wears off.'

The corporal sniffed again and restarted the engine and two minutes later we were there. I peered out to make sure the corporal wasn't dumping me somewhere in revenge but the sign was just legible in the damped light from his lorry.

'If you change your mind...' he tried hopefully.

'If I lose it, you mean.' I opened the door and jumped down. 'Thanks for the lift.' I meant that last remark. The porter's *mile or two* had been at least four and, as far as I could tell, we had gone directly there.

77

THE DUNWORTHY GHOUL

The Dunworthy Hotel was an anonymous-looking brick building, a square block dumped on the edge of the village for no reason that I could think of.

I went inside, slightly surprised to find the door unlocked. Good old Reginald Foort was pumping 'Keep Smiling' out of his good old organ on the wireless but that was as cheery as my greeting got. If the woman who emerged through a curtain behind the desk had done something with herself she might have passed as drab. Her greying fawn hair looked like the last time it had seen a brush it had fled in confusion.

'Yes?'

I had had a better welcome from Gerry Froop, the forger, when I led a raid on his gaff.

'Yes what?' I challenged.

There was no need to ask if this was the same receptionist who had been there on the night of the murder. I had seen a photo and Maggie Morgan-White did not look like an unkempt squirrel.

'What d'you want?' What she lacked in looks was not quite made up for by her charm.

'Do you do this for a living?' I asked in genuine surprise.

'Wouldn't call it a livin'.' She wafted the air as if I had fouled it.

'I need a room for the night,' I told her, wishing already that I didn't. 'Room 14 to be precise.'

The uncordial face of the Dunworthy Hotel slid into a sneer. 'I fought you was one of them. Ghouls you are.' She slammed the register shut. 'We don't need your sort.'

I wouldn't have thought they could pick and choose but I had a problem. Without permission from the Essex Constabulary, I had no right to be sniffing around their patch.

'I'm a journalist,' I announced, 'for *The Times of London*.'

The sneer got sneerier. 'And I'm the Queen of Sheba.'

'Then you have aged remarkably well over the last two thousand years.' She hadn't but I was brought up to be polite. I reached into my handbag. 'This is my press card.' I flashed my warrant card, thumb over the official stamp, just quick enough for her to see the photo.

'Pluck me, so you are.' She jerked her shoulders one at a time. 'Now clear off.'

'One of the reasons this establishment is doing so badly,' I continued, 'is that many people believe the murderer still works in the hotel or lives close by, but I have evidence that he lives in Cornwall. If I can prove it, people may not be so frightened of coming here.'

It must have been quite a gristly thought for the receptionist spent a long time masticating it. The idea of bribing her flashed through my mind but I only had just enough on me to pay for a room. I delved into my coat pocket.

'Aniseed ball?' I offered and she perked up immediately.

'Oh, thank you very much.' She snaffled the whole bag. There must have been at least eight sweets in there.

'You don't look like a—'

'Ghoul,' I chipped in helpfully.

She turned to the rack behind her, rattling her chewed fingers through it. 'It's room 15 now. We get a lot of—'

'Ghouls,' I offered again.

'That's the word,' she said gratefully, 'or the other sort what don't like to sleep anywhere near it.'

Judging by the lack of empty hooks, people didn't want to sleep in most of the other rooms either.

'Do you have any other guests at the moment?'

'Just two commercial travellers,' she admitted.

'I suppose the gas leak didn't help.' I slipped the key off the desk.

'Only four of them died,' she protested.

'And how many guests did you have at the time?'

She scowled. 'Three. A chambermaid came a cropper as well.'

'How long have you worked here?'

'I own it,' she snarled. 'Didn't think I'd be back on the desk until all this happened.'

'So you must be Mrs Villier Jameston.'

'Seems I must,' she conceded.

'But you were away on the night in question.'

'Isle of Wight.'

'What happened to Maggie Morgan-White?'

'You've done your homework,' she conceded. 'Maggie left.'

'Where is she now?' I reached for the register.

Mrs Villier Jameston inhaled through her nose like she was appreciating a damask rose. 'Don't know. Don't care.' She put up her hand like I would to stop a car. 'You don't have to worry about filling that in.'

'Oh I shan't worry,' I assured her and picked up the pen. It was the law after all – plus I wanted to see who else had been there at the time. But this was a new book.

'I suppose the police took the other register away.'

'You suppose correctly.' Mrs Villier Jameston dragged it off me.

'Do you have a porter?'

'No.' The receptionist scrutinised my signature with a dedication that would have done credit to a forensic graphologist.

Some officers pride themselves on having a nose for a lie. This one floated into my nostrils and made itself at home there.

'So who uses his office?

'Nobody.'

'Then I had better go and put the light out.'

'Hang on. You can't...'

But I already could. I strode through the yellow pool oozing from under the door at the bottom of the stairs, the one with a sign saying *Porter*, and turned the handle.

An elderly man was dozing in a chair with a folded newspaper on his lap that was almost as crumpled as him. He had a sparse whiskery moustache, as white as his meagre scattering of hair but with yellowed tips on the left, from smoking, I assumed.

'Good evening, Mr Bright,' I greeted him. Harry Bright was still easily recognisable from his picture in the *Express*. It was an old one taken when he had rescued a puppy from the sea. He had aged since then but who hasn't unless they've been embalmed?

'Oh, Harry, I thought you had gone to bed,' Mrs Villier Jameston, suddenly at my shoulder, said as convincingly as my father expressing surprise with the socks my mother gave him without fail every birthday.

78

THE NIGHT-AND-DAY PORTER

For all his advanced years Harry Bright could still get quite a sprint on up the stairs, but my long legs had no difficulty in keeping up and I was not the one who was wheezing by the time we reached the top.

The corridor was long and dimly lit, the carpet through to the backing in places, the wallpaper so cheerlessly washed out that, if it had been a cup of tea, you would have sent it back.

I let him fumble on the chain for his master key. Not every hotel had them and I wanted to know if that part of the account was true.

'Don't like coming in here, Mrs,' he told me.

'Miss,' I corrected him. 'So do you ever?'

'When I have to.' He had a red jacket on, shiny at the elbows and it looked too big for him. Perhaps he had shrunk more than it had.

'I believe you opened the door.'

'With this.' He put the key in. 'The door hit the wardrobe but I managed to squeeze in.'

'That was brave of you.' I stepped through the opening. 'Not knowing what was going on in there.'

It had taken all my nerve to do the same.

'Stupid more like.' Harry followed warily like he thought the murderer might be lurking round the corner.

'Brave,' I insisted and looked about me. Room 14 was quite a good size, a similar layout to the one in the Royal George but larger. The hotel had probably been converted from the home of a wealthy Victorian family, the large number of rooms being required for their prodigious breeding habits, the multitude of servants required to pamper them and the obligation to be ostentatious. There is no point in being rich if the world cannot see you are. It would be like buying an expensive dress to lock in your wardrobe.

The double bed with its brass bedstead was straight ahead. There was a wide sash window at the back of the room to the left of it. The paper was brown-and-yellow striped, hanging away at the top corner. There was a sink on the right-hand wall and a single wardrobe on the wall to the left as we entered. It appeared that not only were the crimes here and at the Royal George similar, the rooms were too, but then – as I reminded myself – so were countless rooms in thousands of Britain's dreary hostelries.

Harry Bright was curling and uncurling his fists at his sides. He blinked slowly, loath, I thought, to open his eyes but afraid to keep them closed.

'Do you know where Maggie is now?' I shut the door.

'She left a day or two after. Couldn't stand it – the memories and the newspaper reporters. Went back to her parents in Brighton, I think, but I never heard any more.'

'Has anything been changed since that night?'

Harry Bright glanced about. 'Don't think so.'

'So the bedding, carpet and wallpaper are all the same?'

'Well, of course not.'

I never quite understood why, whenever I point out something stupid that people have said, they talk to me as if I'm the idiot.

'What else then? And can you look around properly this time, please?'

Harry made a show of surveying our surroundings but I could see his mind was elsewhere.

'The curtains,' he decided. 'All of those things were burned after the police unsealed the room.'

'The furniture's the same?' I double-checked.

'Even the bed,' Harry replied peevishly, 'with a new-old mattress.'

'Show me how the victim was lying on it.'

'Not likely.' Harry backed off.

'All right.' I sat on the bed. 'Tell me.' I lay back, making sure my skirt came over my knees.

Harry rubbed the back of his neck. 'Are you sure you're not a copper?'

'Do I look like one?' I tried to remember what an uncopperly expression was and settled for an uneasy smirk.

The porter gave me the once-over. 'More like what's-her-face,' he decided.

'People often mistake me for her.' I put my arms over my head. 'His hands were tied to the brass rails?'

'You're not going to ask me to do it, are you?'

'No.' *Because you might.* 'How about his legs?'

'By the ankles to the frame.'

I spread-eagled. 'Like this?'

Harry surveyed me critically. 'A bit more loosely.'

'So he had enough slack to writhe about?'

The porter winced. 'If you put it like that, I suppose so.'

'And he was gagged.'

'Yes, with blood everywhere.' It was obvious that he didn't want to play any more.

'The sink and taps? Were they bloodstained too?'

'Yes.'

I sat up, swung my feet onto the floor and went to look out of the window. It was starting to get dark. The clouds had considerably parted and I could make out a long garden with an area of what I guessed was uncut lawn, with a few scattered trees – apple, I thought – and a path straight down the middle, sheathed in a long tumbledown rose arbour.

'I heard there were footprints in the garden.'

'A man and a woman's, judging by the heels.' Harry Bright stood close behind me. 'The ground was boggy. Inspector Clements said the man had a limp in his left foot because the right print was deeper than the left. He showed me in case I recognised them.'

'And did you?'

The porter stuck his thumbs in his faded scarlet waistcoat. 'What do you think?'

'What kind of a limp?' I asked in forlorn hope.

Harry pulled a face. 'How many kinds of limp are there?'

'Four. An ankle injury shows shallow dips; a knee is slightly deeper with a bit of a drag; a hip is a long deep drag; a combination of any two or all tends to be a long scuff.'

Aunty M would be proud. It was her who taught me that.

Harry ruminated. 'I'd say ankle but I wouldn't put my wages on it.'

'I believe a ladder was found.'

'The glazier left it.' Harry's voice was getting huskier all the time. 'We'd had some windows broken – kids with an air rifle on the back lane. It had been thrown to the side but there were dents in the lawn just below here.'

'What's that structure?' A cat was sitting on the roof.

Harry looked over my shoulder. 'Mrs V J calls it a summer house but it's just a shed really.' He hesitated. 'Know what I think?'

'I'd rather you told me.' I tried the lower sash. It didn't want to go up on one handle but I forced it.

'About a month later I went in there. We stored deckchairs so people could sit out and have a drink when it was warm enough.'

'Go on.' I leaned out, keeping a hold of the sill. I had not forgotten how Dexter 'Crazy Dog' Devlin had tried to tip me out of a window and nearly succeeded. I let go for long enough to reach for the old iron drainpipe. It was well beyond my reach or anybody else's.

'When I carried the table out there was blood on the floor underneath it. I think the murderer hid in there after he escaped through the window.'

'So while Noble Jones, the ARP warden, was searching the garden the kidnapper was only a few feet away with his victim,' I mused. *Dear God, what must that woman have gone through, hearing all the commotion? Did he hold a knife to her throat to silence her?* The cat was washing its back leg. 'Did you tell the police?'

'Mrs V J said not to and she made the cleaners scrub it all out – said a fox had killed a rabbit in there. She was hoping the story would blow over.'

I came back in. 'Is that why she told me you weren't here?'

'That and she's put it about that all the staff who were here on the night have gone.'

'So why does she keep you on?'

'They call me the night porter but I'm the night-and-day porter now 'cause the other one quit.' Harry found a stain on his lapel and rubbed at it with his handkerchief. 'I don't make a fuss when she doesn't pay me. It's a roof over my head and three square meals.'

He gave up rubbing and I wasn't sure why he had bothered. It didn't look any worse than the other stains to me.

'She's not exactly welcoming.' I shut the window.

Harry plucked at his moustache. 'She got an inheritance and didn't want to put it into this place but Mr V J twisted her arm. Two months later he realised she was right and buggered off with a waitress. Excuse my French.'

'I think the French have a different word for that,' I murmured, resolving to ask Jimmy. He had had a girlfriend from Marseilles once. 'Tell me about the woman.'

'Small, well dressed, dark glasses, headscarf, like a film actress that doesn't want to be recognised.' It was obvious he was reciting what he had said countless times and that I was not going to get anything fresh.

'I must be keeping you up.'

Harry fished out an old pocket watch from his waistcoat. 'She'll have locked up and gone to bed now, so I will when you're done.'

'Mind if I use your office?' It was warmer than this room and I had a horrible suspicion that something from the bed was feeding on me.

'So long as you don't put any more coal on.'

'I won't do that,' I promised as we went back into the corridor. 'So the woman didn't speak?'

'Not a word.' Harry accepted without a comment or glance the coins I dropped into his hand. 'Except when she banged her funny bone on the bannister and said "*Ouchy-wouchy*" like a little girl.'

I was just about to close the door when there was a loud sharp scream behind me. I spun round.

'Fox,' Harry said.

'I know.' And I did but it had still startled me.

I liked to think I wasn't superstitious but then I liked to think all sorts of things – that I was still eighteen, for example, and that I wasn't half the things Adam had called me.

This was not so much a copycat crime, I pondered, as a carbon copy of events at the Royal George. Why then did it deviate into abduction? I shivered. What had the kidnapper done with his victim? Had she been killed or was he still doing it now?

My phantom limb was still so convincing that, although the

stump had hardly troubled me since my operation, my hand – forgetting it had been pickled – had terrible cramps and I had an absurd desire to massage the thin air where it should be. I crooked my imaginary fingers.

Ouchy-wouchy, I mused as I fell into a troubled sleep.

79

THE SUFFOLK UMPIRE

There was a corpse in Brigsy's chair, only I had got used to that now. One day, I reflected, Sergeant Briggs would actually be dead and wouldn't jump out of his skin when I lifted the report book over my head to let it crash down on the desk just in front of him.

'Bwuff.' Brigsy jolted awake with his now-traditional cry and obligatory addenda of, 'What's going on?' and 'Can't you see we're closed?' He rubbed his eyes. 'Oh, hello, madam. I wasn't asleep.'

'I know you weren't,' I said gently.

'Oh.' The gears of his brain crashed into first. 'You've done and bin away, you have.' He struggled to his feet.

'I know.' I smiled.

'And you're done and come back, you are.'

'I am,' I agreed.

Police sergeants don't offer their hands to police inspectors and the inspectors don't take them but Brigsy did and I did. 'Welcome back, madam.'

'It's good to be back,' I told him.

Brigsy screwed his cadaverous face into a died-of-shock expression. 'Really?'

'Really,' I said as much to my surprise as his and I suddenly realised it wasn't just the job I'd missed, it was all the incompetent idiots who I did it with – or some of them. Or perhaps just Brigsy.

My sergeant let go of my hand and appraised me. 'They didn't go and graft a new arm on you then?'

'Not yet,' I told him. 'They trimmed a bit more off and made it comfortable though. I hope to have a new false one fitted soon.'

'Oh.' He looked disappointed. 'Don't know how the men will take to tha'. They've gone and got used to calling you—' He stopped in embarrassed confusion.

'Old Stumpy,' I finished his sentence for him.

'How d'you know tha'?'

'Have to be deaf and stupid not to.'

Brigsy chewed my statement over. 'Well, you int deaf,' he decided.

'Is anybody else here?'

'Apart from me?' He considered the question.

'Yes.'

'And you?'

'Yes.' I was feeling a little less glad to be back already.

'Wellll, Nippy Walker he do be on the East Sackwater beat, I do believe.' He rubbed his moustache so hard I was worried he might erase it. 'Annnd the Snipe Twins they do be off duty 'til eight of the clock, they do. Annnd—'

'I don't need to hear about everyone who isn't here.' I put my helmet on the desktop.

'Oh?' Brigsy had obviously decided I had got that wrong. 'Then you won't want to know about Old Scrapie.'

I had told them all off many times for calling a superior officer that in my presence but now I let it go.

'Chivers told me he was detained by the French authorities. Is he back then?'

'No.' Brigsy folded his arms in great satisfaction. 'And you won't want to know why not, I take it.'

This could take longer to play than the average game of Monopoly. 'Yes I do.' I surrendered before he had even passed the Old Kent Road.

'Wellll, there was another bit of bother on the way back.' He stopped.

'Nothing serious?' I forced myself to add, 'I hope.'

'Wellll,' Brigsy ruminated, 'rumour do have it, when the British authorities goo an' check the Shark's papers to try to get him released, they found out his father was Austrian but Old Scrapie do goo and change it to Australian on his birth certificate when he applied for a passport.'

'So now he's an enemy alien, a spy and a forger.' I shook my head. There was a certain poetic justice in the first charge but I found it difficult to rejoice in his troubles.

'I always thought there's something funny in the way he walk,' the man who lumbered like a zombie observed shrewdly because, as every Englishman knows, foreigners all mince about – except Germans, who strut out of uniform and goose-step in it.

'Who, if anyone else, is here?' I leafed through the charge sheets. We did not seem to have made many arrests lately, except a man calling himself Old Trafford who confessed to being the Suffolk Umpire. He was kept overnight for being drunk and disorderly.

'Wellll, Supernintendent Vesty is sort of here' – Brigsy nibbled his lower lip – 'but he don't be the same since he heard tha' explosion.'

'Wha' explosion?' *Oh Lord I'm turning Suffolk.*

'Blew up the end of the pier, they did, the army.'

'Put the kettle on.' I went down the corridor and knocked on the end door.

'Who goes there?' came faintly through the door.

'Inspector Church, sir.'

'Friend or foe?'

This was the second game in two minutes I didn't want to play. I went in. Superintendent Vesty was crouched behind his desk, head tilted to the right, his war-issue police helmet on. His elbow rested on the desktop, his left hand cupped like he was begging for alms, and it was only when I noticed the right hand below his shoulder, first finger crooked, that I realised he was sighting me with an invisible rifle.

'Halt or I fire,' he yelled.

'It's me, sir.' I took a step forward and closed the door behind me.

'Password,' he rapped, training the rifle on me as I widely skirted the desk.

'Mustard,' I chose at random and he swung his weapon back towards the entrance.

'Come quickly, man.' He jerked his neck. 'And keep your head down, for God's sake. There's a sniper over the—' He stopped, unable to connect his memory with what he was actually seeing, and I crouched beside him.

'That war is over, sir.'

'They've surrendered?' he asked incredulously.

'There was an armistice but there is another war now and you are a policeman.'

Major Ian Vesty DSO touched his sunken skull with trembling fingertips. 'It still hurts, you know.'

'I know, sir.'

'What about your arm?' He lowered his fingers to an inch above my sleeve.

'That hurts too.' I got up and held out my hand and, after a nervous glance over his shoulder, the superintendent took it.

'The Somme?' Vesty struggled to his feet.

'No, sir. I wasn't in the war. I'm Inspector Church and you are unwell.'

He looked about. 'Don't let the men know. Frightfully bad for morale and we have a big push coming up tomorrow.' He stroked his brow. 'No we don't, do we?'

'No, sir.' We were still holding hands as we went back down the corridor.

Brigsy looked up. *Please don't say anything stupid*, I thought.

'Can you call Dr Jackson, please, Sergeant Briggs? Superintendent Vesty is unwell.' *Please don't say anything stupid*, I prayed.

'Certainly, madam.' Brigsy picked up the phone.

*

Vesty sat quietly in the back room sipping the mug of tea Brigsy had made him.

'Ypres,' the superintendent muttered. 'Filthy business. It broke my heart but it did not break me.' He swept his hand back over his head.

'Wipers.' Brigsy nodded. 'I missed that, thank the good Lord, but I got a bellyfull of the Somme.'

'I suffered a head injury, you know,' Vesty told him.

'So I do believe.' Brigsy nodded sagely. 'But I heard you got four men out.'

'Four?' Vesty cried out. 'Only four?'

'Four who would have died if you hadn't carried them one by one.'

'Good lads.' Vesty lowered his head. 'Only four. It broke my heart.'

We sat in silence for a long time, Vesty ducking twice as something went overhead.

Dr Jackson came. He would drive Vesty home to collect some things before they went to the hospital.

'He's been like this before,' he whispered. 'He'll be all right.' He raised his voice. 'Fancy a walk, Ian?'

'Wouldn't say no to a round of golf.' Vesty perked up.

'When you're better.' The doctor slipped an arm through his

patient's and, as Brigsy stepped aside, I saw that he was saluting – not his usual sloppy wave but in a proper military manner.

'Carry on, Sergeant.' Major Vesty returned the salute with an unseen swagger stick and strolled out into the sun.

'I'm glad Inspector Sharkey wasn't here,' I said as the door closed.

'I'm not,' Brigsy muttered. 'Might have given me the perfec' excuse to break his jaw, he might.'

I wasn't sure Brigsy could best Old Scrapie in a fistfight but I would have loved to see him throw the first punch before I broke it up and I was failing to reprimand him when the phone rang.

'I shall s'licit Inspector Church's presence,' Brigsy said after a brief conversation and handed it over.

I held the mouthpiece to my jacket. 'Who is it?'

'Mr Wicks,' Brigsy told me as if it could not possibly have been anybody else. 'Won't say what it's about.'

'Hello, Mr Wicks, this is Inspector Church.'

'Is this a joke?' the caller demanded. 'You're that bloody woman who pestered my wife.'

'I'm that bloody policewoman who helped your wife,' I told him, 'and I am also the senior officer on duty.'

'Where's Sharkey? I want to deal with him.'

'Away on police business so it's me or nobody.' My fingers were crossed he would take the second option.

'Oh great,' he growled. 'Well, you'll have to do then. Come to my house immediately. You know where it is.'

He had a nice baritone voice but that seemed to be where the niceness started and ended.

'Can you give me some idea of what—' but I was talking to a click and then silence.

80

THE REASON FOR EVERYTHING

could have ignored the call. I could have rung back to insist that he explained himself. I went to Cormorant Road and knocked on the door of Felicity House.

'We don't need any dusters and we have enough lucky heather,' my mother called through the coloured glass door.

Enough for what? Starting a grouse moor?

'It's me, Mum.'

'Why don't you use your key?'

'You took it off me.'

'Oh for goodness' sake,' she said and sighed in exasperation. 'I suppose I'll have to let you in.'

The door clicked and swung open.

'I hope you haven't come to upset poor Dodie.'

'Hello, Betty, how lovely to see you. How did you get on in hospital? Is your arm better? Sorry we didn't visit or ring or send a card,' I raged.

'Well, that's a nice greeting, I must say,' my mother fumed because, of course, she had welcomed me with tears, hugs and kisses.

My father came out of his surgery and I wondered why he had even gone into it. The waiting room was empty.

'If you've come to cause trouble.' He wagged a warning finger.

'If I've come to cause trouble what?' I demanded. 'Will you send me to my room? Oh no, you can't because I haven't got one.'

'Hello, boss.' Dodo skipped down the stairs.

'She came to see me,' I told my parents.

'Oh dear.' My mother clapped her hand to her forehead like nobody does in real life. 'Are we back to you getting all sulky because we forgot to get you a cake on your ninth birthday?'

'You forgot my ninth birthday full stop!' I shouted.

'What is a birthday full stop?' Dodo puzzled. She had a pretty floral dress on that just about covered enough of her to stop her being arrested. 'I have never had one.'

'Get your uniform on,' I commanded. 'We are going to Pinfold Lane.'

'Oh goody.' Dodo clapped her hands. 'Lavender Wicks and Pooky – what fun.'

'Pooky?' my parents chorused in bafflement.

It was then I knew I had my big chance. I hadn't told them that she was working in Treetops House and had asked Dodo not to. I hadn't wanted to hurt their feelings by explaining that their old maid detested them. Now that I had the opportunity and excuse to get a bit of my own back I found myself saying weakly, 'It's a very common name.'

'Oh but...' Dodo began, then, suddenly catching sight of my grimacing and hand-waving, changed tack to, 'it is. Especially in Daddy's part of our beleaguered country.' And she was doing quite well except that she had her fingers crossed in full view of us all. 'I shall go to get changed now,' she said and set off meekly back up the stairs, 'and hope I do not go to hell for telling a whopper.'

'What has happened to the little Bettyboo I used to dangle off my knee?' my father moaned.

I couldn't remember him ever doing that but I took his word for it. 'Why didn't you come to see me?' I asked.

'Is your journey really necessary?' my mother quoted piously from the posters.

'Every drop of petrol we use is one less for our brave boys on land, sea and air.' My father glared at me as if I had sabotaged a fuel depot.

'You could have written.'

'Don't you know there's a paper shortage?' my father came back at me.

Of course I knew. We were being encouraged to use the back of old forms to make new reports.

'Or rung me up.'

'Ah,' my father cried in triumph. 'There I have you. I did ring and they told me they had no patient by that name in any of their wards.'

'Though they did have a Mr Church who was absolutely charming. We had a lovely chat,' my mother said as if that made it better.

'When was this?'

'Yesterday morning,' my father said.

'Well, he could hardly have rung this morning.' My mother laughed tartly.

'But I was discharged on Monday and spent a few days at Aunty M's. I wrote and told you. I wrote you a lot of letters.'

'Ufff, we haven't had time to read all those.' My mother flapped her hand up high above her head. 'And your father was very upset to have missed you.'

'Really?' I softened a little.

'Very,' he confirmed. 'I wanted to see if you could find me a nice wheel of Stilton before you left London.'

'Why—' I started to backtrack.

'Because he likes Stilton.' My mother rammed her fists onto her hips. 'Is that against one of your precious war laws? Are you going to arrest your own father for liking cheese?'

I turned to him in the hope of a more sensible response. 'Why couldn't you have rung this morning?'

'Does there have to be a reason for everything?' my mother demanded.

'Yes,' I replied.

'The phone isn't working.' My father, never very good at eye contact but even worse at taking an interest in décor, suddenly seemed to be fascinated by the wallpaper.

'Have you told the Post Office?'

'Oh that's right,' my mother said scornfully. 'Try to get him into even more trouble.'

More trouble?

I folded my arms. 'What's going on?'

'It wasn't ringing.' My father inspected his fingernails closely. 'So I decided to fix it.'

'There's a lot of confusing wires in telephones,' my mother contributed. 'Instead of persecuting your poor father, you should be arresting the telephone people.'

'Has it occurred to you it wasn't ringing because...' But I couldn't do it. I couldn't bring myself to put it to them that the phone hadn't rung because nobody ever rang. I heard footsteps on the stairs. 'There might be a fault at the exchange,' I finished lamely, it seemed to me, but entirely reasonably, it seemed to them.

'That must be it.' My mother clapped her hands. 'The exchange and the complicated wiring that broke itself.'

'And that smell that you said was the drains—' my father began.

'*I* said?' I broke in indignantly.

'It was those horrible eggs you gave me from that horrible man,' my mother said ungratefully. 'They all went bad under the stairs.'

'But that was weeks ago,' I protested. 'And I told you to put them in waterglass if you wanted to keep them longer.'

'Oh.' My mother propped up her breasts. 'I thought you said to keep them in glasses of water.' She wobbled them side to side with her folded arms. 'They all exploded. It was disgusting.'

'But I told—'

'You need to learn to speak more clearly,' my father lectured me.

'You can speak clearly enough when you're cheeking your father,' my mother contributed.

Dodo rejoined us, looking much more the part.

'And don't go getting sand in poor Dodipops's shoes,' my mother scolded. 'It took your father hours to clean them properly.

'But you never cleaned mine,' I burst out.

'I think,' my mother folded her arms, 'that you are old enough to do your own.'

'Bye-bye, Doadie-Woadie,' my father grinned soppily.

81

THE FILM STAR AND THE FEW

Pooky admitted us.

'He's had a few,' she warned us.

'A few what?' Dodo wondered. 'Noses?' she asked in surprise when Pooky tapped hers.

'Drinks,' Pooky clarified.

'Tea would be nice.' Dodo watched her own reflection. 'If it is made properly but not if it is not. Oh, what happened to that looking glass?'

'He threw a shoe and the mirror cracked from side to side.' Pooky jiggled her profuse eyebrows. 'Wait there.' And went through the whiteness into a new whiteness, announcing, 'The cops are here,' in the same voice you might tell someone they've trodden in something.

'I cannot believe we are going to meet Ajax Clarke, Private Eye.' Dodo hopped excitedly.

'Neither can I,' I agreed, 'because we are not.'

Dodo skipped. 'Owwy-zowwy. I forgot it was poorly-sorely.' She bent to rub her ankle. 'Why did you not remind me, boss?'

'I did not know you had forgotten.'

'You could have asked.' She pouted.

'Send them in,' the same deep voice I had heard on the phone said curtly and then, with the easy charm we all associated with Thurston Wicks, 'You took your time.'

He was a tall man – not much under six feet from his brown-toed white-topped co-respondent shoes, his tan slacks and his rust-coloured pullover to his carefully slightly tousled much-too-black hair – not as big as he looked on the screen but I didn't suppose anybody was. I had looked Thurston Wicks up in a couple of the stack of magazines Dodo had brought into work to show me.

'I had no reason to believe it was urgent, *sir*.' I emphasised the last word to show that I had some manners even if my host did not.

'I told you to come immediately.' The big tumbler of whisky looked comfortable in his fist. 'It doesn't take much intelligence to know that means *right now*.' There was an odd mix of faux upper crust and fake New York in his accent – how you might imagine Noël Coward imitating Humphrey Bogart.

'It takes even less intelligence to know that the police are not at your beck and call and that, if you need an officer to come to your house, you should give her or him a good reason to do so.' I looked into his eyes. Something of what I had seen described as *emerald* had been rinsed out of them and the lower lids were not exactly baggy but were losing their tone.

'Where's Sharkey?' Wicks demanded. His jaw might still have been what Hollywood liked to call chiselled, for bone is strong, but the flesh was weak, hanging slackly in soft jowls. 'He knows his manners.'

'What a pity he did not teach them to you,' Dodo murmured and Thurston looked at her sharply, not quite sure if he had heard correctly.

'What?'

'Inspector Sharkey is unavailable,' I told him, which was all he needed to know.

'Do you think he is being rude because he is drunk, boss?' Dodo asked as if the man in question had just left the room. 'Or do you think he is always rude?'

'Why don't you ask me that yourself?' Wicks challenged, squaring up like she was a mobster on the streets of Chicago.

364

Dodo cleared her throat. 'Excuse me, sir, are you being rude because you are drunk? Or are you always rude?' she enquired nicely.

Wicks's face broke into a grin, a brief flash of the suave, slightly roguish heroes he had made his reputation playing. 'A bit of both, young lady.'

'I ceased to be a young lady when I put on this uniform,' she told him with great dignity.

Thurston Wicks nodded amiably. 'Point taken.' He put his glass down next to a coaster on a glass-topped table. I was fairly certain Mrs Wicks would not be happy to see him doing that. 'As is my wife.'

I replayed his words. 'Your wife is taken?'

'In a word' – he picked up a letter from beside a white vase filled with dead white roses – 'yes,' and handed it to me.

I HAVE YOUR WIFE. PAY ME £5,000 CASH OR
SHE WILL DIE. DO NOT TELL THE POLICE.
INSTRUCTIONS FOLLOW.

I read, realising too late that my fingerprints were on a vital piece of evidence and that his would be all over it too. The words were printed in pencil, so straight and regular that they must have been done with a ruler. It was signed, also in block capitals:

NAPOLEON SPARTA THE SUFFOLK VAMPIRE

I glanced at the back of the letter – it was blank – and put it on the coffee table in front of where Lavender had lounged when I met her. 'Nobody touch it,' I said, better late than never. 'Where is the envelope?' *Please don't say you have burned it.*

'It didn't have one.'

'So it was just put through the letter box like that?' Dodo asked.

'Naked as the day it was born,' he agreed.

'How rude.' Dodo tutted.

'Did your maid touch it?' I asked.

'She gave it to me.'

'And she knows the contents?'

'Unless she's illiterate,' Wicks agreed obliquely.

'Napoleon Sparta?' I wondered.

'Oh that is easy-peasy-lemon-squeezy.' Dodo jiggled animatedly. 'Napoleon Sparta is a master criminal and Ajax's arch-enemy.'

'Oh,' I said. 'I don't think I've seen that one.'

Thurston Wicks recoiled. 'He is in every episode,' he told me.

Which showed how memorable I had found them.

'You were very good in *Scarface*,' I reassured him, not sure why I was bothering.

Thurston Wicks winced. 'That was Paul Muni.' If it had been a hot summer's day, I might have been glad of the ice in his voice, but it wasn't and I was quickly coming to two conclusions: one, I hadn't seen Thurston Wicks in anything at all and two, I had done too much pandering already. Here was a man whose wife was allegedly kidnapped and he was getting sniffy about being mistaken for another actor.

'When did you get this?'

'Half a bottle of bourbon ago,' he told me. 'First thing this morning.'

'And I assume your wife is missing,' I said.

'Why would I call you if she wasn't?'

'You might be worried that it arrived too soon and that there is a plot to kidnap her,' I reasoned.

'Indeed,' Dodo chipped in supportively. She had settled onto the same chaise longue she had shared with Lavender before and picked up the ball of knitting half-hidden under a cushion.

'That's a fair point,' he conceded. 'Yes, Inspector, Lavender has been missing these last ten days.'

'Were you not worried?' I wondered.

'Lavender is hardier than she looks.' Thurston Wicks flapped a hand. It was rather small and pasty for a supposedly tough guy. 'She had to be with her upbringing.'

'Were her parents poor?' I asked.

'What parents?' He waved the idea away.

'Oh but why did you not think to inform the police that your lovely wife had vanished?' Dodo was inspecting Lavender's work with a critical eye. 'Or did you think to but not get round to doing it?' She tugged at a loose loop. 'Or did you think you could rescue her yourself like you did in *The Black Hand*?'

'*The Black Hand* is a silent movie with Anthony O'Sullivan,' he snarled.

'So why have you waited?' I asked. Was I the only one interested in Lavender Wicks's fate?

Thurston Wicks rubbed his face in both hands. 'I only got home last night and I found this.' He passed me an even more mauled note and Dodo clipped on her spectacles to peer round my arm at it.

'Darling, gone to stay the night with Poppy. Be back soon. Love and cuddles ex ex ex,' she read out as loudly as she might have in a school assembly. 'Oh how sweet – that's me saying that last bit, not the letter.'

'You think I haven't read it?'

'No.' Dodo removed her glasses with great care before saying, 'But your maid might not have.' And then even I heard her – scuffling away down the corridor.

'She's seen it all right,' Thurston Wicks assured us.

'And who is Poppy?'

'Lavender's sister. She does secretarial work in her own

muddled way. I rang her but she said she hadn't seen Lavender in weeks, even though she lives locally.'

'When did Wilson last see your wife?'

'The afternoon of Tuesday the third.'

'That was the day—' Unusually, Dodo stopped herself in time.

'I know about the goings-on in Essex,' Thurston Wicks said grimly and suddenly he was a lost child. 'But I suppose it could just be a coincidence.'

'I do not think you are wise to suppose that,' Dodo told him and he nodded.

'Neither do I.' His gaze dropped. 'I read this woman wore a yellow scarf with birds on it. Lavender has one like that.'

'They are very popular this year,' Dodo enthused, 'for ladies.'

'Has she gone missing before?' I kept a hold of both notes.

'Never.'

'Do you think it possible, Mr Thurston Wicks,' Dodo asked slowly, 'that your wife, Mrs Lavender Wicks, was having an affair of the heart?'

'No.' Thurston Wicks threw a bit more ice into the atmosphere. 'Lavender is not interested in other men.'

I noted his emphasis on the last word with interest and wondered how much heart-throb Thurston really knew about her guests in her snug.

'But the woman who went into the Dunworthy Hotel with that man did so voluntarily,' I pointed out.

'Did she?' Thurston Wicks challenged. 'How do you know what threats had been made to make her go in? How do you know he did not have a knife or a gun on him?'

'Does Poppy confirm that Lavender was going to see her?' I asked.

'No.' Mr Wicks tipped his head back. 'But my wife often goes to stay with her sister without calling.'

'Does your wife normally—' I began.

'Normally? You think this is a normal occasion?' He took up his tumbler in that not-as-great-as-you-might-expect fist again. 'Know what I think?' Thurston Wicks did not wait for an answer, though Dodo was shaking her mop of hair as vigorously as a dog getting dry. 'I think Lavender set off to see her sister but got kidnapped on the way.'

'Where is her car?' I wondered. I could not imagine Lavender walking or cycling into town and Pinfold Lane was not on a bus route.

'In the garage. She must have been waylaid as she stepped out of the front door.'

'Have you asked the neighbours if they saw anything?' Dodo asked, very sensibly, for a change.

'I am Thurston Wicks—' The man in question tossed his head.

'Dodo Chivers,' my constable introduced herself.

'I don't think Mr Wicks had finished,' I told her and she dropped her outstretched hand.

'My reputation is everything,' he announced so proudly I didn't have the heart to tell him I had only become aware of him recently. 'Do you think Ajax Clarke goes trotting round old ladies' houses asking if they have seen his wife as if she were a lost kitten?'

'Well, if he wanted Mrs Ajax Clarke back, it might be a start,' Dodo reasoned.

'You think I don't?' Thurston Wicks threw back the rest of his whisky.

'It could be less alarming than it seems,' I speculated. 'Somebody, knowing that you don't know where your wife is, may be trying to make you think they have her.'

'D'you think that is likely?' he asked in undisguised desperation.

'No,' I conceded. 'But neither is kidnapping for money. Despite what you may have seen or acted in the cinema, it is a very rare crime indeed in this country.'

'I have never come across it,' Dodo weighed in with her vast experience.

Wicks was pouring himself another.

'You are away a lot,' I observed.

'What of it?' Thurston Wicks swung his arm round, showering me, the arm of the chaise longue and the carpet, but not himself, with Connemara Malt. 'It's the nature of my job and I give her everything.'

'Do you remember when Agatha Christie went missing?' I asked. 'She was found safe and well claiming to have amnesia, but most people think—'

'You think Lavender is doing this for publicity or to get my attention?' Thurston Wicks demanded. 'She has been taken, goddammit. My wife has been kidnapped and is locked in some cellar or God knows where, frightened out of her wits.' He flung the glass, shattering it against the far wall. 'Oh Christ, she'll kill me when... if...' He took a shuddering breath. 'If I get my hands on whoever has done this, I will tear him limb from fucking limb.' He closed his eyes. 'Excuse my French.'

'Which was the French word?' Dodo wondered as Wicks slumped into a sofa.

'Have you done anything to try to find her?' I asked. 'Apart from calling us?'

Wicks suddenly looked Malt tired. 'I've rung every friend who has a phone that I know of.'

'I shall need their names plus all the friends and relatives she has without phones.'

The door burst open and Pooky hurtled in, my mother's attempts to teach her deportment all in tatters. 'Just come through the door.' She was holding out a photograph to her employer. I took one glance, barged her aside, ignoring her 'Oy', disregarding her 'cheeky madam', and raced into the hall. Dodo jumped up.

'Are you running away because you're frightened?' she called as I flung open the front door.

There was nobody in sight. I glanced down at the sandy path. My helmet was on the hall table. I whipped it up and plonked it on the ground.

'Leave my helmet alone,' I yelled.

'I never touched it,' Dodo retorted indignantly.

She was hard on my heels as we raced across the front garden and onto the road. A figure was disappearing round the corner. If we had had our bikes, we might have caught up with it, but we didn't and it had too big a start for us to outrun it.

'*Haqq*,' I swore.

'Was that French?' Dodo fiddled with her helmet strap.

'Maltese.'

'Is that worse?'

'Can be.' I squinted into the distance.

'Did he look familiar to you, boss?'

'Yes.' I peered over on the off-chance that whoever it was would double back but it was a slim and forlorn hope.

Tall in a floppy-brimmed hat and a long dark coat, the figure looked all too familiar to me.

82

SNAP AND THE BOX

We watched the road for a while.

'So we are both agreed that was definitely the Suffolk Vampire,' Dodo told me, though I had done no such thing. 'Although,' she twirled her forefingers round each other, 'we must say nothing to Mr Wicks – and what a grave disappointment he is but there is a lesson in that for you, boss. Never meet your heroes.'

'I don't have any.' I pushed Gary Cooper to the back of my mind, where he had a tussle with Clark Gable.

'Also we must keep this info – which is an informal abbreviation for information – from Pooky because they will both panic because members of the public are not as brave as we are, are they, boss, also—'

'Shut up,' I snapped, then, seeing the wounds appear on her face, added, not even slightly convincingly, 'as they might say because they are not as patient as me.'

A breeze whipped the light sand into a miniature storm.

'Owwey-wowwey,' Dodo cried. 'I have a piece of sand dune on the front surface of my eyeball.'

'Don't rub it,' I said, rubbing the grit out of or into mine. I found a fairly clean handkerchief, twisted the corner and performed my Rufus Verdigris I'm-a-doctor routine without the romantic intent but just as efficiently. I had practised on patients when I helped my father and he got chips of enamel in their eyes from his electric drill.

'Oh bless you, boss.' Dodo blinked. 'You're better than an accountant.'

We went back up the path to where I had left my helmet and I crouched beside it.

'I am going to lift my helmet and I want you to pay very close attention to what is underneath,' I told Dodo Chivers and she shrank back.

'What is it? Is it a frog or a toad? – I don't mind them – or a rat or a serpent? – I do mind them, especially if they're alive – a ssss ssss' – she steeled herself to hiss it out – 'sssspider?' as if she was playing some demonic game of snap.

'None of those.' I took hold of the rim. 'Watch it very carefully.'

Dodo bobbed down beside me.

I whipped the helmet up and there it was in the sand – a small flat round-toed shoe with parallel cleats in the sole. I tried to shelter it with my hand but the breeze blew the insole out and the outsole in so that soon there was just a faint blur on the path.

'Well, that was not very scary.' Dodo sighed.

'Did the shape remind you of anything?' I asked.

Dodo had a think. 'Well, one ant looks much the same as another to me,' she decided.

'The footprint,' I insisted.

'Oh yes, of course.' Dodo jumped up like she was in a skipping game. 'It reminded me of Robinson Crusoe when he found Man Friday's footprint in the sand and rescued him from...' she clapped a hand over her mouth so that her next word was mercifully muffled but not quite enough, 'cannibals.'

'Well, she's a fine piece of work.' Thurston Wicks came up behind us sounding suddenly Hibernian and I scrambled to my feet. 'Did you see it?'

'The ant or the footprint?' Dodo enquired. 'We saw both.'

'This.' He thrust out the photo.

'Oh my awful Aunty Angela's ankles,' Dodo cried. 'She looks like she's been hit.'

'She has been hit,' Wicks insisted. 'My beautiful Lavender has been given a fucking pasting.' He didn't sound so suave now, though I could not blame him.

I took the photo from his outstretched hand, trying to hold it just by the corners but stop it blowing away. Lavender Wicks did not look good. Her pure complexion was bruised and bleeding. Her immaculately set Jean Harlow hair was now a strewn mess, as if she had been thrown around by it.

Pooky wandered out. 'Oh Miss Betty, you've got all sand on your skirt, what will your vile mother say?'

'Did you see this come through the letter box?' I held up the photo.

'Well, of course it came through the letter box,' she said. 'I picked it up off the mat and I couldn't have done that if it hadn't, could I?'

'Yes but—'

'It's not *yes but* it's *no but*.'

'Did you see this being delivered?'

'Well, of course it's been delivered!' Pooky threw up her hands in exasperation at having to deal with such a stupid girl.

'You were in the hall when the letter box clattered,' Dodo told her. 'I heard your clean white starchy apron brush against your pretty port-wine dress.'

What was it about dresses? March Middleton could hear them rustling in hallways; so could Dodo Chivers. Why the hell couldn't I?

'If anything else comes through the door can you both try not to touch it?' I requested. 'Use tweezers or wear gloves. Then we might be able to get a fingerprint of the kidnapper.'

'Except yourselves,' Dodo put in helpfully. 'If you come in through the door, you do not need to use tweezers or gloves. Or if we return—'

'They know what I mean.' I shook the sand out of my helmet. Dodo hadn't got hers on yet.

'I don't,' Pooky said, out of cussedness, I suspected.

I turned the photo over and on the back in the same measured block capitals was printed:

HAVE THE MONEY READY FOR MY NEXT
INSTRUCTIONS OR SHE COMES BACK IN A BOX,
NAPOLEON SPARTA THE SUFFOLK VAMPIRE

'I think the bit about a box means a coffin,' Dodo explained for my benefit, then, for everyone's benefit, declared, 'It is probably not the real Napoleon Sparta, you know. In fact' – she put her feet into that oddly overlapped facing-opposite-directions way that I think is the fifth position in ballet – 'I do not know why a vampire would have to give himself a made-up name anyway.'

'So that we would know him from anybody else sending messages claiming to be from the vampire,' I suggested, wishing I was that flexible but not quite sure why.

'An impersonator?' Dodo shuddered with alternating shoulders. 'What a terrible insult to the real Suffolk Vampire.' She sniffed. 'Small wonder he behaves so badly.'

83

THE FOLDER

sorted through the tea chests. Carmelo had been very patient and let me keep them in the hold but space is always precious on a boat, even a landlocked one, and, though I hadn't – thank God – seen a rat yet, *Cressida* was home to at least one family of mice. A favourite old sweater of mine had provided them with nesting material and I didn't want my godmother's archives to provide more. One of the boxes was crammed full of newspapers as far as I could feel without emptying it out. In the second box I only had to lift the protective top layer of brown paper to see it lying on top – a file dyed in distinctive Grice's Lilac with a rectangular stamp diagonally over the cover:

MARCH MIDDLETON, 125 GOWER ST, LONDON

I wondered why she never used any of the titles she had been awarded before her name or any of the letters after it. If I had half her accolades I would have them filling my headed notepaper, but Aunty M was a modest lady. She had given her life to investigating crimes to help people, not to cover herself in glory.

The pot on the range was two-thirds full and still hot. I filled an enamelled mug and sat at the table in the wheelhouse. The natural light was much better there and, when I glanced up, I could watch a family of moorhens – or skitty coots, as I had heard them called – tocking along the side of the bank in search of food.

Sidney Grice would never have thrown a seemingly irrelevant ant's egg away once he had put it in a test tube and he had built vast vaults in London and Dorset to store his collection. His goddaughter was more selective, in her opinion – or slapdash, in his – about what she thought worth retaining. Her four boxes might have been thirty in his day and she only kept those in case a verdict was ever questioned years later.

I opened the folder. It was encouragingly thin – no more than thirty or forty pages – and I had years of practice at skimming paperwork to extract what I needed to know. The notes were handwritten in March Middleton's small, unfussy, highly legible hand and I settled down with a cigarette to read them.

*

Vernon Willowdale was an impoverished parson's son raised in Whitechapel. Against his father's wishes, he married, but his wife died giving birth to their daughter, Drusilla. He began training for the clergy but, after his father's death, Vernon discovered that, if three other men died prematurely and in the right order, he would inherit Lord Blockett of Coniston's title with a sizeable fortune. With this in mind, Vernon Willowdale quit the clergy and set his mind to murder. The first victim, Snitchel Roewader, was an easy task. An elderly man, his life's work after retiring as a marmalade manufacturer was compiling the seven-volume *Roewader's Encyclopaedia of British Canals*. It was an easy matter to brain him with a cudgel and make it look like he had slipped and hit his head, falling into the locks at Rufford and drowning. The coroner had no hesitation in declaring death by misadventure and releasing the body for burial.

*

I lit another cigarette, one of the five I kept pre-rolled in a tobacco tin with my Zippo lighter. Willowdale sounded an interesting character but I couldn't see why my godmother had thought he was relevant to my enquiries. I read on.

*

Vernon Willowdale's triumph shrivelled into disappointment. There is little point, he thought, in being clever if nobody knows that you are. So he decided to perform a more public murder for his next victim. Pagan Gatherpole was a garden pest exterminator, who employed so many men that it was his proud boast that he had made a mountain out of a molehill.

Gatherpole had an office on Tottenham Court Road. As he arrived at Euston Square tube station in the rush hour on Monday 16 March 1925, he fell to the platform, clutching his neck. He had two deep wounds in his throat and the best efforts of two nurses, who had been fellow passengers, could not staunch the haemorrhaging. By the time a doctor was summoned from UCH, all she could do was declare Pagan Gatherpole dead, confirming the public's belief that the few women in the medical profession were a few too many.

Witnesses spoke of a man running up the stairs and turning left towards Gower Street. He wore a long cloak and a broad-brimmed hat. There were two wounds about an inch deep and half an inch apart in Mr Gatherpole's neck. They were not made with a knife but with two spikes or – as the press had it – fangs. And so the legend of the Camden Vampire was born.

Despite there being so many witnesses, or perhaps because of so many conflicting accounts, the police were at a loss as to the identity of the killer. March Middleton, living 300 yards away, took a keen interest in the case. She was able to demonstrate that the killer had stood behind the man and was taller than him and that the wounds had been inflicted simultaneously or in very quick succession, but despite speaking to eighteen witnesses at length, she could find no other information about him.

*

I drank my coffee, reread that section in detail and turned the page.

*

The only man standing between Vernon Willowdale and his inheritance now was Fradigor Strynge. Strynge was a not-very-successful portrait painter. While his paintings were pleasing, his manner was not. He browbeat small children and sweet old couples into holding uncomfortable poses until they seized up so that he could depict them at his leisure. Like Willowdale, Strynge was acutely aware of the wealth and position tantalisingly just out of his reach. So, when he learned of Snitchel Roewader's demise, he was elated. When he was informed that Pagan Gatherpole had also been removed from the list of heirs, he was ecstatic. He only had to wait for the elderly Lord Blockett of Coniston to fade away and all would be his.

But then Strynge found out that Gatherpole had been murdered. His immediate concern was that this made him the primary suspect. Had he taken his customary Monday trip to London, he realised, he might have had difficulty in clearing his name, especially as he had abnormally long canine teeth. Fortunately for Fradigor Strynge he was able to prove that at the time of the murder he had been bullying a terrified five-year-old Lady Veronica Hyde into sitting for him with a peevish vulture on her arm at the family seat in Stranraer.

It did not seem to occur to Strynge that he might be the next victim, nor that it would have been simple to determine who had most to gain by killing him. He went about his business as usual, accepting, without question apparently, an invitation to meet a stranger on Hampstead Heath to discuss a commission. It was while he was sitting on a bench ignoring the view that a little girl turned up and started chatting to him. Strynge tried to shoo her away but she was very persistent.

Vernon Willowdale had devised his own weapon, adapted from a knuckleduster with two long spikes on the palm side. This could be folded back until required, then hinged out so that he only had to clamp his hand over a victim's neck to pierce the throat. While Strynge was distracted by the little girl, Willowdale struck, but missed his target so that the spikes went painfully though not deeply into the side of Strynge's head.

Strynge was not an especially powerful man but he was desperate and he fought back. As the two men engaged in their life-and-death struggle, Hickory Brawn, a passing cowboy from Wyoming, lassoed and tied them both back to back to a beech tree before moseying off in search of a sheriff.

Vernon Willowdale claimed that it was he who had been attacked by Fradigor Strynge and, given Strynge's reputation, he might have been believed, especially as Strynge had ripped the device from Willowdale's fingers and put it onto his own. But March Middleton was not so easily fooled. By examining the crushed stalks of acidic grasses and moss in the area, she demonstrated that Willowdale had crept up upon and lunged at Strynge. Willowdale confessed and went into great detail about the crimes but he clammed up when asked about the little girl, leading to suspicions that it might have been his daughter, Drusilla. She was such a delightful child, however, that enquiries about her were not vigorously pursued.

Vernon Willowdale was hanged but Fradigor Strynge did not live to inherit his birthright. His head wounds became infected and he died four minutes before Lord Blockett, leaving all his estates to Commissaire Sampson Perroquet, a retired policeman from Luxembourg.

*

'Oh shit,' I said.

The captain was coming out on deck. He had been in the saloon listening to his radio and he did not look well. His face was grey and his body bowed. I closed the file, put my mug on top to stop anything blowing away and hurried out.

'Are you all right, Carmelo?'

'*Madonna Mater Dei.*' He crossed himself. 'I have just heard.'

Oh please God not Jimmy. 'What is it?' I took his arm.

Captain Sultana could not look at me.

Oh dear God it is Jimmy, isn't it?

'The *Royal Oak.*' He leaned on the side, staring out towards the ocean we could not see.

'The battleship?' He had told me about her, how she had fought in the Battle of Jutland.

'Sunk,' he said, 'safely moored, or so they thought, in Scapa Flow. A German submarine sneaked in... torpedo.'

'Was anyone killed?' I asked stupidly. He would not have been that way over an empty old ship.

'Eight—' He choked over the number and I nearly told him it could have been much worse, but he was forcing the next words out, 'hundred men and boys.'

I took his right hand off the rail, slipped myself in between it and him and put my arm round him, hugging hopelessly at his misery. But there was nothing I could do to help Carmelo or to stifle my own despair at all those cruel killings in Sackwater and a wider world hell-bent on slaughter so soon after the war to end all wars.

381

84

SHEEP

t was wet. Unlike in London, where the rain falls vertically and you can put up an umbrella to keep it off you, on the east coast the wind blows the rain almost horizontally. It was gusting so strongly that afternoon that the few people foolish enough to try their umbrellas instantly found them snapped and turned into inverted cones.

Dodo and I battled on, relieved to have turned the corner and be heading up High Road East so that the worst of the weather was being hurled at our backs now. Our faces glowed from the cold showers they had received.

Brook's Hardware had a special offer on – two free wooden stakes with every mallet – and I wondered how long it would be before some innocent sleeping man was mistaken for a vampire and impaled through the heart.

I still couldn't wear my false arm – my stump was too sore for that – but Carmelo had stuffed the sleeve of my coat, unscrewed the hand, put a glove on it and sewn the glove onto the sleeve for appearances. He had been a fisherman all his life and learned needlework repairing sails.

'At least it never ever gets any worse than this,' Dodo chattered as we passed Ye Olde Tea Shoppe reluctantly. I was tramping around Sackwater with Dodo because WPCs were too delicate to walk the beat on their own and couldn't be accompanied by a policeman in case they were overcome by carnal desires on the street. The twins were on night duty – something else women can't possibly do, for they might meet intoxicated or frisky men and unbalance their delicate female constitutions – and we were too thinly manned to put three officers on one round.

'You should be here in a storm,' I told Dodo.

Her eyes opened wide. 'Is this not a storm?'

I pulled my collar tighter round my neck. 'When it gets really rough the waves come crashing over the promenade and the sea spray lashes at you and you can hardly stand upright in the gales.'

'Crippety-crikey, boss.' Dodo shuddered. 'Is that how the last WPC here got swept out to sea and eaten by a giant cod?'

'Who told you that?'

'Constable Walker.' Dodo skipped over a little puddle into a larger one. 'Oh blipperty-botheration.'

'And you believed him?'

'I was a little sceptical.' Dodo Chivers shook her wet foot like a nurse with a mercury thermometer. 'But Constable Bank-Anthony assured me that it was true, as did Constable Rivers, so it must be… true, I mean.'

'They were pulling your leg.'

'The rotters,' she fumed. 'I shall tell them a story about a man constable who got swept out to sea and eaten by a giant haddock and see how clever they feel then.'

'I don't think they will believe you.'

There were footsteps sploshing quickly behind us and I twisted round to see a man, bare-headed and coatless, racing up the hill, weaving through the pedestrians, crashing into an indignant corporal, stumbling away and staggering in our wake.

'Save me,' he panted. 'They're going to cut my throat.'

85

AGAINST THE DRIVING RAIN

narrowed my eyes against the driving rain and peered back. A woman was trudging along with shopping in one hand and trying to drag two struggling infants up the hill with her other, but there was no sign of any sword-wielding homicidal maniacs.

'Who is?' I scanned the scene carefully.

The man raised an arm, pointing down the road so dramatically that the woman, who had drawn close, ducked and said, 'Bleedin' Nora, bleedin' Nazi,' and the man, realising he was giving a straight-armed salute, lowered his arm and told me, 'Down there.'

He had no hat on and his mackintosh was flapping unbuttoned around him.

'I can't see anyone,' I said.

'Oh no,' Dodo cried. 'Have you gone blind, boss? Shall I call a doctor?'

'No and no,' I replied.

The man jumped and looked over his shoulder. 'He must be hiding in a shop doorway.'

'Who is he and is he armed?' I asked.

'Save me!' The man grabbed my hand and pulled. There was a loud ripping noise as it came half away. The man looked at it and me in profound shock and, before I could reassure him, swooned limply onto the pavement.

'Catch him,' I yelled and Dodo just managed to grab a good handful of air before his head bounced off a lamp post to clunk on the kerb.

'Ouchy-wouchy,' she cried because somebody had to and he couldn't. I knelt in the gutter to check his pulse. Until that moment, I had thought I couldn't get wetter. A steady stream of drain water into my left shoe proved me wrong but at least the stranger was alive. His expression was almost serene now. He was well but badly dressed in the sense that his three-piece suit was of good quality but it was crumpled and his shirt collar was grubby. He needed a shave – there was a two-to-three day raspiness on his well-filled cheeks – and his eyes were under-ringed and breath sour from more beer than his body could absorb.

I glanced up. People were still hurrying by, heads down, but a gawkily constructed woman in her thirties paused.

'Disgusting,' she tutted, 'what the police will do to innocent citizens. Did he look at you sideways?' She had such a schoolmarmish air that I half-expected her to slap my legs with a ruler. 'Fascisti.'

'No he pulled my inspector's arm off,' Dodo chipped in.

'He...' The woman looked at my sleeve, which was dangling at a very odd angle now. 'Oh my sixpenny straw hat. Do you need an ambulance?'

'No, thank you. It's all in a day's work.'

'It was cut off below the elbow,' Dodo explained for me and for a second I thought the woman would crumple into the road, which would have been very inconvenient because a warrant officer was speeding by on his motorbike and sidecar, proving that it was possible for us to get even wetter still. But the woman walked unsteadily away.

'That's what happens when you skip Sunday School,' a man trudging past warned his son.

Our man was starting to come round.

'Oh my head.' He touched the back of it, his eyes flicking wildly. 'Oh Lord.' He looked about him.

'Nobody has come after you,' I assured him.

'Not to kill you anyway,' Dodo reassured him. 'We are trained to notice if people are being murdered.'

He struggled to a sitting position. 'Your arm?'

'It's false.' I got up a great deal damper than when I had got down. 'Why did you think somebody was after you?'

'Ohhh.' He rubbed his head gingerly. 'I can't think straight.'

'I think you need to see a doctor.'

'No.' He waved the idea away with spanned fingers.

'How much have you had to drink?' I held out my real hand to help him up but he shied away.

'Not enough.' He clambered to his feet, clinging to the lamp post. 'The trouble is, I haven't slept for three days.'

The rain had eased to a heavy drizzle now.

'You need a coffee.' I tried to straighten my glove but it was hanging limply by the cuff. 'Come on. I'll get you one.'

'Oh goody-goody-gosh.' Dodo kicked her toe playfully through a puddle, filling my other shoe. 'And we cannot have coffee without chocolate cake. It simply is not done.'

Ye Olde Tea Shoppe was still open but, by the sour greeting Mavish Brittle, the manager, gave us, she had been thinking of closing for the day.

'Don't drip on my clean floor.'

'Do you have a dirty one we are allowed to drip on?' Dodo asked so sweetly that neither Mavish nor I could tell if she was being silly or smart.

We hung our coats on the stand by the door and settled around the nearest table.

'Yes?' Mavish hissed as if we had roused her from bed at dawn to ask if she was seeking salvation.

'Three coffees please and do you have any chocolate cake?'

'What if I do?'

'Then we would like three slices.'

'At this time of day?' She rested her red knuckles on her narrow hips. 'You'll ruin your appetites for dinner.'

'I think we'll risk that.'

She shrugged. 'It's your funeral.'

'Is the cake poisoned?' Dodo whispered loudly and moistly in my ear. 'If it is, you can have my slice. Daddy told me never to eat poison. It is very bad for my health.'

'Funeral?' Our guest ran his fingers through his hair in bewilderment, wincing when he reached the crown.

Mavish was off. She had an odd walk, as if the two halves of her body wanted to go in opposite directions, and she managed to make the short journey back to her counter look like an unrehearsed three-legged race.

'So who frightened you?'

'I feel very stupid now.' He checked his hand but there was no blood on it. 'I went to Casanova's for a shave but there was quite a queue so I sat in the corner. I think I may have fallen asleep for when I woke up, Mr Casanova was waving a razor and saying "*You're next.*" I panicked and ran.'

'Is that where you left your hat?' Dodo asked.

'Hat? I suppose it was.'

'Do you have your name in it?'

'Name? Yes, I suppose so.'

'Good.' Dodo spoke as if declaring checkmate. 'Then we shall know if you are lying when you tell us what your name is.'

'Which is now,' I informed him.

The man dug into his trouser pocket for a soiled handkerchief to wipe his hands. 'My name is Maurice Leaf,' he announced with great pride and a toss of the head that I think he regretted.

'Where do you live?' I asked as he winced in renewed pain.

'The Mallards, Mallard Road.' His chin was up and with some reason. Mallard Road was home to the cream of Sackwater – not exactly in the Rothschild league but way beyond my means, unless I seduced Mr Leaf, which I felt no inclination to do.

'Do you often panic?' Dodo asked. 'I do.'

He eyed her quizzically. 'Not until recently.'

Three very milky but not very hot coffees arrived with the last two pieces of chocolate cake. There was only that or ginger and nobody liked ginger, especially me. I hate ginger. So I got a Nice biscuit that wasn't especially. It smelt musty.

'So what's happened recently?' We were given one lump of sugar each. I lowered mine in, watching the coffee rise up, before I realised I was being childish and let it sink.

Maurice Leaf crunched on his sugar. 'You don't know?' He snorted. 'All those deaths – Ardom Dapper, Skotter Heath Jackson, Ian Henshaw – and you haven't noticed?'

Dodo dropped her sugar lump from six inches up, splashing coffee into her saucer onto the until-now white cloth and, of course, me.

'Well, of course I've noticed. I was there when Ardom Dapper died,' I protested. 'But why would you think you're next?'

Dodo tried to cover the stain with her cake plate but only smeared it further.

Maurice Leaf took his coffee cup in both hands but he was shaking too badly to drink it. 'Because I'm one of *them*,' he said.

THE RAMS OF SUFFOLK

watched Maurice Leaf slopping coffee over his cuffs.

'One of whom?' Dodo had chocolate crumbs round her mouth.

He loosened his tie, which was already quite loose. 'It's supposed to be a secret.'

'One worth dying for?' I asked and he clattered his cup down.

'The Rams,' he blurted out.

'Which rams?' Dodo asked with great interest as if she knew several.

'The Suffolk Rams.'

I had heard of them. 'Aren't you a bit like Freemasons?'

'Sort of,' he admitted, mopping his wrists. Mrs Leaf would have quite a job getting that handkerchief clean, I pondered. 'But it's more of a social thing really.'

'Then why the secrecy?' I pressed.

Mr Leaf looked abashed. 'Our activities are sometimes not...' he struggled for words, 'the sort of thing we might want our wives to hear about. I don't mean other women,' he hastened to explain, 'but drinking games, pranks, that sort of thing.'

'So not really like the Masons at all.' Dodo sprayed crumbs onto the tablecloth before whispering to me, 'Daddy is a Mason but that's tippity-top secret.'

'We are all businessmen well known locally so, when we book a room in a pub or hotel, we all wear ram masks to avoid being recognised,' Leaf explained, then averted his eyes. 'It sounds a bit childish when I say it.'

'I don't think so,' Dodo assured him. 'It sounds *very* childish to me.'

Leaf shrugged. 'Doesn't seem to matter now.'

'So all those men you mentioned were Rams?' I clarified. 'What about Freddy Smart?'

'What, that hoodlum?' Leaf scorned. 'Hardly our type of person.'

'What about Hamish Peatrie?'

'Who?'

'Mr Hamish Peatrie was his name,' Dodo explained indistinctly, her cheeks bulging with the last of her cake.

'Never heard of him.'

'You have now,' Dodo pointed out.

'Grant Herring?' I suppressed a shudder. The memories of what I found after I forced my way into that room were all too vivid.

'The one at the Royal George?' Maurice Leaf looked to me for confirmation but I had my poker face on. It never won me much money at cards but it was useful for interviews.

'He wasn't one of us,' Leaf said, 'and I haven't a clue who the woman was.'

'Ian Henshaw at the Dunworthy Hotel in Essex,' I prompted and Maurice Leaf reacted as if I had presented him with the cadaver.

'Happy Henshaw, we called him.' Leaf turned a paler shade of pale. 'He was a founder member and thoroughly good egg. Everybody liked him. He didn't deserve—' Leaf shivered uncontrollably.

'Do you know who his companion was?'

'The one who got kidnapped?' He shook his head. 'Not Mrs Leaf is all I know.'

'How many members are there?' I nibbled my biscuit.

'None now,' Leaf told me. 'Everyone quit after Skotter Heath

Jackson. Didn't save Henshaw though.' He picked at his cake with his fingers before pushing it aside.

I could have eaten that.

'I shall need their names,' I told Leaf and he grimaced.

'I had to vow to drink my own urine if I betrayed their names.'

'Well, you cannot do that in here,' Dodo said severely.

Though it might be better than the tea, I thought.

'I could just arrest you for obstructing our enquiries,' I suggested.

'Might be safer in jail,' Leaf snorted but then thought better of it. 'I'll send you a list first thing in the morning.'

'Do you have any idea why somebody might want to kill you all?' I dunked my biscuit in the hope that this might make it taste better. It didn't.

'Apart from you all being silly, horrid men,' Dodo chipped in helpfully.

'None at all.' Leaf spread out his palms. 'I'd be the first to admit we've been a bit boisterous at times but we've always paid for any damage. Nobody has ever refused to take a booking from us except SLAG, the anti-drink people, and our secretary only approached them because he misunderstood what they were about.'

'We shall need to speak to you again,' I told him.

'Oh, do we have to?' Dodo moaned.

'And I strongly advise you to get that bump on your head seen to. Is there a Mrs Leaf?'

'I hope so.' Maurice Leaf half-rose to stuff his handkerchief into his trouser pocket. 'We had a big row about my recent... erratic behaviour. I couldn't tell her I'm scared shitless.'

'I should hope not,' Dodo scolded.

'Closing now.' Mavish Brittle came over. 'Boil my beets! It's like a chimps' tea party in here.'

'I haven't made a mess,' I piped up virtuously, just before a soggy bit of my dunked biscuit splotted onto the cloth.

*

Thurston Wicks rang the station. He had heard nothing more but demanded to know what I was doing. I explained that Lavender's kidnap was being investigated by another force as she had been kidnapped in another county. Understandably, he was not impressed.

I got hold of Superintendent Thatchman of the Essex Constabulary, who was charming and only very slightly patronising. He told me he had all available men on the case and would appraise me of any developments, which I took to mean he would let us know when they had a result.

'Trust a Suffolk girl to get herself kidnapped,' he sniped.

'Let's hope we can trust an Essex policeman to rescue her,' I replied but there must have been a fault in the line because it went dead.

I rang Thurston Wicks back and advised him to badger them and let me know if he heard anything. In an attempt to steady himself he had had a few drinks since we spoke, but only succeeded in unsteadying himself.

'She's not as strong as she likes to make out,' he assured me, choked with emotion, 'not a tough old bird like you.'

'I'll get our superintendent to find out what's happening,' I promised. 'But he's unwell.'

'Vesty?' Mr Wicks sneered. 'When isn't he? You need a proper man in charge, not that tinhead.'

And, much as I hated the sentiment and the way he expressed it, I feared Thurston Wicks might be right.

SWIMMING WITH PIRANHAS

We had coffee before the Ipswich conference started. I was, of course – apart from the waitresses and secretaries – the only woman there. We had six women constables in East Suffolk now and there were rumours one was to be given stripes, but I remained the only one ranked high enough to attend. Vesty should have gone but he was still unwell and we couldn't send a sergeant, so I left Brigsy to bask in the glory of being the top policeman in all of Sackwater and District – heady stuff indeed, given our current plague of crimes, for an officer whose greatest triumph to date was catching a sheep rustler.

Superintendent Browning made a beeline for me. He had been introduced to us all as chairman of some committee or other.

'He-llo.' He put out a hand so high I thought he was making a grab for my left breast and maybe he was, but I managed to divert it in a clumsy shake. 'Nice to see a bit of glamour in the force.'

'Yes, it would be,' I agreed.

He stepped back to appraise me. 'Nice legs.'

I stepped back to appraise him. 'Not quite as nice as yours, sir.'

Browning took two steps forward and dipped his head until it almost rested affectionately on my shoulder. 'Heard talk about you.' He lowered his voice to seduction level. 'And the general feeling is you're not quite as good a copper as you think. Sharkey, he's a good solid officer, worked his way up from the ranks.' So had I but I didn't get a chance to say so. 'He's sent in a couple of worrying reports—'

'About what?' I broke in, but Browning tapped his nose in an infuriatingly Pookyish manner.

'The whisper is that the only reason you got promotion is because you stole Heartsease's case by—'

'Chief Inspector Heartsease gave me that case because he was getting nowhere and thought I wouldn't either,' I burst out, quite a bit louder than I had intended. I was aware of voices stilled and heads turning.

'The only reason,' Browning continued as if I hadn't spoken, 'you weren't kicked out for getting yourself crippled is because you are Grice and Middleton's bastard child.'

There were too many things to object to in that sentence so I homed in on *bastard* and was about to tell him he better fitted that description than me when a chief superintendent breezed between us like a boxing referee and, like any good referee, stopped the fight before it got too bloody.

'I see you two have already met, splendid. Chivers is the name.' He grasped my hand firmly and looked at me straight with his bright harebell eyes. 'I believe you know my daughter?'

'Dodo? Yes, very well.'

'Dodo?' He had a light easy laugh. 'Is that what she calls herself now? She's always been Dolores to me – at least that's what she chose to call herself.'

'Chose?' I wondered. There was something puzzling about his puzzlement.

Fido Chivers nodded thoughtfully. 'This coffee tastes like it came out of a camel's arse.'

'I'll take your word for that, sir.'

'Fido,' he insisted.

'Betty.'

'Fancy a proper drink?' he said brightly. 'They'll spend the first hour reading the minutes of last month's meeting and congratulating each other. The bar should be open in the members' lounge – the only reason I joined this stuffy mausoleum in the first place.'

We were in the Guildhall of the Ancient Order of Shrivers, though it had lost any religious significance a very long time ago.

'Sounds good to me.' Some women don't know when they're being picked up. I do and this was not one of those occasions.

The bar was all dark oak and deserted, apart from ourselves and a barman who looked like he might have been an original feature. We settled into two worn, sagging but very comfortable leather armchairs by a bay window overlooking Tavern Street. There was no need to cross these windowpanes with tape; they had been crossed with lead about four hundred years previously.

A waiter brought us two large whiskies with a silver jug of water.

'Wouldn't pay too much attention to Biffo Browning.' Fido raised his glass in an unspoken toast. 'You were supposed to flutter your eyelids and giggle like all his typists do.'

'I'm not much good at fluttering.' I raised my glass in reply.

'I don't suppose you are.' We both took a slug. 'I hope the war ends before this runs short.'

I rolled it around my mouth. 'Old Pulteney?'

'You know your whiskies.' He raised an impressed eyebrow. 'So how are you finding life in Sackwater?'

'You know I was born there?' I asked. He nodded and I continued, 'Not as strange as I thought I would. I expected to keep bumping into childhood friends and finding it awkward but because I went away to school—'

'Roedene Abbey.'

'You've done your homework.'

'Good coppers like us always do.'

I accepted the compliment with a smile. 'Most of the men have accepted me surprisingly quickly.'

'Except Inspector Sharkey?'

'I don't think we will ever be friends.'

'I'm not sure it would be wise to be his.' Chief Superintendent Chivers tossed down his drink while I was still halfway through mine, and most people would agree I can knock it back. 'How's Vesty getting on?' He asked this slightly too casually for my liking.

'His doctor tells me he should be out soon,' I lied. Dr Jackson had told me he was having doubts his friend and patient would ever be well enough to return to work.

'He was a good man in his time,' Chivers mused. 'If he did have to be invalided out it would be with honour.' He waved a hand impatiently at himself. ''Nuff said.'

'I presume you have heard about the kidnapping case.' I watched the chief superintendent slip a fat cigar out of a triple-tubed cigar case.

'Lavender Wicks? Who hasn't?'

'Essex Police are not being very cooperative,' I complained.

'Nor will they be.' Chivers rustled a fat cigar between his thumb and first two fingers under his bulbous nose. 'Chief Superintendent Drinkwater has taken charge of that case. Rest assured he would resist an invasion by the Suffolk Constabulary more vigorously than if we were crack German troops. You've met the famous Thurston, I take it?' He slipped the cigar away without even clipping it. 'Break a few ladies' hearts if they found out about him.'

'Being married?' I asked in surprise. 'I thought that was common knowledge.'

'Being a fairy,' Fido corrected me. 'Never had a girlfriend, though they used to get various starlets to attend functions with him. Rumours were still rife, though, so Thurston was told to get himself a wife. Then he was photographed with a German diplomat a few years back. All had to be hushed up, of course, but the studios got wind. They were terrified it would get out and they would lose their investment, so they told him to make himself scarce for a few months until it blew over.'

That, I supposed, explained why he and Lavender had set up home in remotest Suffolk.

'And did it?' I asked.

Fido shrugged. 'Don't really keep up with showbusiness gossip but I gather the film-makers found they didn't miss Thurston as much as they thought they would and gave his part to someone younger who could actually act.'

For a man with no interest in gossip, Chief Superintendent Chivers seemed to know a lot of it.

'Crispin Staples,' I recalled.

He chuckled, then fell silent, shuffling in his seat so much I was half-expecting him to get up and go when he asked suddenly, 'How's Dolores getting on?'

I hesitated. 'Have you asked her?'

'Good fudging.' He grinned. 'I don't need to. Dolores tells me she is getting on splendidly. She sings your praises to the heavens.'

'And yours,' I assured him.

'Let me make this easy for you.' He tipped a little more water from the silver jug into his Scotch. 'She's bloody hopeless, isn't she?'

'Well...'

He put up a hand. 'You don't need to deny it.' Chief Superintendent Chivers puffed and unpuffed his cheeks. 'When Dolores tried to join, I rang the applications board chairman to insist that I did not want her to be given special treatment. He obviously took this as a veiled threat and they accepted her. How the hell she got through the medical beats me.'

God and Inspector Church knew the answer to that but one of us wasn't telling.

'To be fair, she was very good in a crisis,' I told him.

'The railway station murder?'

'She acted very quickly to try to save his life,' I told her father. 'But she is – how can I put this – an unusual person.'

'Well, there's an understatement. Drink up.' He signalled to the barman for two more.

'I'll fall asleep during a lecture at this rate,' I warned.

'Why not? I always do,' he snuffled. 'Anything worth knowing goes into the leaflet they send to every station anyway.'

'Dodo never mentions her mother,' I ruminated.

'Hardly knew her.'

'Did your wife die when Dodo was a baby?'

Fido Chivers looked at me curiously. 'You don't know, do you?'

I swirled my whisky in the tumbler.

'What don't I know, Fido?' I urged softly, though I knew this must be the main point of our tête-à-tête.

'Dolores's birth name was Drusilla.' He sat back to let the penny drop. 'Vernon Willowdale, the Camden Vampire. She's his daughter.'

Oh poor Dodo.

Chivers continued, 'She had a bad time when her father was hanged. She was sent to St Jerome's, a particularly brutal workhouse in the East End. There was no attempt to hide her true identity and she was bullied terribly. I had no role in the case but Rea, my wife, heard about the little girl, made enquiries, visited her and brought her straight back to our home. Dolores was a sweet child. We fell in love with her instantly and adopted her but then my wife died – consumption.'

'Does Dolores remember all this?'

'Oh yes, she was seven at the time. As I say, we gave her our surname but it was Dolores's idea to change her Christian names.'

I finished my first drink. 'Did you ever ask if she was used – wittingly or unwittingly – as a decoy?'

Fido breathed heavily. 'How can you ask a child a question like that?'

I poured a little water from the jug and tried not to think about it.

'Poor Dodo,' I said aloud at last. When I was seven my biggest worry was if I would get the doll I had seen in Palmer's Toys of Anglethorpe.

'She's a lovely person,' Chief Superintendent Chivers assured me. 'Very loving and loyal.' He chuckled. 'I'm making her sound like a pet poodle.' His face became serious again. 'I sometimes think she behaves so childishly because she still wants the childhood she never had. Her father was a brute, by all accounts.' He finished his second drink – I had hardly started mine – and stood up. 'I have to go to give a report now but, if I were you, I wouldn't bother going to any of the meetings – seriously. Finish your drink and have another on me, if you like.'

'I'm sorry, sir,' the barman called, 'but there's no unaccompanied ladies in the members' lounge.'

'An excellent rule,' Fido Chivers told him wholeheartedly. 'But there is no such thing as a lady police officer.' He winked at me. 'Dolores told me you said that.' His voice dropped. 'I just wanted you to be aware in case anybody else finds out and makes trouble for you both.' He smiled grimly. 'You are swimming with piranhas and they will strip you to the bone given half a chance.' I stood and we shook hands. 'Anyway. Tell her not to forget me.'

'I hardly think that's likely,' I assured the chief superintendent. 'She thinks the world of you.'

'Be nice if she turned up occasionally to tell me that in person,' he commented wryly.

But Dodo told me she had, flicked through my head. But maybe he was like my parents, complaining about me neglecting them when they were the ones who made no effort.

Fido Chivers rebuttoned his jacket and I wondered if I or any woman would ever get a crown on their epaulette.

'Anyway, enjoy your drink,' he was saying. 'You are obviously a connoisseur.'

'Shall I tell you a small truth?' I broke down and confessed. 'I saw the bottle.'

I didn't finish my drink but I did spend a long time peering into it. As usual, there were no answers there.

'Oh Dodo,' I said, unintentionally aloud. *So little and wide-eyed even now. What must you have been like then?* I lit a cigarette.

I had been so mean to her, treating her as a silly soppy girl when she had endured a tougher, nastier world than I could even imagine.

'I'm sorry,' I whispered.

'That's all right, miss,' the barman reassured me. He was polishing the next table and staring at my legs.

I didn't bother asking what he thought I was apologising for.

'Inspector,' I corrected him.

'Yeah.' He winked. 'But only for the duration.'

'And what will you do,' I enquired nicely, 'when the real barmen get back from the war?'

88

THE CAT AND THE CANARY

Back in Sackwater I decided to take the twins for a walk.

'Ohhh, mam, but our feet are so very footsore,' Algy moaned.

'Chin up, Algernon,' Sandy urged. 'I'll mek you a nice mustard bath when we get 'ome.'

'For goodness' sake,' I said. 'We're hardly halfway there yet.'

''Alfway?' Algy staggered sideways like I had caught him with a spiked mace. 'I think I'm going to 'ave one of me little turns.'

'With a nice mug of 'ot milk,' Sandy promised and his brother calmed down.

'Let me tell you something' – I increased my pace – 'that policemen do not have – ever.'

'Oh no, please mam, let uz guess,' Algy begged.

'Rolls-Royce cars,' Sandy tried.

'No.'

'But they don't,' Sandy objected.

'Chief Superintendent Browning has two,' I lied. 'Anyway, you're supposed to guess what I was going to say.'

'But 'ow can we do that when we don't know?' Algy puzzled.

'A camel,' Sandy speculated. 'Or does Chief Superintendent Browning 'ave a gaggle of them?'

'Don't be silly, Lysander,' his brother scolded. 'Camels come in flocks.'

'Herds,' I said as we made our way down Featherstone Lane.

'So is that the answer?' Sandy curled up his lip in disgust. He and his brother had asked permission to start growing moustaches the previous day and were already putting Brigsy to shame with quite promising flaxen adornments.

'No.' I toed a pine cone back into the dunes.

'Goal!' the twins shouted, slapping each other's backs and running towards me with arms outstretched before thinking better of it.

'A notepad,' Algy guessed.

'Well, that was a more sensible suggestion,' I encouraged him, 'but, if you think about it for a minute, you have both got notebooks and so have I.' I tapped my breast pocket and looked from one to the other as they exchanged guilty glances. 'You *do* have notebooks, don't you?'

I stopped and they did too.

'Well...' Sandy screwed up his face like he was sucking on a lemon. 'Yes.'

'Indeed,' Algy concurred uneasily.

I thrust out my hand. 'Show me.'

'Well, we didn't say we 'ad them on uz.' Sandy dragged his words out carefully.

I dropped my hand onto my hip. 'Explain.'

'Well, they rub,' Algy obliged.

'We 'ave very sensitive nipples,' Sandy expanded.

'Do you seriously think that your nipples are more sensitive than—' I just managed to stop myself saying *mine* – not a conversation I wanted to enter into with my constables, 'anybody else's?'

'Yes,' they insisted in unison.

'We could never wear starched cassocks when we wuz altar boys,' Sandy recalled.

'Well, why couldn't you put them in your side pockets?'

'We tried,' Sandy said.

'But they ruined the lines of our jackets.' Algy patted his slender waist to emphasise the statement.

'Listen.' I strode on with them lolloping either side of me like a pair of Afghan hounds. 'Regulations require that you carry a notebook and pencil at all times.'

'Oh but pencils can be very sharp.' Algy flapped.

'For the very good reason that, in the unlikely instance of either of you arresting anyone, you will be required to produce your notebook in court.'

'She said *unlikely*,' Sandy pointed out to his twin.

'That wasn't very kind,' Algy simpered.

'I am not trying to be kind,' I told them.

'And not managing to be,' Sandy murmured.

'What did you say?' I spun towards him, nearly toppling over my own feet and grabbing his lapel to steady myself.

'Ohhh, Algernon,' he shrieked, 'mam is going to beat me up.'

'Tell 'er you'll bring your notebook in future,' Algy urged.

'I will,' he vowed.

'So will I,' Algy promised and I released my grip.

'What was the answer to your guessing game, mam?' Sandy asked as we turned down Pinfold Lane.

'Little turns,' I replied. 'Policemen never have little turns.'

'Ohhh, that's not fair,' they chorused.

'Because *we* do,' Algy explained.

'Then you are to stop it immediately.' I came to a halt. 'Have you stopped it?'

'We're trying.' They wrung their hands like the poor widow with no fuel when it is snowing in the first scene of a melodrama.

'Right, wait here.'

'Which one...'

'Of us?'

'Both of you.'

'Ohhhhh.' They threw their hands up in as much despair as the widow being evicted by wicked Squire Jasper in scene two.

'An old woman lives alone in that house,' I explained. 'What will she think if she sees three police officers marching up her drive?'

They scratched their heads like Stan Laurel at his most perplexed.

'It's difficult for us to think what she'll think,' Sandy decided.

'Because we don't know 'er,' Algy put in.

'She will be alarmed,' I said.

'Do you know 'er then, mam?' Sandy asked.

Oh good grief!

'I explained all this at the station,' I reminded the twins and they scratched their heads in gestures of puzzlement that Stan Laurel would have been proud of.

'Oh yes,' they remembered.

'But we weren't realleh—' Algy began.

'Listening,' Sandy concluded.

'It's where you are going to keep look-out,' I snapped.

'Oh we thought that was... just—' Sandy said tentatively.

'Make pretend,' Sandy confessed.

I took a long deep breath before deciding not to waste it.

'Wait here,' I ordered and went up another twenty feet to the driveway of Sandy View – aptly named, for there was sweet damn all else to see except that, crucially for me, it backed onto Pinfold Lane. Even more luckily, this was a dormer bungalow with two hip windows in the red-tiled roof overlooking the Wickses' Treetops House across the road.

'I don't think Stumpy knows her either,' Sandy whispered. 'I think she is bluffing.'

Either I had superhuman hearing – and I don't think I did – or the modern generation had not been taught how to whisper. Dodo was hopeless at it and they were little better.

In contrast to the unkempt rear of the property, there was a nice little garden at the front with a path curving round a rockery stocked with doubtless a great variety of heathers, although they looked identical to me.

I rang the bell. It was answered almost immediately by a little old lady with a pleated linen mob-cap Jane Austen's great-aunt might have worn and an overly large apron with shoulder ruffles and a pattern of what looked like little swastikas but were, I decided, faded pansies or butterflies.

'If you've come about my George, it was her fault for leaving the cage open.' She trembled.

'George is your cat?'

'And her canary flew into our garden.'

'Has she made threats against you?'

'She threatened to call the police,' the old lady quavered, which was no use to me. I wanted to be doing her a favour rather than begging one that she could refuse. 'Then she said she would drown George in the bath.' That wasn't much but it would have to do.

'Well,' I said, 'we take these threats very seriously Mrs... I'm sorry, I've forgotten your name.'

'Violet Scrup.'

'Oh, I had an aunt called that.'

'Scrup?' She lit up. 'Really? It's not as common a name as you might think. We must be related.' She held out her arms for an embrace that was never to be consummated. 'You must call me Aunty Vi, dear, and I shall call you Deirdre.'

'Inspector Church might be better while I'm in uniform,' I suggested.

'Oh!' She shrieked so suddenly and loudly I thought she might have been stabbed by an unseen assailant. 'Your poor poor arm. What have they done to you, darling?'

'It's just gone for repair,' I said. This seemed to satisfy Mrs Scrup, which was more than most of my inventions did with most people.

'It's wonderful what they can do these days,' the woman who would never be Aunty Vi to me enthused while I struggled to get back to the reason for my visit.

'We take these threats very seriously, Mrs,' I repeated, 'Scrup, and we have assigned two policemen to guard you until the threat is over.'

'Sergeants?' Mrs Scrup's face lit up. 'Oh I love a sergeant.' She clasped her hands joyfully.

'Constables.'

'Burly?' The light had dimmed but was almost instantly rekindled. 'Oh I love a burly constable.'

'I can let you have tall.' I hadn't been expecting to haggle.

'With ginger hair? Oh, I—'

'In the right sort of light,' I hastened to say as confidently as I could be bothered and motioned them over. 'This Constable Grinder-Snipe will keep watch in one of your rear upstairs windows.'

'But George mainly uses the front garden,' she objected.

'Our intelligence tells us to expect an assault from the roof, madam,' Sandy said, with commendable quick-wittedness but rather spoiling the logic of my next announcement.

'And this Constable Grinder-Snipe will hide in your potting shed at the back.'

Mrs Scrup blinked repeatedly. 'They look very similar.'

'We have to mass-produce them in wartime,' I told her. 'Not handcrafted like the older officers. Well, I shall leave you in their capable hands, madam. And please don't feel the need to offer them anything. They might pretend to want tea or food but that's just their little joke.'

'Ohhh,' they both gasped.

That'll teach you to call me Stumpy *within earshot*, I thought and whistled as I went back up the road, which was all the more enjoyable because I had been brought up with the belief that ladies never whistle.

89

THE ALLIGATOR AND THE CHAIN

The phone rang on the hour. I know for certain when it was because Rivers' shift had finished. In motion Rivers reminded me of an alligator I had seen in Anglethorpe Zoo. It had drifted in a concrete moat like a log. 'It's a fake.' A smart young lad in a sleeveless pullover had leaned over the railings and prodded it with a stick. In an instant the water was a foaming mass and the alligator had whipped round and ripped that stick out of the intelligent child's grasp, tragically not quite dragging him in with it.

The moment the minute hand of the station clock clicked into place, Rivers the waxwork became Rivers the rival to Jesse Owens and was out of the door.

Brigsy was doing what Brigsy did best – brewing up a big brown pot of tea – so I picked up the handpiece. 'Sackwater Central Police Station.'

'Church?' I recognised that voice immediately.

'Yes this is Inspector Church, Mr Wicks. Have you had any news about your wife?'

'I have received instructions about the demand.'

'Was this by letter in the same way again?'

'Yes.'

'Did you remember what I said about not touching the note?' I asked.

'Of course I fricking did,' he assured me in the enchanting and sober manner that had become his trademark as far as I was concerned.

'What does the note say?' I pressed on.

'Tell Inspector Church to be at your house in one hour. Delivery instructions to follow.'

'He asked for me by name?' I said in surprise.

'I have just said so,' Thurston Wicks pointed out with every justification.

I briefly mulled it over. Why would the kidnapper choose me? Was it because he had read about my connection with the 'vampire' murders or had Lavender given my name as somebody who could be trusted?

'And it has just come?'

'Hot off the press.'

'Did he say anything else?'

'Do you think I wouldn't have told you if he had?' Thurston Wicks sneered.

'I'm on my way,' I told him.

The Wolseley was parked round the back but I couldn't drive any more and Brigsy had never learned. I briefly explained what had happened and got out my trusty Raleigh Ladies' Popular.

It was already late crow-time when I freewheeled off the forecourt.

'Good evening, Inspector.'

I wobbled in surprise as Toby Gregson appeared at my side on the pavement.

'Oh hello, Toby. You aren't here on police business, are you?' I hoped not. I was glad to see him but I had no time to spare.

'No, just on my way home from the office.' He stepped back into the shadows. 'Any information on the killings?'

'I'm sorry, Toby, I'm in a bit of a hurry.'

'Perhaps we could have another drink and talk things over?'

'I'll give you a ring,' I said and meant it but, for some reason, it sounded like I didn't.

It was only after I had pedalled off that I thought about it. Toby Gregson lived in Mafeking Gardens, the opposite direction from the *Gazette*'s office on Straight Street.

90

THE TRACTOR, THE CAT AND THE RAT

The evening was surprisingly mild though still damp after the heavy rain earlier. An ambulance went by, but it seemed in no great hurry so I assumed it was nothing too urgent. The sun was low and, of course, straight in my eyes so I kept my head as low as possible. A tractor chugged past with a pile of manure on a trailer, two farmer's lads sitting happily on top of it.

One put his fingers in his mouth and blew a piercing whistle. 'Keep those legs pumping, darlin'.'

'She int got no crossbar,' the other jeered. 'Want to straddle my crossbar, darlin'?'

'Bet that muck didn't smell half as bad until you climbed onto it,' I muttered to myself but did my best to maintain a dignified aloofness – not easy when I was pedalling along the gutter to avoid the filth showering onto the road. Luckily I was at my turning and they were soon out of view, only their wolf-howls and even more obscene suggestions following me down Pinfold Lane.

I never understood why men did that. Did they really imagine their leers and jeers would entice me to roll abandonedly in cow shit with them?

There had been a drift of fine sand a few inches deep and my bike wheels were spinning uselessly on the higher ridges, so I dismounted and walked to Treetops House. Across the road was the back of Sandy View, Mrs Scrup's home. I could clearly see the potting shed in her back garden. This was where Sandy was supposed to be hiding but the door was wide open and, unless he had taken camouflage classes, my constable was not inside.

'Grinder-Snipe,' I bellowed, terrifying a pheasant out of cover but failing to get my constable to break his.

I stacked my bike against a gorse bush and scrambled up the low dune. One reason I had chosen Sandy View and not the next house along, which had just as good a view of the front of the Wickses' home, was that it had no rear fence so Sandy, on getting a signal from his twin, could burst out and nab whoever delivered the ransom instructions. This was perhaps not very subtle but I was confident that, if we could catch the kidnapper or his accomplice, we could persuade him to reveal the whereabouts of Lavender rather than face a more severe charge, kidnapping and murder carrying a mandatory death sentence. It seemed a better plan to me than trying to follow the messenger and risk losing him, or simply paying the ransom and relying on the kidnapper keeping his side of the bargain.

I was fully aware that the Essex force regarded this as their case since the crime was committed on their territory but, as far as I was concerned, the victim came from my patch, I had been instructed to deliver the ransom and it was my duty to try to save Lavender Wicks.

I trampled down the other side of the dune, snatching at a clump of marram grass to stop myself sliding.

'Grinder-Snipe,' I yelled repeatedly, bulldozing through a patch of bracken and traipsing over an uncut, ankle-high lawn.

I had almost reached the back door when it flew open.

'Ohhhh, mam.' Sandy stood flapping his fingers. 'It's all gone 'orribly wrong.'

I marched up to Constable Lysander Grinder-Snipe.

'How?' This had better be good. If they had fallen asleep or left their posts for a tea break, they would find themselves on the uncomfortable side of a disciplinary hearing before the week was out.

'It's Algernon, mam. 'e's...' Sandy choked, swallowed and tried again. ''E's...' Sandy burst into tears and then I remembered the ambulance. It had been travelling quite sedately – but then it wouldn't bother rushing for a fatality.

'Is he—?' I began.

'Yes.'

'Is he—?' I began again.

'Been tekken to 'ospital,' Sandy managed.

'Is he—?' I tried a third time.

'Broken leg.' Violet Scrup came into the kitchen behind the constable, her mob-cap flopping forlornly. 'And it's all my fault.'

She didn't look capable of breaking anybody's leg but then, I suppose, neither does a swan, which everybody tells you can do that with its wing.

'What happened?' I glanced at my watch. It was four thirty and the dark was creeping up steadily. 'And make it quick.'

'I screamed,' Mrs Scrup confessed shamefacedly. 'George brought a rat in and was running upstairs with it. Your brave boy in blue came running down to save me, tripped over George and fell headlong into my umbrella stand. There was a horrible crack. I thought it was the nice ebony cane Mr Scrup used to take to chapel on Sundays but it was poor Constable Gutter-Snipe's hind leg.'

'Did you see anyone go to Treetops?' I asked Sandy.

'No, mam,' he sobbed. 'And I did go straight upstairs even though...' he coughed back his misery, 'poor Algernon was in such pain and not being in the least bit brave about it...' At least, I consoled myself, Sandy had had the dedication and initiative to take over his brother's watching post – but then he spoiled that delusion by admitting, 'Because I couldn't stand the racket any longer and the potting shed is very uncomfortable.'

'I gave the poor wounded man a cup of tea and an iced bun,' Mrs Scrup assured me, which was good news because we all know those things heal a broken leg and, if you need an anaesthetic, it's always a good idea to have a full stomach.

'If I come out of Treetops and wave both arms, come out for instruction.'

'You will 'old your left one 'igh up, won't you,' Sandy mithered. 'Only...' He fumbled for words.

'I have noticed that it's shorter,' I assured him. 'If I wave just one arm – my right – you may go to see your brother.' I awaited his gratitude.

'Do I 'ave to, mam? I 'ate 'ospitals. They remind me of illness.'

'Yes,' I insisted. 'But on your way, let them know at the station what's happening and say not to do anything until they hear from me.'

Sandy Grinder-Snipe wrinkled his forehead. 'The railway station?'

'The police station.' I missed out an expletive after *the* in deference to Mrs Scrup.

'Whatever you were up to, it's a fucking cock-up, isn't it?' she suggested sweetly.

91

THISTLES AND THE TEARDROP COUPÉ

I raced back through the garden.

'Mind my flowers,' Violet Scrup called after me but, apart from daisies, died-down dandelions and a lonely thistle I could see nothing the head gardener at Kew might recognise as a flower.

I hurtled over the dune back onto the road, seeing my bike at the last moment and hurdling it in a leap that would have got me straight back into the athletics team Miss Addison removed me – but not Hortensia Bogwhist – from for smoking even though Hortensia had given me the cigarette.

Cars rarely came down Pinfold Lane but a very sleek and very, very expensive cherry-red Talbot-Darracq Teardrop Coupé that was clearly exempt from all traffic regulations came skidding to a halt.

'Get off the bloody road, woman.' The driver honked imperiously. I straightened myself up, turning for him to see POLICE printed in black on my helmet. *Oh sorry, Officer*, I imagined him saying, but only getting, 'Bloody bobby should know bloody better.' As he swept away I recognised the driver as Arthur, Lord Stovebury's son. We had danced together once at Stovebury Hall a long time ago. I never forgot him, so dashing and aloof, but to him I was just another local girl getting a taste of noblesse oblige. He had better not park on the pavement outside the Stovebury-Furnace Estates Office while I was in the area again.

Pooky came to the door.

'Oh it's you.'

'Thank you for that invaluable information.'

Pooky turned her head from side to side like I was a modern painting that nobody was quite sure which way up to hang.

'Give them a uniform and the power goes to their heads.' She sniffed.

'Exactly what I was thinking.' I gazed at hers and Pooky sniffed again.

'Come in and wipe your feet.'

I did as I was bid, unable to resist saying, 'Kindly announce me to your master.'

Pooky's face went rancid but she didn't have a chance to respond because a door flapped open.

'Inspector Church.' Thurston Wicks strode into the hall, glass in hand. 'You took your time.'

I wanted to ask who else's time I could take, and I certainly wasn't going to apologise for having had to cycle to his inconveniently situated house.

'Have you had any more messages?' I asked and he scowled.

'If I had, your men would have told you.' He drained his glass and let it fall unharmed onto the thick-pile carpet.

'They were called out on an emergency,' I lied.

Wicks clenched his fists. 'A bigger emergency than this?'

'We think it relates to this case but I cannot tell you any more at present.' And it flicked through my head how Sister Millicent had warned that little lies lead to bigger lies and so on ad infinitum and that, if anybody should know, she should. 'Can I see the latest letter?'

'I never touched it,' Pooky insisted, though I had not even asked her. 'Well, only quickly.'

'Come to my den.' Mr Wicks led me down the long whiteness that was his hall. He had a long easy stride and kept his head level – like Sister Millicent had taught us to do with a Bible on our heads because she knew that we would make sure not to commit the sin of letting God's holy word slide to the floor – but I noticed he weaved like Stanley Matthews on his way to score a goal, except with considerably less grace.

We passed Lavender's snug on the right and took the next door on the left.

The word *den* had conjured up an image of the tree house I had built in our sycamore despite my father's assistance, but this room was a bit more sophisticated than that – there was not one nail jutting through the floorboards when we went from the whiteness into a yellowness that turned out to be his study.

This room was wood-lined and everything in it – the panelling, the desk and chair, the bookcase, the ceiling – was painted in slightly different shades of yellow. Only the floor wasn't painted and that was because it was carpeted – in yellow.

It was rather a nice colour but, as I was told by Sister Millicent – who seemed to be cropping up in my thoughts an awful lot lately – you can have too much of good thing. I never believed it until she gave me a whole bag of sugar to eat one lunchtime.

The only breaks in the colour scheme were pictures, every one of them featuring Thurston Wicks's one true love. A large framed poster of Thurston, swooning brunette draped over his arm, cocktail in his free hand, hung over the fireplace. Portraits of Thurston adorned the walls, including a life-sized one behind the desk that had him breathing smoke through his nostrils from a cigarette in a long holder. Photographs on the mantelpiece showed him with glamorous women, one of whom might have been Bette Davis, and a signed picture on a table was definitely Edward G. Robinson, but I was not going to flatter Mr Wicks by peering closely at them. We had a rather more important matter at hand.

'You saw nobody?'

The letter lay unfolded on the desk.

'We kept away from the windows for fear of frightening him off,' he said reasonably, resting his fingertips on a picture of himself and Katharine Hepburn and not seeming to notice that he had knocked it over.

'And it came just like this – no envelope.'

'Exactly.' Thurston Wicks looked up at me. 'And there is nothing on the back.'

He had weighed down the edges with little wooden rulers, creating a makeshift frame.

'INSPECTOR CHURCH,' I read,

BRING THE MONEY IN YOUR HANDBAG TO THE KING'S OAK AT SIX THIRTY-FIVE. HANG IT ON THE HOOK IN THE HOLLOW. IF ANYBODY GOES INTO THE TREE BEFORE THEN THE DEAL IS OFF. MR WICKS WILL STAY AT HOME AND AWAIT MY PHONE CALL. COME ALONE. DO NOT BE LATE OR LAVENDER WICKS WILL DIE. NAPOLEON SPARTA THE SUFFOLK VAMPIRE

A butcher's hook had been driven into the inside of that tree many years ago. Some said a poacher used to string his rabbits on it to hide them. Others said a man had hanged himself on it. If so, he must have been a midget, for it was only about four feet from the ground.

'Wilson said you will know where that is.' Thurston casually rotated Groucho Marx towards me. The comedian was puffing a big cigar.

I nodded. 'So whoever wrote that demand must have detailed local knowledge.' I looked at my watch. It was eight minutes past six already. I would have a job to get there by then. 'Have you got the money?'

Thurston Wicks pointed. 'Behind the desk.' He poured himself a brandy from a cut-glass decanter, sploshing it over the cuff of his shirt.

I went round to find a green canvas duffel bag tied at the mouth. I untied the cord and pulled the mouth open. There were bundles of ten-pound notes inside, each wrapped in a gummed white paper band. I stacked them on the desk, twenty-five of them, all old, as far as I could see randomly numbered.

'Did the bank not question why you wanted this much money?'

Thurston Wicks shrugged his left shoulder. 'Who said anything about banks?' He downed the drink in one and slopped out another.

'You keep this much money in the house?'

'And more,' he told me.

I blew out between my lips. 'You do make a tax return, don't you, Mr Wicks?'

'My accountant does.'

'Ever heard of burglars?' I asked.

'Ever heard of the Depression?' he countered.

'Like everybody else, I lived through it.' I didn't tell him my maternal grandfather had lost a fortune investing everything in a hair oil company. He had owned Tringford Hall but ended up in the attic of Felicity House.

'I want my money where I can get my hands on it whenever I want it.'

'I hope you have a good safe.'

'It would take an expert just to find it,' he boasted. 'And I doubt the one in Martins Bank has a better lock.'

'I'll have to empty my handbag.' I unpacked it into his duffel bag and stuffed my torch into my jacket pocket and the money into my bag, just managing to force the clip shut. 'I had better get going.'

'Oh God...' Thurston suddenly seemed to realise this was really happening. He rubbed his brow. 'I am drunk and being stupid.' He crumpled somewhere in the middle. 'It's this constant need to keep up an image.' He ran his fingers through his not-so-carefully-more-than-slightly-tousled-now hair. 'Oh shit.' Thurston Wicks staggered one step sideways. 'I love my wife, Inspector, and I want her back.'

I went towards the door and he shot an arm across it in the way drunks do when they think they might get a kiss. But Thurston Wicks was not leering. He was pale and nobody can fake that on demand. His voice was steady but his gaze flickered.

And, looking into those eyes, I believed it. 'I know you do.'

'You will bring her back safe, won't you?' Thurston begged, all at once transformed by fear.

'I will do everything I can,' I promised because that was all I could promise.

92

DANCING WITH THE MARQUIS

rushed outside, jumped on my bike and, within one revolution of the wheel, I knew something was wrong. For a second I thought it was the sand or that the chain had slipped but, as soon as I climbed off to push it over the drift, I saw that the rear tyre was flat.

'Bugger-bugger-bugger.' I threw it back to the side of the road and ran. It was hopeless unless... I saw two almost-painted-out headlights approaching and, before I had even waved, slowing down. The rich purr of the engine sounded very familiar. It pulled alongside.

'Are you all right?' Arthur, Marquis Stovebury called through his wound-down window. 'I'm so sorry for my rudeness earlier but it's Father's car and I'm terrified of denting it. I came back to apologise and saw your bike so I've been cruising up and down ever since.'

I went round the front of the car and opened the passenger door. 'Take me to the King's Oak.'

'You can't order me around like that,' he said in half-amused indignation.

'Under the Emergency Powers Act I can,' I assured him, not quite sure if I could. 'I can also requisition your car if you refuse and I don't think you'd like me to be changing gears on corners.'

'King's Oak it is.' He smiled. 'Can I ask why?'

'Of course you can,' I assured him, 'but I won't tell you.'

And the marquis set off at a speed I should have flagged him down for, sand spraying in his wake like water from a speedboat.

'It's Betty, isn't it?' my new chauffeur said, not so worried about the bodywork as to avoid squealing into Manor Road on the wrong side and straightening up so violently that I was flung against him. 'I'm Arthur. You won't remember me but we danced together at a Hunt Ball, the first after the Great War. I never forgot you in that gorgeous pink dress, your golden hair, the way you swayed to the music. You were a terrible flirt.'

'I was not,' I retorted but I was. It only surprised me that he had noticed.

'You jolly well were.' We accelerated along a not-very-straight stretch. 'What happened to your arm?'

'I got fed up with it.'

'Limbs can be such a bore.' The marquis nodded. 'I'm down to my last four now.'

I laughed. The speed, dangerous and illegal, was intoxicating.

Arthur glanced over. 'You won't give me a summons for speeding?'

'Of course not,' I promised. 'You are going about urgent police business.'

'I'll give you a lift more often,' he vowed.

'Not if you go into the gate you won't,' I said.

The level crossing was closed.

'Bloody hell.' Arthur slammed the brakes on, skidding to a halt two feet from the barrier, and breathed a sigh of relief. 'Sorry, can't get used to them being blacked out. Good job one of us was paying attention to the road.'

'I'd prefer that person to be you.' I looked at my watch abstractedly.

'In a hurry?'

'I must be there by half past.'

Arthur sounded his horn and the old signalman stuck his

head out of the signal box window. 'Be another four minutes yet.'

I twisted to wind down my window. 'Then you have time to open it. Urgent police business.'

'Heard that one before, I have,' he mocked and I climbed out to show myself, flashing the torch briefly on myself.

'Can't be helped.' He shrugged. 'Rules is rules.'

Arthur poked his head out. 'Hello, Harry, how's young Albert getting on at the estate?'

The signalman squinted. 'Oh, good evening, my lord. I didn't see you there.' And, miraculously, the gate swung open.

I leaped and just had time to slam the door before the car set off again, forcing me back into my seat.

'Can you actually see where you're going?'

'Eyes like a cat,' he assured me, bumping over the kerb and nearly throwing me out of the seat he had just thrown me back in. 'Damn.' He dropped back onto the road. 'I imagine the police will compensate for any damage incurred.'

'You have a vivid but inaccurate imagination,' I told Arthur as he swerved round the shadow of a dustbin.

'Know why it's called the King's Oak?' the marquis enquired, seemingly more intent on me than on the public highway.

'Is it one of the five hundred trees Charles II is supposed to have hidden in?' I guessed.

'Don't know.' We veered sharply and without warning to the left. 'Thought you might.'

'I'm afraid not.' He wrenched the wheel and slammed on the brakes. 'Here we are.' He slid an arm over the back of my seat. 'Fancy a nightcap?'

A few years ago I would have jumped at the chance.

I slid out. 'Thank you but you have to go now.'

'Another time then.'

'I'll give...' My mind went through the possibilities. What the

423

hell was the wife of a marquis called? '...the marquisess a call,' I told him uncertainly.

'Would you like me to wait for you?'

It was starting to drizzle.

'I need to be alone.' I hoped I didn't sound too much like Greta Garbo but at the same time a bit of me hoped I did.

'As you wish, Greta.' Arthur tipped his hat and it was only after he had sped off that I remembered it was a marchioness.

93

THE HAUNTING

The Soundings was not so attractive at night as it had been when I had strolled through with Dodo after our first visit to Treetops House, but few places are in the dead of night. I made my way to the oak, a massive silhouette in my dimmed torchlight. Some said Etterly Utter haunted that tree and that they had heard her calling out at night. I didn't believe them but, when you hear these stories from people you know to be honest and reliable, you can't help wondering.

Vandals had smashed the locks off the pine door twice and nobody had bothered to replace them the second time. I drew back both the bolts. Somebody had lubricated them recently. The bars slid easily despite the metal being rusty and I could smell the oil on my fingers. The hinges had been similarly treated so the door swung open without complaint. Obviously whoever had sent me there had not done so on a moment's whim.

I hesitated. The slit can't have got any narrower but I hadn't got any smaller. It was an elongated triangle, about four feet tall at the apex, and I had to bend just to be able to shine my torch inside the tree. The interior, which had been a good-sized den to play in once, was more like a chimney now. I poked my head in, running the beam around inside. It still looked a long way up to the top opening but at least I could be sure there was nobody else hiding in there.

Here goes. I looked around me. As far as I could tell, there was no one else about but there were a dozen other trees a person could hide behind. I took off my helmet, putting it on the ground inside the tree, and was just about to follow it when I was attacked. There was a sudden rush behind me and I pulled my head out just in time to be cracked across the skull, fall to my knees and feel myself blacking out.

94

FOXES AND FASCISTS

S omehow I managed to jolt back to consciousness and grab hold of a jutting piece of bark to steady myself, half-rising and swinging round to try to lash out, but a hand went into my face and rammed me back, smashing my head against the tree.

'Struggle any more and I'll beat the faecal matter out of you,' a man's voice threatened. 'Nazi vixen.'

I had been called a Nazi before, by people who thought anyone in uniform must be a fascist, but there was something in the way my assailant made the accusation that sounded as if he thought I actually was one.

'I am a police officer,' I managed to gasp.

'Like fun you are.' A torch went on, blinding me. 'Oh flip, it's you.'

My attacker stood back and turned his torch briefly on himself and I saw it was Teddy Moulton, the bookseller, and that he had his warden's uniform on now – well, a helmet and armband at any rate.

'Yes,' I said usefully.

'Oh Betty!' He shone the light on me. 'I'm so sorry. I thought you were signalling to the foe.'

I rubbed my head. 'In a tree?'

'The beam was projecting through the superior aperture into the heavens.'

'You've been reading too many of your own books.' I had a splitting headache now.

'I'm sorry.' He took my arm to help me up and, for once, I accepted. 'Look, we've got a kettle in the shop. Let me make you a cup of herbal tea.'

'That's kind of you.' A large Scotch would have been kinder. I put my fingers to my temples to hold my battered skull together. 'But I have to ask you to leave, Teddy. I'm on police business but I can't tell you what. Can you go to Sackwater Central and tell them where I am?'

'You want backup?'

'I want them to stay away.'

He looked at me uncertainly. 'Are you sure you're all right? Only you're haemorrhaging onto your forehead.'

I put a hand up and found he was right. 'What the hell did you hit me with?'

'My torch,' he admitted. 'Still works but there's a deuce of a dent in it.'

'I've got a matching one in my scalp,' I told him. 'I'm sorry, Teddy, but I really need you to go now.'

Teddy hesitated. 'If you're free from doubt.'

'Go... please.'

Teddy, the bookselling ARP man, clumped away into the night.

I checked myself over. I was in pain but that was all. I'd been in worse pain and most pains go.

'Put that bloody light out,' I heard distantly from the man who had once banned a customer for saying *Blast* when she dropped a sixpence through a gap in the floorboards.

I crouched again and squeezed through the gap until I was inside the tree, and was getting to my feet when there was a bang. At first I thought it was in my head, because the noise sent a jolt through it, and that I must have been concussed – but I looked back and saw that the door had been slammed shut. I threw myself against it but even before I crashed into the planks I could hear the bolts being slid home.

'Shit.' I had hurt my right shoulder and jarred my head even more. 'Shit. Shit.' I sat heavily on the ground and kicked out with both feet but it was hopeless. I was shut inside a tree.

95

THE WHISPERER

f I screamed now somebody would hear me and they would probably call for the police to rescue me – but police officers don't scream and I would rather stay trapped than suffer Sharkey's mockery when he found out.

For some reason I suddenly remembered that I hadn't signalled to Sandy Grinder-Snipe when I left Treetops House and I was just working out if that mattered when I heard it.

'Betty?'

I must have imagined it.

'Is that really you, Betty?'

It must have been the wind through the branches.

'Who's there?'

'Why did you leave me, Betty?'

'Etterly?' Her name was wisped away to the clouds.

'Why, Betty?' The voice was coming through a knot hole near the top of the door.

'I didn't know you were here.' I listened hard.

'Liar.'

'I've come back for you, Etterly.'

'Liar.' The door rattled furiously. 'Filthy filthy liar.' I leaped towards it, switching on my torch, and saw an eye, the pupil screwing into a black dot, and heard a small grunt of surprise before it shot sideways, leaving me with a tunnel view of nothingness except the bark of a birch tree reflecting white in the distance.

'Nice game,' I shouted at whoever it was. 'But she never called me Betty.'

I banged the side of my fist on the wood uselessly and kicked it with my toe. I'm not claustrophobic but I am frightened of being trapped, and with good reason. I had been trapped before and nothing good ever came of those experiences. They say breathe slowly when you feel panic rising but one of the things about panic is you don't feel you can breathe at all. I was getting hot and unbuttoned my coat. There was nothing I could force my way out with. My penknife might have been helpful but it was amongst the things I had emptied into Mr Wicks's bag and the blade would probably not have been sturdy enough to do anything useful anyway.

'Shall we play another game then?'

I tried my torch again but only got the same view of the same tree. The whisperer had learned from the experience and was to one side of the knot hole now.

I said nothing.

'Shall we?' More playfully, but still I held my peace. 'I think we shall,' the voice continued. 'Let us have a race. You should be good at running with those lovely long legs.'

'Where to?'

'To where?' the whisperer corrected me. 'I shall leave you a message in the phone box on the corner of Gordon Street.'

'And how will I get out?'

'You will break the door down.' The more that was said, the more sense I got of the accent. It didn't sound much like anyone's idea of a Transylvanian count.

'That should give you a few days' start.'

I heard a sniffy snigger. 'I shall pull back the top bolt. I have already loosened the hasp on the lower, so a few kicks should do the trick.' The precise enunciation did not sound forced. 'I shall say *go* when it's done. Ready?'

I did not reply. I was too busy listening. I did not think the bolt could be drawn back without my hearing it so, if I could break out with one effort, the whisperer would have hardly any start on me at all. I pressed my ear to the wood and thought I heard footsteps running over the grass, going away. Was it possible I had missed it? But then I heard the barrel slide back.

I sat down heavily, leaned back against the inside of the oak tree, pulled my knees up and kicked out as hard as I could on the lower crossbar. There was a crack and the door flew open. I clambered up, stumbling out into the glorious wet fresh night air, torch in hand, sweeping the green. It was not possible to have run or cycled out of the square in the few seconds it took me to escape and I had not heard a car engine, but there was nobody in sight. Was he hiding behind a tree?

'Where are you?' I shouted uselessly. 'You can't get away.'

There were footsteps racing, fading away. I rushed round the tree and caught my foot, nearly tripping – a length of garden twine tangled round my feet and I saw that the end was tied to the upper bolt. It was difficult to be sure which way it had gone after my clumsiness, but it seemed to point towards the south-eastern exit of the Soundings heading towards the sea. I hurried along it and saw that the other end, about thirty feet away, I guessed, was tied to a stone. Somebody had retracted the bolt with the twine and thrown the end back towards the door. It could have come from any direction.

There was nothing for it but to head north-west, back into the town centre and Gordon Street as instructed.

A group of men and women were coming out of the Leg O' Lamb. Saint Jaspar Divers must have been doing a good trade for they were not exactly sober. They were not exactly disorderly either, though they were belting out 'If I catch you bending I'll saw your legs right off' from that bloody awful 'Knees Up Mother

Brown'. Elsie and Doris Waters – lovely as they were – had a lot to answer for. I dashed past.

'He went that way,' a man in a donkey jacket called and I spun round to see him pointing in both directions at once, the little scallywag.

'Oh you are a card.' His female companion slapped him on the back. I could have done that and much harder, if I had had the time.

I turned down Germaine Street. It used to be German Street before the Great War and there were calls now to rename it after Haig. The street was cobbled and wet cobbles are slippery. I skidded, fell sideways and hit my stump on a wall.

'Whoops-a-daisy,' they catcalled after me, these people I was sworn to protect.

'*Foxx kemm ghandek*,' I muttered – a Maltese obscenity Adam had taught me – and ran on, trying to keep to the narrow pavement, blocked in places by dustbins because the houses had no backyards.

Germaine Street joined Gordon Street about halfway along. I turned right and ran to the phone box on the corner. This was on a crossroads, where I stopped and peered in every direction. There was no sign of anyone, the only sound being Mother-bloody-Brown coming out of the Three Farthings accompanied by a badly tuned piano. Was our strategy – in case of invasion – to annoy the Germans to death?

Those two scraggy girls were crammed into the box, the door wedged open with an empty rusty tin of bully beef.

'Farewell my own true lover,' the scrawny girl was sobbing.

Her scrawnier friend nudged her. 'Tell him you'll write,' she prompted.

'Oi'll write every day.' She covered the mouthpiece. 'What's his name?'

'Dunno,' her friend said, 'just call him *darlin*'.'

'My darlin',' she concluded, then raised her voice. 'No, I don't want to put any more money in, thank you, operator lady. I do got two more darlin's to ring yet. What d'you mean he heard tha'? Well, tha' was a waste o' fourpence.'

I pulled open the door. 'I'm sorry, police business.' And to my surprise they acquiesced cheerfully.

'Come on. Just got enough for a pack of fags.' The scrawny one rattled the coins in her pocket. 'And there's tha' new aircraft engineer with the big...' she giggled, 'piston.'

So off they went, the flower of English womanhood.

I opened the door and realised why they had propped it open. Somebody had decided it made a good urinal and it smelt like many of his friends had agreed with him.

The phone rang and I put my hand on the receiver.

'Oh,' Scrawny cried, 'that'll be Jethro.'

'You jus' spoke to him,' Scrawnier reminded her.

'Or Jed.'

'Could be Jed.'

'Go away.' I picked up the receiver. 'Hello.'

'You took your time,' the whisperer said.

'Well, I...'

'Willy. She said *Willy*,' Scrawny yelped in excitement. 'She's trying to make off with your Willy.'

'But I don't know any Willys,' Scrawnier puzzled, 'except...'

I forced the door shut but could still hear them squawking.

'Last game,' the whisperer said. 'You have fifteen minutes to get to the Pier Pavilion. The right-hand side gate and the front door are unlocked. Be in the stalls with the money or the girl dies.'

'It's quite a long way.'

'Fifteen minutes,' the whisperer said. 'Starting... *now*.' And the line went dead.

96

THE SLAUGHTERHOUSE

dialled. 'Come on.' It seemed to take for ever for the dial to whir back before I put the next number in. At least it was a direct line so I didn't have to wait for Maggie, the Sackwater Telephone Exchange night operator, to put down her darning and try to strike up a conversation. 'Come *on*.'

There was a click, a lot of throat-clearing and a 'What now?' from Brigsy.

I didn't have time to ask if he meant: Good evening, Sackwater Central Police Station.

'Briggs, this is Inspector Church.'

'Oh gawd I thought it do be Algy playing silly boogers again.'

'Is anybody else there?'

'Welllll...' A brief pause. 'No.'

'I am going to the Pier Pavilion.'

'I do believe it's closed, ma'am,' he warned to avoid disappointing me.

'I know. Try to contact the men on the beat and tell them to stay away but, if you don't hear from me in exactly one hour, you are to send as many officers as you can get hold of, regardless of whether they're on duty or not. Got that?'

'Including Old Scrapie?' he said.

'Yes.' I put down the phone. *If I'd have known the bugger was back I'd have thrown a party.*

I looked at my watch. It had a good strong luminous dial. Thirteen minutes to go. The scrawnies were still squawking.

'The fret of it is, I do love 'em all.'

'But there's not one as you want to marry.'

'Gawd no. They're fraugsy?'

Fraugsy? I hadn't heard that one before.

The streets were quiet now. Nobody wanted to socialise in the pitch-dark and tales of wicked men loitering unseen were spreading feverishly – in fact there were more definitely true stories than there were men in the district.

I was off. Most of Victorian Sackwater had been built within a twenty-year period and laid out on a grid system. The older part was more the product of evolution, streets following old lanes or heading towards dairies or tanneries long since gone. Slaughterhouse Lane hadn't had an abattoir in my lifetime but it was still wider than most of the lanes, for driving animals to their deaths.

At the corner of Derby Street the police phone was ringing. Brigsy would be doing his best. In peacetime there was a light on top of the boxes that flashed to alert any constables to a call. Now you just had to hope they heard it or a member of the public told them.

I cut through Tiny Rupert Square but decided against Divine Alley in case Bressinghall's the butcher's had blocked the far end with their van. I skirted round Amity Street, taking the long way round Chapel Street and Peacock Lane, only to find Bressinghall's had left their van where they had no right to and were blocking the exit to Dorking Road. There was no room to squeeze round it and I could not climb over or wriggle under it. There were six minutes to go. I tried the back doors and found them unlocked. The van was filled with wooden trays on runners. It had a solid barrier between it and the driver's cab, so I couldn't get through the vehicle. I ripped half the shelves out into a heap on the cobbles and, using them as rickety steps, managed to scramble onto the roof and over it and slide down the windscreen to land on the cobbles, skittering on both feet and catching my stump on the bumper in the process.

'*Haqq qahba kurnut,*' I cursed and stumbled on my way.

Peacock Lane leads out onto Dorking Road, parallel with High Road East and sloping down to the promenade, with a clear view of the old pier before me. The pavilion stood at the entrance to the pier, a sort of cross between a railway terminal and a cathedral with a nod to the Orient. It was a tall rectangular building with an arched roof and a tower at each corner topped by onion domes. In happier times the great glass windows would be lit up with crowds surging between the two crenellated gatehouses onto the planked forecourt lined with long-gone slot machines, a sea of faces swelling around the carriages of the wealthy and the cabs of the comfortably off. Now the building stood gloomily empty, the high iron-railed gates shut and topped by rolls of lethal-looking military barbed wire and signs on the railings warning:

WAR OFFICE – KEEP OUT
TRESPASSERS WILL BE
PROSECUTED

A heavy chain had been wrapped round both gates and secured with a padlock the size of a Scotsman's sporran. It might not have presented much of a problem to an invading panzer division, but it certainly kept any vandals out and would have presented me with a problem if I had not been given my instructions. The padlock on a gate to the side of the right-hand gatehouse had been unlocked, with the shank pressed only slightly into the body so that I could easily slip it open.

Somebody had been busy with their oil can again for the gate swung open without a squeak. I passed through, leaving it fractionally ajar so that, if any of my men did need to follow, they wouldn't be shredding themselves trying to clamber over the top, though the image of Sharkey impaling himself on top of the main gates was fleetingly pleasing.

The forecourt was deserted, the wind whipping the rain from the remnants of the pier into my face and stirring the sea into restless waves breaking invisibly onto the shingle ten yards beneath my feet.

The front door was open. Once I had skipped through it with Pooky holding my hand to see *Aladdin*. My parents never went to the panto, mainly because my mother found it unsettling, though she could not explain why, but also because my father thought it a waste of money. He had grown out of such things, he declared, oblivious to the fact that I had not.

Nine o'clock on the dot.

The foyer was a forlorn sight, the ticket office window closed with a sign hanging over the window declaring as much. Cobwebs were draped like dustsheets over hanging non-glittering chandeliers and the gold-painted scrolled mirrors fixed all around.

The floor and the long runner going down the middle of the foyer were carpeted in heavy dust. There were several scuffs in the dirt but no clear footprints. The double doors with their tarnished brass handles were closed but they pushed creakily open. Once liveried footmen had held the doors back while pretty usherettes in daringly short red dresses saw members of the audience to their seats.

Now the auditorium was filled, not with laughter, applause or cheers, but with the stench of decay. The claret velvet seats were mouldy and the gold paint peeling off their arms, springs sticking through some of the upholstery. The ceiling so gaily painted with trumpet-blowing cherubs, laurel crowns and shepherdesses was stained by water from the leaking roof – lead thieves had been on it years ago – with sections of plaster collapsed over the stalls and overfilling one of the upper boxes.

A lot of seats at the front were missing or tilted forward.

Most worrying of all was the smell of rotting wood and the way the floor felt spongy and sagged. The wind and sea sounded much louder than they should as I stepped carefully down that central aisle. I put on my torch and saw that the runner abruptly disappeared ahead of me. As I edged forward, the reason for the devastated front rows became obvious. The floor had caved in, creating a jagged-edged chasm some six to ten feet wide. Fifty feet below, the sea swelled and crashed against the barbed-wire-tangled seaweed-and-barnacle-covered posts that – I hoped – supported the derelict theatre. The air gusted up with sudden vigour and I stepped hastily back from the edge.

On the other side of the ditch were the tumbled remains of the orchestra pit and, beyond that, the raised stage. The safety curtain had been lowered, with the remnants of the original grand drapes at the front hanging raggedly at either side. I turned to look up at the balconies but from what I could see they were deserted.

'Hello,' I called, my voice curiously flat and dead, and I remembered hearing a leading lady complain once about the poor acoustics of the pavilion. There was a crash behind me and I spun back to see the safety curtain collapsing into billowing clouds of debris to expose a dust-fogged stage. The curtain toppled forward and fell, tumbling into what was left of the pit.

With a loud click the footlights went on and behind them was a drawing room scene, very Terence Rattigan – all chintz with potted palms – and I half-expected to see a maid appear to vacuum up the debris. She couldn't have been doing her job properly for years. The figure that did stagger onto the stage from the right wing was not dressed in a servant's outfit, however. She was all in black and, as my eyes became accustomed to the sudden blaze, I saw quite clearly that this was Lavender Wicks.

'Please don't kill me,' she sobbed and sank to her knees.

97

THE INVISIBLE MAN

avender Wicks put out a hand to steady herself against a sofa. Her platinum hair was unclipped and hanging over the left side of her face.

'Mrs Wicks,' I shouted above the surging sea. 'Are you hurt?'

Lavender hauled herself up and looked about in confusion.

'Who is it?' She squinted through the lights towards me.

'It's me,' I called stupidly, then added, more informatively, 'Inspector Church.'

'Inspector?' She made a peak of her hand to shield her eyes. 'Can it really be you?'

'Is anybody with you?'

'Oh thank God.'

'Where is the kidnapper?' I put the bag down on a hinged seat that had fallen open as if the invisible man was sitting on it. If he was, he didn't make a fuss.

'I knew you would save me.' She let go of the sofa and took a faltering step forward.

'Don't get too close to the edge,' I warned. 'It's not safe.'

Lavender Wicks grabbed the back of an armchair as her knees buckled, but she managed to keep herself upright.

'Have you paid the ransom? Are they letting me go?'

'I've brought it. Who are they? Do you know where they are?'

'Oh Betty,' she cried and this did not seem a time to stand on my dignity over my rank. 'I thought they were going to kill me. Is that really you? Come forward a little more where I can see you.'

I took a couple of cautious steps and saw a second figure to the back of the stage rising from the floor. I was just about to shout out a warning when I saw that it was Dodo, with her finger pointing to her nose in the way she thought meant *shush*. She was in a pretty, unseasonably summery frock and had a racquet in her right hand, as if she was going to bound across laughing lightly, *Anyone for tennis?* But Dodo's expression was deadly serious as she crept towards Lavender, raising the racquet over her left shoulder.

'Are you all right, Lavender?' I called, hoping I didn't sound as confused as I was.

'Oh Betty,' she sobbed. 'It's been awful. I thought I was going out of my mind. Thurston must have been frantic with worry. Was it him who paid the ransom?'

'Yes,' I replied. 'Do you know where they are – your kidnappers?' I looked about me anxiously.

'I can't see you very well.' Lavender leaned towards me.

Dodo was almost behind her now.

'I'm worried about the floor,' I told her. 'It's rotten.'

Lavender reached behind her back.

'Watch out, she's got a blooming gun!' Dodo yelled and, with a great flourish, whacked Lavender Wicks full on the temple with the side of the racquet, knocking her out cold.

98

THE LAYING OUT OF LAVENDER WICKS

Dodo dropped the racquet and caught Lavender Wicks as she fell, lowering her to the floor.

'I told you she was the guilty one,' she reminded me, pinching Lavender's wrist.

'For crying out loud, Constable Chivers,' I bawled across at her. 'She was the victim. The kidnapper is probably still in the building.'

A terrible idea was crystallising in my mind that I might be speaking to the kidnapper and murderer at that very moment. Was it possible that Drusilla, having allayed suspicions of being an accomplice to the murder of Fradigor Strynge, by her air of childish innocence, was trying the same trick again? Her 'blooming gun'; her sprained ankle; the way she had clutched Ardom Dapper's throat at the railway station; her lie about the train being late when the accountant, Skotter Heath Jackson, was murdered in his office; the mysterious woman at the Dunworthy saying 'ouchy-wouchy'. So many loose ends suddenly intertwined into one line of evidence.

'I am sorry, boss,' Dodo crossed Lavender's arms over her chest as if laying out a corpse, 'but – without wishing to be as contrary as a cod – have you forgotten that I noticed her direct gaze?'

'And for that you concussed her?' I yelled. 'I assume you haven't killed her.'

'Oh dear.' Dodo grimaced. 'Unfortunately I have...' she checked Lavender's pulse, 'not.'

I hesitated. 'Why did you say, *Watch out, she's got a blooming gun?*'

Dodo laughed hollowly. 'Because she had one.'

'But why did you use those exact words?' I asked carefully.

'Because that's what someone shouted at Slackwater Railway Station.' She rolled her eyes. 'So it must be how people warn each other.'

I had another thought. 'How did you know I was here?'

'Oh.' Dodo rubbed her front teeth with the knuckle of her thumb. 'Brigsy told me.'

'How?' I asked. 'Did he ring Felicity House?'

'Err...' Dodo crossed her feet. 'Maybe.'

'But the practice phone isn't working.'

Dodo tangled her fingers. 'Oh...' She had almost chewed her knuckle off by now. 'They must have had it fixed.'

'So how did you get here so quickly?'

Dodo was rooting about behind Lavender.

'I cut down Divine Alley like you taught me.'

'But the alley was blocked.'

'Not when I skipped down it.' Dodo gave me the direct gaze that she had told me denoted guilt.

'Go on.'

Dodo cleared her throat. 'And then I saw the gate unlocked,' she recited in a curious monotone. 'And then I thought I saw a light round the back and then I went in through the stage door and along a tunnel and up a ladder into here.' Her voice rose an octave. 'There were spiders, spiders everywhere, hundreds of them, thousands.' She brushed her shoulders frantically. 'But I braved them for you, boss.' Her voice fell again and hardened. 'Not that I suppose you will thank me for that.'

And Dodo rose very slowly, like an overloaded lift. She had an odd disturbed look on her face and a revolver gripped in her hand.

99

THE FINGER ON THE TRIGGER

I watched Dodo very carefully. I couldn't see if her finger was on the trigger but I had no reason to suppose it wasn't. To add to my worries, from where I was standing, it had looked like Dodo had taken that gun out of her own handbag.

'I think you should give me that,' I told Dodo and she laughed in a sarcastic way I hadn't heard before.

'But how do I do that, boss?' she asked. 'I am as hopeless as a holiday at throwing but, even if I manage, it could go off when it lands.'

'You could take the bullets out first.'

'Then it will be no use to either of us,' she reasoned with a new coldness.

'Have you ever handled a gun before?'

'Oh yes.' Dodo smiled menacingly. 'Daddy used to take me to the range. I am a crack shot with a revolver.'

She certainly seemed to be handling it with confidence.

I tried a new tack. 'I met your father in Ipswich, Dodo.'

'Daddy?' Dodo's face shone brighter than the limelights. 'You mean *my* lovely daddy, not your horrid one?'

'I thought you liked my father?'

'Oh I do,' she assured me. 'We have lovely games of hide-and-seek and piggy in the middle in the evenings and sometimes old maid with crinkled playing cards but you must admit that he is especially horrid.'

I couldn't deny that. I was just surprised Dodo had noticed;

but she was surprising me in a lot of ways tonight.

Not for the first time it occurred to me that Dodo had been absent for every murder except the one where she had clamped her handkerchief over the victim's throat.

I got back on track. 'The morning Skotter Heath Jackson, the accountant, was murdered in his office you said you had visited your father. But he told me he hadn't seen you in ages.'

'Oh, did he indeed?' she said defiantly. 'Well, if Daddy said that it must be true because Daddy *never* lies.'

'But you did,' I pointed out.

'So I made up a fib.' Dodo uncrossed her feet and stamped the left one.

'He told me about your first father.'

Another, even newer, expression appeared on Dodo's face – a sort of cold fury.

'He told you…' She was lost for words. 'Why would Daddy do that? You must have tricked him but you are not clever enough to do that. Perhaps you are lying. But you do not lie.' I did sometimes but this was not a good time to tell Dodo that. 'I am confused.' She was scraping her right foot along the boards now like a bull about to charge the matador.

Lavender Wicks groaned and raised her face. 'What…'

'Keep still, blast you,' Dodo shrieked and took a swingeing blow, contacting Lavender's occiput with a sickening thud.

Lavender's head thumped down again.

'Christ, Dodo, you nearly decapitated her.'

'Thou shalt not take the name of the Lord thy God in vain,' she lectured me. 'So what if Vernon Willowdale *was* my father? Am I to be blamed for that? I do not blame you for your odious-but-kind-to-me parents. The police never pressed any charges against me. What are you saying, boss? Do you think I am the Camden Vampire?'

'No, of course not.' *Possibly the Suffolk Vampire though*, I thought, but this was not a good time to mention what I had read about his clamping a handkerchief over his victim's neck. 'I'm just a bit worried about Mrs Wicks, Dodo. I can't see her breathing.'

Dodo hardly glanced down. 'Oh, she is breathing all right.'

'The murderer at the Dunworthy had a limp,' I reminded myself – in an inaudible mumble, I thought, but it's funny how a voice will carry in poor acoustics when you don't want it to.

'That does not mean anything,' Dodo reasoned. 'So do I.'

Maybe I would wait until we were in company and more evenly matched in weaponry, I decided, before I asked about the spikes I had seen in her handbag.

'Put the gun down, Dodo,' I urged but she shook her head.

'I am afraid I can't do that, boss.'

'Put it down,' I said firmly. 'And that is an order, Constable Chivers.' I took a step towards her. We might have been separated by the Grand Canyon for all the threat I posed, but Dodo raised the gun in both hands and pointed the barrel straight at me.

'Stop right there.'

'The others will be here soon!' I shouted.

'But not soon enough to save you,' she raged.

'Dodo,' I held out my hand to show it was empty, 'whatever you've done, it's over.'

But I could see she was not listening to me by then. 'Stay where you are.' There was a controlled frightening intensity I had not imagined Dodo Chivers had in her until that moment. 'I will not warn you again.'

'I can't hurt you from here, Dodo.'

'Stop!' Dodo screamed. 'Do not make me kill you.'

I took a step back.

'I warned you.' She levelled the gun a fraction more, crouched slightly to brace herself. 'I am sorry,' she whispered and pulled the trigger.

I thought you couldn't feel a bullet immediately. But I did.

'**O**h God,' I said but I could not hear it.

There was a pain in my head and it made the pain Teddy Moulton had inflicted when he battered me seem very tame indeed. It was sharp and it burned. I felt the hot blood burst down the left-hand side of my face.

I staggered back, clutching myself. 'Oh God, Dodo. What have you done?'

'Oh fiddlesticks, that hurts,' somebody gasped as if I needed telling, especially in such a silly way. 'You have killed me.'

'Drop it or I shall,' Dodo said with steeliness and something landed clattering at my feet.

It was a walking stick.

'What the hell?' I turned and saw a woman behind me. She was grasping her right shoulder as if her life depended upon it – and possibly it did to judge by the way the blood flowed steadily between her fingers. She wore a wide hat with a heavy veil that made her look like a bee-keeper. If that was the fashion, I wouldn't be following it.

'Don't shoot!' I shouted.

'Why would I?' Dodo puzzled.

'If Mrs Wicks comes round again, do *not* hit her.'

'Not even a teensy-weensy likkley-wickley tap?'

'No.'

I had one handkerchief in my skirt pocket and I needed it for me so I used it for me, clamping it against my ear with the side of my stump.

The woman behind me had a tawny woollen coat on. I pulled it off her left shoulder.

'What are you doing?'

'Helping you,' I said. 'Slip your arm out.' She obeyed in a daze.

'Ouchy-wouchy. It hurts.' She was starting to look familiar in the gloom, or maybe it was her voice.

'Of course it hurts – you've been shot.' I adjusted my pack. 'So have I,' I added pointedly.

'Sorry, boss,' Dodo said. 'But your ears do stick out a bit.'

'No they do not.' I had never been told that before and I felt sure my parents would have mentioned it.

'One of them still does,' she affirmed. 'Anyway, you moved your head.'

'Was I supposed to stand still while you fired at me?'

'I was aiming at her but you got in the way.'

'I'm so sorry,' I retorted.

'Apology accepted.' Dodo smiled like a hostess pretending she doesn't mind wine splashed on her new Axminster.

'Take your coat off,' I barked.

The woman obeyed gingerly but without wincing. She was probably numb. I wished I was. My ear was on fire as I ripped her shirt open, buttons pinging off.

'Look what you've done,' she burst out. 'That cost me twelve shillings in Jarvis's.'

'Ten shillings and eight pence.' I had looked at the same shirts myself but they were too small for me. I pulled hers down over her right hand.

'Ouch. Oh flip. Excuse my language.'

'I think I may have heard worse.' I took a look at the wound.

'She has,' Dodo called over. 'Sergeant Briggs, who we call Brigsy, often says *boogy*, which is very rude indeed, apparently.'

I bunched the free side of her shirt up. 'Hold that over it. You've just got a flesh wound on the outer edge of your upper arm. The bullet has gone clean through.'

'Oh but it will leave a horrid scar,' she moaned and started to trudge off, our conversation clearly at an end.

'At least you can cover it. I can't hide mine unless I go around looking like Van Gogh.'

'He had a beard,' Dodo chipped in helpfully.

'I'm still working on mine,' I muttered and snatched the woman, swinging her back by her left arm, though from the yelps you'd have thought I had grabbed the other. 'Right, let's have a look at you.'

I let go of her, took hold of the front of the veil and raised it. The woman tried to bury her head and turn away but I had seen enough to confirm my suspicions.

'You,' I said, meaninglessly to anyone except me and her when I thought about it. 'The woman who fell down the Leg O' Lamb cellar steps. I never did discover your name.'

The woman raised her head to look me full in the eye.

'Poppy,' she told me. 'Miss Poppy Castle.' She swallowed. 'Is Lavender all right?' She peered round me.

'And what is she to you?' I asked.

'Haven't you guessed yet?' Poppy Castle taunted as if it was a game we'd been playing for hours. 'Lavender Wicks is my big sister.'

THE WEIRD SISTERS

Perhaps it was hearing her name that roused her. Lavender Wicks began to rise groggily.

'No,' I warned Dodo, who was poised to give her a hefty backspin.

'Dohhh,' Dodo moaned in disappointment but lowered the racquet.

'Are you all right, Sissy?' Poppy called.

'Oh of course I am.' Lavender got onto all fours. 'Never happier than when I'm crawling around filthy stages getting concussed with a sledgehammer.'

'It was actually a Bancroft Super Winner,' Dodo said. 'I had one at school. Once, on a Thursday afternoon, I knocked out Mrs Driver, our sports mistress, but by mistake in her case.'

'You got off lightly.' Poppy briefly removed my makeshift wad to demonstrate. 'She shot me.'

'And me,' I reminded them but nobody paid any attention to that.

'Shot? How?' Lavender got onto her haunches and patted herself. 'That's my husband's gun. Give it back this instant.'

'The only way you'll get this back is one slug at a time,' Dodo snarled in a passable imitation of Humphrey Bogart, though I didn't recognise the quote – *The Petrified Forest*? I hadn't seen that when it came to London. I was too busy chasing real, though less charismatic, tough guys.

'Right.' I tried to establish some order. 'What *exactly* is going on?'

'Well, I should have thought it was quite obvious,' Dodo – who

the question wasn't aimed at – proclaimed. 'Lavender Wicks –
who I so wrongly suspected because of her direct and honest
gaze and because I am jealous of her dizzly-dazzly beauty – was
kidnapped by this evil-as-eggs, ugly-as-umbrage weird woman
posing as her sister while—'

'Weird?' Poppy fumed.

'She *is* my sister,' Lavender insisted.

'Then why does she need to pose as her?' Dodo puzzled.

'So why did Mrs Wicks have a gun?' I objected. *And why,*
I thought, *am I interrogating my constable when we have two
criminals in our custody?*

'Well.' Dodo put her left hand on her hip for, all at once, I was
the class simpleton. 'If you were being kidnapped, would you not
want to have a gun to protect you?'

'Quite so.' Lavender hauled herself up on the side of an armchair.
'Well, thank you so much for rescuing me, Inspector Church...'

'Aided by Constable Chivers,' Dodo reminded her.

'I was coming to that,' Lavender insisted snappily and Dodo
stuck out her tongue.

'And your sister crept up behind me with a stick because...?'
I queried.

'Because—' Poppy began.

'Because she had come to rescue me and thought you were
the kidnapper,' Lavender assured me. I had to admire how she
made one of the most implausible explanations I have ever been
offered sound only just implausible, but I battled on regardless.

'So how' – I held up my hand in the stop sign – 'and this
question is just for you, Miss Castle, did you know that Mrs
Wicks was being held here?'

'Because...' Lavender blustered.

'Don't be greedy,' I scolded. 'You will have plenty of your own
questions to answer soon enough.'

'Because' – Poppy looked about for an explanation – 'I got a ransom note as well.'

'As well as what?' I jumped in.

'As well as you?'

'Who said I got one?'

'How else would you have known where to bring the money?'

'What money?'

'The ransom money.'

I blinked. 'I don't understand.'

'Oh for goodness' sake, it's perfectly simple.' Poppy folded her arms crossly at my incomprehension. 'The £5,000.'

'Shut up, Poppy,' Lavender called.

'A bit late for that,' I remarked. 'Why, Mrs Wicks, did you pretend to be kidnapped?'

'Because...' Poppy began.

'You must have been very annoying children,' I speculated, 'if you kept trying to answer each other's questions.'

'I will offer you seven to one on that,' Dodo calculated. 'Because you are both as annoying as artichokes now that you are adults.'

'Because you were on to us,' Lavender explained. It was news to me that I had been hot on their trail. 'I knew you knew when you said I would be handcuffed.'

I had only meant what I said – that she would have no difficulty in finding someone willing to play her games – but, if Lavender Wicks thought I had evidence against her, I was not going to deny it.

It occurred to me that she did not have the facial injuries I had seen in the photograph sent to Thurston – but she was probably skilled in using make-up, having been an actress.

'I did think it odd that, when we returned your licence, you didn't ask where your handbag was.' I had realised this too late, but not too late to seem cleverer than I was.

'That was stupid of me,' Lavender admitted.

454

'Shut up, Lavvy,' her sister warned, too late, as most warnings, in my experience, are.

'Oh what's the point?' Lavender slumped into the armchair.

'Was that a rhetorical question, boss?' Dodo hissed.

'I think so.' I picked up the cane. It was unusually heavy. Did it have a lead core to turn it into a cosh?

'We were going to disappear,' Lavender confessed, 'start a new life somewhere where we couldn't be extradited from.'

'That would have to be out of England then,' Dodo calculated. 'And you probably couldn't take your furniture with you – that pretty white baby grand pianoforte, for example.'

'We needed money,' Lavender continued. 'Thurston is very generous but I couldn't ask him for that sort of money.'

'So he doesn't know this was a charade?' I checked.

'Oh I love charades.' Dodo clasped her hands.

'Of course not.'

'Did you not feel beastly at deceiving him?' Dodo enquired severely. 'I know I would feel as guilty as a giraffe.'

'Not in the least,' Lavender said defiantly. 'Husbands are made for deceiving.'

'He'd have been even more upset if Lavender had gone to the gallows,' Poppy piped up.

'Not just me,' Lavender Wicks cried indignantly.

'Not that we had anything to do with those other things,' Poppy hastened to add. 'Nothing to do with them at all.' She looked from me to her sister to Dodo to back at me. 'Absolutely nothing. We don't even know what you are talking about.'

And with that it was as if I had thrown a jigsaw puzzle into the air and all the pieces had fallen the right way up and slotted together.

'Murder,' I murmured, 'or rather murders, at least eight of them.'

Was it really possible that, at last, I was confronting the Suffolk Vampire?

D odo opened her mouth. 'Sorry? What was that, boss?'
'All those murders,' I said wonderingly.
'But' – Dodo stamped her foot again – 'you told me, the
first time we went to her nice interiorly monochrome – that is a
big word for a little constable to use, is it not? – Treetops House
in Pinfold Lane, that she was not guilty.'

'It's very rude to talk about me as if I wasn't here.' Lavender
sniffed.

'As if I *were not* here,' Dodo corrected.

'No I did not,' I reminded her. 'I said that you needed more
proof than saying that Mrs Wicks looked straight at you with
her lovely periwinkle eyes.'

'Did you really say that, Constable Chivers?' Lavender
simpered.

'Yes I did.'

'Oh thank you.' She turned them on Dodo.

'Although they look more forget-me-not in this light,' Dodo
decided.

'Mr Wicks says that.' Lavender clicked on a smile that any
Luftwaffe pilot could have seen from five thousand feet.

'And she said I was jealous of your dizzle-dazzle beauty,' Dodo
misremembered.

'I think you said that yourself,' Lavender corrected her mildly.

'So I did,' Dodo brayed. 'But that was only because I was.'

My stump was competing with my ear and contending with

my skull as to which hurt the most. Though it was a close-run thing, the ear was fractionally in the lead.

I left them to it and turned to Poppy. 'Do you have anything to say?'

'In bright sunlight they are more like bluebells,' she contributed.

I lowered my left arm and the handkerchief stuck, dangling from the side of my head.

'About the murders,' I prompted.

'Oh those.' Poppy threw up her arms like I was a boring parent telling her to tidy up her room. 'They all deserved to die.'

'Except that first man, Freddy Smart,' Lavender chipped in.

'Well, he did sort of,' Poppy argued. 'He was an absolute beast.'

'Yes but we didn't know that,' Lavender said.

'You mistook him for Ian Henshaw,' I realised.

'Oh, are we speaking to Little Miss Disapproving?' Lavender mocked. 'I suppose you've never made a mistake?'

'Murder is murder,' I pointed out and Poppy stuck her tongue out to prove that Dodo wasn't the only one who could do that and to make it clear how priggish I was being about it all.

'Only if you call it that.'

'Not just me. The law does as well.' I bent to pick up the stick.

'Then the law and you will have to prove it.'

'Actually,' Dodo put in thoughtfully, 'the law does not prove anything. You prove things *in* law, not with it.'

'Why were you carrying this?' I waggled the stick in Poppy's direction and she winced.

'Because—' Lavender began yet again.

'Shut up,' Dodo snapped, 'or I'll show you the rest of my tennis strokes.'

'Because I injured my ankle when I fell into that stupid cellar.'

A cellar is an inanimate structure and no more capable of

457

being stupid than you are of being intelligent, I recalled Mr Grice telling his maid, Molly, to her confused delight.

'You didn't limp at the time.'

'It didn't hurt until the next day.'

'It's not a very ladylike stick.' It was a Victorian gentleman's ebony cane and the style of its silver ball handle was very familiar.

'It's my father's. I borrowed it.'

I peered closer and found what I was looking for – the intertwined letters *S* and *G* etched on the top. I turned the handle. There was a click and a blade about an inch long slid smoothly out of the ferule.

'My godmother's godfather had these manufactured,' I told her.

'Well, I never knew it did that before.' She threw out her arms like she was going to serenade the performers on stage.

'But they didn't sell very well because people kept having accidents – stabbing themselves or their companions in the legs. The manufacturers had cut costs by using a flimsier safety catch than he had specified.'

'Well, thank heavens I never had a mishap with it.' Poppy laughed in that annoying way sopranos do in schoolgirl productions of Gilbert and Sullivan.

'Oh but somebody did,' I told her. 'Someone accidentally stabbed Mr Ardom Dapper with it from the train at Angleford Railway Station – twice.'

'That wasn't me,' Lavender raged.

'No,' I agreed. 'It was your sister.'

'How dare you?' Poppy threw up her arms, every inch the affronted maiden.

'My inspector dares all sorts of things.' Dodo tossed her hair – vermilion in the glare of the footlights – proudly. 'She is not even afraid of...' my constable paused dramatically, '*spiders.*'

I was a bit but I could never admit it, especially not now.

I dabbed the edge of the blade. It was still razor sharp but chipped.

'I don't know which of you stabbed Freddy Smart, but whoever did it, the tip snapped off. We have a very thorough pathologist here and he discovered it buried in Mr Smart's brain. I will bet you a pound to a penny that the two pieces will fit exactly.'

'Those are very good odds,' Dodo advised. 'I for one would be inclined to take them. Even if you only risk a shilling you could get twelve pounds back.'

'This is the first time I have ever used this cane,' Poppy said airily.

'Plus your stake,' Dodo added.

'So are you putting the blame on your father?'

'Free of tax,' Dodo remembered.

'My father is dead,' Poppy snapped, 'and so is my mother. I live all alone in Straw House.'

'Oh, that's the horrible house we looked at on my first morning,' Dodo recalled.

'It is *not* horrible. It is beautiful and crammed with memories...'

'And dry rot,' Lavender added.

'Only a bit,' Poppy retorted.

'The bits that don't have wet rot,' Lavender jeered.

'You never liked that house.'

'Of course I didn't. It's a dump.'

'We can't all be married to millionaires.'

'Girls, girls.' I did my schoolmarm act. 'Can we actually stick to the subject?' They clammed up and I continued. 'You, Mrs Wicks, were at the station as well, dressed in a hat and cloak. When you were far enough away to be mistaken for a man, because of your clothing and having the height to carry it off, Poppy drew attention to you and away from herself by

459

shouting, *He's on the bridge. Watch out, he's got a blooming gun.* You fired a shot in the air. You obviously didn't aim at anyone because the bullet was never found and there was no damage at the station. When everybody looked towards you, Poppy leaned out of the train. Her first stab didn't go very deep. You were either too tentative or he was slightly beyond your reach. The second stab was more than deep enough though. It penetrated his carotid artery.'

Poppy greeted my news without the slightest concern. 'I remember now,' she told me. 'I found that stick on the way here this evening.'

'All Grice Patent Swordsticks—' I began.

'It looks more like a spike stick from here, boss.' Dodo leaned forward, screwing up her eyes.

'The shaft is telescopic,' I explained. 'If I had two hands I could demonstrate that it will slide into itself to bare a blade about two-thirds of the stick in length.'

'A bit like a telescope with a sword inside it,' Dodo explained to Lavender in case Mrs Wicks had been unaware of that.

'All Grice Patent Swordsticks,' I began again, 'have a serial code. The suppliers will easily be able to tell us who purchased that particular cane so, unless it was resold privately...'

'Oh dear,' Lavender said with just enough smirk to let me know that this was not a concern.

How stupid of me. The pattern on the imprint on Mr Peatrie's neck didn't say *5G, 27*. It was *SG, 27* I realised.

'In this case, however, the stick was stolen. Do I have to tell you where from?'

'Yes please.' Dodo nodded keenly.

'From Mr Peatrie's antique shop,' I said.

'You will have trouble proving that,' Dodo told me, rather unhelpfully.

'Actually' – I tried to fix her with a stare but you can't do it across a chasm and an orchestra pit, especially when the lights are in your subject's eyes – 'I can. Mr P—'

'That's what she calls Mr Peatrie,' Dodo explained.

'—kept very detailed records. This stick along with its serial number will be recorded in his ledgers, plus the fact that it had not been sold.'

I didn't point out that proving the stick was stolen didn't prove that they had stolen it, nor that they had murdered him with it, but neither of them seemed to realise that and, if Dodo did, she was keeping her thoughts to herself for a change.

'Darn.' Poppy chewed her lower lip.

'We didn't plan to kill him,' Lavender claimed.

'You, Mrs Wicks, grabbed the stick to steal it and ran out of what you thought was the back door,' I surmised. 'Only it was the door at the bottom of the stairs and Mr P chased after you. He grabbed your leg – hence the faint bruise on your left calf that I noticed when I visited you alone. You jabbed twice back at him with the stick, so hard that it left an imprint in his throat. He fell back and broke his neck and you left him propped inside the door.'

Lavender applauded in slow sarcasm. 'You should do this for a living.'

'Why didn't you just buy the stick?' Dodo asked. 'You must have had enough pocket money between you.'

'He wouldn't sell it to us,' Poppy complained.

'Mr P was a pacifist,' I explained. 'He would only sell weapons to people he knew were genuine collectors and would not use them.'

'Well,' Poppy sighed. 'That's got us bang to rights.'

'Looks like we might have to execute our first backup plan,' Lavender called back.

'What is your first backup plan?' I asked warily for I didn't like the way Lavender had said that. I would worry about any subsequent plans if and when they entered the conversation.

'In that case,' Poppy replied as if I hadn't spoken. *This is worse than being with my parents.* 'We might as well come clean.'

103

THE CLASSIFICATION OF FLAMINGOS

D odo flopped onto the sofa. 'If this is going to be a long story, I need to rest,' she declared. 'My fetlocks are as frazzled as a fossilated flamingo.'

I didn't think there was such as word as *fossilated* and resolved to check in the dictionary Jimmy had left behind. He had taken his little rhyming one with him.

'What plan?' I asked with mounting unease. Murderers' plans rarely involved being kind to the police.

'We are coming clean first.' Lavender brushed me aside like an irritating fly.

'Then why don't we start with Freddy Smart?' I suggested and Dodo put up her hand.

'Can I just explain something?' she asked and, seeing no dissent, continued, 'When Inspector Church asks why don't we do something, she is often suggesting that we do it – rather than inviting a debate on the advisability of doing so – and I think that this is one of those occasions.'

'She must be a very confusing person to work with,' Poppy mused and I was not sure if she was sympathising with me or my constable.

'Smart wasn't,' Lavender declared, pausing for the laughter that never came.

'He was easy.' Poppy plugged the gap.

'We just knelt on his doorstep and called *Cooee* through the letter box and *hello big boy* until he came to the door. The instant

he crouched to look out, I thrust. The first jab went into his face.'
Lavender beamed.

'You burst his eye,' I told her.

Poppy jiggled about. 'Oh, I hoped you had.'

'And then he fell backwards,' Lavender recalled.

'He grasped the blade to stop himself.' I remembered the gashes in Freddy Smart's hands.

'I thought he did.' Lavender nodded thoughtfully. 'But I couldn't see very well. Anyway, it cost him his worthless life because it stopped him falling out of range and, when I stabbed again, I saw the metal go into his throat and out the other side.'

'I couldn't see very well at all.' Poppy pouted but instantly brightened as she recalled, 'But I heard him gasp and gurgle.'

The two sisters smiled at this special memory.

'But you got the wrong man,' I pointed out. 'Not very smart of you either.'

'It was an easy mistake,' Poppy protested. 'Henshaw lived in Bath Avenue. How was I supposed to know it wasn't the same as Bath Road?'

'I did say it didn't look like the right sort of house for a well-to-do businessman,' Lavender reminded her little sister.

'I should have listened,' Poppy conceded. 'But it was all right. He was a horrid man anyway.'

'But you didn't know that,' I pointed out.

'God knew,' Lavender told me piously and I knew better than to argue about God. I had tried that before but, in some matters, apparently, he had confided exclusively in Sister Millicent and, in others, in Adam.

104

THE SILENCE OF THE SEA

D odo wiggled a little finger in her ear. 'Who has known the mind of God?' she quoted and, as if in response, the wind whooshed upwards, spraying us all with water from the crashing sea.

'Skotter Heath Jackson,' I shouted above the sudden roar and was gratified to hear it die down like a class of naughty children being reprimanded.

'Ah yes,' Poppy recalled dreamily, 'the chartered accountant. He was great fun.'

'You went to kill him a week earlier,' I calculated, 'but he was off ill with a heavy cold.'

'Men are such fussy-fusspots,' Dodo complained. 'Why, Mr Church made an awful commotion when I spilled a pan of scalding water over his bare foot – just because it hurt a big lot and came up in an enormous blistery blister that he had to burst with an old scalpel.'

'You went to his office to kill him only to find he wasn't there. That was when you dropped your driving licence,' I postulated.

'It must have been when I got my lipstick out of my handbag,' Lavender agreed. 'A girl likes to look her best.'

'For murder?' I protested.

'For everything,' she told me. 'But I don't know why it took so long to find it.'

'Can I do that one?' Dodo kicked her feet like an excited child in soft sand, knocking into and rocking an occasional table. My mother would have told me off for the rest of my life for behaviour like that, but Dodo, apparently, could do what she liked. 'Mrs Daphne Milligan, Mr Skotter Heath Jackson's plain and sharp-tongued ex-secretary, told us,' Dodo continued, 'that Mr Heath Jackson's cleaner had gone to make Spitfires just like Lavender's maid Wilson alias Pooky had pretended she was going to do.'

'Pooky?' Lavender wrinkled her nose.

'I think I made the name up when I was learning to speak,' I admitted shamefacedly.

'Well, you should have learned to speak better,' Poppy huffed, for my crime was incalculably worse than any of theirs.

'And she had not been replaced – as you could have guessed by the state of his floor, which is worse than Slackwater Central Police Station and nearly as bad as Felicity House, 2 Cormorant Road, Slackwater, where I currently lodge with Mr Harold and Mrs Muriel Church—'

'Is that the dentist's?' Poppy asked. 'I went there once. It was ghastly. He had smelly fingers and smelly breath and he hurt me.'

'He can make sweet animal shapes out of napkins,' Dodo said.

Could he? The only thing I had ever seen my father make of a napkin was a crumpled mess.

'You reported the licence missing because you didn't know where you had lost it,' I continued.

'Why are you telling her that, boss?' Dodo lay back like Cleopatra on her barge. 'I think she knows.'

'I am letting her know that I know.' I sighed. 'One of you went back to Corker's Coffee House and left the handbag in the ladies' cloakroom.'

'That was me,' Poppy boasted. 'I felt like Mata Hari.'

'You do not look like her,' Dodo chipped in.

'Then you returned the next week to commit the murder—' I continued.

466

'Excuse me,' Poppy butted in indignantly. 'These were not murders. They were executions.'

I digested that statement. 'We will come to the motives later.'

'You bet we will.' Dodo toyed with the tennis racquet as if it was a ukulele, and I was only relieved she didn't burst into a George Formby song.

'So you went upstairs—' I conjectured.

'Whose story is this?' Lavender pouted. 'I went first in case he recognised Poppy.'

'So he knew her?' I clarified.

'How else could he recognise me?' Poppy asked, logically if tetchily.

'He was easy,' Lavender told us. 'I told him I was a new client but first he must humour me by closing his eyes and – can you believe it? – he did. I had a shopping bag with two knives and a sack.'

'Also a bottle of lemonade in case we got thirsty,' Poppy reminded her sister. 'But we didn't,' she reassured me, because that had been my greatest fear.

'I took out the bag and slipped it over his head,' Lavender recalled wistfully. 'And he made a silly noise like people do when you creep up and put your hands over their eyes.'

'Then I went into his office,' Poppy continued the account. 'He looked ever so silly wriggling about with a sack over his head and he was saying, *Oh come along now, madam. I can take a joke but enough is enough.*'

'And then he said,' Lavender giggled, '*Did the others put you up to this?*'

'And I said,' Poppy chortled. '*No, the others will die just as you are going to.*'

'I expect you alarmed him when you said that,' Dodo speculated.

467

'Not as much as when we got out the knives and started stabbing him,' Lavender replied. 'We took turns. He became very distressed then – shouting at first, when he thought we were punching him, then, when he realised he was being punctured, screaming and begging.'

'Begging for mercy,' Poppy confirmed. 'But I said, *What mercy did you show me?* And he said, *I don't know who you are* so I lifted the sack and said, *Remember me now?*'

'And he,' Lavender took the anecdote over, 'said, *No, I don't think I do.* Can you believe it? The nerve of the man.'

'We had made our own knuckleduster thing with metal teeth,' Poppy declared like a child telling a parent about her schoolwork, 'from one of Thurston's leather belts and a couple of old farrier's nails.'

'Lavvy pulled the sack down,' Poppy galloped on. 'And I drove the spikes deep into his throat. That soon shut him up.'

'Well, he did shout *Oh no!* and gurgle quite a lot,' Lavender chipped in.

'Yes.' Poppy thumped her brow. 'I didn't say he shut up immediately.'

'She said, *That soon shut him up*,' Dodo recited like a court stenographer.

'And then' – Poppy extruded her lower lip – 'he died.'

'We stabbed him a few times more,' Lavender concluded, 'but ours hearts weren't in it when he didn't react.'

'We took our sack off him and looked at him for a while until we got bored and went home,' Poppy concluded sadly.

'His receptionist was coming in as we went out.' Lavender sank into her chair.

'But she couldn't see us because we had our veils on.'

'And Lavender said, *We know where you live* and showed her the knives.' Poppy laughed.

'And Poppy said,' Lavender choked with mirth, '*And we know you stole the money*. And the receptionist said…'

'*I was going to pay it back*,' they chorused with precision that would have done credit to the Grinder-Snipe twins.

I thought her attitude was strange, I said to myself before asking, 'What about Millicent Smith?' But their blank expressions were enough to convince me they knew nothing about her. I had known in my heart that Crake Smart, Freddy's father, had found Millicent before we did.

Dodo strummed the tennis racquet. 'When I'm cleaning windows,' she began but, catching three disapproving tuts, gave up and threw the racquet over her head to bounce off the stage, slither and disappear down the trapdoor from which she had made her dramatic entrance.

105

THE ETIQUETTE OF MURDER

took the opportunity of the distraction to have a think. Why were these two women confessing so readily? Were they just attention-seekers? So far they had told me nothing that they couldn't have read in the papers, possibly supplemented by taking one of my constables for a drink. Bantony would not be averse to impressing a couple of pretty young women, I speculated.

'Let's talk about the Royal George,' I suggested and Dodo clapped her hands.

'Oh yes, do let us, please.'

'The Royal George,' Lavender ruminated. 'We were after Ian Henshaw again. He had already eluded us when we got Freddy Smart. Probably not our finest hour.'

'It actually took two hours to finish him off,' Poppy corrected her. 'But you can't really blame us for that one.'

'I feel confident that we can,' I assured her.

'It was another case of mistaken identity,' Lavender admitted.

'What a couple of sillies you must think we are.' Poppy simpered.

'But we did make sure we had the right man this time,' Lavender explained. 'Only we got the wrong room.'

'So Ian Henshaw had two lucky escapes,' I observed.

'The devil looks after his own,' Lavender quoted.

'We tried very hard,' Poppy protested. 'We followed him for ages hoping to catch him alone.'

'We didn't want to go to his home because we were sure Mrs Henshaw was innocent and we heard they had a child.'

'A little girl,' I said. 'My sergeant and Constable Chivers had to go and tell them while I was in hospital.'

'They cried.' Dodo's lower lip quivered at the memory. 'A big lot.'

I scrutinised the two sisters but neither showed any remorse at that news.

'They are better off without such an iniquitous husband and daddy,' Poppy decreed before returning to her narrative. 'Lavender watched the front of the hotel as he went in and I watched the back. I saw the porter go and close the blackout curtains and I counted which window it was ever so carefully.'

'Poppy waited over an hour to make sure nobody else came along,' Lavender defended her sister, 'but we weren't to know that that couple, the Herrings, had gone into the hotel just before Mr Henshaw and that he didn't go to his room immediately.'

'He didn't go to his room at all,' I remembered. 'He walked straight out. The receptionist thought it was because he didn't like the place. More likely he was afraid of being recognised and lost his nerve, leaving the woman he intended to meet to nurse a port and lemon by herself at the bar.'

'But he would have had to go out of the front door,' Poppy objected, 'so Lavender would be sure to have seen him.'

'Well...' For the first time since I had met her, Lavender Wicks looked embarrassed. 'I did pop round the side of the building to get out of the wind so I could light a cigarette. But I was only gone a minute at most.'

I waited for an outburst from Poppy but she tinkled a light laugh. 'Oh well,' she giggled. 'Worse things happen at sea.'

'Not to Grant Herring and Timothea Cutter, they don't,' I pointed out. 'You went to the room...' I prompted.

'I knocked, saying I had brought them champagne, courtesy of the management,' Lavender declared.

'He answered and I had run him through his arm before I realised it was the wrong man and that he had the wrong woman with him,' Poppy recalled.

'But you still went ahead and killed them both,' I objected.

'What were we supposed to do?' Poppy protested like I was an unreasonable parent. 'They had seen us.'

'Luckily she fainted,' Lavender recollected. 'So we were able to make him lie on the bed and tie his wrists to the bedstead before she came round, when we did the same to her.'

'They thought we had come to burgle them,' Poppy said. 'And we told them if they didn't struggle we wouldn't hurt them – which was a big porky admittedly – so they let us tie their ankles and put their stockings as gags in their mouths.'

'Oh.' Dodo shuddered. 'How unhygienic.'

'And then you killed them,' I said, sickened by my own words. 'Did you take one each and kill them both at the same time?'

'What kind of monsters do you think we are?' Lavender rounded on me. 'Even in murder manners matter.'

'Ladies first?' Dodo guessed.

'Exactly,' Poppy called up to her approvingly.

'So was it good manners to torture them?' I rounded on Lavender furiously.

'It was good practice,' Lavender replied coolly, 'for when we got the real Mr Henshaw.'

'But they were innocent people,' I objected, not sure yet why the rest of their victims weren't.

'Innocent?' Poppy scorned. 'Pah. They were married,' she paused to let the full horror of her next words sink in, 'but not to each other.'

'We have very strong views on the sanctity of marriage,' Lavender explained.

'Also she had a silly name.' Poppy sneered. 'Timothea – that's just a man's name with an "a" on the end.'

'And for that she deserved to die?' Dodo asked incredulously.

'I knew you would see it our way,' Poppy told her.

'You went to see Mrs Wicks while I was in hospital, didn't you?' I accused Dodo.

'Might have.' She sniffed. 'Well, all right, I did. I wanted to trick her into telling me something but I did not and she did not.'

'But she tricked you,' I pointed out. 'You told her my name was Betty, didn't you?'

Dodo shuffled her whole body. 'Possibly.'

'And you told her about the oak tree.'

Dodo crossed her ankles. 'Might have.' She twined her fingers. 'She said you despised me. I said you didn't but she said yes you did because you would never confide in me about anything personal so I said well you had told me about your friend Utterly Etterly but that was all. I didn't tell her about how you broke the vase or your teddy bear Mr Fluffly or those love letters from Roger Ackroyd you hid under that loose floorboard.'

'Roger Arkwright.' I had forgotten about his letters.

'Especially the one about that night when—'

'Let's concentrate on another night,' I broke in. 'The one in the Dunworthy Hotel.'

106

THE JUSTICE OF JUST

L avender Wicks lounged sideways on the arm of the chair like a Roman noblewoman waiting to be fed grapes.

'We had been lucky with our mix-ups over Bath Road and Bath Avenue and the wrong rooms in the Royal George,' Poppy told us, 'because the people we killed deserved to die anyway but we decided to make sure with the man in Bocking.'

'Ian Henshaw in the Dunworthy Hotel,' I said.

'What is there to say?' Lavender shrugged. 'Henshaw was a fool. He believed all the stories about a vampire so he didn't think twice about trusting me. I mean to say, do I look like a vampire?' She walked her fingers down her thighs to the hem of her dress.

'More like a vamp,' I commented and she radiated charming malice.

'If you mean to say it you should say it,' Dodo instructed and Lavender tinkled with laughter.

'Henshaw was easy,' Lavender scoffed. 'I invited him for a drink on the pretence that it was business and made it clear there was only one kind of business I was really interested in. Give a man a few compliments and he thinks he's Rudolph Valentino.'

'He's dead,' Dodo declared so accusingly you might have thought the sisters had finished him off thirteen years ago.

'No!' Poppy tottered two steps sideways and one step back. 'I wondered why he hadn't made any films recently.'

Lavender threw back her head. 'Henshaw wasn't known in Essex,' she continued. 'He lived in Sackwater and so he felt quite safe when I suggested going to that hotel. We had never actually *done* anything but the promise of doing it was enough to lure him. I told him I had a special game. He had to get undressed as quickly as he could and lie on the bed. He let me tie him up without a murmur. Mrs Henshaw would never join in anything like that – he bleated. And when I told him I had a sister who would very much like to meet him, he almost burst with anticipation.'

'We arranged for a ladder to be there by smashing all those top windows with our catapults so the glazier would need to bring it and we did it too late for him to be able to repair them all in one evening, with the blackout in operation, and we hoped he would leave his big ladder overnight,' Poppy told us breathlessly, 'and he did!'

'Hoo-rah.' I clapped sarcastically.

'Poppy came over the wall,' Lavender related.

'The ladder was ever so heavy,' her sister complained.

'You carried it under your right arm,' I realised.

'How could you possibly know that?' Poppy asked sharply.

'Because you were leaning that way with the weight of it. The right footprint was deeper than the left.'

'Oh well done, boss.' Dodo bounced on her perch. 'That was like being a proper detective, better than Miss Prim.' She wrinkled her nose. 'Is that why you were so interested in my limp?'

'Of course not,' I lied and she nodded vigorously.

'I did not think it could be.'

'He was ever so thrilled to see me come in through the window,' Poppy said, 'but he still didn't recognise me, though he asked if we had met before as I looked familiar.'

'And had you?' I watched her.

'Oh don't spoil the story,' Lavender protested.

'He asked if I had ever been a typist at Jackson-Ruperts, his family firm.'

475

'And had you?' Dodo joined in.

'Do I look like a typist?' Poppy yelled.

'Well, you have ten fingers if you include thumbs,' Dodo pondered.

'You tortured and killed him.' I steered the conversation back before we got too far off the topic.

'I tried drinking his blood,' Poppy made worms of her lips, 'but it was all salty and sticky and disgusting so I had to spit it out.' Her lip trembled. 'It made me feel quite poorly.'

Oh you poor little mite, I thought.

'That decrepit porter nearly did for us,' Lavender recalled. 'With all the excitement I forgot to leave the key in the lock. It was just as well we'd pulled the wardrobe across. We hardly had time to do our speeches and escape before he forced his way in.'

'*What are you doing?*' Poppy reprised her lines with a giggle. '*No. Don't hang me... please.*'

'*Come on or I'll snap your pretty neck.*' Lavender put on a gruff baritone voice so well that, even watching her, it was difficult to believe a man had not spoken.

Both sisters did little bows.

'I am glad you find it so amusing.' I turned from one to the other.

'Inspector Church is probably being sarcastic when she says she is glad,' my constable clarified. 'She is almost certainly appalled.'

'Why should Mr Henshaw have recognised you, Miss Castle?' I asked.

Poppy turned purple. 'Because' – she clenched her fists – 'he was one of them.'

'The Suffolk Rams?'

'You knew about them?' Lavender asked incredulously. 'And you did nothing?'

'As far as I know they are just a bunch of rowdy Round Table rejects,' I replied.

'Just?' Poppy shrieked, then, deciding that it hadn't had the right effect, did it again but louder and in my face. '*Just?* That's what he said when we tortured him. *Just a bit of fun*, he said. Oh yes indeed, he tried to apologise when we set to work on his arms but sorry doesn't cover it. Anyone can be sorry when they are paying the price.'

'So these men assaulted you?' I clarified.

'Assaulted?' She swept an arm just past my nose. 'They insulted my womanhood. They...' she almost vomited the next word, '*abused* me. Every one of them. Henshaw was the ringleader. That's why we left him to last and made him suffer the most.'

'How did you know who they were?' I asked.

'Because I do secretarial work part-time,' Poppy announced.

'A typist,' Dodo insisted.

'I deal with their accounts and membership letters and keep minutes at their meetings,' Poppy told her fiercely.

'Some secret organisation.' I shook my head in wonder.

'I disagree, boss.' Dodo rooted about her hair like she was looking for something dropped in a field. 'I do not think that was very secret of them at all.'

'I took a vow of silence,' Poppy protested, suddenly loyal to the men she had slain.

'Then it was very naughty of you to break your oath,' Dodo lectured. 'God will be very cross when you meet him.'

'Oh dear.' Poppy chewed her lower lip. 'I didn't think of that.'

I clasped my head, avoiding my ear and forced myself to concentrate.

'But why this kidnapping charade?' I wondered. 'You must have known it would attract all the attention to you.'

'Because, as Lavender has already explained,' Poppy told me with frayed patience, 'she knew that you were on to her.'

'Actually I wasn't,' I confessed.

'I was,' Dodo announced but both our statements were greeted with indifference.

'And you wanted to escape your marriage,' I calculated.

'Escape from Thurston Wicks?' Dodo chortled. 'Why would anyone want to do that?'

'Rumour has it he is not interested in women,' I told her delicately.

'Well, of course he is not. He is a married man.' Dodo hesitated. 'Oh, you do not mean... Oh, you do.'

'I was fully aware of that when the studio paired us up.' Lavender stretched lazily. 'And it rather suited me.' She yawned. 'He had his boys. I had my girls.'

'But you do not have any children,' Dodo objected.

'What then?' I asked.

'Because he was such a bore,' Lavender said, 'always whingeing about Crispin Staples getting his part by sleeping with the director.'

'But that is silly.' Dodo tossed her head scornfully. 'If I were a director I should want my actors to stay awake.'

'I was on the brink of stardom,' Lavender declaimed, arms akimbo like this was the cue for a song, but then they fell into her lap. 'And I thought a little of his fame would rub off on me but, when Thurston was seen dancing with that Kraut from the embassy, I was forced to drink from the same poisoned chalice and my career was ruined.'

'He tried to poison you?' Dodo exclaimed. 'Good for him.'

'I don't think Mrs Wicks meant it literally,' I informed her.

'He might as well have,' Lavender rejoined bitterly. 'You can't get much deader than Sackwater.'

A squall rattled the roof tiles and the whole building creaked.

'But it is lovely here,' Poppy argued indignantly. 'And you told me you were coming back to help look after Daddy.'

'Fortunately, he died within a week of our return.' Lavender sniffed.

'Fortunately?' Poppy shrieked, adopting a pugilistic pose with her little fists clenched. 'Or did I mishear you?'

'Yes. I said *unfortunately*,' Lavender muttered unconvincingly.

'I thought you must have.' Poppy relaxed.

'Did you never think of going to the police?' Dodo suggested.

'What the hell would you have done?' Lavender demanded.

'Well, clearly you knew who they were,' I reasoned. 'We would have questioned and arrested them, if we found your story to be true, and they would have been severely punished.'

'How severely?' Poppy sneered. 'Bound over? A fine that they could pay without thinking about it?'

'More than that,' I assured her. 'They would have got long prison sentences. The law takes rape very seriously.' I was about to add that they would be given a rough ride by the other prisoners too, when Poppy gathered her lips into a seething sphincter and spat out at me, 'Rape? Don't be dis-*gusting*. Who said anything about rape?'

I blinked, somewhat taken aback by her vehemence and slightly confused by her question, but it was Poppy's older sister who ended the pause.

'But you told me they had—' she said quietly.

'No I didn't,' Poppy burst out. 'You asked if they had touched me and I said yes.'

'You said you were outraged,' Lavender said, aghast.

'And so I was.' Poppy threw back her head. 'Their behaviour was outrageous from start to finish. They insulted me with lewd remarks—'

'Such as?' I interrupted her.

'I don't like to say.'

'Try.'

'Well...' Poppy hung her head, 'about not touching me with a bargepole, for instance.'

'Hang on,' I said. 'They insulted you by *not* wanting to touch you?'

Poppy flushed. 'Well, wouldn't you be offended?'

'What exactly happened, Poppsie?' Lavender asked in a stage whisper.

'Well, I had had a few glasses of champagne—'

'But you don't drink,' Lavender reminded her. 'Who gave you those?'

'Well, I sort of helped myself,' Poppy admitted. 'I just wanted to know what it tasted like and it tasted very nice and made me feel all warm.'

'And woozy?' Dodo asked.

'And woozy,' Poppy agreed. 'But I only had five or six little glasses.'

'And then?' I prompted.

'Well, then I asked Mr Henshaw if he wanted to dance but he said there wasn't any music. I said that didn't matter and I started trying to teach him a foxtrot but I ended up sort of hanging round his neck with him trying to unclasp my fingers behind his neck.'

'You don't know how to foxtrot,' Lavender objected but her sister carried on talking.

'One of the others, Mr Dapper, the seed merchant, said something like, *I didn't know you were that desperate, Ian* and that's when Mr Henshaw made his remark about bargepoles and I tripped backwards into a sherry trifle.'

'Custard in your hair,' I remembered.

'And they all started laughing and making fun of me.'

'The swine,' Dodo breathed.

'One of them asked how much I charged and another said I should be paying him. It was very embarrassing. I ran out onto the street.' Poppy swallowed. 'That's when they did start threatening me. One of them, Mr Heath Jackson, the accountant, shouted, *Come back or you'll get hurt.*'

'I suspect he meant it more in concern,' I suggested.

'Oh.' Poppy put a hand to her mouth. 'I hadn't thought of it like that.' She mopped her brow with her forearm. 'It was awful and, when I ran away, they chased after me.'

'Are you sure?' I asked.

'Of course I am,' she said uncertainly, 'I wouldn't have fallen into the cellar if I hadn't been running.'

'No I mean are you sure they chased you?'

'Well, I heard footsteps and one of them threatening that I would fall under a bus.'

'It sounds awfully like they were trying to help you,' Dodo remarked.

'It wasn't like that,' Poppy insisted. 'One of them shouted for me to come back because I'd dropped my handbag but the next day it was left on my front doorstep so they must have followed me home.'

'Or looked at the address in your driving licence,' I suggested.

'What about you?' Poppy demanded with renewed fire. 'While they were attacking me, you stood by and watched and shouted, *Come on, boys* to encourage them.'

'No I didn't. I met you running away after your fall and looked after you,' I pointed out. 'I took you to hospital.'

'Is this true, Poppy?' Lavender asked hoarsely and Poppy ran the fingers of both hands through her hair.

'Well, it might be. I was quite confused.'

'So all those people we killed were just laughing at your drunken attempts to seduce Ian Henshaw and engaging in a bit of banter and, when he said it was just a bit of fun,' Lavender gasped unbelievingly, 'it was.'

'Well, I don't know.' Poppy huffed. 'Bits of it got clearer over the weeks and that blow to the head seems to have helped.'

'But it was me that got hit.' Lavender touched her scalp indignantly. 'Twice.'

'Yes but it sort of jolted me back to reality,' her sister explained.

Lavender looked at her in disbelief. 'So we killed them all for making fun of you?'

'It was very embarrassing,' Poppy protested.

'And we lured Inspector Church here for nothing.' Lavender lit her cigarette.

'Oh that is awfully bad for you,' Dodo told her. 'Makes you windy when you play lacrosse.'

'I don't.'

'Lured?' I repeated.

'Oh yes.' Poppy brightened. 'You will never get out of here alive.'

107

THE LAST RESORT

Dodo sat up. 'Do not be silly,' she said. 'Inspector Church has the spikey walking stick and I have a gun with five dangerous bullets in the twirly bit.'

'It only had one bullet,' Lavender told her. 'And you have fired it.'

'Then you won't mind if my constable pulls the trigger,' I challenged.

'It was a bluff,' she admitted.

'So how can you possibly stop us leaving?' Dodo demanded crossly.

'Quite easily.' Lavender Wicks smiled, coldly for once. 'This whole pier is rigged to be blown up in case of invasion.'

'Gracious,' Dodo gasped. 'That sounds like a very noisy thing to do.'

'Don't worry.' Lavender put her hand down the back of her seat cushion. 'You'll be dead before you even hear it.'

'I do not wish to start an argument with somebody as skilful at sadistic killing as you appear to be – assuming you are not telling us porky-pies – but I do not find that as reassuring as you anticipate,' Dodo decided. 'Perhaps I should just shoot you now.'

'And risk detonating...' Lavender's hand came out from behind her cushion, 'this.'

'Oh.' Dodo watched with interest. 'Is that a stick of Sickwater rock?'

'No,' Lavender replied. 'It is dynamite.'

'In that case I would be a little less blasé about waving it about,' I told her. 'I don't know much about dynamite but I do know it is highly unstable. The slightest knock can sometimes set it off.'

'Which is exactly what I intend to do.' Lavender looked straight through me and I was disconcerted to hear how steady her voice was and see how steady her hand was as she told me that.

'But I thought you intended to flee to Paris,' Dodo said. 'At least I hoped it was Paris. I saw some pictures in a magazine called *Paris Fashions* – I'll show you tomorrow, if you like.'

'There won't be any tomorrow,' Poppy forecast.

'Oh do not be silly,' Dodo told her. 'It's Wednesday today and there is always a Thursday every week.'

'Actually it's Saturday,' I told her, as if it mattered.

'Oh bother-bother-botheration,' Dodo cried. 'I am a silly sandwich. I have missed another hair appointment.'

'Actually I rather like your hair as it is,' Lavender told her and Dodo primped the fiery ball that enveloped her head.

'Oh thank you' – she grinned – 'which reminds me – I was going to say they have some lovely clothes in Paris. You would look radiant in some of their gowns.'

'What about me?' Poppy asked plaintively.

'Oh, I do not have to toady to you,' Dodo replied airily. 'You do not have a stick of dynamite in your hand. Mind you...' She sat up to peer more closely and put the gun into her lap to slip on her little round glasses. 'That does say *TNT* on the wrapper.'

'It's the same thing,' Lavender said sniffily.

'If you say so' – Dodo took her glasses off – 'but I think it is much more powerful.'

'All the better,' Poppy called. 'There are crates of the stuff under the stage, ready to be put under the supports.'

'There are indeed,' Dodo agreed readily, 'enough to blow up half the town, I should think.'

I suddenly realised something. The army would never leave something like that unguarded and a couple of privates usually stood outside the main gate with bayonets fixed. 'Where are the sentries?' I asked.

'Feeding the fish,' Lavender told me.

'Well, that's very kind of them,' Dodo responded, 'but I really think they should be on patrol or they will get into awful trouble.'

'They are beyond that,' I explained.

'We invited them in and cut their throats.' Poppy chortled.

'Badly?' Dodo touched her own neck anxiously.

'Ear to ear,' Lavender confirmed.

'I expect you mean *ears to ears*,' Dodo corrected her.

'How dare you criticise my grammar?' Lavender fumed. 'You are as bad as those damned bitches at—' She stopped dead but Dodo completed the sentence almost seamlessly: 'St Jerome's.' She clicked her fingers. 'I knew I had seen you before. I thought it might have been in *How Dark It Doth Groweth* but it was at St Jerome's Workhouse. You were much older and in charge of my dormitory but I do not suppose you even noticed me.'

'Noticed?' Lavender echoed scornfully. 'How could I not? I had been in that stinking hole for six years but you were hardly there six months before that stuck-up policeman's wife took a fancy to you. She had been interested in me until you turned up, Little Miss Goody-Two-Shoes clinging to her skirts. *Oh please be my mummy*,' she mocked in a baby voice, her fist blanched as she continued, 'I was there another year before the Castles turned up looking for a sister for Daddy's darling Poppy.'

'I was always Daddy's darling.' Her sister smiled dreamily.

It was then I remembered Thurston Wicks telling us that his wife had had a hard childhood without any parents. I had thought nothing of it at the time. Mr G would not have been impressed. *You should always think something of everything*, he used to tell me.

'In case you did not realise it, that explains why you do not look like each other,' Dodo informed them.

'And also why you tried to frame my constable,' I concluded.

'Which one?' Dodo enquired with interest. 'Surely not Rivers. He has not got the energy.' She wiggled her nose clockwise. 'Oh you mean me.' Her nose went into reverse. 'But why would you do that?'

'Call it poetic justice.' Lavender toyed with a loose strand of her long blonde hair. 'You got away with being an accomplice to the Camden Vampire—'

'I did not!' Dodo burst out. 'I didn't even know he *was* the vampire until he was arrested and even then I didn't believe it.' She picked up the revolver and waved it at everyone like an overwrought conductor. 'But I have paid the price for my father's crimes all my life.'

'Well, you couldn't expect us to know that.' Poppy shrugged, making everything all right.

'No more than I could expect you to believe I was guilty.' Dodo's eyes narrowed. 'Well, I have to say you really are a couple of stinky-winky beasts.' Dodo got up and pointed the revolver at Lavender, who tinkled merrily.

'This whole chair is stuffed with explosives. If you shoot me at that range the bullet will go straight through me and blow us all to kingdom come.'

'Oh dear.' Dodo sat down. 'I am not sure what to do for the best now.' She looked across. 'What would you suggest, boss?'

'You would probably be best making a run for it,' I advised.

'But I cannot leave you,' she cried.

'You will have to if I order you to.'

'Think I shall sit and watch you go?' Lavender unclipped her handbag.

'You do not have to watch if you do not want to,' Dodo reassured her. 'Anyway, it might not explode when you throw it.'

'Think I'm stupid?' Lavender brought out her lighter.

'Well, you have done some very silly things,' Dodo told her. 'Shall I go now, boss?'

'It would be best,' I agreed.

'Well,' Dodo Chivers got to her feet and gave a little wave, 'goodbye.'

'This is it, Poppy!' Lavender yelled, flicked the top off her lighter and spun the wheel. The flame rose on her first attempt.

'I'm ready, Lavender.' Poppy, forgetting her sister's prediction about not hearing, put her fingers in her ears.

Lavender held the flame under the stick and the wrapper caught fire.

'Damn it,' she swore as the flames licked her fingers. She dropped the stick and the fire went out.

'TNT doesn't explode with heat,' I told her as she picked it up and tried again. 'It needs a small explosion to set it off.'

'You were right to say a bullet would set it off though,' Dodo said.

Lavender Wicks flung the stick furiously into the orchestra pit, where it bounced harmlessly away.

'How do you two know so much about explosives?' she asked, all of a sudden deflated.

'We went to see *The Dawn Patrol* with Errol Flynn,' Dodo told her. 'In it,' she added in case Lavender thought he had accompanied us to the pictures, and then explained, 'though not together and not at the same time.'

'Was it not *Gunga Din* with Cary Grant and Douglas Fairbanks Jr?' I queried. 'No don't tell me. It was...'

'*The Gold Miners*,' we said in unison.

'Is that the one where they get trapped by a rockfall?' Poppy asked. 'I would quite like to see that.' Her lower lip wobbled. 'But I don't suppose I will now.' She raised her voice. 'Shall we use our last-resort plan, Lavender?'

'It would be preferable to awaiting the hangman.' Lavender pursed her lips. 'On the count of three?'

'One... two... three,' they yelled in unison and ran straight towards each other and the gaping hole in the floor with the wind-whipped sea crashing far below.

'Stop!' I shouted, uselessly, but you have to shout something.

I was not sure they even heard me. Lavender, getting there first, waited for Poppy to catch up. They stood on the brink, looked at each other, nodded and leaped over the edge, just managing to clasp hands before they disappeared into the abyss.

108

THE ABSENCE OF LISTENERS

edged carefully along the old red carpet towards where it dipped away.

'Oh yuckity-yuck.' Dodo shivered.

'Ouchy-wouchy,' wailed Poppy.

'Oh fucking hell that hurts,' Lavender shrieked.

'Wash your mouth out,' Poppy scolded.

'Wash your stupid brain out, you stupid cow,' Lavender retorted. 'All that for being jostled by some drunken rams.'

And then it clicked. *'Inshulted by seep,'* I recalled. 'She was trying to tell me she had been insulted by sheep.'

I turned on my torch to see the two sisters lying, Lavender face-up and Poppy face-down, on the bales of barbed wire that packed the space to stop anybody getting access to the explosives.

'The more you wriggle the more entangled you will get,' I cautioned.

'I do not think they are listening, boss.' Dodo watched the two women squirm.

'No,' I agreed. 'I do not suppose they are.'

'Do you think we have enough evidence now?' Dodo asked and I would have replied in the affirmative if the double doors from the foyer had not crashed open and the figure of a man appeared on the threshold.

109

THE WATCHER IN THE SHADOWS

I didn't have to look twice to recognise the newcomer.

'Inspector Sharkey,' I greeted him. 'You took your time.'

He looked at me standing in the aisle and Dodo on the stage, both peering down the hole.

'Well, I got him,' he cried in triumph.

'Who?' I asked.

'Inspector Church wishes to know who you have got?' Dodo explained.

'The kidnapper, of course,' Sharkey crowed. 'Told you it takes a man to sort out a real case.'

'But who?' Dodo asked and I was glad she had beaten me to it, so that she didn't have to clarify my enquiry.

'Bring him in, men.' Sharkey clicked his fingers and the Grinder-Snipes made their entrance, dragging another man between them. 'Caught him loitering in the shadows outside the gates.' Sharkey pumped out his chest, every inch the matador standing over his despatched bull. 'Obviously waiting for you to leave so he could pick up the ransom money.'

'Hello, Inspector Church.' Toby Gregson raised his head and I saw blood trickling down his lips onto his chin.

'Did you hit him?' I accused and Sharkey snorted.

'Resisting arrest,' he said, his confidence clearly waning now that he could see who his suspect was.

'I didn't know he was a policeman,' Toby protested. 'When

490

a man jumps on you in the dark, without saying anything, of course you fight back.'

'Ohhh 'e did a lot of wrigglin' when we detained 'im,' Sandy told me.

'It were like 'e didn't want tu be detained at all,' Algy remarked in surprise.

'I thought you had a broken leg,' I told Algy.

'So did I, mam,' he agreed.

'And me,' Sandy endorsed his brother's statement.

'But it were me truncheon,' Algy rubbed his thigh, 'what snapped. It felt like me leg though. It reeeelly 'urt.'

''E's got a shocking bruise,' Sandy assured me.

'I'm glad you were able to come back on duty.' I nodded approvingly.

'I couldn't leave Lysander to patrol alone,' Algy said stoically. 'He's reet afraid of the dark.'

'I am that,' Sandy confirmed.

I sucked in some air and walked up the steps. On closer inspection, I was delighted to see Sharkey's left eye starting to close up.

'Were you following me?' I asked Toby sternly.

He greeted the question defiantly. 'Of course I was. You wouldn't tell me anything so I've been trying to do my job. Besides,' he winked, 'you promised me a drink. I didn't realise you worked with Himmler.'

'Let him go,' I ordered the twins, and turned back to my esteemed colleague. 'You must tell me all about your trip to France.' I smiled. 'In the meantime, we have the murderers and kidnappers in custody down there.'

Sharkey pushed past me to have a look.

'Bloody hell,' he breathed. 'Snared in barbed wire.' He viewed me with a new respect. 'And I thought I was ruthless.'

'What will happen to Lavender Wicks and Poppy Castle?' Dodo asked as she skipped back through the town with me. 'Will they be hanged by their very pretty and quite pretty necks until they are dead? Or will they hire a clever ruthless lawyer who gets them acquitted on a technicality or concocts a cast-iron alibi? Or will they stage daring escapes to South America?'

'They will not be acquitted.' I jumped over a puddle and hoped Dodo did not think I was joining in her game.

'Oh well done.' She applauded, my hopes dashed.

'But I doubt they will be hanged.' I lit a roll-up and sucked the smoke in. 'Judges don't like hanging pretty women. I don't think a good lawyer will have much trouble finding plenty of doctors to testify that they are insane – and, perhaps, they are.'

'Of course they are.' Dodo jumped with both feet together over the shadow of a plane tree. 'Anyone must be mad who thinks that they can fool you.'

'Well, I wouldn't go that far,' I protested modestly.

'I would, boss,' Dodo asserted confidently. 'You always know everything. Why, only this morning, Sergeant Briggs asked me how long is a piece of string and I said that I did not know but you would.'

'Well, it's not that simple—' I began.

'So how long is it, boss?' Dodo broke in, her big eyes looking trustingly up at me.

'Seventy-nine units,' I told her.

'*Du hast schöne brüste*,' she cried in astonishment. 'Excuse my French but the man on the train taught me that means *well done*. I simply *knew* you would know.'

My German wasn't up to much but I could take a fair guess at what part of a woman *brüste* referred to.

'Let us play I Spy,' Dodo suggested as we crossed the road. 'You first.'

Oh good grief, I thought and was about to refuse when I remembered that Dodo had saved my life that night.

'I spy with my little eye something beginning with "s",' I said. I had no idea what but there must be something that would fit the bill nearby.

'"S"?' Dodo stroked her chin and swivelled all the way round. 'Oh that's an easy one – cigarette.'

110

THE CORPSE IN BROWN PAPER

used the reconnected phone in my office to ring March Middleton.

'I shall not say that Mr G would be proud of you,' she told me, 'for I am not sure he was ever proud of anyone except himself, but I am, Betty, very proud.'

Coming from the woman who had solved the *Mysterious Affair of the Sties* this was high praise and, since that woman was Aunty M, I felt a lump in my throat.

'I am sorry, darling, but I must go. Winston is getting sulky at being ignored,' she told me. 'Now he is trying to take my last garibaldi.'

'So all the time I have been chattering on,' I gasped, 'you are entertaining Mr Churchill?'

'Well, somebody has to.' She chuckled. 'Put that back, Winnie.'

'We shall fight over the biscuit,' a voice rumbled in the background as my godmother bade me goodbye, 'but I shall *never* surrender.'

'Goodbye, Aunty.' I stubbed out my cigarette.

There was a silence when I went back into the lobby – not the normal quiet but the sort of thing you get as a woman when you enter a men-only bar – and I was almost sure I had heard shushing. Brigsy was behind his desk. His head bobbed down just late enough for me to be sure he had seen me.

'What's going on?' I looked suspiciously around.

'Nothing,' Nippy Walker said nonchalantly but didn't ask, as any innocent person would, '*Why?*'

'Absolutleh nothing...' Algy insisted.

'At all.' Sandy closed the sentence for him.

Rivers leaned against the desk from the public side trying to whistle something jazzy, but just made the sort of noise my father makes blowing through his briar pipe to clear the stem.

'Why?' Bantony enquired too late to be convincing.

I breathed hard. 'If somebody has done something wrong, it will only make things worse playing silly games.'

Brigsy was scratching around with his matches, no doubt lighting his foul pipe to calm himself before breaking whatever bad news it was.

'Ready,' Brigsy called and then I knew. They were going to play some stupid prank and I would be expected to laugh to show what a good sport I was when I wasn't. That was why Dodo wasn't around. She wouldn't have joined any practical joke against me.

Dodo came out of the back room. Her arms were behind her back in an ostentatiously casual manner.

'Games?' Superintendent Vesty materialised.

'Welcome back, sir,' I said enthusiastically.

Sharkey stuck his head nosily out of his office, scowled and stuck it back in again.

Two other figures struggled out from the back room – my parents – what the hell were they doing in there? – lugging what looked like a corpse in brown paper between them.

'What—' I began but Dodo burst out with, 'Happy...' and Brigsy was lifting something. It was a cake with innumerable candles and everyone joined in, 'Birthday to you.'

And then I realised.

'Happy birthday to you.'

Why was I the only one who hadn't known?

'Happy Birthday, dear' – and here there was a mixture of *Inspector/Inspector Church* and a *Betty* from Vesty while I joined in with my guess of *Superintendent* – 'Happy birthday to yooooo.'

'You thought we'd forgotten, didn't you?' My father laughed.

'As if we would,' my mother protested as if I had directly accused them of such an act, 'especially not your fortieth.'

'I'm thirty-eight,' I said weakly.

'Oh don't be so vain,' she scolded.

'Mumsy and I made it,' Dodo declared with immense pride at the sunken lump on a plate. 'Ginger, your favourite.'

Ginger? I hate ginger.

'Lovely.' I sighed.

'That is how I knew you were at the pavilion,' Dodo burbled merrily. 'Because I was here getting things ready for your wonderful surprise when the telephone rang.'

That would explain why Brigsy hesitated before telling me nobody else was there.

'Goodness,' I breathed.

'Blow out the candles, boss,' Dodo urged and so I did.

'Presents.' She clapped, wild with excitement. 'You first,' she urged my parents and they plonked their gift on the floor. Its shape was looking all too familiar by now and made an all-too-ominous clinking sound.

'Oh for goodness' sake, you've broken it,' my mother snapped at me, though I had not had any contact with it yet.

'Just like the vase that went on it,' my father reminded me grimly and then the wonderful surprise as well as the wonderful present were ruined.

'Well, open it,' my parents urged and so I did.

'Lovely,' I greeted the smashed pedestal.

'You can probably glue it,' my father reassured me.

'Thank you.' I kissed my mother's cheek.

'We know you've always wanted it,' she said.

'Don't be soppy.' My father wiped his cheek as if a strange dog had licked it.

'Me now.' Dodo thrust a white paper bundle tied with white string at me. 'Open-it-open-it-open-it,' she chanted and so I did. 'Nobody else has bought you anything.'

'We thought about it,' Brigsy assured me.

'But we,' Rivers said.

'Decided...' Bantony said.

'Against it,' the twins chorused.

I struggled with Dodo's knots. 'Has anybody got any scissors?'

'Try this, madam.' Brigsy passed me his tar-coated pipe-knife and I sawed through the string. A set of sharp implements clattered onto the desk, including two spikes.

'You saw those in my handbag,' Dodo reminded me. 'But I crossed my fingers and told you they were nothing.'

'What are they?' I asked.

'Well' – she beamed like a proud mother showing off her firstborn – 'I remembered you said you couldn't knit with somehow mislaying your arm, so I got you a leather-working kit.' She lifted a lethal-looking curved knife. 'You can cut the leather with this.' She picked up a spike. 'And this is for creating holes,' she enthused because, of course, these would all be so much easier to manipulate one-handed than simple needles. 'You will be able to make yourself a new pair of shoes,' Dodo promised. 'They'll be much nicer than the ones you normally wear off duty.'

'Thank you.' I forced a smile.

My father cleared his throat. 'I would just like to say, on this auspicious occasion' – he tucked his thumbs into the pockets of his red velvet waistcoat – 'how very proud we are to see you in that uniform, my darling.' For the second time in five minutes I had trouble swallowing. My father rarely praised me and very rarely

497

called me that, especially not in company, and I was struggling to form a reply when he concluded, 'Dodo.'

That did it.

'Actually...' I began but I still couldn't do it. I couldn't bring myself, after all the trouble everyone had gone to, to point out that this was October and my birthday is on 28 April.

'I got you a little something,' Superintendent Vesty confessed, quite shyly, I thought. 'Forgot to wrap it though.'

'Oh that doesn't matter, sir,' Dodo assured him. 'Not with all your head problems.'

'Head?' Vesty touched his forehead in surprise. 'I was having a chat with old Mr Bell,' he reminisced.

'At the left luggage office?' I queried.

'That's the fellow.' Vesty nodded, blister ballooning. 'And he told me you needed one of these.' He reached inside his jacket and brought it out – a bottle of smelling salts.

'Thank you very much, sir,' I said faintly. 'I probably do.'

December --
2020

A letter from the publisher

We hope you enjoyed this book. We are an independent publisher dedicated to discovering brilliant books, new authors and great storytelling. If you want to hear more, why not join our community of book-lovers at:

www.headofzeus.com

We'll keep you up-to-date with our latest books, author blogs, tempting offers, chances to win signed editions, events across the UK and much more.

 @HoZ_Books

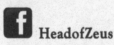 HeadofZeus

 @HeadofZeus

HEAD of ZEUS